✔ KU-264-554

A PREGNANCY,
A PARTY
& A PROPOSAL

BY
TERESA CARPENTER

MILLS & BOON

All rights reserved including the right of reproduction in whole or in part in any form. This edition is published by arrangement with Harlequin Books S.A.

This is a work of fiction. Names, characters, places, locations and incidents are purely fictional and bear no relationship to any real life individuals, living or dead, or to any actual places, business establishments, locations, events or incidents. Any resemblance is entirely coincidental.

This book is sold subject to the condition that it shall not, by way of trade or otherwise, be lent, resold, hired out or otherwise circulated without the prior consent of the publisher in any form of binding or cover other than that in which it is published and without a similar condition including this condition being imposed on the subsequent purchaser.

® and ™ are trademarks owned and used by the trademark owner and/or its licensee. Trademarks marked with ® are registered with the United Kingdom Patent Office and/or the Office for Harmonisation in the Internal Market and in other countries.

Published in Great Britain 2015
by Mills & Boon, an imprint of Harlequin (UK) Limited,
Eton House, 18-24 Paradise Road, Richmond, Surrey, TW9 1SR

© 2015 Teresa Carpenter

ISBN: 978-0-263-25111-1

23-0215

Harlequin (UK) Limited's policy is to use papers that are natural, renewable and recyclable products and made from wood grown in sustainable forests. The logging and manufacturing processes conform to the legal environmental regulations of the country of origin.

Printed and bound in Spain
by CPI, Barcelona

MORAY COUNCIL LIBRARIES & INFO.SERVICES	
20 38 55 81	
Askews & Holts	
RF	

Teresa Carpenter believes that with love and family anything is possible. She writes in a Southern California coastal city surrounded by her large family. Teresa loves writing about babies and grandmas. Her books have rated Top Picks by *RT Book Reviews*, and have been nominated Best Romance of the Year on some review sites. If she's not at a family event, she's reading, or writing her next grand romance.

For Gabrielle, the younger twin,
pragmatic, dedicated, witty, and a very hard worker.
You're going to make a great pharmacist.
I love you, babe.

CHAPTER ONE

"'TWO LINES MEANS PREGNANT.'" Lauren Randall read the early detection instructions. "'One line, not pregnant.'"

Simple enough. Perched on the side of the bed in a long blue robe, heart beating a mile a millisecond, she scrunched her eyes closed—a cowardly act entirely unlike her—and then opened them to look at the stick.

Two lines.

She blinked. Looked again. Still two lines.

"Oh, boy." She blew out a pent-up breath. Her mind spun with the news. She was going to be a mother. Strolling to the bedroom's picture window, she stared unseeing at the Pacific Ocean.

Her hand went to her waist. She was expecting a baby.

Ray Donovan's baby. Mind-boggling. This type of thing didn't happen to her. She was too organized, too controlled. She didn't have unprotected sex. She *hadn't* had unprotected sex. But a broken condom might have changed her life…forever.

She glanced at the stick in her hand. Yep, still two lines.

"Oh, my." A baby.

A tiny part of her was thrilled at the knowledge. She was having a *baby*! Would he or she have Lauren's blond hair and light brown eyes? Or Ray's sandy, slightly darker locks and blue eyes?

Just thinking about it sent the more rational side of her reeling. A child was not in her current five-year plan.

Certainly not a child with a domineering man incapable of standing still for two whole minutes.

The sound of pounding drew her gaze down. Below her the lush garden of the Santa Barbara estate was being transformed into a wedding paradise. The day had dawned sunny and bright and, according to the meteorologists, might reach seventy degrees. Given it was Valentine's Day, they were lucky. February weather could be unpredictable in Southern California.

The event promised to be spectacular. On the edge of the property a white-columned gazebo stood against a backdrop of green hedges and long-standing trees, beyond which the vast Pacific Ocean flowed on forever, symbolic of the unending devotion about to be declared.

Short columns on which sat rose ball topiaries created the aisle. White chairs with silver sashes provided seating for the guests. A huge white tent graced the middle of the lawn and wood flooring had been put down. The tent-poles had been encased in columns to match the gazebo and thousands of white lights were being draped across the ceiling to give the impression of dancing under the stars.

More rose topiaries acted as centerpieces on the round tables at the dining end. Curved couches ringed the dance floor at the other end. The overall vision was elegant, yet understated, and *her* By Arrangement team had pulled it off beautifully.

Co-owners of By Arrangement, Lauren and Tori had both taken on new assistants at the start of the year. They were working the event, but the rest of the jobs had vendors in place, thus freeing their staff to attend as guests.

Shortly Lauren would be walking down the aisle toward Ray. Not as bride to his groom, but as maid of honor to his best man. Today was not her big day, but her twin's. Tori would marry the man she loved in a romantic ocean-view ceremony in a little over two hours.

If that gave Lauren a pinch of envy it was only because her sister was so happy. Difficult not to want that for herself.

But it was only a pinch. After a bad scare in college, she'd put her career in front of romance. So far she had few regrets. Lauren liked where she was in life. Of course she'd need to recalibrate now she was going to have a child to consider.

So, a wedding for her sister and a baby for her. The timing of the discovery was extraordinary. Was this some kind of karmic message? Or perhaps a spiritual nudge?

Now, *there* was a cosmic joke—because "marriage" and "Ray" were two words that didn't belong in the same sentence, or even paragraph. Heck, they wouldn't be in the same novel.

And if she hadn't been playing ostrich—again, totally unlike her—she would have known she was pregnant a week ago. She'd certainly suspected, with the nausea and the tenderness in her breasts. But she'd been busy and in denial—a slick combination for avoiding the inevitable.

There'd been too much to do, what with last-minute details for the wedding and family coming into town for the rehearsal. Seeing Ray again was what had prompted her to pick up the early pregnancy testing kit. She couldn't contemplate walking down the aisle to him without knowing the truth. Not that knowing the truth helped now that it was a yes.

Well, no time to brood about it now.

Tossing the stick in the trash, she moved to the closet to take down her dress. It was past time to join Tori and their mother in Tori's room to get ready.

A knock sounded at the door. Carrying the dress, she opened the door to her mother.

Like Lauren, her mom already had her hair and make-up done. Garrett, Tori's fiancé and owner of Obsidian Studios, had arranged for three professional hairstylists and make-up artists to come to the house to prepare the wedding party for the event. Her mom looked lovely, with her hair swept up in a sleek French twist and the expert application of cosmetics. But then she looked just as pretty with no make-up and her hair in a ponytail.

To Lauren, she was just Mom.

"Oh, Mom." She launched herself into Liz Randall's arms, letting the scent of lavender comfort her.

The news of her baby nearly tripped off Lauren's tongue. She pressed her lips together to prevent the words from spilling. This was Tori's special day. Lauren would never do anything to disrupt her twin's wedding day.

"Hey." Her mother's arms closed around her, careful not to crush the dress she held. "Are you okay?"

"Yes," she lied. She wouldn't be okay until this day was over and the certainty of running into Ray no longer existed. And, truthfully, the hug did make her feel better. She forced her mind to switch gears. "Our girl is getting married."

"I know." Liz gave her another squeeze before stepping back. "She won't be right next door anymore, but we have to remember we're not losing her—we're gaining a new son and brother." She tweaked the ends of Lauren's hair and studied her closely. "Are you sure you're okay? You're a little pale."

"I'm fine." Lauren hooked her arm through her mother's as they walked down the hall to the master suite. "I'll still miss her."

"She's your partner. You'll see her nearly every day."

"It won't be the same."

No, and their lives were going to change even more drastically than her mom knew.

"Different, yes, but in a good way." Liz was a glass half-full gal. "Especially when we start getting little ones to play with. You two will be twenty-nine in a couple of months. I've waited a long time to be a grandmother."

Yeah, well, her wait was nearly up.

"Oh!" Liz exclaimed. "Maybe she'll have twins."

Lauren's stomach did a little flip. She swallowed hard. Okay, she wasn't ready to think about having twins.

Down the way a door opened and Ray Donovan stepped into the hall. He wore jeans and a muscle-clinging green T-shirt. His shaggy dark blond hair had been trimmed considerably since she'd seen him last night. It was brushed back at the sides and a little wild on top. He looked entirely too yummy for her peace of mind.

He hesitated at the head of the stairs, his blue gaze traveling between her and her mother. He lifted his camera, aimed it in their direction.

"Ray, stop that. We're not dressed yet. Where are you going?" Her mother pointed to the car keys in his hand. "You should be getting ready."

He pocketed the keys. "I have an errand. I'll be back in plenty of time." With a last glance at Lauren, which she avoided, he headed downstairs.

For a wild moment she wondered how he would deal with twins. But her mind refused to wrap around the concept so she pulled her focus back to Tori.

"Mom, I think we should let her get through the wedding before we have her barefoot and pregnant."

"Sweetheart…" Liz patted Lauren's hand "…who are you kidding? Tori will be barefoot before the end of the night."

The statement was so true they were giggling when the door in front of them opened and Tori stood there in sexy curls, a silky white robe, and bare feet. "Where have you two been?"

Lauren met her mother's golden gaze, so like her own, and they both burst out laughing.

Ray Donovan shifted his wide shoulders in the custom-made tuxedo. Weddings gave him hives. *Been there, almost did that, never plan to do it again.* A fact not even his good buddy Garrett knew. It had happened so long ago Ray liked to pretend it had never happened at all.

Pacing the study, or "the groom's room", as Lauren's new assistant had corrected him, Ray twitched at his tie. He was slowly suffocating.

Thinking of Lauren didn't help at all. Contrary woman. The honey-eyed blond was the hottest armful he'd ever held, but way too stubborn for his taste when they weren't locked in a clinch. Their fling, for want of a better word, was over.

Until two days ago he hadn't seen her since Christmas, when she'd called time on their trysts.

How stunning to realize he'd actually missed her. But any hope of expending his nervous energy by reigniting the chemistry between them while they were hooked up for the wedding festivities had fizzled out when she had refused to meet his gaze at the rehearsal. Or any time since.

Okay. Message received.

All for the best. In spite of his hopeful initial reaction, he'd been truly unnerved as he'd watched her walk down the aisle toward him. The sight had been a punch to the gut. He hadn't stopped twitching since. Confirmation that he'd been smart to keep it casual, to let her end things between them.

He paused in front of a gilded mirror. He smoothed his short sandy hair back into place and straightened his tie. *Pull it together,* he silently chided himself. *You're sounding more like a wuss than a director known for going into the trenches with his stuntmen and actors.*

"Relax," Garrett said from his place behind the desk. "Anyone would think it was you getting married instead of me."

"I don't know how you can be so calm."

Ray dropped into the chair in front of the desk, picked up his camera and shot the groom. To occupy his hands, as well as his mind, he'd decided to give the bride and groom the gift of an insider's perspective on their wedding: pictures and videos no photographer would have access to.

"The waiting is excruciating. How much longer before this gig gets going?"

Garrett's gaze shifted to the mantel clock. "Soon. And it's easy to be calm when you're sure of what you're doing."

"Marriage is a trap for the unwary. Standing up there in front of everyone is a lonely place to be."

Okay, he knew that was warped even as the words slipped out. His memories had no place here.

"I won't be alone." Garrett laughed off the outrageous comment. "I'll be joined by the woman I love. Until then you'll be by my side."

Garrett opened the bottom drawer in the solid oak desk and pulled out a bottle of aged whiskey and a single crystal glass. After pouring a good dollop into the glass, he pushed it across the oak surface to Ray.

"Maybe this will help settle your nerves."

"No, thanks." Ray turned down the shot. Normally he'd accept and relish the burn. Today he'd remain stone-cold sober. The way he felt, adding alcohol was not a good idea.

"I don't understand you, dude." Garrett shook his head. "You're the one who told me I'd be safe with Tori."

"It's easy to see she makes you happy." Ray ran a hand over his jaw. Just because marriage wasn't for him didn't mean others couldn't benefit from the bond. "And of course you have that whole Spidey sense of approval going for you."

Apparently the twins were natural matchmakers and got a special "feeling" when they saw two people who belonged together. Lauren had gotten the feeling about Garrett and Tori, but hadn't said anything until after they were engaged.

Garrett arched a dark eyebrow. "Mock if you want. I'm reaping the rewards."

"Sorry. The truth is you deserve the best. Don't mind me—weddings make me twitchy."

"So you said when I asked you to be my best man. Thanks for doing this for me."

"You're the closest thing I have to a brother. Of course I'm here for you."

"What's your deal anyway?"

Ray shook his head. "Ancient history. Too depressing for the occasion."

Too depressing, period. He didn't talk or think about those times.

A knock sounded at the door and Lauren's assistant stuck her head in. "It's time, gentlemen."

"We'll be right there," Garrett assured her, and surged to his feet. He looked at Ray as he rose too. "Are you ready for this?"

Ray waved Garrett forward, then clapped him on the back when he passed. "Let's get you hitched."

Outside, Ray stood at his friend's side in the shade of the gazebo as music filled the air and the bridal party started toward them. Nick Randall escorted his mother to the front row. As soon as they were seated, Lauren began her journey down the rose-strewn runner.

Ray couldn't take his eyes off her. She wore a strapless, figure-hugging silver gown, showing her curves to sweet advantage. The fading sun gleamed in golden curls swept to one side, leaving one creamy shoulder bare. She grew more stunning the closer she got.

He completely missed the bride walking down the aisle as his gaze lingered on the maid of honor. Watching her, he remembered their first heated encounter in the laundry room of his home on Thanksgiving. Desire stirred.

Not wanting to embarrass himself, or his friend, he turned his attention—and his camera—to the ceremony. The officiate spoke, and then Garrett and Tori exchanged the poignant vows they'd written themselves. Weddings might make Ray itch, but as a film director he recognized powerful dialogue when he heard it.

He received the signal to hand over the rings. Garrett kissed his bride. The officiate introduced the couple as Mr. and Mrs. Black. And finally the time came for Ray to touch Lauren as they moved to follow the couple up the aisle in a reverse procession.

As before, she refused to look at him as he linked her arm around his.

"You look beautiful." He laid his hand over hers and squeezed. Forget her decree. He wasn't ready to let her go yet. Changing her mind was exactly the distraction he needed.

She bunched her fingers into a fist, but didn't look at him.

"You girls outdid yourselves with the decorations."

She rolled her amber eyes. "You could care less about the decorations."

"Not true. As a director, I admire a well-organized scene."

"I'm sure Tori will be glad you approve. It's her vision."

They reached the end of the aisle. Lauren immediately pulled free of him.

"Don't wander off. We'll be doing photos in a moment."

"Yes," he tossed out with droll humor. "I got a copy of the itinerary."

That drew her gaze as she narrowed her eyes at him. "Behave."

He lifted an eyebrow. "Where's the fun in that?" He leaned close, inhaled her sweet scent—honeysuckle and soap—and whispered, "Meet me in the laundry room in twenty minutes."

A blush added color to her rose-dusted cheeks. But, oh, such warm eyes weren't meant to give off chills. Her hands went to her shapely hips, but before she could speak she was drawn into a hug as friends and family descended on the wedding party.

"You're a piece of work," she managed in an aside between greetings. "What about your date?"

"I'm stag tonight." He shook hands and nodded as people stopped in front of him. In a short break between one guest and the next he sent her a sultry look over his shoulder. "There's been no one since you."

"What? I'm supposed to feel sorry for you?" She snorted, then had to paste on a smile when her grandmother gave her an odd look. "Spare me, please. You're a world-class director. You could have a woman on your arm with the snap of your fingers."

"I pine for you," he said, and lifted Grandma Randall's hand to his mouth to kiss her fingers. "So nice to meet you. It's easy to see where Tori gets her beauty."

The older woman twittered prettily and moved on.

"Flirt," Lauren admonished him.

He grinned. "She loved it."

"Only proves my point. You won't be alone for long."

"Come on—I barely know anyone." There were a few film industry people here, but the biggest portion of guests was made up of Tori's family and friends. "You're maid of honor to my best man. We're scripted to be together."

"Hmm. You've spent half the time behind that camera. I don't know why you need company at all."

Implying he was lacking at his duties? Why did he allow her to get to him? Yes, she was lovely, but he'd dated some of the most gorgeous women in the world. She was a bit of a brat, and she constantly challenged his authority. But one whiff of her scent and he could think of only one thing: getting her alone.

The thinning crowd shifted, bumping Lauren into Ray. He grabbed her to keep her from toppling. His fingers framed her hips as he drew her close.

He lowered his head and kissed the vulnerable curve

of her neck. "The laundry room door has a lock. We won't be gone long."

She melted against him. The corner of his mouth kicked up in satisfaction as he mentally tracked the fastest route to the utility room. They both had bedrooms inside, but the laundry room held sentimental value. Best of all, no one was likely to look for them there.

In the next instant she'd elbowed him in the gut and twisted from his grasp. "Hands off."

He immediately held his hands up in a sign of surrender. He looked at her more closely. "Are you okay? You're a little pale."

She looked away. "I'm fine. I just choose not to let my hormones rule me today. It's my sister's wedding. I'm not going to steal away with you."

Lauren's assistant appeared, ushering the wedding party back to the gazebo.

"No one will miss us after the photos are done."

"Just *stop*." She planted a hand in the middle of his chest and lifted a pleading gaze to him.

He stepped back. "Pardon me."

He'd never forced himself on a woman and he wouldn't start now. If she didn't care to act on the desire her stand-offishness couldn't completely disguise, he respected her decision. He'd only pursued her because she helped distract him from the wedding heebie-jeebies.

Shoulders back, he gestured her forward.

For the next twenty minutes he stood where instructed, smiled when told, and snapped his own shots when he wasn't needed. Finally the photographer released the wedding party. He trekked to the reception with Lauren's brother Nick.

They exchanged pleasantries. "How's work?" Ray asked.

"Busy. I know I shouldn't be happy about that." Nick ran the trauma unit at a Palm Springs hospital. "But I prefer action to twiddling my thumbs. How about you? Is there a new film I should be looking forward to?"

"I wrapped up *Gates of Peril* in December. It'll be out over the summer. I'm still in the planning stages of the next one."

"I'm going to hold you to that invite to a premier you issued at Thanksgiving. Not only will I enjoy the movie, it'll be serious chick points."

Nick introduced Ray to more family and he got some nice group footage. Lauren had a large, fun family. Grandma Randall did like to flirt. She snagged his arm and showed him off. It made him think of his own family. He owed his grandmother a call. She had raised him from the age of ten, when his parents had died in an auto accident. Her birthday was this week.

Having delayed as long as possible, he wandered over to the head table. Along the way a curvy redhead caught his eye. She showed her interest with a come-hither gaze. He kept on walking. He already had all the woman he could handle tonight.

At the head table he slid into his seat next to Lauren. Tori's parents sat on the other side of the happy couple. Unwilling to sit in uncomfortable silence for the duration of dinner, he turned on the charm.

He kept the conversation light and impersonal, which put Lauren at ease. Stories from the set were always entertaining, and he finally drew a laugh from his companion. It gave him almost as much satisfaction as when she had melted against him earlier.

She'd been overly tense all day. Probably from having to hand control over to her assistant. The woman was nothing if not bossy. The deejay announced the first dance: a waltz to *When You Say Nothing At All*. Tori and Garrett took the floor, and after a few minutes Ray led Lauren out to join them and pulled her into his arms.

"Close your eyes," he bade her. "It'll be over in a minute."

She glanced at him through her lashes. "You're being very nice."

"Hey, I can take a hint when it slaps me in the chest."

"I'm sorry." She laid her head on his shoulder. "I've been such a brat."

He tightened his arm around her waist. "No more than usual."

She laughed. "You're just saying that to make me feel better."

"Is it working?" He laid his cheek against the silk of her hair. "Should I brave another invitation to move indoors?"

She pulled her head back, eyed him speculatively. "To the laundry room? There are more comfortable rooms available inside, if you're truly interested in tempting me."

"Hey, I have fond memories of you in a laundry room." He kissed a path to her ear. "Remember?"

She sighed. "I remember. It wasn't one of my finest moments."

"Oh, I disagree." He twirled her and brought her back against him. "You were more than fine—you were extremely hot."

"My parents were playing poker in another room!"

"You wild child, you."

She grinned. "It *was* rather naughty."

"Excellent." Blood surged hot through his veins. "Let's go."

With her hand in his, he started off the dance floor.

"Stop." She dug her heels in. "Fun as this is…" she waved between them "…there's no future to it. I can't keep dodging into closets with you."

"Why not?"

"I'm a responsible adult. I have to think of…my reputation. Eventually someone is going to notice if we keep disappearing together."

He scowled, positive that wasn't what she'd been going to say. "Dynamite, this is Hollywood—being seen with me can only up your reputation."

"Humble, much?" She shook her head. "Seriously, whatever was between us is over."

He stood watching her walk away, appeased only slightly by the look of regret he'd seen in the depths of her eyes.

This night was never going to end. Lauren gathered empties and carried them to the tray near the bar. And turned to be confronted by the bride.

"What do you think you're doing?"

"Nothing." Lauren fought the urge to hide her hands behind her back. She waved them instead. "See? Nothing."

"Uh-huh." Tori grabbed one of her hands and drew it close as she wrapped her arm around Lauren's. "Because it's *my* day, I'll pretend I didn't see you clearing the tables."

"Forgive me. Blame it on habit."

"Only because I had to stop myself from doing the same thing twice."

"Oh, that would never do."

"That's what Garrett said."

As they neared the dance floor Lauren demanded, "Where are you taking me?"

"Here." Tori drew her right into the middle of the dancers swaying to a soft ballad. "I've danced with all my favorite people today except one. You."

Lauren's stomach jolted at the idea of swirling to music even as her heart overflowed with joy. She stepped into her sister's arms and hugged her close. If she moved slowly enough she'd be fine.

"Be happy," she whispered. "More than anything, I hope for your happiness."

"I am. Happier than I've ever been," Tori assured her. "Garrett *gets* me."

"And you get him. It's why you click."

"I want this for you." Tori's eyes glittered with happiness, with a need to share her bliss with the world. Her gaze flitted to the head table, where Garrett and his best man lounged back with a couple of beers. "Maybe you and Ray?"

"Oh, no." Lauren automatically shook her head. "Sorry to disappoint, but that's ancient history."

"Why?" Tori challenged. "Because he causes you to act spontaneously? To have a little fun? I think he's been good for you."

"Good for me?" She laughed. Oh, he did wonderful things *to* her. But good *for* her? Not by a long shot. "Think about it. He's a master manipulator."

"He's a director," Tori reminded her. "It's what he does, not who he is. He's not Brad, Lauren. He'd never hurt you."

Easy for Tori to say. Lauren would rather not risk it. Something told her Ray's power to hurt would put Brad to shame.

"Ladies, you make such a pretty picture we had to come join you." Garrett smoothly stepped between them and brought their linked hands to his mouth, where he kissed the back of Lauren's fingers before twirling her around and passing her over to Ray.

Her world spun as he moved off with Tori.

"Hey." Ray's strong arms held her steady. "Are you okay?"

"Yes. No." She leaned her forehead on his chest, prayed for her stomach to settle. No such luck. "I'm going to be sick."

Lifting her skirts, she took off at a run. And, *oh, goodness,* she wasn't going to make it. But then a hard arm curved around her back and swept her along. She reached the bathroom off the kitchen with no time to spare.

Ray held her hair while she emptied her stomach. She

was mortified—and grateful. She wanted him to go but was also glad he was there.

"I'm so sorry." She flushed and slowly lifted her head. Wait—why was she apologizing? It was *his* kid causing this inconvenience! A fact he was sure to catch on to with this display.

"No need to be. We've all had a tad too much bubbly at one point or another." He pressed a damp cloth into her hands.

She lifted it to her face, reveled in the coolness. When she lowered the cloth he held a dripping bottle of water out to her. She gratefully accepted it.

"Oh, man, I could kiss you right now."

He smiled and tucked a loose tendril behind her ear. "Sorry, Dynamite. All trips to the laundry room have been cancelled for the night."

CHAPTER TWO

A TRILL OF BEEPS sounded from Ray's phone. And another, and another. He ignored them as he navigated the hill to his Malibu home. He'd skipped out on the post-wedding breakfast. With Garrett gone, Ray's duties were done. No need for him to linger. Nope, he was happy to put all things wedding-related behind him.

Another beep. Sounded like media alerts. He guarded his privacy, so he liked to stay on top of his media exposure. Such as it was. Better, in his opinion, to be on top of an issue than blindsided by it. With that in mind he had an assistant producer set to tell him whenever his name appeared in the news. Being best man at a major Hollywood wedding—an outdoor wedding, at that—would probably have the darn thing beeping all day long.

Once he reached his place, he dumped his garment bag at the bottom of the stairs, set his camera case on the foyer table, and wandered into the living room. He aimed the remote at his sixty-inch TV and powered it up. He'd barely tuned in to a basketball game before his phone beeped again.

He picked it up and started flipping through the alerts. Just as he'd thought, most were about the wedding. Pictures were already plastered across the internet. Distant and grainy, most gave a sense of the event but the people were unrecognizable unless you knew who they were— which would suit millions of viewers just fine.

A few obviously came from within the event. Garrett would have a fit about that.

Ah, crud. Just his luck—one of the up close and personal shots was of him bent over Lauren, kissing her neck. The look on her face spoke of wistful desire. So she hadn't been as indifferent as she'd pretended.

Too bad the knowledge wasn't worth the hassle it would bring. The photo had already gone viral. And, yep, right on cue his phone rang. The ringtone, an Irish ditty, announced that his grandmother waited at the other end.

"Hello, Mamó. How are you on this bright winter morning?"

"What do you know of winter? I saw on the news it's seventy degrees in Los Angeles. We've snow up to our knees. *That's* winter."

"I hope you aren't shoveling the drive again? I hired someone to keep the drive and walk clear."

"Wasted money." Annoyance flashed down the line. "We don't need it more than half the time."

"That's not the point." His brows drew together. It wasn't like Mamó to be grouchy. Thrifty, yes, but generally good-natured. He sought to distract her. "What do you have planned for your birthday?"

"Oh, they're making a fuss and I don't want it."

"They" being his aunt Ellie and his cousin Kyla.

"Nothing special about being another year older when I have nothing to show for it."

Knowing she meant great-grandkids, he dropped his head onto the back of the sofa. Lately she'd been more and more verbal about her desire for him to settle down and start a family.

"Are they taking you out to dinner?"

"No. They have a party planned at the community center. I keep telling them it's a waste of space and time."

"Everyone loves you, Mamó. I'm sure the place will be packed with your friends."

"It is difficult these days. My friends like to crow about their grandchildren and great-grandchildren. I have nothing to share."

"Mamó…"

"I know you don't want to hear this. But it is my life."

He frowned over the despair in her voice. He'd never heard her so depressed.

"I'm sorry—"

"Stop." A loud sigh blew in his ear. "Listen to me rant. Forgive an old woman her bitter babbling. I miss you, my boy. It would cheer me greatly if you could come to my party."

"A visit?" he mused. He might be able to manage that. A trip would help him to put Lauren out of his mind again.

Goodness knew there were a few harrowing memories waiting there for him. Perhaps it was time to put them behind him.

"Yes." Mamó showed a spark of life. "And you can bring your girlfriend with you."

Uh-oh. "Girlfriend?"

"Yes. I saw all the pictures of the two of you on the internet. You look so handsome." Her voice contained a world of excitement. "The two of you look just like a bride and groom yourselves."

In her stunning silver dress Lauren *had* looked like a bride. He remembered the stutter of his heart when she had started down the aisle toward him. In the midst of a harrowing day, she'd been the ideal distraction.

Now that played against him, giving Mamó unrealistic hopes.

"She's a lovely girl. I'm so excited to know you're seeing someone. Say you'll bring her."

This was going downhill fast. Mamó was setting herself up for disappointment if she believed a future existed for him and Lauren. "Listen—"

"You can't fool me. It's clear in the pictures you care for

her. Please, Ray?" Mamó beseeched. "You have to come and bring her with you. It's my dearest wish. And this may be my last birthday."

She was always saying things like that, but one of these days it would be true.

Comfortable in yoga pants and a cap-sleeved tee, Lauren sat on her beige sofa, feet kicked up on her ottoman coffee table, tea at her elbow, trying to focus on the mystery book she'd been saving for her vacation. Her mom, dad and brother had left for Palm Springs after breakfast, leaving Lauren free to head home and officially start her vacation.

With Tori taking two weeks off for her honeymoon, Lauren had decided to have a much needed break as well. She saw it as a great opportunity to let their new assistants take the lead on the two events scheduled for the coming week. The women had done a great job at the wedding and were ready for more responsibility.

Only a week off for Lauren, though. Hollywood's premier awards ceremony aired on Sunday, and By Arrangement was hosting Obsidian Studios' after-party.

The event represented a major goal for the company. Yes, Tori was now married to the owner, but Lauren took pride in the fact that By Arrangement had earned the contract *before* they'd got engaged. Their work for Obsidian at the Hollywood Hills Film Festival had become legendary.

For the past two months they'd been getting more work than they could handle. She'd gotten three new calls just this morning.

Much as she loved her family, Lauren had been glad to see them go. Being around her mom and not telling her about the baby had just felt wrong. But Lauren wasn't ready to confess her condition yet. Not just because she wanted Tori to be there when she revealed the news, but because Lauren needed to get used to the idea herself.

Which also explained why she wasn't ready to talk to Ray.

In a perfect world she wouldn't have to talk to Ray at all. She could dismiss him as a sperm donor and go about her life raising her child as she pleased. Unfortunately she possessed too much integrity for that option. Plus her work and his crossed paths too often for a pregnancy to go unnoticed.

A knock at the door drew her brows together in a frown. She couldn't think of a single person who might be calling. Setting her teacup on the ottoman, she made her way to the door. Where she caught sight of herself in the mirror over the hall table.

She skidded to a halt on the hardwood floor. She didn't have a lick of make-up on. After a bout of morning sickness she'd scrubbed her face clean and changed into comfy clothes. She'd barely run a brush through her hair before throwing the mass into a ponytail. She looked like a slightly hungover sixteen-year-old.

With any luck it would be a Girl Scout selling cookies. Lauren could buy a box of chocolate mints and send the child away without too much embarrassment.

A glance through the peephole proved she wasn't that lucky. Ray stood on the other side of the door. Geez, how did he even know where she lived?

Maybe if she didn't answer he'd go away. As soon as that thought registered she reached for the doorknob. It smacked of cowardice—something she refused to allow.

"Hey," Ray greeted her.

Of course he looked sensational, in black chinos and an olive lightweight knit shirt under a black leather jacket.

"Can I talk to you? It's important."

She'd bet her "important" beat his "important." But she wasn't ready to go there yet, so she really had nothing to say to him.

"I don't think that's a good idea." She blocked the door. "We pretty much said everything yesterday."

"Not this. I have a job for you."

Uh, no. "You'll need to call the office. I'm on vacation."

"I know." He kissed her on the temple as he pushed past her. "That makes it perfect."

Gritting her teeth, she followed him down the short hall to the open-plan living-room-kitchen combo. She had no doubt his "never take no for an answer" attitude had contributed greatly to his success as an award-winning director. On a personal front, she found it highly annoying.

"I don't think it's wise for us to work together at this time." She lingered in the opening between the hall and living area, watching as he made himself comfortable on her overstuffed couch.

"No one else will do for this particular job," he said, with such conviction it sparked her curiosity.

But she refused to be drawn in. She needed these next few days to herself, to re-evaluate and plan. To consider his part in her future.

"I'm sure that's an exaggeration."

"It's not, actually." He picked up her teacup and sniffed; he took a sip and nodded. "My grandmother's birthday is this week." He went to the kitchen and began opening cupboards until he found a mug. "I talked to her this morning. I've never heard her sound so down. All her friends are great-grandmothers and she's pouting because she doesn't have a baby to dangle on her knee."

"I'm sorry to hear that." Lauren took the mug from him and set it on the counter. "What does that have to do with me?"

"She asked me to come to her party. I'm hoping if I go it will cheer her up."

"Good luck with that." She did wish him luck, knowing how stubborn *her* grandmother could be when stuck on that topic. "I still don't see how By Arrangement can be of assistance. We have no connections in New York. If we'd had more warning we could have put something together for you, but at this late date—"

"I don't need your expertise as an event coordinator," he broke in. "I need a date."

She blinked at him; let her mind catch up with his words. "You want me to go to New York with you?"

"Yes. We leave tomorrow morning. I've already arranged the flight."

Of course he had. She pointed toward the door. "Get out."

"Lauren, I'm serious. I need your help."

"You're insane if you think I'm going to New York with you."

"I don't expect you to drop everything for nothing." He treated her to his charming smile. "I want to hire you."

The attempt at manipulation and the reminder that his request was a job offer only made the whole thing worse. Fortunately it had the benefit of reminding her he was a client and as such deserved a respectful response.

Drawing on her professional persona, she breathed deep, seeking calm. "As I already mentioned, I'm on vacation."

"Name your price." He would not be deterred. "I need you. Mamó saw that tabloid picture of us a couple of months ago, and now all the internet pictures of us at the wedding, and is excited about the idea of me having a girlfriend. All she wants for her birthday is for me to bring you with me."

"I'm not comfortable with the idea of deceiving your grandmother. If that's what you're looking for I'm sure there are any number of actresses who would be pleased to help you."

"It's not like that." He scowled. "It has to be you because you're the one in the pictures and because we do have a relationship."

"Did." She corrected him. "We had a fling." Calling

their frantic rendezvous a relationship seemed a stretch. "It's over."

He stepped closer, played with the ends of her ponytail. "It doesn't have to be. We could have fun on this trip."

Gazing into his cheerful blue eyes, she experienced the irrational desire to lunge for what he offered. She didn't think when she was in his arms—she just felt. An option that held huge appeal when her mind still whirled from the fact she was expecting his baby.

"No." She spun out of his reach, crossed her arms in front of her—protecting herself, protecting their child. "We couldn't. I told you, there's no future for us. I like to be in the driver's seat and so do you."

"I don't mind riding shotgun to a beautiful woman on occasion."

"Liar."

He laughed. "Okay, you got me. But we manage okay. What's wrong with having a little fun?"

"It's not me." Which was true—even if there wasn't a child to consider. "And I'm too busy. Don't forget the awards are this weekend. We're handling the Obsidian party."

"But you're on vacation. And we'll be back by Saturday."

"I prefer to be available in case the new assistants need help. And, believe me, I have things to keep me occupied." Like planning a new future. Making an actual doctor's appointment. Strategizing how she was going to handle him.

Ray stepped back, propped his hands on his hips. He appeared truly perplexed by her refusal. "Lauren, it's my *grandmother.*"

Okay, he knew what button to push. She didn't wish his grandmother ill. She actually admired his attempt to help the older woman. But she couldn't let her sympathy lead her down a dangerous path.

"I'm sorry. She's going to have to make do with you."

"Right." His blue eyes turned cold. He turned away. "Sorry to have bothered you."

She closed her eyes rather than watch him walk away. A moment later she heard the front door close behind him.

Lauren's conscience niggled her all morning and into the afternoon. For all his forceful charm and pre-planning ways, Ray had genuinely been concerned for his grandmother.

And, though they were no longer and never really had been seeing each other, the tabloid and internet pictures gave the appearance they had. Ray's penchant for privacy—well known in Hollywood and no doubt by his family—only added credibility to his grandmother's assumption.

But every time she considered changing her mind her heart raced and she remembered how insane his proposal was. If she agreed to go with him she'd be the unbalanced one. The man rode roughshod over everyone. Case in point: he had bought her airline ticket without even getting her agreement first.

So arrogant, so controlling… She shuddered. So not a good combination.

Except her life was now irrevocably linked to his. The trip to New York would present the perfect opportunity to see Ray in the midst of his family. What better way to learn what family meant to him? His concern for his grandmother was already an eye-opener. How could she refuse to help him and then expect to have a harmonious relationship going forward?

Simple—she couldn't.

A child grew within her. Ray's child. Mamó's great-grandchild. Which meant Lauren had no choice but to go to New York.

She consoled herself with the knowledge that the trip

would provide the perfect opportunity to tell him the news of their pending parenthood.

She hated making spur-of-the-moment decisions. She liked to plan, set goals, make lists. Order prevented chaos, allowed her to be prepared, in control. She hadn't reached that point when it came to the baby. Or Ray.

If she was going to go to New York with him she wanted to lay down some ground rules.

Mind made up, she changed and drove to Ray's hillside home in Malibu. It took close to an hour. She pulled in to his flagstone driveway and parked. He lived alone except for the middle-aged couple who took care of the house and gardens. Fred and Ethel lived in a small villa on the grounds.

Lauren smirked as always at the couple's names. They were poignant reminders of home. You didn't grow up in Palm Springs, rich with old Hollywood history, without being familiar with *I Love Lucy*.

She rang the doorbell, listened to it echo through the house. Given the size of the place, she gave it a few minutes before ringing again. Ray's home took up four acres and consisted of five buildings: the four-thousand-square-foot main house, a multi-level garage with a heliport on top, a guest house, a pool house, and the caretakers' villa. The grounds were terraced and included a tennis/basketball court, a pool, and two spas.

He also had top-of-the-line security with high-end electronic capabilities. Ray loved his gadgets. She didn't look into the camera above the door, but she knew it was there.

She frowned and glanced at her watch. Maybe he was out. But if that were the case why had she been let in the front gate? Lauren had allowed plenty of time for someone to respond to the bell, which meant he was here and making her wait or he was refusing to acknowledge her.

Now who was the coward?

"What do you want?" His disembodied voice came from no discernible source.

"To talk to you," she replied, keeping her gaze fixed on the ground. If he wanted to see her face he needed to open the door.

"I believe it was made clear there was nothing further to discuss between the two of us."

She crossed her arms over her chest. This was why they weren't compatible—the constant play for power. "I'm not having a conversation through a door."

"What?" he mocked her. "Am I lacking graciousness as a host?"

"Fine." She turned on her peep-toed heels. "Forget it."

All the better for her. No awkward acting required in New York, and she'd made the attempt, so he couldn't hold her earlier rejection against her.

The door opened at her back and a strong male hand wrapped around her upper arm. "Please come in." He led her inside to the large, open living room. "I wouldn't want you to come all this way and not state your business."

She walked past him and took a seat on an oval suede sofa in rich beige. *Shoot*, an already difficult discussion had just got harder. Because he looked yummy. He wore the same pants and shirt he'd had on earlier, but he was sexily disheveled, with his sandy hair mussed up, the start of a five o'clock shadow, and bare feet.

When she didn't answer he dropped into a chair across from her, knees spread, arms braced on muscular thighs.

She swallowed hard.

"No door, Dynamite." He gave her his full attention. "What do you want? If you'll remember, I have some packing to do."

Seeking composure, she straightened her shoulders and crossed her hands over her purse in her lap. "I've reconsidered my earlier decision. I'm willing to help you with your grandmother."

He considered her for a moment, his blue eyes assessing. "What's it going to cost me?"

Annoyed at the mention of payment, she seared him with a glare.

"By Arrangement is an event-oriented business. We do not get involved in family dynamics. I would be doing this as a favor for a friend."

Okay, that was stretching it. She'd be doing it to get to know her child's father better.

"So now we're friends?" He lifted one brown eyebrow.

She shrugged. She'd like to think they could be friends, but the chemistry between them made the ease of friendship a difficult prospect.

"The point is I'm willing to help. And it's not going to cost you anything more than a few common courtesies."

His eyes narrowed. "I knew there'd be something."

"Just a few ground rules so we don't get tripped up."

He sat back. "Such as?"

"Well, to start with I think we need to be as truthful as possible."

"Agreed."

"It'll be less complicated. And I prefer to be as honest as we can."

"No argument. What's next?"

"I want separate bedrooms."

He cocked his head. "It's my grandmother. I'm pretty sure that's guaranteed."

She relaxed a little. So far, so good. "No fostering false hope that our relationship will mature to the next level."

"'Mature to the next level?'" he repeated. "Who talks that way?"

"Nice." Her shoulders went back. "You know what I mean."

"Don't get her hopes up that we'll get married." He frowned over the words. "You really don't have to worry about that."

"I'm not expecting a proposal." A long-suffering sigh lifted her breasts, drawing his attention downward. How predictable. "I want you to promise you won't let concern for your grandmother sway you into implying something you can't deliver. She'll only be hurt in the long run."

"You can be assured I'm not going to do anything to hurt Mamó."

Uh-huh. She believed his love and concern were genuine. But she also knew his penchant for control, and that he had a compulsive need to fix things. She easily saw one emotion feeding into the other.

"The last is no unnecessary touching."

He threw back his head and laughed. "You've got to be kidding. The point is that we're a *couple*. How do we portray intimacy without touching?"

She understood his confusion. The man was very tactile —he couldn't *not* touch…things, materials, people.

"I didn't say no touching. Of course there will need to be public displays of affection. But you're a master director, brilliant at evoking emotion. I'm sure you can manage with the minimum of physical contact."

"So PDAs are okay?" His gaze ran over her as his mind connected the dots. He was to keep his hands to himself in private. "So businesslike. I thought you were doing this as a friendly gesture. Why so strict?"

How to answer that? The baby motivated her to help him, because she needed to maintain a position of power. But that wasn't the only reason. Before she'd known about the baby she'd fought her desires because they turned her into someone she wasn't. Reckless, abandoned, acquiescent.

She'd subjugated her will to a man once before. It had changed who she was—a mistake she'd never make again.

She considered telling him about the baby—just putting it out there. But, no. He was already dealing with a distressed grandmother. It wouldn't be fair to drop the baby news on him, too.

"I've put what was between us behind me. Yet there's no denying the sexual chemistry between us." She gave him the lesser truth. "I don't want to jeopardize the progress I've made. This is a deal-breaker, Ray."

"Okay, you win." He threw his hands up in surrender. "I promise to keep my hands to myself."

She knew she'd have to remind him of his pledge, but it would do for now.

"When is our flight?"

The limousine pulled to a stop in front of Lauren's home and Ray stepped out. He knew she co-owned the bungalow-style duplex along with her sister. The arrangement allowed the twins the proximity they enjoyed, yet gave each of them their privacy. Perfect for sisters who were both friends and partners, or so she'd told him.

Of course that would all change now Tori had married Garrett. Would the twins keep the property and rent out Tori's side? Or would they sell, leaving Lauren to find a new home?

In a flash he saw her at his place, bringing order to his chaos, watching daily edits with him in the media room, claiming the gaming loft as her home office.

He froze with his hand poised to knock.

His head shook along with a full-body shudder. Must be residual fallout from the wedding. His overactive imagination tweaking on domestic bliss overload.

He knocked. He still puzzled over why Lauren had changed her mind and agreed to accompany him to New York. Nothing really made sense except that family mattered to her.

He'd seen that first-hand last Thanksgiving, when he'd learned that Garrett was spending the day alone, with nothing to occupy him but memories of his father's passing and the shattering of his own body in a car accident the previous year.

Of course Ray had invited his buddy over for Thanksgiving dinner, and then made an emergency call to Lauren to see if By Arrangement could pull off a miracle.

She'd been about to sit down to dinner with her family, but had named a couple of restaurants he could try. He'd cut her off to invite her family to join him and Garrett. The home-cooked deal had appealed to Ray, and additional people would help to distract Garrett.

And, of course, thinking of Thanksgiving brought back memories of their laundry room tryst.

Luckily the front door opened, keeping him from remembering the details of their heated session on the washing machine.

"Good morning." Lauren came out, pulling a small suitcase. "Can you grab the garment bag?" She motioned to the blue bag hanging over the hall closet.

He stepped inside and grabbed it. "Just the two bags?"

"You don't have to be sarcastic." She glanced at her luggage with a frown. "I know it's a lot for a week, but you didn't mention anything except your grandmother's birthday so I have to be prepared for anything."

"I wasn't being sarcastic." He handed her bag to the driver, who also took the roller bag, then held the back door for her. "If you're prepared for anything I'm surprised you don't have twice as many bags."

She gave a small smile and slid across the seat. Her jacket dragged on the seat behind her and he swept it out of the way as he slid in after her.

"Is this your heaviest jacket?" He fingered the fleece-lined raincoat. "The forecast in Queens is for snow."

"I'm sure it'll be fine." She pulled the fabric free and tossed the coat over her purse on the other side of her.

"Fine for Southern California is not the same as fine for New York. You'll freeze if that's all you take." The car pulled away from the curb. "I'll have the driver swing by Rodeo Drive."

He reached for the intercom. Her hand intercepted his, pushing it down.

"Forget it. I'm not buying a coat I'll only wear for a week."

She quickly retracted her touch. The woman did like her rules.

"I brought sweaters and a warm scarf. I'll be fine."

He snorted. "Let me know when you change your mind."

She glanced at him over her shoulder. "Why? So you can say, *I told you so*?"

"So I can take you shopping." He trained his gaze on the muted TV monitor across the way. "The *I told you so* will be strictly implied."

Out of the corner of his eye he caught her grin. He relaxed back into his seat. The trip might not be the total cluster bash he feared.

"Please. Hold your breath," she advised, all sweetness and light.

He turned to address her sass, only to stop when she pressed a hand to her stomach. A glance at her face revealed she'd lost all the color in her cheeks. Concern tightened his chest.

"Lauren, what is it?"

She sat very still, slowly drawing in a deep breath. "I wasn't ready for that last turn. It sent my stomach spinning."

"What can I do?"

"Can you lower the partition?" She swallowed repeatedly. "I think it will help if I can see where we're going."

He picked up the remote and did as she'd asked. The additional light showed her color was returning. "If you're not feeling well we can delay our flight for a day."

"That won't be necessary." She dug in her purse and

pulled out a dry protein bar. "I should have eaten something earlier. I'll be all right once I have a couple of bites." She looked at him oddly. "You're awfully cavalier about our departure time."

"It's not a commercial flight. I called a friend and he's agreed to lend me his jet. Barring emergencies, it's at my disposal for the next week."

"Must be nice." She closed her eyes and leaned her head back as she chewed. Her hand lingered over her stomach.

"Rest." He ran a knuckle down her cheek. "I'll let you know when we get to the airport."

Instead of flinching away, she leaned into his touch. After another sweep of her silky skin he left her to rest. He took heart from the exchange. If she could take comfort from him, the connection between them wasn't entirely extinguished.

Strong enough, he hoped, to convince his family for a week.

And maybe to allow for one more hook-up?

Because Lauren might see them as over, but he wasn't doing well with the whole cold turkey approach. He watched the soft rise and fall of her breasts and struggled with the desire to pull her into his arms.

No, his feelings about their relationship didn't match hers at all. Sure, he believed in keeping things short and light, but *he* usually called the where and when.

And when he looked at her he saw unfinished business.

CHAPTER THREE

LAUREN ACCEPTED RAY'S suggestion to rest as an opportunity to avoid conversation for the rest of their trip to the airport. She shrugged out of the brown cropped jacket she wore over a cream sweater and jeans, then settled back against the seat and watched the road through the veil of her lashes.

Thank goodness seeing where they were headed had helped to calm her queasy stomach.

One thing was for certain. She needed to get this morning sickness under control or she'd be making explanations before she was ready. Ray was too intelligent not to put the pieces together with them living in each other's pockets.

And then there was his grandmother, aunt and cousin. Hopefully they'd be too caught up in Ray's visit and Mamó's birthday to pay much attention to her.

At the airport they departed from the commuter terminal. Expedited VIP service streamlined their boarding process and within minutes she climbed the steps to a mid-sized jet. The scent of fine leather hit her as soon as she entered the plane. Fortunately the baby had no objection to the smell.

Lauren made her way down the aisle between half a dozen armchair-style seats in creamy beige. The second half of the cabin contained two face-to-face couches of the same color in a soft ultra-suede fabric. At the end a door stood open on a full-sized restroom.

Just *wow*. This was totally going to spoil her for flying coach.

Pretending a sophistication she didn't feel, she turned to Ray. "Where do I sit?"

"Wherever you want." He indicated two armchairs facing each other. "Why don't we start here? I asked the attendant to bring you some tea once we're in the air. She'll also bring you something to eat. Do you want eggs and bacon? Bagels or muffins? Fruit?"

"I don't care for anything right now." She sank into the chair next to the window.

"A few bites of protein bar aren't much," he protested. "You need something more."

"Welcome aboard." The attendant, an attractive brunette in a gray pantsuit, appeared at her elbow. "My name is Julie. I'll be serving you today. If you need anything you can call me via the remote, or just push this button." She showed Lauren on her armrest. "I'll bring tea when we've reached cruising altitude. What more would you like?"

"Nothing for—"

"Thank you, Julie." Ray cut Lauren off. "Please bring a selection of bagels, fruit, and yogurt."

Lauren slammed him with a glare at his arrogant disregard for her wishes. She should know if she was hungry.

"May I take your things?" Julie offered. "There's a closet at the front of the cabin. You'll have full access during the flight."

Lauren handed off her purse and coat. She waited until the other woman had disappeared before addressing Ray.

"If you hope to get along on this trip you will refrain from treating me like a child."

"Then don't behave like one."

His gaze roved over her. She felt the weight of it everywhere it touched.

"You're still pale. Food helped in the car. I can only

assume it would be better if you had something more. It would please me if you ate. But the choice is yours."

She gritted her teeth. To argue further would only make her sound petty.

Luckily the pilot's voice filled the cabin. "Please fasten your seatbelts. We'll be departing momentarily."

Avoiding Ray's gaze, she glanced out the window as the plane began to move. His reasonableness did nothing to appease her. In fact it only annoyed her, putting her in the position of being unreasonable—an intolerable situation, which was totally his fault.

It would please him if she ate? Seriously?

Right this minute she felt fine. She hoped to stay that way through takeoff. And the thought of food…? Not helping.

As a view of the airport, planes, and air traffic personnel flowed by the porthole window she marveled once again at her current circumstances. The only explanation she could come up with was she must have royally ticked off Lady Karma in another life, because she should not be pregnant.

She'd started on the pill. Ray had worn condoms. Yeah, they'd been frantic for each other, but they'd also been responsible. Okay, there had been that once when the condom broke. Yet—hello?—still on the pill. Sure, her doctor had warned her that it took time for the body to adjust, but it had been a month. Well, almost.

The force of takeoff pushed her back in her seat as the plane began to rise. Her fingers curled into fists on the armrests, her nails digging into the soft leather. She closed her eyes, willed her stomach to behave.

"Are you okay?"

Ray's voice sounded next to her ear at the same time as a warm hand settled over her clenched fingers.

Her eyes flew open. When had he moved next to her?

More to the point, when had his touch become an instant soother?

It had to be the distraction, her logical mind asserted, but she didn't care. She turned her hand over, threaded her fingers through his and accepted the warmth and comfort he freely offered.

Tension eased away, taking the rising nausea with it.

"Thank you." She gave him a feeble smile.

"Nervous flyer?" he sympathized.

"Mmm…" She made a noncommittal sound. Poor guy. Her hormones were all over the place, her emotions likewise. Talk about mixed signals. *She* didn't know how she felt—how could he begin to guess?

"Not usually." She made an effort to participate in the conversation, hoping the resulting distraction would continue to work on her mind and stomach. "I guess I'm nervous about the whole trip. We haven't truly discussed how we're going to handle things. I'm not comfortable lying to your grandmother."

"Me neither," he said. "So we don't lie."

Eying his stoic expression, she felt the muscles in her shoulders begin to tense again. "If you're suggesting—"

"I'm not." He squeezed her fingers. "We're friends. At least I hope you consider me a friend. That's what we put out there."

Because his touch felt too good, she pulled her hand free of his. On another level she noticed the plane had leveled out. "But everyone has an expectation there's more between us."

"Exactly. We'll just be ourselves and they'll see what they want to see."

She tapped her fingers on the armrest as she considered his approach. "Still seems a little artificial."

"The power of illusion comes from a collective awareness. People believe what they want to believe. Directors use viewer expectations as a tool to manipulate the audience's emotions all the time. It doesn't make what they feel any less real."

"Do you hear the words you're using? *Manipulate... audience*. This is your family we're talking about, not a theater full of moviegoers."

She understood the concept he presented, and, yes, she expected it would work as well as he stated. The truth worked for her. Leaving his family with preconceived notions that went well beyond reality was more iffy.

"Look." His gaze earnest, he picked up her hand, swept his thumb over the pulse at her wrist. "I know the girlfriend front isn't ideal. Ordinarily I wouldn't even consider it. But you have no idea how upset my grandmother sounded." Concern darkened his eyes to a soft azure. "If this plan lifts her spirits, it's worth a little discomfort on my part."

"Okay," she agreed. And again removed her hand from under his. Bottom line: his concern was genuine. And, if she were honest, it wasn't as if she and Tori hadn't occasionally manufactured events to gain their mother's cooperation to get something they wanted.

His family—his call. She'd agreed to come, so she'd do as he wished.

"Teatime."

Julie had arrived with a cart. She reached past them to pull a table from a wall slot, trapping Lauren next to Ray. The sudden intimacy suffocated her. She wanted to protest. Of course she didn't.

She was too strong to give in to weakness, too smart to reveal it to the opposition.

Onto the table Julie slid a tray, artfully displaying an array of bagels, both toasted and non-toasted, along with a healthy heaping of cream cheese, butter, and jellies. There were containers of yogurt and a lovely selection of fresh fruit. Next came steaming pots of hot water and a small basket of teas.

A midsized plate and linen-wrapped silverware were

placed in front of each of them. "May I serve you?" Julie asked.

"We'll help ourselves, thank you." Ray's charming smile caused the poised woman to blush.

"Please buzz me if you require anything more," she bade them, and then disappeared to her niche in the front of the plane.

Lauren waited for her stomach to revolt. When it didn't she reached for the basket of teas, chose a soothing de-caffeinated blend and steeped it in one of the pots. When it looked the right color, she poured the brew into a delicate teacup.

Ray slathered cream cheese on a cinnamon bagel and slid melon, pineapple chunks and a few blackberries on his plate.

"Can I fix you anything?" he asked, after she'd taken her first sip.

"Perhaps half a plain bagel, with a light spread of cream cheese."

He nodded and a moment later placed it on her plate. She cut it into quarters and picked up a corner to nibble on.

"You know, I'm all for sticking to the truth and all..." She set her cup back in its saucer. "But the details are still going to be a bit sketchy. You do realize we've never been on an actual date?" She stabbed at a plump berry on his plate and ate it.

His eyes narrowed in thought. He reached for a carton of peach yogurt, opened it and scooped in a few berries. He took a couple of bites before pointing his spoon at her.

"We've kept a low profile."

Her brows lifted. "You're a little too good at this."

He grinned and offered her the yogurt carton. "I'm a director. It's my job to invent and interpret."

"Convenient." Not even thinking about it, she accepted the yogurt.

The flavors, peach and blackberry, exploded in her

mouth. A few more bites finished it off. She sighed. A glance at her plate revealed he'd gotten his wish. She'd eaten all her bagel plus fruit and his yogurt. And she felt great. More energized than she had in forever.

"Finally you've a little color in your cheeks."

She gave him a cool glance. "Saying *I told you so* is unbecoming."

He shook his sandy head. "I'm just glad you're feeling better."

"Thanks." What else could she say without sounding petty? To his credit, he appeared sincere.

To break the moment she pushed the button on her armrest. Julie appeared within moments to clear the table. But all too soon she and Ray were alone again. It was all she could do not to twitch in her seat. How to get him to move away?

Turned out she didn't have to do anything. Phone in hand, he stood up.

"If you'll excuse me, I have some calls to make?"

She nodded and he moved across the aisle and up to another row of seats. Able to breathe freely, she refused to acknowledge she missed the heat and comfort of his proximity. Some alone time to think was exactly what she needed. She felt the best she had in days—make that weeks.

Maybe she'd actually be able to concentrate and come up with a course of action for this abrupt change in her carefully crafted life plan. So far she hadn't quite been able to wrap her mind around the enormity of the fact she carried a child within her. And that kept her from making sense out of the chaos in her head.

Which left her feeling out of control and desperate to get her life back.

Panicked, really.

The last time she'd given up control, she'd lost a part of her soul.

Lauren couldn't go through that again—especially

when she had a child to think of. She required her lists, her goals, her plans. She craved order, needed to be in charge. Only then could she cope.

She stared unseeing out the window.

Some things were obvious. Once Tori returned Lauren would tell her family. She would continue to work. She would tell Ray. It all sounded simple and straightforward. It couldn't be more complex.

Even telling her family. Sure, they would love and support her. She had no doubt of that. But there'd also be disappointment and concern. And questions. Personal questions, not easy to answer.

Continuing to work would require compromise and sacrifice. Deciding between daycare and a nanny was only one decision to be made requiring careful research. She also needed to consider housing—whether to sell the duplex and move to a bigger place in a family-friendly area. It didn't need to be done now, but it was already on her mind. A part of the mix keeping her from finding the necessary peace to deal with everything.

Telling Ray. Yeah, she'd been playing ostrich there. She knew she had to give him the news. Yet the where and when were still questions. She had no idea how to approach him, but she did know it wouldn't be before this deal with his grandmother played out.

It wouldn't be fair to distract him at this time.

And, truly, everything else hinged on his reaction. Any plans she conceived were contingent on how involved he'd want to be.

Her stomach roiled. The realization threatened the scant control she'd managed to muster.

She drew out her phone and powered it up. She had a couple of her own calls to make.

About forty minutes before they were scheduled to land Ray roused Lauren. Halfway through the trip she'd stretched out on one of the couches and slid into a solid sleep. She hadn't moved an eyelash when he'd dropped a blanket over her and stuffed a pillow under her head.

She was slow to awaken. He had no idea if that was natural or not, as they'd never actually slept together. He tended not to sleep with the women in his life. Too messy.

How fragile she looked. He traced the shadows under the fan of her lashes. She said she wasn't sick, yet she was tired and pale and a couple of times he'd caught an expression on her face that made him think she might be fighting off nausea. Perhaps it was the aftereffects of stress. Handling her sister's wedding during Hollywood's biggest party season must have been a challenge, even for a pro like her.

She was such a strong woman—quick and intelligent and in control—he tended to overlook the fact she was quite delicate.

"Lauren." He ran his hand up her arm, gave her shoulder a gentle shake. "Wake up, Sleeping Beauty."

"Hmm?" She sighed and shifted onto her side. "Ga-way."

He grinned. "No, I'm not going away." Leaning over her, he pressed his lips to hers. "But I'll join you if you'd like." That ought to wake her up.

"Ray…" Her lips opened under his and an arm snaked around his neck, pulling him close.

The action put him off balance. He went down on one knee to keep from tumbling on top of her. He'd happily follow up on his offer to join her on the couch as soon as he knew her mind was as engaged as her body.

Meantime, he sank into the kiss.

Instantly the chemistry ignited between them. Angling his head, he slid his tongue past her lips to taste the honey of her mouth. Her sleepy response seduced him into a slow, deep exploration. The meandering journey pulled them down a path not yet taken. The softness of the moment was different but every bit as hot as their bolder encounters.

She sighed and shifted fully onto her back. The drag of her fingers through his hair was a dreamy caress, a subtle demand for more, for longer, for slow and sensual. He willingly set the pace, lingering over each touch, each taste, each smell, satiating all his senses. Her breath sighed over his cheek and he took satisfaction in each little moue and gasp.

Never had he burned for a woman like he did for her. And she was right there with him, her responsiveness inspiring him to new depths.

The gradual, sultry building of passion urged him to tenderness, to lengthy kisses and gentle insistence. He worked his hand under her sweater and glided up her silky skin, seeking the bounty of her breast.

She suddenly went very still and her hand came down on his, effectively pushing the stop button on his attempt to move their embrace to the next step.

"Not a good idea," she mumbled in a sleep-husky voice.

He groaned and tested her resolve, sweeping his thumb across the warm flesh of her stomach. She gasped and tightened her hold, but the knit of her sweater separating her grasp from his was a thin barrier to his persistence.

"Shh, Dynamite," he whispered against her lips, "you're dreaming."

"Liar." Her lips lifted in a smile under his and then she turned her head aside. "My body is too alive for me to be asleep." She pulled his hand free of her clothes. "We agreed no touching."

"You started it, wrapping yourself all around me." He kissed a path up her jawline to whisper in her ear. "Let me finish it. We can start the no touching when we get to New York."

She moaned deep in her throat—a sound he took to

mean she was tempted, if the look in her golden eyes meant anything.

"Uh-uh." She planted both hands on his chest and pushed. "I did not start it. You kissed me first. When I had no resistance. Unfair, Ray."

He let her up, slid onto the couch next to her when she pushed into a sitting position. "Spoilsport."

An arch glare came his way. "Really?"

The show of ire along with her mussed hair and just-kissed lips was too sexy for words. Made him want to take up where they had left off. Forget about apologizing. Besides, he still maintained she'd started it. His had been a mere peck on the lips; she had taken it to the next level.

Not waiting for a response, she rolled her eyes, then glanced back at him. "Why did you wake me?"

He checked his watch—much safer than contemplating her. "In ten minutes we begin our descent. I thought you'd like to freshen up before we buckle up."

"Oh. I would, thanks." She made her escape.

While she did her thing he went through his email and texts. The car service he used in New York advised that a driver was waiting. His meeting with the mayor was confirmed. And Mamó couldn't wait to see him.

With a sigh he slipped the phone into his pocket. This trip was long overdue. Sure, he saw his family regularly, stopping off in New York or flying them to him two or three times a year. But he rarely went back to the old neighborhood. Certainly not for any length of time. Too many memories he'd rather not deal with.

Lauren came back, looking as calm and fresh as when she'd first boarded the plane. Something he envied, considering he still ached from their recent bout of passion. He earned another glare when he settled in the seat next to hers, and those luscious lips opened ready to protest, but the pilot came on, demanding they buckle up.

The landing went well and soon Ray saw Lauren seated

into a sleek black town car. She promptly slid to the far side of the bench seat, leaving at least a foot between them, and pulled out her tablet, effectively shutting him out. Within a few minutes they were swallowed by the late-afternoon traffic headed through the borough of Queens to Queens Village.

His grandmother lived in a two-family, two-story pitched-roof house on a postage-stamp-sized lot. He'd tried to upgrade her to a bigger house on a larger lot in a better area, but she refused to move. She'd lived in her house since she'd moved in as a bride and intended to stay until the day she died. Rather than argue, he'd paid off the mortgage, bought out the neighbors so his aunt could move in, and made sure the house remained sound and safe.

"We're here," he said as the pale gray building with its white filigree fence came into view.

Lauren leaned close to look out the window. "Quaint house."

He explained his attempt to relocate her. "I told you she was stubborn."

Cars overflowed the driveway and street, forcing the driver to double park. Ray stepped out and turned to help Lauren. Leaving the driver to bring their bags, Ray threaded their fingers together, more for his benefit than hers, and climbed the brick stairs to the front door. It flew open before his knuckles connected with the wood.

"Ray!" Aunt Ellie pushed open the screen and pulled him into a big hug. "It's so good to see you. Come inside." She stepped back, dragging him with her, and by extension Lauren. "Everyone—Ray is here."

Pandemonium broke out. Women of all ages launched themselves at him. He barely recognized most of them but he hugged them anyway, one-armed. Because he was not letting go of Lauren. Behind him he heard her fielding greetings.

"Hello."

"Hi."

"Nice to meet you."

"I'm Lauren."

These were his grandmother's, aunt's, cousin's friends. He got that they were proud of him and wanted to show off. So he smiled and nodded and forged ahead.

He froze when he spied Mrs. Renwicki. The smug look on her face reminded him of her granddaughter, Camilla. And, *bang*, the past was right in his face.

Turning his back on it, he finally broke through the crowd of people and furniture, and there was Mamó. Short and plump, her white-gray hair woven into a braid and pinned in a bun on top of her head, just as he always pictured her. She rose from her floral wingback chair and framed his face in her wrinkled hands.

"Ray, my boy, I'm so happy to see you." She kissed him on the cheek.

"Mamó, you look great." He gave her a full-on hug. "I've missed you."

"Then you should visit more often." She admonished him. "But you're here now, and you've brought the beautiful Lauren with you."

"Yes." He met Lauren's guarded gaze as he wrapped his arm around her waist and drew her forward. She was a trouper for putting up with this gauntlet. "Thanks," he whispered before turning to his grandmother. "Mamó, this is—"

"This is Lauren!" Mamó broke in, taking Lauren's hands in both of hers. "Your fiancée."

CHAPTER FOUR

LAUREN BLINKED AT Ray's grandmother, the word *fiancée* echoing through the room. Or was it just through her head?

"Oh…" Lauren's smile froze in place while her mind scrambled for an appropriate response. Did she carelessly laugh it off, politely deny the allegation, or go along with the crazy suggestion?

This broke so many of her rules. What was Ray thinking? Was the tight grip on her elbow warning or encouragement?

She angled her head up and around, her gaze meeting his. The shock in his eyes reassured her that his surprise matched hers.

"Mamó—" he began, and Lauren sighed, willing to let him handle the unexpected claim. "We're not—"

"Forgive me," Mamó rushed in, cutting him off. She kissed Lauren's cheek, color high in her cheeks and a look of pleading in her pale blue eyes. "I know you wanted it to be a surprise, but I couldn't resist sharing the news with my closest friends." Her gaze flitted to an older woman across the room before lifting to meet her grandson's eyes. "Please say it's all right."

Behind her, Lauren felt Ray's chest expand in a heavy sigh. "Mamó, I don't know where you got your information, but—"

The hands holding hers shook as the older woman nearly crushed Lauren's fingers.

"Of *course* we forgive you," Lauren rushed to say. It was good to know Ray would uphold his promise to her, but she couldn't let him embarrass his grandmother in front of all her friends.

The way he suddenly relaxed told her it had been a difficult decision.

"Thank you," Mamó breathed in Lauren's ear as she hugged her.

A chorus of congratulations rang out and a few people rushed at them to offer a new round of hearty handshakes and some hugs.

Ray handled it like a pro, reminding Lauren of his short stint as an actor before he'd moved behind the camera.

"I want to see the ring," Kyla demanded, pushing to the front. She grabbed Lauren's hand, only to frown at her naked ring finger. Kyla turned the look on her cousin. "Where's the ring, cuz? I expected to see at least a couple of carats."

"We thought we'd ring-shop while we're in town."

Oh, he was good. He handled the crowd of women like a pro. He charmed them all. He was attentive, a little flirtatious, and slippery as an eel. But Lauren didn't relax. There were too many questions, too many people, too many opportunities to mess up.

"Food's ready," Ellie called out.

Lauren hid a grimace, the thought of food too much, but her stomach growled. She placed a hand on her belly, trying to decipher her body's mixed signals as the rest of the guests eagerly moved into the dining room.

"You okay?"

Ray appeared in front of her. It was the first moment they'd had alone since walking through the door.

"Listen, I'm sorry about the whole engagement thing. Especially after I promised nothing like this would happen. I'll talk to Mamó and see if we can't get it all straightened out."

Lauren shook her head. "I think it's too late for that."

"Yeah," he agreed, a frown pulling his golden-brown brows together. "She got herself into a pickle. Thanks for not embarrassing her."

"Of course." She sent him an arch glance. "She obviously wants to see you settled down."

"And bouncing a baby or two on her lap," he bit out. "It's no excuse for putting us in this position."

Mention of a baby put a tremble in her muscles. She locked her knees and tried for practical. "We knew she was hopeful of a deeper relationship when we headed east," she reminded him. "If we stick to our rules we'll be fine."

"I'm glad you're taking this so well." He placed a hand in the small of her back and directed her toward a table laden with food. "You can still expect an apology."

She sighed, seeing his persistence as a need to control the situation. But she also respected his desire to honor his promise and protect her. Then she reached the food table and all thought left her head as hunger took over.

Grabbing a plate, she filled it with salads, fruit, and meat. She reached for a roll as Ray handed her napkin-wrapped utensils.

"Good to see you have your appetite back." He kissed her on the top of her head.

Okay, she could take that as patronizing or affectionate—neither of which suited her. Deciding to ignore him, she took her plate and found a single seat next to his cousin Kyla. He frowned at her choice and ate standing up near the mantel.

Lauren smiled around a bite of potato salad and listened to the surrounding women talk about tomorrow's party. They were excited because there'd be dancing, but a comment about lack of partners had Lauren glancing around the room. Many of these same people would be guests at the party, and the ratio hit at about three women to each man. Hmm, maybe she could help with that.

A tall, gray-haired gentleman with a dignified bearing hovered around Mamó. A flare of awareness tingled through Lauren, signaling a connection between them. Interesting… Must be a strong link. She rarely experienced the matchmaking sensation without Tori nearby to bolster their shared talent.

The topic moved on to where she should shop for her wedding rings. She stiffened for a moment, then gave a mental shrug. What the heck? She could get behind a fictitious shopping trip.

Thirty minutes later Ray was standing chatting with Mamó's neighbor when Mrs. Renwicki joined them. She gushed over his engagement.

"I'm *so* happy you've finally put Camilla behind you."

Mamó's neighbor nodded and patted his arm as the other woman went on.

"My granddaughter is happily married, expecting her third child. It's time you found some happiness too."

The woman had some nerve, throwing Camilla in his face. He wondered if she knew of the great-grandchild her precious girl had thrown away. Having nothing to say to her, he excused himself and walked away.

The confrontation confirmed his worst fears. His most humiliating moment remained fresh in the minds of the community that had borne witness to it.

His faithful friend was at the ready, and he lifted the camera to his eye and took a few shots. He sought out Lauren with the lens. Seeing her soothed his ravaged nerves. She balanced a half-empty plate on her lap. Her honey-brown eyes blinking repeatedly spoke of her fight to stay awake. It was barely nine—six by west coast timing—but she couldn't keep her eyes open. Knowing her, she had started her day before six. And travel could be exhausting enough without suffering from a stomach ailment.

Ray strolled across the room to rescue her tilting plate. "Time for you to go to bed."

"The party is still going on," she protested as he pulled her to her feet.

"And it can continue without us." He handed her plate off to his cousin and led her to his grandmother. "Mamó, Lauren is exhausted. We're going to leave for the hotel."

"Oh, no." Mamó waved off his statement. "You're both staying here. I made up your room special for you, with new sheets and towels."

He gritted his teeth. He loved his family, but he preferred the privacy and autonomy of a hotel in the nation's largest city.

Plus, he hadn't missed the singular use of "room"—as in Lauren and him in the same sleeping quarters. He couldn't do that to Lauren. She'd already made a huge concession by allowing the faux engagement to stand. He wouldn't force her to share his room.

"We don't want to put you to extra trouble." Ray chose an explanation she'd understand. And it was true, too. "Plus I have appointments in the city."

"Oh…" Disappointment turned Mamó's smile upside down. "But we've already taken your things up to your room." Resignation rang heavy in her voice. She turned to Lauren. "Would you prefer your own room, dear? Is that it? There's a daybed in the sewing room. It's a bit dusty in there—I confess I haven't been in the room for several months—but it won't take long to spruce it up."

Drat. He should have had his assistant call her with his itinerary, but he'd been busy arranging siting plans with the mayor's office. Ray usually stayed in the city when he visited. He never stayed long, for precisely this reason.

He hated seeing his grandmother upset. A glance at Lauren showed her following the conversation with a slight frown drawing her delicate eyebrows together. Her sleepy eyes lifted to his and he saw the words forming on her tongue. He forestalled her so she'd know exactly what she was getting herself into.

"It's best if we go to the suite at the hotel. I did promise Lauren her own space. Plus, it's your birthday. You
shouldn't have to be concerned about caring for house-
guests."

"You know I don't mind. But if it's what you prefer…"
All animation drained from Mamó's face. "I was so looking forward to cooking you breakfast, like old times."

Lauren reached for his hand and gave it a squeeze. "It's
okay, Ray. I'm fine with staying here if you'd like."

Now he really felt torn. He'd much rather stay at the
hotel, but the option of holding Lauren in his arms through
the night brought a whole new element to the situation.

Generally he arranged his amorous adventures so he
ended up alone in his own bed. He found it helped alleviate
complications over the long haul. But for once a woman
was less inclined for entanglement than he was.

In their month-long fling only one memorable encounter had occurred in a bed. He'd run into her at a hotel where
she and her sister had been working a holiday party for
Garrett. Ray had dragged her out a side door for a few
heated moments. She'd quickly put the brakes on because
she'd been working, but he'd sent a room key to her and
after the event she'd met him upstairs.

It had turned out their stolen moment hadn't been as
private as he'd thought, because the next morning a picture
of a torrid embrace between the two of them had hit the
tabloids. Who would have predicted that moment would
have led to this one?

"If Lauren is okay with it, then I'm not going to say no
to your pancakes."

In the end his purpose for being here motivated his
decision. His worry had lifted during the party as Mamó
had seemed like her old self. Watching the light fade out
of her now tore at his gut. The fatigue stamped on Lauren's fine features added weight to Mamó's request. Staying here benefited both women at this point. And, truly,

if he wanted to get Mamó out of her funk he needed to give a little too. Disappointing her on his first day was not a smart move.

"Excellent." Mamó clapped her hands together. "I'll show you up."

"No need." He kissed her cheek before pulling Lauren after him toward the stairs. "I know the way."

"It was a lovely party," Lauren said over her shoulder.

"Thank you, dear. I look forward to getting to know you better tomorrow."

"Goodnight, Mamó," he called.

Upstairs, he opened the door to his childhood room and ushered Lauren inside. He half expected the room to be the same as when he'd left for UCLA fifteen years ago. Luckily the movie posters, twin beds, and blue plaid bedspread were long gone. Instead the walls were painted a pale green and a queen bed stood in the middle of the room, covered by a sage comforter with brown swirls. A large rug in reverse colors was spread across the hardwood floor.

Well, most of it had changed. He grinned when he focused on the art. Movie posters, but instead of being tacked to the wall these were framed behind glass and they were posters for *his* movies.

"Nice touch." Lauren walked to the window and pulled the chocolate-brown curtains closed. "She obviously keeps up with your work."

"When I left for Los Angeles she asked me to send her memorabilia of all my work. I didn't realize it was going on the walls."

"She loves you. It was sweet of you to agree to stay."

He shrugged. It shouldn't be a big deal. It wouldn't be if his grandmother had agreed to move from this neighborhood. He felt powerless here.

"I'm not the one who wanted separate rooms," he pointed out, slowly stalking her into the corner of the room. When her back hit the wall, her hands hit his chest.

"Stop right there." She cocked her chin up and looked down her pretty little nose at him. "Nothing has changed."

He groaned and dropped his forehead on hers. "Please don't tell me I'm going to be sleeping on the floor."

"That won't be necessary." She kissed his cheek, then slipped away. Their suitcases sat at the end of the bed and she moved to lift one of hers onto the comforter. "We'll share the bed, but the no touching rule still stands. As much as possible, anyway. We'll sleep facing away from each other."

He laughed and picked up his camera. "You're joking, right?"

"I'm not, actually." She rocked on her heels, frowning at the lens directed at her. "I don't have the energy to joke."

With her confession he realized she was actually swaying on her feet.

She pulled a toiletries bag from her case along with a nightgown. "New rule: no nudity in this room. Including socks."

"Socks?" He got the no nudity—not that he liked it. But what was the deal with socks?

"Yes, socks. No stripping down to your socks and pretending you're not naked."

He cocked his head and tugged on the end of her pale ponytail. "It sounds like you've used these rules before."

"No," she denied. "But I know how men think. So don't bother pushing the limits. Not only would it be a cop-out, but let me just warn you: the socks alone look isn't sexy."

"Don't worry—it's not a look you'll ever see on me. Now, *you*…" he leaned close to whisper in her ear "…are free to prance around in stockings anytime you want."

"Not going to happen." She used the hand clutching her nightgown to push him back. "The rules are for both of us. So do you agree?" She scowled at him until he came out from behind the camera and nodded. "Good. Now, if you don't mind, I'd like to use the bathroom first."

"Go ahead." He pointed to a door in the corner. "You can use that door or the one in the hall."

"Thank you." She skirted around him. "Quit aiming that camera at me. The rules make this a safe zone. There's no need to hide." And with that she disappeared into the bath.

He set the camera down. How did she do that? See straight to his soul?

No one had ever questioned why he carried a camera. He'd picked up Mamó's small automatic camera not long after his parents had died. Happy to have him show an interest in something—anything—she had given it to him. For a long time he had hidden behind it. It was a world he controlled. He supposed old habits died hard.

Lauren wasn't herself tonight. Sure, she'd pressed her rules on him, but she lacked her usual sass and fire. The trip had obviously taken a lot out of her. Hopefully the faint shadows under her eyes and her low energy would go away after a good night's sleep. It unsettled him to see her out of sorts. At least her stomach seemed to have settled down.

While he waited for her to finish in the bathroom he checked the dresser and found the drawers were empty. Hiking his suitcase onto the bed, he swept the contents up in one arm and dropped them into the bottom drawer.

He eyed Lauren's open case and decided to help her out. Her stuff went in the top and middle drawers. Then he emptied her garment bag into the closet. Their shoes went on top of the stacked luggage in the bottom of the closet.

Once he'd finished the unpacking he settled in the lone armchair and tapped his fingers on the brown Pleather arm. He glanced at his watch: just after ten. No way was he sleeping anytime soon. Especially in that tiny bed with Lauren tucked up next to him. Not with a no touching rule firmly in place.

Hell. He scrubbed his hands over his face. It was bad enough being back in his old neighborhood, with all the memories waiting to trip him up, now he had to deal with a faux engagement.

He closed his eyes and just for a moment pretended it was real, that he and Lauren were on the brink of starting a life together. He saw the future spread out before him, complete with Lauren at his side and a beaming Mamó cradling a baby in her arms. The wonder of it felt so real he had to shut it down.

The shower was turned off in the next room. He walked over and gave a brief knock. A muffled acknowledgement came from the other side.

"Hey, I'm going to rejoin the party for a while."

The door opened a crack and one golden eye peeked at him. "Okay, thanks for letting me know."

"Leave space for me," he taunted her, hoping to spark some of her fire.

"I will," was her quiet response. "Goodnight."

"Night." He sighed.

The door closed. He pressed his hand to the wood and assured himself she'd be her old self in the morning. Then he grabbed his camera off the dresser and headed back to the party, the option of spending time with the matriarchs of his old neighborhood only slightly better than the torture of lying awake in a platonic bed with Lauren.

Lauren leaned against the bathroom door until she heard the bedroom door click. The door of the bedroom she shared with Ray Donovan.

What had she been thinking?

She'd been so careful to outline her conditions for accompanying Ray, with separate rooms right at the top. Plain and simple: Mamó had got to her. The pleading in her eyes, the resignation on her face… Until that moment Lauren hadn't seen the depression Ray feared, but seeing the loneliness in the older woman's eyes had made Lauren sad. No way could she deny her. Lauren loved her family, and couldn't imagine her mother's reaction if she tried to stay at a hotel when she visited.

Of course not every family was as close as hers. How she longed for a cuddle with her mom.

Wanting to take advantage of Ray's absence, she hurried to brush her teeth and slip into her nightshirt—an oversized T-shirt that fell to her knees and hung off her shoulder. It was the most comfortable and least appealing sleep garment in her wardrobe. She'd brought it for the comfort, but was glad for its lack of allure now she was sharing with Ray.

Yawning, she moved into the bedroom. The thought of unpacking filled her with dread. Her limbs felt so heavy she could barely lift them. The bed looked inviting. She wanted nothing more than to pull back the comforter and climb in.

Wait. She blinked at the empty spread. Where did her suitcase go?

She scuffed around to the other side, thinking Ray must have set it aside. *Nope.* Next she opened the top drawer of the dresser. She stared down at the contents, blinked, and stared a moment more, her mind slow to accept the notion of Ray unpacking for her. But there was the evidence.

Tears stung her eyes. How sweet. Seriously, she could kiss the man.

Good thing he wasn't around or she might break another rule.

The contents of the drawer needed straightening, but it was good enough for tonight. She tucked her dirty clothes into a corner and shoved the drawer closed. All things considered, Ray had been pretty decent today—taking care of her, sticking to the rules even when it upset his grandmother, unpacking her things.

Well, except for the kiss on the plane.

She pressed her lips together to squash the smile tugging at the corner of her mouth. She would *not* let the man seduce her again. No doubt he'd be back to his regular dictatorial self tomorrow. She'd be better able to deal with him then.

Giving in to her weariness, she burrowed into the queen bed, staying strictly to her side.

After all, rules were rules.

Mamó fell asleep in her chair as the last guests were leaving. Ray helped Kyla and Ellie on cleanup by carrying the dirty dishes to the kitchen while they put the food away and loaded the dishwasher. When he came back from taking out the trash, Aunt Ellie shooed Kyla off to bed.

Kyla folded her dishtowel and hung it over the stove handle. "Only because I have work in the morning." She stopped by Ray to kiss his cheek. "Welcome home."

He punched her in the arm. "Good to see you, too."

"Ow! That hurt." Rubbing her arm, she made for the door leading next door. "Bully."

"Girl."

"And proud of it. Night, Mom." Kyla stuck her tongue out at Ray just before she disappeared.

He grinned and turned to his aunt, slipping his arm around her shoulder. "It's good to be home." He nodded toward Mamó. "How is she doing?"

"Sound as an old horse. But she's been down a lot lately. It was good to see her so up tonight. You being here is going to be good for her."

"I hope so." His gut clutched at the concern in his aunt's eyes. "Don't they have meds for depression these days?"

"Yes, but she wouldn't take them even if she agreed to go to the doctor and get properly diagnosed. You know how she is about taking medicine. I've been checking out the internet to find natural remedies through diet and exercise."

"That sounds great."

"Of course the best thing would be—"

"For me to get married? Come on, Ellie, that's not fair.

And announcing it to the neighbors isn't going to magically make it happen."

Ellie groaned. "I know. I'm so sorry."

"Oh, I know where to place the blame. And we'll be talking in the morning."

"Don't be too hard on her. Mrs. Renwicki was being particularly obnoxious about Camilla—going on about her expecting her third child. Not only was Mom upset on your behalf, but I'm sure she was thinking those could have been *her* great-grandkids."

"Not in this lifetime."

"No, of course not. Obviously Mom lost it for a moment there."

All too familiar with Mamó's desire for him to marry and produce a great-grandbaby, Ray rolled his head over the hunched muscles of his shoulders. To keep from giving her false hope was one of the reasons he kept his affairs private.

"Yeah, well, it's not just me she's involved in her fabrication," he reminded his aunt.

"Gosh, you're right." Ellie's worried gaze went to the ceiling, towards where his room was situated. "Will Lauren try to take advantage?"

He barked out a laugh. "Not likely. But there were a lot of people who bore witness to Mamó's announcement."

"Oh." Ellie covered her mouth with her fingers. "You think someone will leak the news? But these are friends of the family."

"Who will see nothing wrong with sharing the knowledge with their friends and family. So, yeah, I expect word to get to the press within a couple of days."

Something he needed to warn Lauren about. She might not have been so quick to give in to Mamó if she'd realized the news would become public.

Which meant he owed her an apology as well as his appreciation.

"Ray…" Ellie fretted, regret in her hazel eyes.

"Don't worry about it. I'll call my assistant, get him started on damage control." He gave her a kiss on the cheek. "Do you need help getting her to bed?"

"No." She patted his hand. "I've got her. I just need to finish cleaning up. You head on up. I hope we weren't too overwhelming for Lauren?"

"No, she'll be fine. She's close with her family so she gets it."

"Good. She seems nice."

"She is." *To most people.* She liked to bust his chops, but he knew she'd get along with his family. If only to spite him. He actually looked forward to her giving him guff again. It would mean she was back to her old self.

"Why don't you take care of Mamó and I'll finish up here?"

"I can't let you do that."

"Sure you can. I'm on California time. I need to kill an hour before I'll be ready to sleep."

Begrudgingly she nodded. "It's good to have you home."

She shook Mamó awake and led his sleepy grandmother down the hall toward her bedroom.

Pulling open the dishwasher, he started loading in more dishes. Memories flooded in. Back in the day he and Mamó had had the routine down to a science and had been able to finish up in ten minutes or less.

He loved her. But she'd put him in quite a fix. He suspected that Lauren would be cool about the whole engagement thing, but in reality she could end up suing him for breach of promise when he failed to marry her. She knew he'd pay. Because no way would he humiliate Mamó by letting the whole thing play out in the news.

It had been a long time since he'd been able to trust a woman.

Fifteen years, to be exact—ever since Camilla had taught him that you never truly knew anyone. He couldn't bring himself to be happy for her. Not after what she'd cost him. So he was petty? He'd live with it.

Dishes loaded, he poured in dishwashing crystals, closed and locked the door, and set the machine in motion. Lauren thought of him as controlling and manipulative. He'd live with that, too. And place the blame right at Camilla's feet.

After drying his hands on the dishtowel, he wiped down the counter.

He'd never be caught unprepared again.

CHAPTER FIVE

LAUREN AWOKE SLOWLY. Her first thought was for the state of her stomach. When there was no immediate revolt her senses began to pick up on other elements. Like the large, muscular man she was snuggled up to.

Her eyes flew open to the yummy sight of smooth skin covering broad shoulders. She reared back, ready to scold Ray for taking advantage, only to find she'd been the one to encroach on *his* side of the bed.

Chagrined at being the one to break the rules, she rolled back to her side and immediately missed his warmth. Obviously she'd been lured by his heat during the night until she'd wrapped herself around him. With any luck he'd slept through her lapse, otherwise he'd razz her unmercifully for breaking her own rules.

She waited for him to move, to awake. When a few minutes passed and he didn't shift, she slid from the bed and fled to the bathroom. Several minutes later she stood brushing her teeth when the door from the bedroom opened and Ray strolled in.

"Morning." He gave her a peck on the cheek, then moved past her to the shower. Dropping his gray knit boxers, he stepped naked into the tub and pulled the curtain closed. Lauren choked on a mouthful of toothpaste.

She spit, rinsed, grabbed her make-up bag and escaped to the bedroom to dress before he finished showering. It didn't take long to pull on jeans and a lavender sweater. She tugged on thick socks and low-heeled boots, and then sat on the side of the bed to put her make-up on, consciously waiting for Ray to make his appearance.

Her stomach hadn't protested yet, but she snagged a soda cracker from her purse stash. Better safe than sorry. Yesterday's queasiness had been explained away with the travel, but it couldn't continue without serious questions arising.

Lauren preferred to tell Ray about his impending fatherhood on her own terms, at her own pace. Which might well be when they were back in California—not while she was half a world away from her support system. Or trying to keep up the pretense of a false engagement.

He wandered into the bedroom, a towel hitched around lean hips.

"Seriously?" she demanded. "You agreed to the rules!"

His bare shoulders were impossibly wide and the muscles in his arms and chest flexed as he rubbed a second towel over his head. The man was droolworthy, with his sculpted abs, tight gluteus, and long, hair-dusted legs. Just watching him walk across the room made her mouth water. Other body parts went straight to tingle.

This was exactly why she'd made the rules.

He glanced over his shoulder at her. "I've honored them." He stepped into a pair of boxer briefs before ditching the towel. "We never discussed the bathroom. Plus, let me just repeat how crazy I think they are. It's not like we haven't—"

"I know we've been intimate." Didn't matter. They'd never been naked together. Their encounters had been too hurried, too frantic. "But that's over."

"So you say." He grabbed a pair of chinos from the bottom drawer, along with a pale blue T-shirt. "I thought you might have changed your mind."

Her hands went to her hips. "What made you think that?"

"The way you cozied up to me in bed last night, for one."

Heat flooded her cheeks. So much for the hope he'd slept through her groping. "That was unintentional," she informed him. "It won't happen again."

"If it was unintentional…" he came to tower over her "…that means you had no control over your actions. What makes you so sure it won't happen again?"

She lifted her chin. "I was overly tired last night. That won't be a problem the rest of the trip."

"I hope you're right." He lifted his right hand, cupped her cheek, and traced the faint shadows under her eye. "Not that I'm complaining. I won't hold you to the rules. Feel free to cozy up to me anytime you please."

"I'm not going to hold you to a standard I'm not willing to uphold myself." She backed up until his hand dropped. "The rules are meant as a mutual show of respect. Is it too much to ask for your cooperation?"

"Not at all—but then I'm not the one trying to pretend our relationship never happened."

Her jaw dropped. "Oh, believe me, I'm well aware that our…fling…*happened*." Knowledge of their child ran deep within her. "And calling what was between us a relationship is pushing it, don't you think?"

"I don't generally say things I don't mean." He cocked his head, invading her space again. "Hurried and hot doesn't necessarily relate to lack of depth."

"Funny, that's exactly how I see it." She locked her knees, refusing to give him any more ground.

"Is that what bothers you?" he asked, all concern, and she was reminded again that he had started his career as an actor. "You doubt my commitment?"

"I have no doubt of your commitment…" she paused "…to getting your own way." She circled him and crossed the room. "Look, I admit the sex was hot. It was crazy and wild and fun. But it was totally lacking in emotional depth.

And that's not who I am." Hand on the doorknob, she met his gaze. "I smell coffee. We should go down."

Ray followed Lauren down the stairs, enjoying the sway of her hips in the well-fitting jeans. She had him in a quandary. She'd nailed his motivation dead-on, but she was also wrong.

His emotions were not as detached as she believed. He'd be a whole lot more comfortable if they were.

Instead he worried about the pallor in her cheeks and whether she had slept well the night before. Now he had her back in his life he wanted to explore the passion between them at a more leisurely pace.

When he'd finally joined her in the tiny bed he'd lain awake for a good hour, tormented by his promise not to touch. He'd stared into the dark while she'd shifted from position to position, as if unable to get comfortable. She'd seemed drawn to him, yet had jerked away if she got too close. Her subconscious was clearly on the job.

Her restlessness had added to his until he'd finally had enough. He'd rolled over and gathered her in his arms, tucking her into the shelter of his body. She'd sighed and gone limp in his arms. Despite the arousal intensified by her nearness, he'd soon followed her into sleep.

Thankfully she blamed their tangled bodies on their subconscious actions. Yeah, that was a confession he'd take to his grave.

In the kitchen Mamó stood at the stove, flipping pancakes. When she heard them on the stairs she turned with a huge smile.

"Good morning." She greeted Lauren and then Ray. "Sit. Sit. As promised, I have your favorite breakfast." She bustled to the stove and returned with a heaping platter she set in the middle of the table. "Blueberry pancakes."

"Mamó, this looks wonderful." Lauren helped herself to one pancake.

"They *are* wonderful." Ray added another to her plate. "Nobody can eat just one," he explained piling four onto his plate. He added warm syrup and dug in.

"He's right, dear." Mamó poured him a cup of coffee, then held the pot over Lauren's cup.

Lauren stopped her. "Do you have decaffeinated?"

Mamó grimaced. "Unfortunately, I do. But it's instant."

"That'll work." Lauren hopped up. "I'll get it. You sit with Ray. I'm sure you have a lot of catching up to do." Before his grandmother could protest, Lauren added, "That is if you don't mind if I make myself at home?"

"Of course, my dear." Mamó slid into the chair next to Ray as she directed Lauren to the proper cabinet. "I want you to be comfortable."

Ray silently toasted Lauren for the brilliant move. She met his salute with a smile and started the microwave. He turned his attention to Mamó.

"Great party last night. Thanks for the welcome."

"Everyone was so excited to see you." Mamó patted his hand. "It's been too long since you visited the neighborhood. They're so happy for your success."

"And apparently for my engagement." He eyed her over his coffee mug.

Mamó's chin lowered and her shoulders sagged. "I'm sorry," she apologized. Then she spoiled it by claiming, "It's your own fault—staying away so long, never giving me any news to share."

"The fact I haven't been back to the neighborhood for a while is not an excuse for lying to your friends."

She stared down at the table, twisted her mug between sturdy hands marked by age and wear. "I wouldn't have to lie if you'd make more of an effort."

He ignored that. Attacking her was not the way to bolster her up. But he couldn't let her get away with this behavior either.

"It's one thing if it were just me." He let the words hang

in the air for a moment. "But you've put Lauren in a difficult position."

A frown pulled Mamó's hand-drawn brows together.

"Oh, but —"

Ray cut Lauren's protest off with a flick of his eyes and
a shake of his head. "It's not okay, Lauren. When we start
getting pestered by the press you won't feel so generous."

"Press?" She bit her pretty bottom lip.

"If it hasn't hit the social media outlets yet, it will soon."
He hardened his heart. Soft-pedaling the news wouldn't
help anyone. "Phone calls requesting confirmation won't
be far behind."

She pushed away from the table. "Excuse me."

"Where are you going?" he asked.

"To text my family and warn them that rumors of my
engagement are grossly exaggerated."

"You can do that from here." He looked at her plate,
pleased to see she'd eaten both pancakes.

"I could, but my mom will be calling two seconds after
she gets the message, so I'll take it to the next room. I'd
be dealing with Tori, too, except she's halfway around the
world on her honeymoon. No telling when she'll call."

"It's pretty early in California," Ray reminded her.

Lauren glanced at the kitchen clock. "Not early enough."

She took off, and Ray arched a brow at Mamó.

"It was just a few friends." Mamó avoided his gaze. Instead she fussed with the syrup pitcher, wiping the edge
and replacing it in the middle of the table.

"Friends gossip," he reminded her.

"Doris Renwicki was the troublemaker." Mamó lifted
contrite eyes to meet his gaze. "I really am sorry. She just
got to me, with all her talk of babies."

"I know." He covered her hand with his. The woman had
gotten to him, too. So, yeah, he understood. But that didn't
mean he could let Mamó off the hook. His career was too

public to have odd announcements like this popping up. Luckily he was here and could coordinate damage control.

"You've put Lauren and me in a difficult situation. If I were serious and had decided to ask her to marry me, you've stolen her moment of announcing it. And that's if she doesn't question my motives and agrees to accept my proposal."

"Oh, Ray, of course she'd accept you." Mamó covered her mouth, true distress in her pale eyes. "But you're right. I've ruined her moment. Do you think she can forgive me?"

Figured she would zero in on the injury to Lauren.

"What can I do?" She began to cry. "I don't want things to be difficult between the two of you."

Damn. This wasn't what he wanted. He pushed his empty plate to the side.

"Stop crying. Don't worry. I'll fix it."

"I'm sorry." She wiped at her eyes.

"I know, and I'm going to fix it. Just stop crying now. Lauren will think I'm being mean."

"It's not you, it's me." She hid her face in a napkin.

"It'll be okay." Her distress made his gut clench. He took her hand in his and squeezed.

"It won't. The press will come."

"I'll handle it," he promised, going around the table to pull her into his arms. "I love you, Mamó. Now, dry your eyes. You want to be beautiful for your party."

"I don't want to go."

"Of course you do. It's just the thing to cheer you up. Everything is going to be okay."

"No. I've messed things up for you and Lauren."

"When I'm done fixing things she'll think I'm a hero."

Mamó's body stopped shaking. "A hero, huh?"

A warm jacket was settled over Lauren's shoulders and she turned to give Ray a grateful smile. As expected, her mom had called right on the heels of Lauren's text. Wanting privacy for the call, she'd stepped outside onto Mamó's tiny stoop, only to discover it had snowed overnight. The overhang protected the stoop and some of the steps, so she wasn't standing in snow, but her sweater did little to ward off the freezing temperature.

"Don't worry. You'll be the first to know," she reassured her mother for the third time. "Ray's waiting for me. I have to go."

"Okay, but I want the whole story when you get home," warned her mom. "Say hello to Ray for me. Bye, love you."

"Love you." Lauren closed her phone. "Thanks for the jacket," she said to Ray. "It snowed."

"It does that here."

"Tori would be so jealous."

Making it snow at his Hollywood manor had been Garrett's Christmas gift to her twin. The romantic gesture had won Tori's heart and the acceptance of his proposal. Lauren still got choked up thinking about it. Here in New York she found the reality of the frozen landscape a bit overwhelming.

"So, did you haul Mamó over the coals?"

He cocked his head. "It felt like it. She cried."

"I'm sorry." She slipped her arms into his jacket. "But you needed to talk to her. It would be bad enough if you were an average guy. Right now you're the hottest director in the country. The press will be all over this. Is she okay?"

"Yeah." He flicked at a piece of paper. "I distracted her by asking after her 'to-do' list. Are you up for doing some chores?"

"Sure I'll help," she agreed easily. "I'm not about to pass up the opportunity to watch the great Ray Donovan at manual labor."

Just the notion had her insides tingling.

"Brat." He tugged on her ponytail. "Such wit. You should consider writing for the movies."

"Oh, no." Even though he'd joked, she literally backed

away at his suggestion. "That's your world, not mine. I'm happy staying in the background, thank you very much."

"You're good with details." He edged forward, eliminating the distance she'd created between them.

He always did that, and had done right from the beginning of their association. Even before they'd become intimate. It was intoxicating and unnerving at the same time.

"You'd make an excellent production assistant."

"I have a job, but thanks for the endorsement."

She inched back again, seeking the space she needed. Seriously, how was she supposed to keep a clear head around him while constantly inhaling the clean, male scent of him?

"What's on the to-do list?"

He consulted the paper. "A broken railing, changing some lightbulbs, and assembling a console."

"That's quite a list. We should get started if we want to finish before the party." Shivering, she tucked her hands in the pockets of his jacket. "Are there home improvement centers in New York?"

"Better. We have Chester's Hardware."

He invaded her bubble again, but a car pulling to a stop in front of the house distracted her. Had the press discovered them already?

A uniformed deliveryman emerged from the car, carrying a large box. He crunched through the snow, opened the gate, and approached the steps. "Delivery for Lauren Randall."

Her brows zinged up in surprise. She wasn't expecting anything—certainly not at this address.

"I'm Lauren Randall." She accepted the package, thinking she should tip the man. She glanced up at Ray. "My purse is inside."

"That's okay, ma'am," the delivery person assured her. "The tip was included. Have a nice day, now." He tipped his head and trudged back to his car.

She clutched the large package to her. "For a minute there I thought the press had found us."

"Actually, I see a fellow across the way with a camera." A hand in the small of her back urged her toward the door. "Why don't we take this inside?"

Her skin itched at the idea of being spied on, so she allowed him to direct her indoors.

She settled on the sofa and placed the large box next to her. "What did you do, Ray?"

"What makes you think it's from me?" He went to the fire and tossed on a log, then took up a spot at the mantel.

"Because nobody knows I'm here."

"Open it."

Eying him suspiciously, she worked off the bright red bow. Was it coincidence that the bow was her favorite color or had Ray asked for red? Coincidence, surely? She doubted Ray knew her favorite color.

She lifted off the lid and dug through mounds of tissue. Her heart began an erratic tattoo as she recognized the famous name blazoned on the inside of the box. Maybe he did know, because the paper parted to reveal a red leather coat trimmed in black fur. *Oh, my.*

"Oh, my…" Mamó echoed Lauren's thoughts. "What a beautiful coat."

Lauren held the garment up. The jacket was long enough to hit her just above the knee. A black asymmetrical zipper slashed across the front and the softest of faux fur lined the inside from shoulder to hem, including a shawl collar that converted into a hood.

"Gorgeous…" she breathed.

"Try it on," Mamó urged.

Lauren didn't need the encouragement. She had already unzipped the jacket and shrugged out of Ray's coat. She slid her arms in and sighed as softness and warmth surrounded her. The smell of rich leather teased her nostrils. Oh, she coveted it.

She turned to Ray, who smirked with quiet satisfaction.

"Thank you," she said as she shrugged out of the lovely coat. "But I can't accept it."

"Oh, but—" Mamó covered her mouth, turned around, and hurried toward the kitchen.

Ellie came through the connecting door to her unit and Mamó detoured to grab her arm and drag her along to the back of the house.

Lauren barely noticed. All her attention was focused on Ray's stormy expression.

"You need a warmer jacket. Your time on the stoop should have proved that."

"I'll manage."

For some reason her refusal seemed to hurt him. But accepting such an expensive gift implied an intimacy she was trying to avoid. She'd told him she didn't need a new coat, and yet true to his controlling nature he'd gone against her wishes and bought one anyway.

"It's too much."

"I can afford it."

"That's not the point."

"You just said it was." He raked a hand through his hair. "You're only here because of me. It's my responsibility to make sure you don't suffer for doing me a favor."

Silently she applauded him for the brilliant argument, but she saw right through him and chided him with a simple, "Ray…"

"As far as I'm concerned it's yours," he said dismissively. "If you don't want it, just borrow it while you're here and I'll have Mamó give it to the Salvation Army when we leave. Whatever you decide, I'm leaving for the hardware store in ten minutes."

He stormed off, taking the stairs two at a time.

Dang the man. By stating his intention to give the coat away to charity he'd taken the power of her refusal away from her. She stroked the silky black faux fur. Would it hurt to wear it during her visit?

Yes. She needed to stand by her principles—to show him she couldn't be bullied or bought. Regretfully, she folded the jacket back into the box. Sometimes being right really, *really* sucked.

CHAPTER SIX

OF COURSE THEY walked to Chester's. The neighborhood store turned out to be only three blocks away. It was easier to go by foot than to shovel the drifts away from the garage. Ray offered to call a cab, but Lauren refused. Not for three blocks.

She slid into her fleece-lined raincoat, borrowed Ellie's snow boots, and met Ray at the gate.

He scowled at her coat but refrained from saying anything. Instead he took her arm. "Be careful. The snow has been shoveled, but it can be slick."

At first they strolled in silence, but several people were out and Ray got hailed a number of times. He tried to keep them moving, which proved difficult when it was someone on the same side of the street.

Shivering as a light snow began to fall, Lauren admired his skillful ability to greet and go. Across the way she noticed the photographer Ray had spotted earlier. The man kept pace with them, yet seemed content to keep his distance.

All in all, by the time they reached the hardware store, she wished she hadn't been quite so quick to set Ray's gift aside.

"Here we are." He held the door for her.

Grateful for the promise of warmth, she stepped inside. She stamped the snow from her boots and faced Ray. Only to find he'd all but disappeared. A knit cap covered his hair, his neck scarf had been pulled up to cover the bottom half of his face, and his shoulders were slumped forward. He'd gone from being a confident, dynamic man who dominated any room he entered to a man most people would overlook. Obviously that was the point.

Considering their trip here, she couldn't blame him. On this Tuesday morning Chester's hopped with clientele.

"Hello, I'm Lauren." She offered Ray her gloved hand. "Who are *you*?"

"Ha-ha." He took her hand and gave her a basket to carry before leading her deeper into the store. "You're a real comedian."

"Sorry, I couldn't resist. It's a very effective disguise. Do you have to use it often?"

"No." He turned down an aisle and stopped in front of an assortment of lubricating oils. He handed her a can and took off again. "I'm not in front of the cameras anymore, so I'm not as recognizable as celebrities on TV or in movies. Then there's the fact most people are too intimidated to approach me. But this is my old neighborhood, so all bets are off."

"Everyone seems happy for your success. And you're very gracious with them. Yet you're also careful to keep them at a distance." She followed him into the lighting aisle. "Kyla said it's been years since you've visited Mamó at home."

"Do you have a point?" His gaze roamed the shelves, seeking three-way bulbs.

"I'm just wondering what you're running from?"

He went totally still.

Giving him time, she reached past him and selected energy-saving three-way bulbs. She placed them in the basket and waited for him to come back to her. His reaction confirmed her suspicion.

Ray hadn't willingly abandoned his neighborhood. Something had sent him running.

Finally he shrugged. "We all have things in our past we'd rather forget."

"True." She hooked her arm through his. "But some stick with us more than others."

"Will you wear the coat?"

She rolled her eyes. Leave it to him to manipulate his own confession. Too bad she had him beat. "Oh, yeah. I already made that decision on the walk over here. I may be stubborn. I'm not stupid."

"Right." He grinned and reclaimed the basket. He held his other hand out to her. "Come on. Time to go play handyman."

"No touching," she said, reminding herself as well as him, and walked around him to the cashier.

Back at the house, Lauren gratefully released her end of the heavy box containing the mahogany console. They'd blown through the fix-it items on Mamó's to-do list and were about to put together the new console table.

Lauren read the directions while he went straight to sorting the nails and screws. When she caught herself staring at his bent head, she decided to press him a little more on his past.

She crouched down next to him. "So, about those things in the past you prefer to forget...sometimes it helps to share."

"I appreciate the offer." He stroked his thumb over the dent in her chin. "It's better left buried."

"I disagree." She blew out a breath. "I don't know if Garrett told you this, but Tori and I had a friend in high school who committed suicide."

"He mentioned it." His shuttered gaze met hers before he focused on lining up the planks by size.

She stood and squared her shoulders. This was never easy to talk about.

"Well, the school provided counseling for those that

wanted it, and because we were particularly close to him my parents continued it for an extra month. There was guilt and anger to deal with, as well as loss and sorrow. Mostly for Tori. I went more to support her. By talking about our experience we were able to gain perspective and work our way through the stages of grief in a healthy manner."

He slowly rose to his feet to stare down into her eyes. "And yet Tori's memories of that time almost cost her her relationship with Garrett."

"Talking about it doesn't take away the importance of an event. But it can minimize its power over you. Once you've shared with someone, the worst that can happen is over. Someone else knows. The fear of discovery is past, making it easier to deal with what follows."

"Really? Because having the whole neighborhood witness my humiliation, pain and disappointment didn't make it easier to bear. I call *liar* on that."

She flinched—more at what he had revealed than at the bite in his words.

"I once let a man control me to the point I almost ditched my family for him." Saying it out loud sent a cold wave down her spine. Her throat clenched. It was her biggest shame. And she had no idea why she'd just told him. Who knew being pregnant led to insanity? Worse, she couldn't seem to stop. "It was a form of abuse that I didn't even see happening."

"Oh, Lauren." He pulled her into his arms. The screwdriver in his hand bumped against her butt. He set it aside, then enfolded her in a tender embrace. "I just can't see it. You're so in control, so strong."

"In a way, that just made it worse. It was subtle and insidious and completely undermined who I was. Tori saved me."

And for a while Lauren had hated her for it.

"When I finally made the break from Brad I couldn't talk to Mom or Tori. I was too ashamed. That fear of discovery… But I remembered the counseling from high school and decided to see if my college provided counselors and I was able to talk to someone."

She'd learned only she had the ability to give her power away.

His hand stroked softly through her hair. Allowing him to hold her like this broke the rules, but she couldn't bring herself to care. Insanity aside, she'd started this in order to help him deal with whatever it was that had driven him away from Queens.

She eased away. "I can promise you nothing is as bad as you build it up to be in your own head."

He cupped the back of her neck, his intent gaze scrutinizing her carefully. "You're such a contradiction. You find it hard to accept a gift but now you've bared your soul for me."

A shrug was all she had to give him. "Different cost values."

He rocked his forehead over hers. "I don't know what to say."

"The point is your secrets are safe with me. You can say anything." She pressed her lips to his cheek before stepping back again. "And I have agreed to wear the jacket, so technically you owe me."

"I'll think about it."

"A little more your way," Ray directed, eyeing the entryway to gauge its center point. "Okay, set it down."

Lauren stepped back to view the finished results as Ray added baskets to the bottom shelf of the console. Thirty inches high and five feet long, it had three deep drawers across the front, with three rattan baskets going in the open slots below the drawers.

"It really is a lovely piece." She held her hand up for a high-five. "Well done, Donovan."

He slapped her palm. "I couldn't have done it without you, Randall."

"Seriously," she agreed, "that was one heavy beast."

He yanked on the end of her ponytail. "We make a good team."

"Hmm..."

She hummed the noncommittal response just to be contrary. Surprisingly, they had worked well together, making fairly quick work of the assembly. Still, after getting all touchy-feely with him it was best not to give him too much encouragement. The man didn't know the meaning of boundaries. Give him an inch and he'd take a mile.

Best not to encourage herself either.

More than once she'd caught herself staring at his hands. Remembering how they felt on her skin. Long-fingered, strong, and competent, his broad-palmed hands were sensual tools of torment, capable of sending her senses reeling.

Oh, yeah, he knew how to use his hands.

"Mamó will be thrilled." She forced her attention back to the moment.

"I think so." He glanced at his watch. "They should be back soon."

Ellie had whisked Mamó off to the hair salon after lunch. Her big birthday bash at the community center started at six and the women were off beautifying themselves for the event.

"Hair and nails for both of them?" She shook her head while stifling a yawn. Every time she slowed down sleep tugged at her eyelids. Must be jet lag. "It'll probably be another hour at least." She bent and stuffed plastic bags into a large cardboard box. "Why don't you grab us a couple of sodas and I'll finish cleaning up here?"

"I have a better idea." He took the box from her. "Why don't you sit down while I take care of this and get the sodas? It's the least I can do after all your help."

"I won't say no."

He headed outside with the box.

She checked her phone for messages, smiled at the

text from her assistant confirming all was set for the party tonight.

Curling into the corner of the sofa, she clicked on the TV. A reality show came on in which brides sought the perfect dress. A secret fan, she rested her head on a closed fist and watched as the bride and her mother clashed over a peek-a-boo corset dress.

She fought off a yawn. Earlier she'd stepped outside to make a few arrangements for tonight's big bash. Events were Lauren's "thing." She felt bad, sitting back and doing nothing for Mamó's party, so she'd reached out to a couple of local connections she'd met at national conferences and arranged for a little something extra.

Which reminded her—she needed to fill Ray in on her plan. Her eyes closed. She struggled to push them open. Hopefully Ray wouldn't object to her interference. It was all meant in good fun…

After disposing of the box and grabbing two cans of soda from the refrigerator, Ray joined Lauren on the sofa. The first thing he noticed was that Lauren was sound asleep. Jet lag, no doubt. Compelled by something bigger than his promises, he gave in to the urge to touch. He swept a silky blond tendril behind her ear, traced the oval curve of her jaw, stroked his thumb over the plump bow of her lips.

So strong, yet so delicate. His gut churned at the thought of her under another man's thumb. Never would he have suspected her of subjugating her will to someone else. Not with the grief she gave him.

An abusive experience sure explained her fierce need for independence.

His fingers curled into a fist as he fought the desire to smash something—preferably the abusive jerk's face. Too bad he was beyond Ray's reach. Slowly he unfurled each finger, because Lauren deserved tenderness and understanding. He wouldn't be responsible for bringing her any more pain.

Dropping his hand to her thigh, he turned his attention to the TV. His brows plummeted into a scowl. What kind of hot mess had she been watching? A woman in a robe was extolling the virtues of some man while a salesclerk waded through a forest of white gowns. Some sort of bride show.

Just kill him now.

He picked up the remote, ready to click it away. The picture changed to a young, dark-haired woman with brown eyes in a round face. His finger froze on the remote. For a moment he saw Camilla standing there. In a blink the resemblance disappeared.

He scrubbed at the back of his neck. He obviously had the past on his mind.

Hard not to when he was smack in the middle of the borough where it had all gone down. All he wanted was to put the past behind him. Yet everywhere he looked he stumbled across reminders of his darkest moment. And Lauren's probing didn't help.

Maybe he should talk to her. *No.* He appreciated her sharing her past with him, but he couldn't reciprocate. Exposing his shame would be like opening a vein. Better to leave it buried.

Aiming the remote again, he changed the channel, finding a hockey game to watch. He settled into the cushions, one hand on Lauren's thigh, the other wrapped around a cold soda. Now, *this* was more like it. An hour alone to enjoy a cold drink, a good game, and his girl. This was the way to relax.

"Here we are, ladies." Ray climbed out of the taxi and held the door for Mamó and Lauren. He escorted them inside, where the three of them checked their coats. Ellie and Kyla had gone on ahead of them. "May I say it's my pleasure to be accompanying the two most beautiful women at the party?"

"Thank you." Pleased with his compliment, Mamó twittered while patting her white-gray crown of curls. She glowed in a jacket dress of bright purple. A dusting of soft rose highlighted the natural color in her creamy cheeks. She looked lovely, and clearly ready to party.

He wrapped her in a gentle hug. "Make sure you behave yourself."

"Where's the fun in that?" She patted his cheek, giving him a wicked smile. "I plan to party hearty tonight."

"Mamó!"

"Leave her alone." Lauren hooked her arm through his. "This is *her* night. Let her enjoy it."

"Thank you, dear." With a flash of her diamond eternity ring, Mamó waved and walked into the hall.

"'Party hearty'?" Ray muttered. "She's seventy-six."

"She's still a vibrant woman with a huge capacity for love. I know of at least one gentleman attracted by her *joie de vivre.*"

Lauren dragged her hand down his arm, over his hand, clung to his fingertips for just a second, then swung around and through the door behind his grandmother.

He was distracted by her touch, by the sheer grace of her in a sassy off-the-shoulder black dress, and her words didn't connect at first. He hadn't been paying lip service when he'd told them he was with the two most beautiful women at the party. Where Mamó was lovely, Lauren literally stole his breath. *Stunning* was the only word to do her justice.

The black dress clung to soft curves, its hem flirting with the silky skin three inches above her knees. The dark color contrasted sharply with her creamy complexion, giving the impression of delicate strength. Light shimmered in her blond hair, flowing like molten gold around her shoulders as she glanced back at him. A daring red lip gloss drew his gaze to her lush mouth.

He followed as if beckoned.

Only when she disappeared from sight did her words slam into him.

Wait—a "gentleman" was interested in Mamó? Not if *he* had anything to say about it.

He rushed through the door. And found Mamó and Lauren surrounded by a bevy of young studs dressed in tuxedos. Heavens, it was like a casting call for a Fred Astaire remake.

Oh, hell, no.

He waded through the throng to Lauren's side and heard the last of the introductions.

"And I'm Chad," a tall man said.

He had a square chin, brown eyes and dark hair. Ray eyed the other four. Not so young after all—which only made it worse.

"I hope you will save the first dance for me?"

"Oh, my." Mamó giggled as the man lifted her hand to his mouth. "I think I can do that."

Giggled. Like a girl. His seventy-six-year-old grandmother.

"What's going on here?" he demanded, making no effort to curb the edge in his voice.

"Oh. Everyone—this is my grandson Ray." Mamó beamed as she made the introductions. "Ray, these lovely gentlemen are here to dance with me."

"I beg your pardon."

"Now, don't be a grouch. Lauren arranged it. I love to dance, and with so many more ladies than men this ensures I'll always have a partner." She took the opportunity to give Lauren a huge hug. "Thank you so much. It's going to be the best party ever."

"You're welcome." Lauren kissed her cheek. "I might have to borrow one myself if Ray's going to be a party-poop."

"I won't blame you." Mamó stepped back and smoothed her hands over her hips. "I should find Ellie."

"May I escort you to the head table?" Chad offered his arm.

"You may." Mamó threaded her arm through his with another giggle. The two moved off and the other men melted away.

Ray crossed his arms over his chest, his gaze narrowed on Lauren. "*You* did this?"

"This?"

"Arranged for my grandmother to be groped by a gigolo." Her tinkling laugh grated over his taut nerves.

"They are *not* gigolos. They're dancers. I noticed a lot of Mamó's friends were single, so I called a friend of mine who arranged for a local dance studio to send over some men to act as stag dance partners."

Okay, it was a nice gesture. He still didn't like it.

"I didn't know you knew anybody in New York."

"I have contacts all over the world. We meet at conferences and trade shows. Events is a pretty small community, actually."

"I imagine you're a league above most of your colleagues."

She lifted one shoulder in a half-shrug. "No, we just have a more elite clientele than most."

"I've seen your work. I would argue you attract an elite clientele because of your above-par work." He looked around the room at the lush floral centerpieces and the billowing folds of white silk draped from the ceiling and cascading down the walls. "I can see your touch in more than the expanded guest list."

"Mamó has graciously opened her home to me. She, Ellie and Kyla have made me feel welcome. It was the least I could do."

He studied her for a long minute. She was wrong. She was a guest. Nothing had been expected of her. Not even a gift, as they were optional. In fact, in a very real way *she* was a gift—from him to his grandmother.

"I'm not sure I approve." He pulled her close and pressed a light kiss to her lips. "But Mamó is happy, so thank you."

"You're welcome." She swiped a thumb over his lips, removing a light layer of red. "Shall we join Mamó at the head table?"

"Sure." He settled a hand in the sweet spot at the small of her back. "On the way you can explain your comment about a gentleman being interested in Mamó."

"I noticed a connection between her and a gentleman at the welcome party the other night—"

"No." He cut her off. "No noticing anything between her and any gentleman. Just turn your Spidey senses off."

She stopped abruptly, blocking his path. He almost tripped over his own feet to prevent himself from running into her.

Hands on hips, she slowly swung to face him. "You just can't help yourself can you?"

"What?"

"There you go, trying to control me. Worse, you're trying to control your grandmother, who deserves any chance at happiness fate hands her."

"I don't want you interfering."

"It's not 'Spidey senses,'" she informed him in icy tones. "It's a very real feeling about a connection between two people."

"Well, aim it elsewhere. Mamó is not interested."

"That's for Mamó to say, not you."

"I'm saying it for both of us." He stepped into her space, let her see he meant business. "Turn it off."

A flash of hurt went through her eyes before they frosted over in a blink. One red-tipped nail poked him in the chest, pushing him back.

"One: don't disrespect the matchmaking." Another poke. "Two: I'm here as a favor to you. Under protest, if you'll remember." Two pokes this time. "Three: you're just mad because I didn't run the idea by you first. I'd never do anything to hurt your grandmother. You're the one who will do that when she finds out our whole relationship is a sham and has been since the beginning."

She twirled on her stylish black heels, obviously planning to leave him in the dust.

He caught her arm. "Don't even *think* about telling her."

She glanced from his hand on her arm to his face. "It's good to know exactly what you think of me, Ray. For a while there you almost had me fooled that you were a decent guy. I thought I'd learned to see beyond a man's act."

He watched her throat work as she swallowed hard.

"Thanks for the reminder."

Stung, he dropped her arm. "Don't put me in league with that monster. I'm nothing like him."

"No?" She rubbed her arm. "You always have to be in control. You want to tell me what to do, who I can talk to, and what I can say. At least I can see it this time." A slight shiver shook her small frame and a hand went to her stomach. "Tell Mamó I'll be along in a few minutes. I'm going to talk to the facility director."

Again, she began to walk away. It struck him that he'd handled this badly. He'd never meant to hurt her. He just wanted to protect his grandmother.

"Lauren, wait." He moved quickly, blocking her escape. "I forgot four."

She nailed him with cold eyes. Who knew gold could cut so sharp?

"We're already done. I've been telling you that for days."

This time he let her go, his mind ticking over ways to fix this. He'd give her a few minutes to cool down. Let her do her business thing. It would help restore her sense of order. At least he hoped so.

Because he still saw that flash of raw hurt in her eyes. And it made him sick to his stomach that he was the one to put it there.

CHAPTER SEVEN

THE ARGUMENT WITH Ray sent her scurrying for the restroom, the bitter taste of bile rising up her throat. Funny how her nausea often coincided with high emotions.

After she'd emptied her stomach, she liberated a few crackers from the buffet. Perched at a table on the edge of the room, she nibbled away and soon felt better. Well, her stomach felt better. Her emotions still felt thrashed.

Ray's behavior hurt. Did he really believe she'd put Mamó at risk? That she used her matchmaking gift to manipulate people?

That was his talent, not hers.

Wanting to avoid the aggravating man, she went in search of the facilities director. She thanked the plump brunette for allowing the last-minute additions to the decorations. The woman waved her off, saying she'd never seen the room look so pretty.

Lauren heard the same message again and again as she slowly made her way to the head table. And the cost had been minimal, as the flowers were recycled from a wedding earlier in the day. The five gentleman dancers accounted for the biggest expense, but it thrilled her to be able to add to Mamó's day.

Spending the night chained to Ray's side…? Not so enchanting.

He tried to pretend nothing had happened. She responded to his attempts at conversation with the briefest of responses. She wouldn't have responded at all except for Mamó. No need to draw her attention to their tiff.

After a while Ray excused himself and took off with his camera.

She didn't know who was more relieved to have him disappear behind the lens—him or her. Kyla slid into his vacant seat.

"You're my favorite person in the whole wide world." She squeezed Lauren's hand on the table. "The room is just stunning. And all the matrons are atwitter about the studs you lined up as dancing partners." She glanced over her shoulder at a couple of the men at the next table. "I'm kind of aglow myself."

Lauren laughed and nudged her new friend's shoulder. "The night's paid for. I say have fun."

"Really?" Kyla nibbled her bottom lip. "You wouldn't mind? You hired them for Mamó and her contemporaries."

"Of course I don't mind." Lauren assured her. "I want everyone to have a good time." She paused and pointed to the ninety-year-old woman chatting up Chad. "But you might not want to get between the men and Mrs. Harris."

Kyla snorted, then quickly clapped a hand over her mouth. "You're wicked." She leaned close. "To return the favor I'll warn you to stay clear of Old Man Tanner. He has wandering hands."

Pink-cheeked, Lauren asked for a refresher course on the names of the people she'd met the night before. "I'm usually good with names, but I was a tad distracted."

"I suppose news of your engagement might do that." With an understanding smile Kyla complied, adding bits of harmless gossip designed to help Lauren remember names.

Ellie broke in to steal Kyla away, muttering something about the cake.

When the music started Ray reappeared and asked her to dance. She declined. But she gladly accepted Chad when he returned Mamó to the table.

Ray's scowl as she walked off with Chad soothed her ravaged heart.

On the dance floor Lauren swayed lightly to a slow tune. Chad was charming and undemanding—two traits she particularly appreciated tonight.

Relaxing, she smiled at him. "You and your fellow dancers are a big hit."

"It's nice to be appreciated." He winked. "Actually, this is the first gig of this type I've heard of. I wouldn't mind if it caught on. It's nice to put a smile on a grandma's face. Is it true her grandson is *the* Ray Donovan?"

Lauren controlled a grimace. "Yes, he's the famous director. And it will thrill her to pieces if you ask her just like that."

"I like his movies. He's not afraid to take on hard core issues." His gaze traveled past her shoulder. "But obviously I'm a bigger fan of him than he is of me."

Lauren felt the weight of Ray's regard and knew Chad had just clashed gazes with her nemesis.

"Don't mind him. He's being a jerk, but it's not personal."

His gaze shifted past her again, then back down to her. "Do everyone a favor. Have pity. The guy is bringing the party down."

He'd barely finished speaking when a hand appeared on his shoulder and Ray asked to cut in.

Chad stepped back, bowed graciously, and disappeared into the crowd.

Lauren shifted her frown from one man to the other. *Men.*

"What's wrong?" Ray demanded as he pulled her close. "What did he do? Should I go after him?"

"No." She arched her eyebrows at him. Ray was the one who needed to apologize. The music stopped. She dropped her arms. "I want to return to the table."

Another ballad started. His arm tightened around her waist.

"Dance with me," he said. When she simply stared at him, he added, "Please. I want to apologize."

"Okay." She relented, sliding her arms up his hard chest to link her hands behind his head. "But only because your tantrum is marring Mamó's enjoyment of the party."

He made a rude noise in the back of his throat. "Hardly! Mamó barely knows I'm here. She's too busy dancing. Besides, I'm not the one walking away, dancing with other men."

Lauren closed her eyes. *Oh, goodness.* The very lack of emotion in Ray's voice revealed the depth of his upset. And it dawned on her that she was showing him up in front of the neighbors he already felt looked down on him.

Dang. She wasn't ready to give up being mad yet. But he didn't deserve another fifteen years of misery either. She relaxed in his hold and let him turn her around the floor.

"You're right. I'm sorry. I forgot your situation for a few minutes. I'll behave myself. But that doesn't mean you get to tell me what to do or mock my talent."

"Oh, I believe in it. Mamó has the same weird juju when it comes to babies. I just wish you could make it go away."

A hot tide of dread ran down Lauren's spine and a hard knot lodged in her throat. Praying that it didn't mean what she thought it meant, she gulped, then cleared her throat. "Mamó has a talent? Regarding babies? What? She can tell the sex?"

"The sex—and she's a walking early pregnancy test. She'll know someone's pregnant before they do. Made for some awkward moments growing up." He shook that off. "But we're talking about your talent. So, can you make it stop?"

A walking early pregnancy test? Nothing to worry about there…

Lauren propped her hands on her hips. "You're not usually so dense, Ray. I know you love your grandmother, and you're concerned. But you should be happy for her, not thinking of yourself." Enough. She'd let this go on too long. "If I'm not going to get my apology I'm returning to the table."

His hands tightened on her. "So hard tonight." He lifted her chin on the edge of his hand until she looked him in the eyes. His held regret. "I hurt you. I'm sorry."

The simplicity of his words arrowed right to her heart.

She lowered her eyes, unable to hold his gaze. Confronted with his sincerity, she was forced to face the truth. Her anger acted as a shield. Otherwise she'd too easily fall into his arms again. Especially at the party.

Every time they'd hooked up it had been at a festive event of some sort, starting with Thanksgiving at his Malibu mansion last November.

She'd gone with him to set up the poker table in the loft. They'd started arguing over nothing, he'd kissed her, and the electricity between them had flared out of control. The open loft overlooked the living room, where her father and brother had been watching football, so Ray had dragged her around the corner into the first room they stumbled across—which had happened to be the laundry room.

To this day she couldn't do the laundry without blushing.

"Lauren?" He breathed her name against her temple. "Am I forgiven?"

"Oh. Of course." She bowed her head. "I may have overreacted a bit."

"No." He pulled back to see her better. "I'm the one at fault. I know you'd never hurt Mamó. And you have no control over the attraction you sense. It's just—"

Suddenly he swung Lauren around until they had a clear view of Mamó, dancing with an older gentleman with a full head of gray hair, a Van Dyke beard and mustache. "It's George Meade, isn't it? He's been sniffing around her all night."

Her stomach took longer to catch up than the rest of her. Lauren leaned against Ray and drew in some deep breaths.

"Hey…" A big hand cradled her head to him. "Are you okay?"

"Just a little dizzy," she assured him.

Regaining her composure, she created some distance between them.

"I know it freaks you out, thinking about her with a man, but having someone to focus on in her life besides you and your potential offspring might be the answer to your problem."

"Huh," he responded, his gaze focused across the room again. "I'm right, aren't I? It's Meade."

"I'm not saying." Lauren refused to throw the poor man to this predator stalking him. From the corner of her eye, she saw Mamó circling the floor in George Meade's arms. The faint glow of their connection reached Lauren across the distance. "Let Mamó have her evening."

"So it *is* him." Ray released her, his intent clear.

She grabbed his arm before he took two steps. "If you interrupt them I'm leaving."

He froze. "You said you'd behave."

"How I behave won't matter if I'm gone."

Taking her hand, he drew her to the edge of the dance floor. "I just want to talk to him. I'll only be a minute." He turned toward his quarry.

"I won't stop until I'm back in Hollywood," she warned him.

He pivoted in his Italian leather shoes to face her. "You wouldn't?"

She crossed her arms and pinned him with a glare.

"That's just mean."

"You have no idea." Her fingers bit into the fabric of his jacket as she pulled him further away from the dancing. "This is your grandmother's birthday party. I'm not going to let you embarrass her in front of her friends."

"You mean her *man* friend." He scowled.

"Him most of all." Aware of the hard muscle under her fingers, she dropped her hand.

Turmoil roiled inside him. She felt the surge of emotion as much as she saw it storm across his features.

"Just because I sense a connection it doesn't mean anything will come of it. It's up to them to act on it. Or not. But if you interfere you'd better believe I will be on the next plane out of here."

For just a second panic flared in his blue eyes. "You wouldn't really leave me alone with these people?"

She blinked at him, totally unprepared for his reaction even though it confirmed her earlier revelation. The flash of vulnerability exposed how difficult this trip was for him.

She took his hand. "Ray, these people are your family, your friends. They all care about you."

His face shuttered. "They like to claim they know me." He glanced around. "But none of them really does. They care because I'm famous and because of Mamó."

"They could hate you for the same reasons, but they don't."

She debated for a moment about her next move. Her confession might freak him out more than reassure him. She straightened her shoulders and went for it.

"Listen, the same vibe that allows me to see a connection between a couple also lets me pick up on high-level emotions. And the overall feeling in this room is positive—to the point it overwhelms everything else."

He stared at her for a moment, then cupped her cheek and drew her to him for a brief kiss.

"What you're feeling is for Mamó," he said.

"Yes," she agreed. "But I haven't noticed any malice or envy around you. And I think I would." She laid her head on his chest, felt the steady beat of his heart. "Just because they don't know all your secrets it doesn't mean they don't care."

And, oh, how she wished the sentiment didn't strike so close to home.

"Ray...Lauren." Kyla joined them. "Look who I have. This is Lulu, my goddaughter—isn't she beautiful?"

Lauren pulled back, but Ray kept his arm around her waist. She focused on the baby in Kyla's arms.

She held a tiny little girl with dark button eyes, pink bow lips, and short dark curls. Lulu couldn't be more than five months old and she melted Lauren's heart.

Her throat closed up at the thought she'd soon hold a baby of her own.

"Oh, my goodness. She's so sweet." She itched to hold the baby, but Ray beat her to it.

"She's a heartbreaker." He plucked the infant from his cousin. "Aren't you, my beauty?" He held her with confidence and ease, his comfort in handling the child obvious.

Lulu grinned, her bow mouth a perfect O, flashing toothless gums and innocent joy.

"Ah..."

Lauren and Kyla echoed each other, which caused them to laugh.

"She likes you." Lauren ran her finger over the petal-soft skin of the baby's hand. Lulu promptly wrapped her fingers around Lauren's digit.

Kyla snorted. "*All* women love him. Not even a five-month-old is immune to his charm." She held up a camera. "Her mama wants a picture." She stood back and clicked a shot of Lauren, Ray, and Lulu. "Thanks."

"What about Mama?" Ray asked. "We should get one with her, too."

Kyla beamed. "She would totally love that. I told her you'd go for it— Oh, my lord, *no*! Those little stinkers are going for the cake. Be right back." She took off at a trot, a fierce glint in her eyes.

"Oops." Ray's gaze followed his cousin's retreat. "Wouldn't want to be one of those boys."

"No."

Lauren couldn't take her eyes off Ray. Watching him with the little girl had charmed her more than she would have believed. He was so natural with the child. Actually, it surprised her. She would have expected just the opposite.

"You're very good with her."

"I'm into kids," he confessed. "I'm godfather to my assistant's one-year-old boy. I love when he brings him to the house. We play catch."

"Catch with a one-year-old?"

"Okay, you got me." He grinned. "We play chase the ball. But it's fun."

Lulu waved her arms and yammered a mouthful of noises. Ray bounced her in his arms.

"Don't worry, sweetness, we haven't forgotten you. Do you want to hold her?"

Lauren nodded and he passed the child to her. She gathered the tiny girl into her arms. How light she felt, yet warm and cuddly. "Well, hello, Lulu."

She received a big grin just like Ray had got. The precious moment lifted her spirits. She held a miracle in her arms. And soon she'd hold her own miracle.

Lulu waved her plump arms and latched onto Lauren's hoop earring. "Oh. Ouch!"

"I've got it." Ray gently held Lulu's arm and worked her fingers free of the gold hoop. His eyes were laughing as he looked down at Lauren. "For someone so small, she's got a good grip."

"She's perfect." Lauren bounced her gently. "But we really should find her mother and return her."

"Just one dance first." Ray wrapped his arms around her waist, swung the three of them onto the dance floor, and set up a mellow sway.

"You really need to learn to wait for an answer," she chided him. But her reprimand lacked heat. "I think she's tired. Her eyes are closing."

"Oh, yeah, she'll be out soon." His unreadable gaze lingered on her and the child. "You look good with a baby in your arms."

"Hmm?" She stalled, her mind flashing to his child in her womb.

It took all her concentration not to miss a step. She'd envisioned a life with just her child and her—based on his single jet-set lifestyle she'd figured he wouldn't want a child in his life. Certainly not disrupting his home. Seeing him with Lulu had put those notions into question.

"You looked pretty good yourself. Surprised me, really."

"They're just little people."

Not really...

"So, you plan to have a few kids of your own someday?" She held her breath, waiting for his answer.

His body tensed and he didn't respond right away, his gaze focused over her left shoulder. "Maybe," he finally allowed. "Never say never, right?"

Breath rushed back into her lungs. What kind of nonanswer was that?

"I want kids," she shared, watching for a reaction. "At least two...maybe three."

He zeroed in on her, heat flaring in his pale eyes, moving over her face and then over the child in her arms. Her body reacted to him, warming under his regard. He lowered his head and she angled hers, anticipating a kiss.

"She's asleep," he whispered.

"Asleep?"

Lauren blinked. In the space of those two seconds her mind had shut off and her body had taken over. It took a moment for her brain synapses to start firing again.

"The baby. Oh, right."

"We should get her back to her mother."

"Yes. You definitely owe her a picture for taking her child hostage."

"I'm putting the blame for that right where it belongs."

He directed her through the other dancers with a hand at the small of her back. "Squarely on Kyla's shoulders."

Lauren shook her head. "Is anything *ever* your fault?"

"Rarely."

"Ha!" *Of course not.* "Why do you say that?"

"Mostly because I don't play the blame game. It's not constructive. I plan and I fix. I provide good directions, and when something goes wrong I come up with a new plan. It's pretty close to the way I've seen you run your events company."

It was *exactly* the way she and Tori ran By Arrangement.

"I'm always excited when an event comes together without a hitch. But I confess it's exhilarating when we pull off an event that's been problematic."

"Right. It's more about the process than the end result."

"Exactly."

Listening to him made her realize how alike their careers were. He created movies and she created events. His were caught on tape and hers were more in the moment, but they both required careful direction and the ability to adjust. "That's what I enjoy most about being an event coordinator—it's an organic experience."

"You've discovered my secret. Now I'll have to kill you." He waved at Kyla, who stood beside a larger version of Lulu. "Or marry you."

"What—? Huh?" She clutched the baby so hard she woke up and squealed. "Shh, baby. I'm sorry." She glared at Ray. "That wasn't funny."

"Oh, but it was." Laughter danced in his eyes. His lips softly touched hers. "Remind me not to propose again while you're holding a baby."

CHAPTER EIGHT

"Mmm. It smells wonderful in here." Mamó strolled over to a lush chair in soft teal and sat. "I might have to take some of whatever that is home." She indicated the seat next to her. "Come. Sit. Ray said he'd see us here at eleven. We're a few minutes early."

Lauren took in the elegant reception area of the exclusive day spa. Ray had swept them away from Queens early that morning, treating them to breakfast at the Plaza before dashing off to a meeting with the mayor. The spa had been a short walk up Fifth Avenue in the thirty-four-degree weather. Mamó had called it pleasant.

Pleasant? Wasn't thirty-two freezing? Thank heavens for the red leather coat.

"Good morning. Welcome to Nouveaux Vous."

A beautiful redhead appeared at the front desk. She wore a classic black dress that contrasted with her milky complexion. Her make-up was flawless, not a freckle in sight. Her serene expression fit perfectly with the elegant pale teal and cream decor.

"Fern Donovan and Lauren Randall?"

"Yes. We're meeting my fiancé here."

How odd did that sound? Apparently they did have an appointment, though Lauren was surprised to hear her name. She and Ray were supposed to be going siting for a movie scheduled to start filming toward the end of the year. Finding out Ray had made an appointment for her was disappointing. She'd been jazzed at the prospect of seeing some of this famous city.

"We have you both listed for a massage, facial, and glamor. Mr. Donovan arranged for you to have your sessions together. Rene and Kim are available when you're ready. May I get you coffee or water while you wait?"

Mamó shook her head.

"No, thank you." Lauren checked her phone. "No message from him. We're going to wait for a few minutes," she told the receptionist.

Aware this was the moment she'd been dreading, Lauren settled next to Mamó in a lobby chair.

Since learning of Mamó's ability to tell when a woman was pregnant, Lauren had anxiously anticipated a confrontation with the older woman. Until now they'd been in company or on the move. She could put it off no longer.

The other woman spoke first, patting Lauren's hand on the armrest between them. "I want to thank you for your gifts. There was no need for you to bother—just having you here is such a joy to me. But the extra decor and having the gentlemen there to dance with was a treat beyond telling."

"I'm happy it added to your day," Lauren responded honestly.

"Oh, it made my year. My friends had such a grand time. No one will top this event for years."

"I'm glad you had a good time." Lauren smiled at Mamó's joy. Then she sobered. "You know, don't you?" She didn't look at Mamó but at the placid seascape on the far wall.

Mamó didn't respond right away. Then her hand covered Lauren's and she squeezed. "It's your news to share. I respect that."

"Ray doesn't know," Lauren said.

"I've gathered that." There was no judgment in Mamó's voice, just curiosity.

"It's hard to see him as a father."

Or it had been before she'd watched him cradle little Lulu in his arms. The sight of the big, strong man confidently holding the precious infant had changed everything. Or it could change nothing. She needed time to re-evaluate.

"He's always been good with kids. I think that's what hurt him most in the breakup." Mamó's hand shook and she pulled it back into her lap. She twined her fingers together until the knuckles showed white.

Lauren stilled. This must be the incident Ray had referenced. "The breakup?"

"He must have told you? It's the one time I truly regretted my talent. But I couldn't let him say his vows without knowing the truth."

"No, of course not," she soothed.

Vows? Questions ricocheted through her head. She wanted to press Mamó for answers but refrained. The older woman was already distressed by the conversation. Better to calm her down before Ray arrived. She'd put the questions to him at a more appropriate time.

Mamó's unusual talent might have pushed up Lauren's agenda to tell Ray, but it didn't change her concerns over his emotional availability to his child. She needed to know about the past before she could make a decision about the future.

"Honesty is important to Ray," Lauren reassured her.

"That's what I told myself even though I knew he'd leave." Mamó wrung her hands. "It was for the best. He's an important man now."

"I have the feeling Ray would be important whatever he did."

"Probably." Mamó nodded. "But he saw no future for himself here. I had to tell him."

"It was the right thing to do."

Curiosity was killing Lauren, but it wouldn't be fair to

pump Mamó. The story needed to come from Ray. Just as the news of their child needed to come from her.

"I'm going to tell him."

"Of course, dear. I won't say anything," Mamó assured her. "Unless I'm asked, I've learned to keep what I know to myself. Well, most of the time."

The shop door opened and Ray walked in on a blast of "pleasant" air. His presence filled the space along with his broad shoulders. Lauren hopped up and he greeted her with a kiss on the cheek. And then he bent to kiss Mamó's powder-dusted cheek. For a man who prized his privacy so strongly he was demonstrative. She'd pretty much given up on the no touching rule. The man just couldn't keep his hands, or his lips, to himself.

And apparently she couldn't keep to her side of the bed. She'd woken up wrapped around him again this morning. This time she'd got caught—literally—while she'd been trying to unfurl herself from him. He had turned over and met her nose to nose.

She'd refused to admit to disappointment when he had merely wished her good morning with a brief peck on the forehead before bounding from the bed to hit the bathroom first.

Oddly, sleeping with him seemed to suit the baby, because her morning queasiness had all but disappeared.

She'd always considered his bid for privacy to have stemmed from arrogance, but now she knew him better she thought it might be more a matter of self-defense. It was something to think about.

"Listen, babe, there's been a change of plans. The master of the Port Authority isn't available tomorrow, so I'm meeting with him today and viewing the docks. That's going to be a cold, dirty trek I'm sure you have no interest in. Instead I booked you matching spa treatments with Mamó. Is that okay?"

Dirty docks or a facial? No-brainer. "Sure."

"Good." He kissed her again, this time on the lips, a gesture of simple affection. Clearly his mind was elsewhere. "I'll pick you up at three and we'll go shopping."

"Shopping?" She was not letting him buy her another thing.

"Yes, the mayor invited me to a black tie reception tonight. I told him I'd be escorting my two best ladies."

"Ray—" The protest had barely passed her lips when a well-attired man with black hair opened the door and nodded at Ray.

"Sorry, Dynamite, I have to go. We'll talk later."

And then he was gone and the redhead was back. Lauren sighed and shared a glance with Mamó, who shrugged.

"He's a busy man."

Yeah, right. But Lauren didn't push it. "Shall we go get pampered?"

"Yes—and we should buy some of that lovely-smelling lotion. I'm sure Ray would want us to have some."

A smile tugged at the corner of Lauren's mouth because she had no doubt he would. "Yes, we really need some lotion."

Four hours later Lauren followed Mamó from the spa feeling refreshed and revitalized. The massage and facial had worked all the toxins and tension from her body. The beauty regimen had pampered her in a whole new way, leaving her feeling beautiful and eager to show off her pretty new look.

She really must schedule a spa day for her and Tori post-honeymoon.

Mamó had a real glow about her, too. Though some of that might have been due to the call she'd taken from Ellie. She'd made plans for dinner back in Queens and Lauren got the impression George Meade might be involved. Seemed Mamó wanted to showcase *her* new glamor, too.

Lauren didn't push for details. What she didn't know she couldn't spill to Ray.

Bright shafts of sunshine fought through the cloud cover and high-rises to warm the afternoon pedestrians. A limousine stood double-parked at the curb. Ray stepped out as they approached.

He flattered Mamó on how lovely she looked, accepted the news she wanted to bow out of the reception with good grace, and sent her off in the limo, suggesting she use the car service to collect her friends for dinner.

"She always gets a kick out of her neighbors' reaction when she comes and goes in a limousine. She'll be extra excited to give them a ride."

Enchanted with his obvious affection for his grandmother, Lauren hooked her arm through his. "Today she feels beautiful and special. You did good."

Satisfaction showed in the form of a smirk. "Good. There's still a sadness about her, but Ellie says she's been better the last few days." He waved down a passing cab. "How was she today?"

"Fine. It was a mellow day. And she seems excited about tonight."

"Good." He nodded and helped her into the waiting taxi. "Bloomingdales," he directed the driver.

Lauren settled into her seat without argument. She'd already decided to treat herself to a new dress for the reception and as a souvenir of the trip. By Arrangement's success over the past year certainly allowed for a little extravagance—which reminded her: the designer of Tori's wedding dress had a loft in New York. Lauren loved her work.

She scrolled through her contacts, made a quick call, and then asked Ray to change their destination.

"I'm glad you're getting into the spirit of tonight's adventure." He swept a loose tendril of hair behind her ear.

"Hmm?" She relaxed against him. "Are we having an adventure?"

"Yes. This is our first official date."

"So it is." Tipping her head back, she eyed his profile. He appeared pleased with himself. "There's likely to be press at this event. How do you want to handle it?" she asked.

"Word of our engagement is out. I already got asked about it a couple of times today."

"What did you say?"

"That I wasn't answering questions. But I'll make a brief statement tonight." He picked up her hand, threaded his fingers through hers. "I'm sorry you got dragged into a lie."

"Thank you, but it's not your fault."

"I had my team put together a news release. I'll show it to you at the hotel. It includes who you are, when we met, how long we've dated and details currently known about the wedding."

"You have a team?"

"I do. Besides my assistant there's my manager, a publicist, a project manager, an accountant, and—to my shame and at my assistant's insistence—a stylist."

She laughed and slapped his knee. "You do *not* have a stylist."

"Only during awards season. Which reminds me—will you be my date for the awards ceremony this weekend?"

"Walk the red carpet with you?"

Her eyes popped and she sucked in a breath before she got herself under control. The awards were a big deal for Ray this year. They were equally important to her career.

"I'm working that night."

"If we make an announcement, everyone will expect you to attend with me."

"By Arrangement is handling Obsidian Studio's after-party." She rubbed her thumb over his knuckle. "It's been our goal since we focused our business in Hollywood to cater a post-awards ball."

"And I'm betting it will be *the* party to beat this year. People are still talking about the job you ladies did for Obsidian at the Hollywood Hills Film Festival. Couldn't you keep an eye on things from the perspective of being my date?"

His request went totally against her work ethic. She shouldn't even be here this week, but preparing and overseeing the biggest event of her career. Work had become her savior, her solace. She took comfort in the discipline and control necessary to pull off a spectacular event.

But with a baby under her heart and a major life decision to make regarding her child's future her mind couldn't focus on work. She owed it to herself, to her baby, and to Ray to take the time to make the most informed decision she could. In the meantime, twice daily updates from her assistant kept her sane on the work front.

She recalled Mamó's mention of vows and realized there was so much about Ray she didn't know. Dates were meant to help a couple get to know each other better. So that was what she would do. Enjoy the night, learn more about Ray, and maybe get some answers about his past.

Whatever his reservations about his old neighborhood, he hadn't deserted his community. On her way to the restroom at the community center last night she'd spied a plaque posted in gratitude to Raymond Patrick Donovan for the donation of a gymnasium and pool.

Dated seven years ago, the timing of the donation matched his first huge success—a film about a wounded veteran saving a small town from a corrupt mayor. He'd blended drama and action into a brilliant display of bravery, sacrifice, and justice that had provided moviegoers with an emotional and visually satisfying experience. The film had made Ray's name a household word—he'd swept the awards that year, and gone on to become part of the Hollywood elite.

And Ray had handed a cool million to his old neighborhood.

"I'll think about it. Let's get through tonight first."

"Deal. We're here." He climbed from the cab, glanced up at the building. "She's stretching the limits of the garment district, here."

"That doesn't really mean anything to me," she said as she joined him. "Did you see Tori's wedding dress? Fabulous. She found it at a small boutique on Rodeo Drive, and of course she had to call the designer to rave about it. The two of them are now email buddies."

Inside, the receptionist directed them to the third floor. Eve Gardner met them at the door.

"Lauren, I'm so glad you called." The slim blond greeted them in her showroom. "I've seen pictures of the wedding. Tori was absolutely stunning—you must share all the details."

"I will, but first let me say your dress was the jewel in her day. I've never seen her look more beautiful."

"As a designer I can promise you *she* made the dress—not the other way around. My phone hasn't stopped ringing all week." She laughed lightly, looking a little shell shocked. "I should have paid her to wear the dress!"

Lauren squeezed her hand. "You deserve the recognition. It was a stunning dress. I'm hoping you might have something for me." She introduced Ray. "We're going to a reception for the mayor tonight."

"Tonight?" Eve's eyes widened as she recognized Ray, but she quickly recovered and pulled Lauren further into her shop, introducing the two of them to her assistant, Christy. "What type of affair is it?"

"Black tie."

"Hmm, what are you? A size five? I think I have a couple of items you might like."

Eve invited Lauren and Ray to sit and then disappeared into the back. Christy offered them refreshments and then followed Eve.

Lauren sat on a dove-gray tufted sofa while Ray roamed the showroom. The white walls provided an excellent showcase for the life-sized framed prints of celebrities and models in Eve's designs. Several racks around the room held vibrantly hued garments.

"Nice." Ray stopped in front of a print of a high-profile actress in a midnight-blue dress on which the bodice consisted of strategically placed bands artfully woven across the breasts and throat while the skirt fell in a straight sheath to the floor.

"That's showing too much skin for me."

He turned back to her, arms crossed over his chest. "You'd be stunning in something like this."

She shook her blond head. "I should have told her something conservative would be best. Preferably in black."

"Absolutely not. Tonight isn't a job. It's fun. You need a dress to play in."

"I won't be working this event," she agreed, mimicking him by crossing her arms over her breasts. "But you will. I need to respect that."

"Dynamite, in my business the more skin you show the better."

"Yes, but I'm only visiting your world. In my world I can wear the dress again at an event I *will* be working."

"If you don't have the guts all you have to do is say so." He strolled over and dropped down beside her, his arm resting on the back of the sofa behind her.

"I don't have the guts."

No need to bluff. And she wouldn't let him dare her into wearing something she couldn't be comfortable in. That was Tori—not her. Classy and conservative suited her just fine.

"Okay," he said easily, tracing a finger over her ear,

making her shiver. The man was always *touching*. "But you have the body for it. Just so you know."

"You're not supposed to be thinking of my body. Remember? It's one of the rules we discussed."

"I thought you gave up on those rules?"

"No. What made you think that?" She should never have let him get away with the constant touching. It gave him the wrong idea.

"I don't know. Possibly the fact I've woken up with you curled around me the last couple of nights."

Heat rose in her cheeks. The hope that he'd slept through her nighttime wanderings ended at this embarrassing revelation. Of course she knew it had been a futile hope.

"That doesn't count," she bluffed. "We can't control what we do while we're sleeping."

He leaned close, bringing the scent of man and spice with him. He whispered in her ear. "That's not what you said the other night."

"Yes…well…" He smelled so good she'd lost her train of thought. *Oh, yeah.* "The point is the rules are in full force. And you're breaking them."

"Wrong. The rules say no unnecessary touching. I can admire all I want."

No. He had to stop. His admiring and his touching were chipping away at her resolve. She'd agreed to their date tonight, to get to know him better. But already she felt her control slipping. Being the sole focus of his attention might be more than she could handle.

"Your admiring is making it hard to breathe." She put a finger in the middle of his chest and pushed. "Behave yourself."

"Okay." He settled back into his place, but didn't remove his arm from behind her. "But you're forgetting the security cameras. Touching is totally within our limits."

Of course he'd be aware of the cameras. Short of pleading, she only had one other option. A good threat.

"Go ahead—have your fun now. Risk putting me in a bad mood for tonight, when I'll be wearing a sexy dress and sipping a nice wine."

"Good point."

His blue eyes narrowed, showing her he'd caught her meaning. The gleam in those eyes sent a message too. He knew he bothered her. And he planned to put that knowledge to good use later.

He gave her ear a tug and pulled out his phone. "I'll just return a few texts."

"You do that." She reached for her purse. Actually, it was a good time to check her own messages. All was well at By Arrangement. Her mom was still waiting for a full explanation. And no word yet from Tori.

"Here we go." Eve returned, Christy on her heels, with a handful of dresses in her arms. "Come with me. I found a lovely cobalt gown perfect for your skin tone."

"Wait." Ray waved his phone. "How long will this take?"

Lauren stared at him blankly, then turned to Eve.

The designer shrugged. "As long as it takes."

Lauren nodded.

He stood, looking back and forth between them as if expecting something more. "Right. I have something to take care of. I'll be back for you."

"No."

"You want me to wait?" He lifted his phone to impart his response.

"No."

He went still and lifted a brown eyebrow, waiting for her direction.

Okay, she had to admit it was heady stuff. Except for her rules, she'd been following his lead for this whole trip. It was nice to have a little power. It might only be over travel plans, but she'd take it.

"You go ahead. I'll catch a cab and meet you back at the hotel."

They had decided to stay in the city for the night, in the suite Ray had originally booked for them.

"Okay." He advised the person on the other end of the phone he'd be there shortly. Then he came over, kissed her hard, and headed out, taking her hard-won power with him.

But not for long.

She turned to Eve. "I hope the cobalt is sexy."

CHAPTER NINE

THE BLUE FABRIC clung to Lauren's curves. A fitted bodice flowed into two straps that both went over one shoulder, creating an asymmetrical keyhole. The straps narrowed to two-inch strips spanning her bare back. The skirt hugged her hips before falling in a straight line to the floor.

Ray sipped a well-balanced whiskey as he half listened to the mayor talking about the summit underway at the United Nations. Undoubtedly it was a worthy endeavor, but Ray found his attention held by two blue straps—or, more specifically, by the creamy skin they didn't cover. His fingers itched to touch.

A few members of the society press were covering the event out front. They'd lit up like kids on Christmas morning when they'd spied him and Lauren. Made him glad he had the press statement ready.

Lauren had handled the congratulations and intrusive questions well, but her poise had failed to disguise the tremors running through her body—especially when an idiot had demanded to know if she was pregnant.

Ray had wanted to plant his fist in the man's mouth. Instead he'd shut the questions off and moved her inside. They'd made it through the informal procession line with no further incident.

He enjoyed having her at his side. She neither preened nor disappeared. Nor did she defer to him, but treated him as he imagined she treated all her dates—as an equal.

Which influenced those around them, easing the burden of his celebrity.

It was a treat he took full advantage of for over an hour. Difficult to enjoy an event when people feared approaching you or made the conversation all about you. This room held important men who wielded real power. Even casual discussions rippled with nuances of bigger things.

It was almost enough to engage his whole attention. But there was always a part of him aware of Lauren, whether she stood at his side or had wandered a few feet away in a breakaway discussion.

Something about the woman got to him.

He'd earned a reputation for being a hardcore bachelor long ago because he guarded his privacy and made it clear to all his companions that they could expect nothing more from him than a good time and a fond farewell.

Generally he stuck to two dating pools when he wanted female company: women in the industry but behind the camera, because they were familiar with what it meant to be in the limelight, or women unconnected with the industry, because he didn't have to worry that they were trying to further their careers.

Lauren straddled the line, giving him the best of both worlds. He was comfortable with her—which might freak him out except for the sizzling chemistry between them.

He wouldn't be used because of his occupation. He wouldn't be used, period. Being seen as a meal ticket and an escape out of the neighborhood had taught him that harsh lesson before he'd ever made it big.

And the price had been the life of his child.

On his wedding day he had truly understood that anybody could be driven to kill. If not for Mamó he might well have crossed the line.

He shook off the memory. Not the time. Not the place.

His fingers itched.

Lauren thought she was safe, standing in deep discussion with the mayor's wife. But she'd set the rules. He could only touch her in public. So, actually, she'd chosen the place. It was only fair he should choose the time.

He'd been very restrained so far. From the stunning moment when she'd stepped from her room at the hotel, through the limo ride to the reception, to having her by his side through the barrage of introductions.

His patience was at an end.

"Are we boring you, Ray?"

Bob, the governor of New Jersey, clapped him on the back, drawing his attention back to the group.

"I know you're not working tonight, but I'll admit I was hoping for a chance to talk to you about using the great state of New Jersey in one of your films."

"I'm afraid I'm not very familiar with New Jersey, other than flying into the airport."

"Well, I'm happy to rectify that. I can arrange a tour at your convenience."

"Thanks, but my time is limited on this trip, and I have several locations to site tomorrow. I expect it to take most of the day."

"I've put an aide and a limousine at his disposal for the day," the mayor interjected.

"A helicopter would be more efficient, and then you could add a couple of Jersey sights."

"A helicopter?" Ray mused, liking the idea. Liking the idea of smoothing his hand over lotion-scented skin even more. Lauren might get a kick out of an aerial tour.

"Have your assistant contact my office with your schedule." Bob pulled out a card. "And I'll have a bird ready and waiting."

"Come on, Bob," the mayor interposed. "Are you trying to steal my revenue stream?" He was only half joking.

Lauren's laugh tinkled on the air, the sound energizing Ray.

Bob shrugged big shoulders. "I just want to show Ray,

here, the diversity of my beautiful state so he can keep us in mind for future ventures."

The mayor harrumphed.

"Thanks, Bob," Ray said. He flicked the card. "My assistant will be in touch. Gentlemen, it's been a pleasure."

"Running off so soon?" the mayor protested, then followed Ray's gaze to where the women chatted a few feet away. A look of admiration chased away the touch of irritation in his eyes. "Ah. I understand. Congratulations, by the way. You're a lucky man."

"Indeed."

He nodded to the men and strolled the short distance to Lauren's side, shaking off the odd combination of pride and anger at the way the other man had eyed Lauren.

He wasn't usually territorial. Then again he didn't usually have a temporary fiancée either. That had to be it.

His fingers connected with the skin of her lower back and he sighed. Satisfaction and desire replaced all other emotions.

Lauren instantly acknowledged him, looking up and back. She continued her conversation but settled into his touch.

"It's really not that difficult to up the interest factor of an event," she explained to the cluster of ladies. "It can be as simple as having a signature cocktail or adding visual props."

"These affairs always look the same," a white-haired matron said, while fingering the diamonds at her neck.

"That usually happens when it's left up to a hotel. Understated elegance is a classic, so it's often the default mode." She responded calmly, as if her audience wasn't sending furtive glances his way.

"What would you have done differently tonight?" the mayor's wife asked.

"We often work with the client to come up with a theme. Lacking that, I'd switch things up. Flowers are a standard, but instead of roses I might have gone with something more exotic. A tropical feel in the middle of winter would be welcomed by most. And I might have replaced a few of the round tables with a conversation area of sofas and chairs."

A hum of approval came from the group.

Lauren shrugged gracefully. "My sister is the truly creative half of our team."

"Ladies," Ray broke in, "I'm going to steal Lauren away. We have reservations for a late supper."

"How romantic," the matron announced. "Enjoy these early days, dear. It's never quite the same once you've said your vows."

"And Marian should know," one of the others volunteered.

"Yes," Marian agreed with a trill of laughter. "Walter is my third husband."

"Let's give Walter something to think about, shall we?" Ray lifted Marian's diamond-laden hand to his mouth and pressed a kiss to the back of her fingers.

Marian flushed pink, her delight in being singled out bright in her smile.

"Ladies…" He winked and led Lauren away.

Watching the world spin away before her sent Lauren's stomach rolling. Not because of the baby this time, but the dizzying ride in a glass elevator. Placing a hand on her belly, she turned away from the rising view.

"You okay?" Ray wrapped an arm around her waist and pulled her close.

"Vertigo." She leaned against him, took comfort in the caress of his hand on her back. "Better now. Thanks."

The elevator opened on the forty-seventh floor. Ray gestured for her to exit. She did so, but questioned him.

"You said we had reservations for a late supper. I thought we were headed for the rooftop restaurant?"

"It's been a long day. I ordered in." He used a card key to let them into the lounge area of their suite. "I hope you don't mind?"

"No, but I'm disappointed. I was looking forward to re-laxing while taking in the rooftop view. New York keeps beckoning, yet I've only seen a slice of the Big Apple."

This was exactly the type of highhanded behavior she found annoying.

"Sorry." Loosening his tie, he bent to kiss her on the top of her head. "I've had enough of being a spectacle today. I had them set the table up by the window, so the view should be nearly the same."

"Oh…" Now she felt bad. She hadn't considered how being "on" all the time must get tiring for him.

Feeling the quiet of the room embrace her, she admit-ted it was a stellar option.

"Good thinking. What did you order for us?"

"Lobster, steak, a full range of sides and desserts." At the dining table he began lifting lids on dome-covered dishes. "I wanted you to have a choice."

"How thoughtful." And it was. Her mood improved. "This looks delicious."

Ray handed her a plate, took one for himself, and they served themselves. She chose both lobster and a small piece of steak, with asparagus and tender red potatoes.

"How's the vertigo?" Ray's concerned gaze ran over her features as he held her chair. "Would you like me to pull the table away from the window?"

Touched, she smiled her appreciation. "No, I'll be fine. It was the motion combined with the view that got to me. Here the table blocks the feet-to-skyline view, so I should be all right. But I think I'll skip the wine, just to be safe."

Finding ways to decline alcohol and caffeine were get-ting harder and harder.

She set her plate down and allowed him to seat her. "This is lovely."

New York in all its glistening glory was spread out before them. High-rises and bridges threaded together with streets of lights. She recognized the Empire State Building and Ray pointed out several other landmarks.

"Where's Queens?" she asked.

"You can't see it from here. Wrong angle." But he pointed out the boroughs they *could* see amidst the myriad buildings. Even from this height and distance the city's flow and movement reached her. New York was a living, breathing metropolis unlike any place else she'd ever seen.

He told her about his day at the docks, making her laugh with his dry sense of humor. She refrained from boring him with details of her day at the spa, assuring him instead that it had been relaxing. "Not as relaxing as this, though."

A gleam appeared in his eyes. He reached over and threaded long fingers through her smaller ones. His touch soothed and aroused.

"I know what you mean. It feels like forever since we've been alone."

Yes. She got that. And the fact she'd missed him was as surprising as it was true.

She felt as if she'd been on edge for days. They'd been together almost constantly, but rarely on their own. To all intents and purposes they were truly alone for the first time since leaving Hollywood. Well, except for the time they spent together in his small bedroom—which was not relaxing in the least.

Baby might enjoy sleeping in Daddy's arms, but Mama found the whole experience nerve-racking.

Tonight the mood was intimate, yet mellow. The amazing view and the delectable food were too good to ruin with bad vibes. The ease between them presented the perfect opportunity to address something bothering her.

Mamó had mentioned vows in connection with Ray, and something to do with a pregnancy. It wasn't hard to connect the dots, but she didn't work well with supposition. She liked solid facts. Much less room for misunderstandings.

The one time she had allowed herself to have faith in her emotions she'd sunk deep in an emotionally damaging relationship. Some—Tori—might call it abusive. Lauren's pride argued that she'd pulled out before it had reached that stage.

The point was she'd learned a tough lesson: not to let her heart lead her head. Especially now she had a child to think of.

"Can I ask you a personal question?"

"Sure. We're engaged—at least for a few more days."

Uh, no, they weren't. But they *were* going to be parents. She figured that gave her a right to know. So she'd run with his permission.

"Have you been married before?"

He stared at her with an unreadable expression for a long moment, until she wondered if he'd answer her after all. Then he stood, pulled her to her feet by their joined fingers and led her to the large, plush couch.

"If we're going to get into something deep, let's get comfortable."

He sat and drew her down next to him, never letting go of her. And still he didn't elaborate. He played with her fingers, his gazed locked on their entwined digits, their hands perched on his hard thigh, because he'd allowed no space between them.

"I suppose someone mentioned it to you at the party?" Bitterness edged his response. "Fifteen years and four major industry awards and I *still* haven't lived it down."

Okay, that didn't sound like a denial. Then again, she'd never heard of marriage referred to as "it" either.

"So you *were* married?"

"No."

An odd sense of relief slid through her.

Ridiculous, of course. And unfounded. It would be unhealthy for a man his age never to have been involved in a committed relationship. So he preferred to be discreet? That didn't mean he didn't have a private life. Or that he didn't care for the women he spent time with.

Okay, so their interaction had been purely physical, with nothing more than a fake engagement to indicate any sense of depth. She'd be a fool to assume all his relationships were so shallow.

But he hadn't cared enough to get married. She supposed that meant something. She hoped hearing his history might give her the answers she needed.

He'd been quiet while she stewed. Brooding himself?

"Painful memories?" She squeezed his fingers and leaned her head on his shoulder.

"Yeah." It was almost a grunt.

"You don't have to talk about it if you don't want to," she offered. She'd be disappointed if he changed his mind now, but she couldn't force him to share. Not when she had secrets she wasn't prepared to reveal yet.

"It was a lifetime ago. Feels like it happened to someone else." He scrubbed his free hand over the back of his neck. "I was just a kid."

"If it happened fifteen years ago, you *are* a different person. We all change and grow. I know *I'm* not the same person I was when I started college."

He flinched, and she knew he was thinking about what she'd gone through. His jaw clenched. But he started talking.

"I was headed for college, with a scholarship to UCLA in my grasp, when my world fell apart. My girlfriend, Camilla, informed me she was pregnant."

Lauren's hand clenched around his. Even though she'd expected to hear a child had been involved after Mamó's earlier comments, Lauren still took the news like a shot to the gut.

Another woman had carried Ray's child.

The knowledge made her raw. She couldn't squeeze a word past the constriction in her throat. She shouldn't care. Theirs was not a romantic connection. Being so cozy these last few days had given a false sense of intimacy. Nothing had changed.

Ray rubbed his thumb over her wrist. "We had one of those on again, off again relationships—mostly because she wanted constant attention and I was wrapped up in making movies. Neither of us was thinking long-term. At least I didn't think so. She knew I'd planned to go to Los Angeles whether I got the scholarship or not. The University of California Los Angeles is arguably the best school for film and television in the world."

"I remember reading an article stating that you won an award for a documentary on homeless runaways that had scholarship money attached to it."

"The Stahling Award. That's when I knew I had a good chance at going to UCLA. The award carries a lot of prestige. Along with my other awards and a short film, it was the complete package."

He hadn't been wrong. He'd gone to UCLA and become one of their biggest success stories. But something wasn't adding up. Something must have happened with the baby. Or maybe there hadn't been a baby at all?

"Was Camilla lying when she said she was pregnant?"

"No. Mamó would have known."

He got up and poured another glass of wine. He held the bottle up, silently asking if she wanted some. She shook her head. Sipping, he stared out the window.

"My world shattered. The last thing I wanted was a kid. But I'd been raised by my grandmother and my aunt—two widows, basically single mothers. I knew the hardships they'd faced. They raised me to take responsibility for my actions. I couldn't walk away from my kid and everything they'd taught me."

"You proposed?" she guessed, feeling for the young Ray who'd had all his dreams disrupted.

"I didn't love her. We'd only hooked up in our senior year. But the kid was mine, so, yeah, I proposed. Camilla and her mother started making rush wedding plans. She told me she wanted the ceremony right away, so she wouldn't be showing in her gown. I was committed. When didn't matter to me. Providing for my family did, so I started looking for a better job."

"You didn't consider taking Camilla with you to Los Angeles?"

"I considered it, but the scholarship was for dorm housing, so I'd have needed to work. And probably Camilla, too, which would be difficult with a newborn. At least in Queens we'd have family support nearby. But I wasn't giving up. I might have to do night courses, but I started putting in applications to New York film schools. Camilla had a fit when she realized."

"She thought she'd be going with you to Los Angeles?"

"Oh, yeah. She said if I could be a director she could be an actress. I laughed at her."

"Uh-oh." The word escaped without thought. Never a good idea to laugh at a woman—certainly not a pregnant one. The fact her aspirations had been somewhat misguided would only have made it worse.

"Not my shiniest moment," he confessed. "But my tolerance was stretched thin by then. I explained my reasoning. She didn't care—said I was jealous of her and insisted we go. I refused. Said I wasn't taking a child to California. She left in a huff."

Lauren closed her eyes, briefly shutting out his pain. She saw the train wreck coming. His stoic delivery as he relived the tragic memory was not fooling her for a moment. Aching for him, she stood and went to him. Wrapping her arms around his waist, she laid her head on his back and just held him. A fine tremor shook his body, revealing the hurt he tried to hide. He laid his hand over hers.

"I'm so sorry," she whispered.

"At that time we were only days away from the wedding. I should have figured out something was off when she stopped yammering at me over details I couldn't care less about. And she'd begun avoiding Mamó. I didn't notice. Hell, I couldn't even put a good face on it at that point. The less time I spent with her the better."

"Oh, Ray."

"I was at the church, dread heavy in my gut, and Mamó came into the little room where I was waiting. She knew how hard everything was for me."

"She never encouraged you to go?"

"No. She supported my decision to stay and raise my child. But she couldn't let me go through with the ceremony when she no longer sensed a child."

"What did you do?"

"I challenged Camilla. At first she refused to see me. Then she tried to deny it. But I knew. When I demanded someone go for a pregnancy test she broke down and claimed she'd lost the baby. She said she still loved me and now we could go to Los Angeles together. It made me sick to my stomach."

"She aborted the baby?"

"She denied it. Still does, as far as I know. But she was lying. She got pregnant to hook me and got rid of the baby when it threatened her plans."

The muscles in his back flexed as he braced his body to control the shaking. To disguise what Camilla's betrayal had done to him.

"You don't believe she ever intended having the baby."

The breath left his body and he unlinked her hands to turn and study her. He cupped her face, stared into her eyes. "How can you know that?"

"I'm beginning to know *you*. Camilla's perfidy was

painful, but having an innocent life trivialized made it worse."

"It wasn't just an innocent life. It was my child. Her treachery crushed me. Her total disregard for my child's life—that destroyed me." His jaw clenched as he fought for composure. "She stole seed from me and tossed a life away as if it meant nothing. All for a trip to Hollywood. How could I go to UCLA when I knew the lure of Hollywood was what had caused my child to lose his life?

"Ray…" Her heart broke for him.

"For about a week I punished myself. Pulled all my applications from the local schools, grabbed my camera, and hit the streets. I found destitution, despair, disassociation, defeat. These weren't the teenagers I had filmed before. They had been survivors. These people had given up entirely. After three days I couldn't stand it and I dragged myself home. Mamó was waiting for me. She embraced me, fed me, scolded me and shamed me. In the face of all I'd seen, her steadfast love humbled me. The next day she told me to get over the self-pity, pack my bags, and leave for Los Angeles, already. I'd seen what defeat did to a person. Damned if I was going to let Camilla steal my soul. So I followed Mamó's advice and never looked back."

"I'm glad you did. None of what happened was your fault."

"I made a child with her. I let her talk me into unprotected sex. *Stupid.* I was an eighteen-year-old boy, and she'd teased me past the point of control. But that's on me."

"The fact that you accept the responsibility makes you a good man. If you'd walked away unscathed you would be no better than her. But you cared. You mourned. You went on to be a brilliant film-maker. Truly, the world would be a sadder place if you had turned your back on Hollywood."

"Thank you." He pressed his forehead to hers. Tension drained from him. "Most of the time I can bury the memories. But being back has brought up a lot of those old emotions. It doesn't help that the gossip continues."

"Do you ever see Camilla?"

"No." A simple yet harsh statement. "I rarely come to the neighborhood."

"You shouldn't let the past keep you away. Mamó is so happy to have you at the house. A few stray comments amongst friends are nothing to some of the stuff I've seen in the tabloids. If you were around more the gossip would fade away from natural attrition—which would be good, because you're going to want to visit Mamó when you find a real fiancée."

Okay, that was too much. She stepped back. No doubt Camilla's escapades would dwindle when news of Ray's impending fatherhood got around.

Should Lauren tell him now?

No. It wasn't the right time. She didn't want him associating her news with the loss he had suffered in the past.

"I'm not interested in another fiancée."

An arm at her waist didn't let her go far. Long fingers traced the keyhole in her bodice. "Did I tell you how lovely you look tonight?"

"You did." And the desire in his eyes had repeated the message over and over throughout the night.

She'd wanted to make him notice her, and she had succeeded, all right. To the point it had almost backfired on her. The searing weight of his gaze had followed her all night, and her body had responded with heightened awareness until she could barely concentrate. There she had stood, rubbing elbows with the rich and powerful, and she'd struggled to put together coherent sentences. Fortunately the fact that a friend of the mayor's wife had heard of By Arrangement had caught her attention and grounded her in the conversation so she didn't actually embarrass herself.

The desire was back in his eyes now, burning brighter

than ever, making her nerves tingle and her body heat. She much preferred seeing passion over pain in his sea-blue eyes. And, oh, he smelled good.

She missed being held by him. So, with luxury surrounding her, New York lit up at her feet, and a hard man pulling her close, she surrendered her control.

Rising on her toes, she kissed the hard line of his jaw. "Are you just going to look? Or do you plan to do something about it?"

CHAPTER TEN

RAY NEEDED NO further urging. He swept her into his arms and carried her to his room. Towards his bed. *Oh, yeah.* Satisfaction roared through him.

The thought of Lauren in his bed touched off something primitive in him.

Probably because it had taken so long to get her there. From the very beginning their sexual encounters had been steamy, exciting and clandestine. They were like flint and paper—sparking off each other until antagonism flashed to passion and they rushed to find the first private space available.

He'd never had better sex.

And it should have been enough.

He wasn't a possessive man when it came to women. Generally he preferred to keep things as unencumbered as possible, going to a hotel or to her place. He didn't trust easily. Women were a pleasure, not a commitment.

Rehashing his past had been like opening a vein: painful and potentially hazardous. What good could come of it? None, in his regard. He never talked about himself. Yet he'd felt compelled to share with Lauren. Bringing her to New York had probably been a mistake. Their closeness gave a false impression of intimacy.

Tonight he didn't care. He couldn't get too close.

Setting her on her feet, he sought out the side zipper

he'd spied during his frequent perusals of her throughout the night.

His hadn't been the only eyes on her during the reception. The attention she'd drawn had caused a low level animosity to burn under his skin.

She was *his*, damn it. Yet he'd also been proud to be with her. Smart, beautiful, poised—she was the total package.

He kissed her, hard and deep, then stepped back. "Take this off for me."

A shy smile greeted his request—unusual for the confident woman he knew her to be—but her delicate fingers went to the alluring blue straps that had tantalized him all night. Enchanted, he perched on the edge of the bed, prepared to enjoy her performance.

With a flick of her fingers the straps were loosened. A shimmy of her hips and the cobalt fabric pooled at her feet.

Sweet, merciful angels.

He sucked in a breath. It lodged in the back of his throat. She stood in nothing more than a black lace thong and mile-high shoes so sexy they made her pretty legs look like they reached clear to heaven.

Being in her arms was as close as he'd probably ever get.

"You should breathe," she advised him, her confidence fully restored.

She walked to him, all creamy skin and soft curves. Wedging herself between his spread knees, she started undoing buttons.

"Your turn."

"I've never seen anything more beautiful than you." He urged her down to him, kissed her lips, her chin, the side of her neck, working his way to luscious bounty.

She hugged his head to her and he felt her mouth against his hair. In that moment he felt cherished. She always brought intensity to their encounters. This was different—slower, softer.

They were different—no longer acquaintances scratching a passionate itch. She'd met his family, they'd traded secrets, slept together without making love; it was more than he'd had with anyone since leaving New York.

And it was more than he wanted to think about. Time to stop thinking and start touching.

Lying back, he took her with him and then rolled over so she lay beneath him, flushed and dewy-eyed.

"You're not usually so shy." She linked her arms around his neck and smiled at him. "This is going to be difficult to accomplish unless you remove these clothes."

"I don't want to stop touching you."

"Excellent argument. But it doesn't solve our problem."

"We have all night, Dynamite, a soft bed, and no need to rush. Short of being evacuated, I plan to make love to you all night long."

"All night? You *are* feeling frisky."

"I've spent the last few nights with this lovely little tush tucked up next to me. But because of your rules I couldn't do anything but hold you." He surged to his feet and stripped off his clothes. In less than a minute he'd joined her back in bed. "Until now. Frisky? Oh, yeah."

"So…oh…you're saying…uh…you cheated?"

Lauren arched under Ray's talented touch. He knew all her hot buttons and stroked them to maximum effect. True to his promise he took his time, building sensation on sensation, his touch in equal parts tender and demanding.

He smiled against her cheek. "Every chance I got."

He did something with his fingers that stole her ability to speak.

She tried to reciprocate, but all she could do was surrender to his erotic assault. She understood that he sought to escape the demons he'd revealed earlier. It had hurt to see him struggle through his vulnerability tonight, but no sign of it remained as he urged her with mouth, hands and body to mind-blowing responsiveness.

He bit her earlobe, nuzzled behind her ear, sending tingles sparking over heightened nerves. *Yesss.* She happily sacrificed her body to help him through the night.

Lauren lay with Ray curled around her and stared out the wide picture window into the predawn sky. Even at this height she saw lights in surrounding buildings, heard sirens and other city chatter. New York really never stopped.

And neither did her mind.

True to his word, Ray had pleasured her well into the night. Her body was boneless with satisfaction. And still Ray's story kept repeating in her head. What a tragic introduction to adulthood. How did someone *do* that to a person?

She rubbed her belly.

How did someone use another life with such capriciousness, such cruelty? It was unconscionable. And it made her question her own decision to withhold news of their child from Ray.

No doubt he'd be upset.

And he had every right to be.

She might be carrying the baby, but he or she was as much a part of Ray as Lauren. It shamed her to remember how easily she'd dismissed his interest in the child because she hadn't wanted to deal with her child's father. How arrogant of her to think he wouldn't want to be a part of his child's life simply because he had a demanding career and a high-profile lifestyle.

He said he loved kids, and the confidence and care with which he'd handled young Lulu proved his claim. Most men were afraid to hold a child that young. Not Ray. He had reached for her with genuine affection.

Suddenly she longed for the day he held their child.

The time to tell him had come.

In fact she worried that she should have told him last night, but she stood by her decision to wait—to give him distance from the misery he'd relived. She couldn't prevent the past from rising up when she told him he was going to be a father, but she could make sure he was in a better frame of mind.

Today they would tour the city. They'd be playing tourist, but Ray would also be working. She'd be careful to give him his space, to watch his mood. And when the time was right she'd share her precious news.

A helicopter! Lauren wavered between being thrilled and terrified. Dressed in jeans and a black sweater under the red leather jacket, she let Ray strap her into her seat. Once he'd settled in his own seat, and they both had headphones on, she reached for his hand.

"Don't let go," she implored him, not caring if the mayor's aide heard from his seat up-front.

"I won't." He brought her hand to his mouth and kissed her knuckles.

"What are you looking for today?"

"I'm doing a futuristic police procedural. The story is set fifty years in the future. I'll be looking at parts of the city with modern elements."

"Oh."

Well, *boo*. She'd hoped to see more than just architecture. So much for playing tourist. Still, it would be fun to see some of the other boroughs. And they were flying. Surely she'd catch a glimpse of something interesting.

"Can we at least fly by the Statue of Liberty?"

He squeezed her fingers. "We're starting with the statue. What would a film in New York be without a shot of the famous landmark? Don't worry. You'll see plenty of sights."

The helicopter lifted off, the world dropping away beneath her. Lauren clutched Ray's hand. They were leaving from the roof of their hotel, so they already had some elevation. For a moment the surrounding buildings seemed too close, but as the helicopter gained height they grew smaller.

Her breath caught. The panoramic view stunned her senses with the sheer vastness of the city. She waited for the vertigo, but it never came. The wristband the pilot had given her must be working.

"We have to land at Ellis Island." The mayor's aide, Felton Smith, a balding Asian American, addressed them through their headsets. "Helicopter landings are restricted at Liberty Island. A National Park representative will be there to greet us and take us over to the statue."

"National Park?" Lauren asked. "So it's not run by New York?"

"No," Felton confirmed. "Coolidge declared the statue a national monument in 1924, and in 1933 Franklin Roosevelt transferred jurisdiction to the National Park Services. You probably aren't going to want to film right on the island. Unless it's integral to the plot, the view is better from a distance."

Ray nodded. "We'll probably replicate the parts we need at the studio, but I like authenticity and it's been years since I've been to see the statue."

Within minutes the helicopter began to descend on Ellis Island. Having the earth rise to meet them got to Lauren, so she closed her eyes, taking comfort in Ray's hold on her hand. The bump of their landing was so skilled she barely felt it.

A park ranger in a crisp green uniform stepped forward to greet them. Ranger Paceco had graying brown hair and a military demeanor. After introductions, he gave a curt nod.

"Ms. Randall, Mr. Donovan—welcome to Ellis Island. How can I be of service today?"

Ray explained his mission as they walked toward a pier where several boats were moored.

Ranger Paceco stopped next to a speedboat. "Let's take you over. We'll give you the full tour."

Lauren looked longingly over her shoulder at the huge brick building housing so much American history. "Will we have time to take a peek inside when we come back?"

Ray wrapped an arm around her waist. "We'll see if we can find some time." He glanced significantly at the mayor's aide, who looked down at his tablet with a frown.

The speedboat made short work of the trip between islands. It seemed longer because of the cold. Lauren snuggled next to Ray on the bench seat, thankful for his body heat and the red leather coat.

From the shelter of his arm she watched the statue grow bigger and bigger, until she towered over their approach, a symbol of welcome and freedom. She was awe-inspiring. Lauren could only imagine how emotional it would have been to see her at the end of a cramped ocean voyage— the embodiment of a new beginning.

The manicured grounds were immaculate—a sign of the respect and pride the rangers took in their care of the lady. The stairs spiraling upward seemed never-ending. But, oh, the view was worth it.

The ranger gave them ten minutes to themselves. Ray whipped out his camera and started shooting, climbing right up to the glass.

No way was she leaning forward to look down. Her heart was already pumping out adrenaline. But she could still see the city in the distance. And New Jersey on the other side. Spectacular. She took a few pictures with her phone.

She admitted to being a homebody. She liked the comfort of having her things around her. Yet standing in a piece of history, with the world literally spread out before her, she acknowledged the appeal of traveling. Especially when you got VIP treatment.

Thinking of Ray, she sought him out. Her heart jumped into her throat when she saw him pressed right up against the glass, filming straight down.

"Ray." She took a step toward him, then stopped.

She wanted to leap across the space, wrap herself around his leg, and demand he come down from there. But the element of adventure was so much a part of him. She couldn't hold him back by placing her fears on him.

To ground herself she wrapped an arm around a newel post and eyed him anxiously.

"Just a minute more, Dynamite." His balance shifted as he bent even further forward.

"Ohmigoodness."

The man had a death wish. If he didn't fall to his death, she'd do it for him. She might anyway. And suddenly the world was spinning—not because he was falling, but because *she* was. Falling hard. For him.

She loved this crazy, thoughtful, manipulative, brilliant, stubborn, funny man.

Seeing him poised on the brink of a two-hundred-foot fall shot that knowledge home like nothing else. And—oh, goodness—the enormity of the emotion dwarfed all previous relationships. Including that dork in college. His name wouldn't even come to mind.

Ray filled her to the exclusion of everything else.

"Hey." Suddenly he stood in front of her, lifting her face to him. "I'm fine. With the glass, there's no chance of falling."

"Tell that to my racing heart." She wrapped her arms around herself.

"It's perfectly safe." He held his camera out to her. "And I got an incredible shot."

She didn't bother to look. "Oh, that's all right, then."

She pushed past him toward the stairs. He'd just become her whole world and he was doing things like testing the weight factor of the glass in the crown of the Statue of Liberty. He was going to get himself killed before he met his child.

His child. Oh, heavens. She had to tell him. To wait

another moment just seemed wrong. Except for the ever-vigilant Felton Smith and Ranger Paceco. You didn't tell the man you loved he was going to be a father in front of an audience.

"Hey, hey, hey." He caught up to her, swung her into his arms. "I'm sorry." He kissed her softly. "It's so amazing I got carried away." He tucked his camera in his backpack. "Here, come with me. Let me show you what I see."

He climbed up next to the glass and held out his hand.

She shook her head. "I don't think I can."

"I'll have you."

He caught the hand she'd instinctively raised to meet his and pulled her up next to him. Vertigo rose, but he wrapped both arms around her. His firmness and strength surrounded her.

"Okay?" he whispered in her ear.

She nodded, her body tense in his grasp. "Don't let go."

"I won't." Holding her close, he pointed. "That's Queens. And over there is Manhattan. See the spire? That's our hotel."

Cradled in his arms, she listened as he brought his world to life for her. Slowly she relaxed against him, enjoying his enthusiasm. He told her about his movie and she saw the wonder of his vision through his eyes.

Paceco finally signaled it was time to go.

Ray carefully helped her down. "Maybe it'll cheer you up to hear that Felton has made time to visit Ellis."

She blinked up at him. She always focused on his need for control, but the truth was he could also be incredibly giving. He was sacrificing part of his siting agenda to let her play tourist. And the timing would work out perfectly. When they got to Ellis Island she'd pull him aside. As soon as she had him alone she'd give him the news.

The ride back to Ellis Island seemed twice as long as the trip over. On the other hand she barely felt the cold, because she was trapped in her head.

Excitement and anxiety played tug-of-war with her emotions.

She didn't know what she wanted his reaction to be. Excitement, of course. But with his history she knew that was a lot to expect. She wanted him to be pleased, to start thinking of a future together.

Heavens, did she *want* a future together? Until yesterday she'd still been contemplating sole custody.

Don't get ahead of yourself, girl, her head warned her heart.

Finally the boat arrived at Ellis Island. As the group neared the building Lauren turned to their guides and upped the wattage of her smile. "Would it be okay for us to just wander around on our own for a few minutes?"

"Of course." Ranger Paceco offered his hand. "I'll leave you to your wanderings. If you need me, just have one of the rangers call me."

"You've been very helpful." Ray shook his hand. "I should have come over more when I was a kid."

"Sometimes we need age to appreciate things. Take care, now." He nodded and took his leave.

"I'll meet you at the chopper in forty minutes," Felton said. He already had his phone in his hand as he walked toward a bench.

"Nice move, Randall." Ray draped an arm around her shoulders. "I was beginning to feel crowded." He nuzzled his nose into her hair. "Mmm. You smell good." Moving toward the building, he asked her, "So, do you have family that came through Ellis Island?"

"My great-great-grandfather on my father's side. He was six when he came over from England in 1908."

"Cool. Mamó's grandmother came over from Ireland. Hey, I'm pretty sure that was 1908. Maybe they stood in line at the same time?"

"It's a romantic notion." She eyed his profile through her lashes. "And I can see a story brewing in that head of yours. This trip is getting to you. You don't usually do relationship movies."

"It's good to stretch yourself. What are you doing?" He stopped when she tried to direct him toward a bench in the sun. "The entrance is that way."

"I know. I need to talk to you."

At the bench her knees gave out and she gratefully sank down on the stone seat.

"I have something to tell you."

"Are you okay?" Dropping down next to her, he tucked a wisp of hair behind her ear. "You've gone pale."

"I'm fine." She gathered his hands in hers, hoped he wouldn't feel the tremors through her gloves, and looked at them rather than at him. This should be easier. Shouldn't it be easy to tell the father of her child?

"Lauren, what is it? You're shaking." He wrapped her hands in both of his and rubbed them to generate warmth.

"You'll be shaking in a moment."

"Now you're scaring me. Just tell me."

Deep breath…slow release. She looked into his concerned blue eyes. "I'm pregnant."

Shock knocked him back. A flash of joy, and then his expression closed down. His eyes narrowed and he looked out over the water.

"A baby."

His flat tone revealed nothing.

"That explains your upset stomach. And your refusal of wine and coffee. How long have you known?"

"S-Since the wedding." Hating the shake in her voice, she cleared her throat, tried for more confidence. "I did an early pregnancy test that morning. I would have confirmed it with my doctor this week, except I've been here."

He stood, thrust his hands in his pockets. "So you've known for four days and you haven't said anything?"

He made it sound unreasonable. "It was unexpected. I needed time to think."

Anguish flashed across his face.

"No!" Her heart constricted in a punishing vice, she jumped to her feet, rushed to him, placed a reassuring hand on him arm. "Not about aborting the child. I'd *never* make that choice."

"Then what was there to think about?" he demanded. "What was more important than telling me I'm going to be a father?" He pinned her with a hard gaze. "I'm supposing I *am* the father?"

Wow. She retreated a step, then two.

"Yes, of course." Offended, she fisted her hands at her sides. "Are you questioning your paternity?"

"I remember the broken condom." He turned away, ran a shaking hand through thick hair. "Though my attorney will want a paternity test. I can't believe this. I must have super-swimmers. You should have told me, Lauren. All week we've been together. On the plane, at Mamó's." He scrubbed his face. "Hell, last night I poured my heart out to you about the child I lost."

"Right—and I was supposed to break into the middle of that story with *By the way I'm pregnant*?" She wrapped her arms around herself, trying to hold herself together as his words tore her apart. "It wasn't the time. This week hasn't been the time. You've been worried about your grandmother, dealing with the whole fake engagement thing, as well as this siting business. I didn't even know about the trauma of confronting your past."

This was a mistake, she thought. *I should have waited.* The backs of her knees hit the stone bench again. She sank down. She'd known after his revelation last night that he'd have a hard time with her news. She hadn't expected him to be thrilled, but after their time together here in New York she hadn't expected him to be hurtful either.

He came to stand over her. "If you're expecting a proposal, think again. I'm not eighteen anymore."

"I'm not expecting anything from you." A slide to the

left gained her some breathing room. "I'm a successful, professional woman. Don't worry. I can take care of myself and my child."

"*Your* child." He dropped down next to her, but half turned away. "I get it now. You weren't going to tell me."

"Don't be so dramatic. Hollywood is too small to hide a pregnancy. Of course I was going to tell you."

"When?"

"Why do you care?"

"What?" He pinned her with an astounded stare over his shoulder.

"You've made it clear you're not interested in the baby." No need to cast a feature film to get that point across. "Fine with me. Consider yourself uninvited to the party."

"Seriously? You're going to pout because I didn't get down on one knee?"

"No, I'm going to live my life around my child. I'm not a self-important prima donna, too worried about protecting myself to know if I'm happy about being a parent or not."

She needed to get away from him. *Now.*

On her feet, she faced him. "Keep your ring. I never wanted it anyway." She hiked her chin toward the helicopter. "You should go on with your tour. I'm going to hang out here for a couple of hours."

Gaze locked on the entrance to the huge brick building, she put one foot in front of the other. She just needed to get inside before she broke down. No way was she giving him the satisfaction of seeing her cry.

After a few steps he grabbed her arm. "I'm not leaving you here alone."

"You don't have a choice," she informed him. "I'm all grown up, Ray. I can make my own decisions and get myself home." She glared pointedly at his hand on her arm.

He released her. "Why?"

"Because you're not responsible for me."

"No, why did you tell me now when you had no plan to do so?"

"You scared me." Giving him half the truth, she waved toward the statue towering in the distance. "I thought you should know you had a kid before you did something foolhardy and died."

"Listen, come with me." His hand dropped away. "I'm not handling this well, and I'm sorry. I need time to process everything."

"And we both know you'll process better without me. I'll see you back at Mamó's.

"Okay." He gave a gruff nod. "I'll arrange for a car to pick you up at Battery Park. I'll text you with the information. They'll take you wherever you want to go."

Home. Could the driver take her to Hollywood?

It was where she longed to be—curled up on her couch with her grandma's quilt tucked around her, surrounded by familiar things, with her sister next door and her mother on the other end of the phone.

The fantasy burst, an impossible dream.

"Thanks," she said, for once happy with his need to manipulate every situation. Then she continued toward the entrance, not wanting to watch him walk away.

She needn't have worried. She barely saw the doors through the tears blurring her vision.

CHAPTER ELEVEN

Staying over in the suite tonight.

LAUREN STARED AT the text, numb both inside and out. Apparently she was supposed to process the fact she was pregnant immediately and then go on to share the news with him, but he needed most of the day and the night, too.

"Ray isn't coming home, is he?" Mamó set a tray on the coffee table and settled into her chair next to the couch, where Lauren sat trying to reproduce the image of home she'd created earlier.

"No. Business is keeping him in the city, so he's going to stay at the hotel again."

"You don't have to cover for him, dear." Mamó leaned forward to pour steaming liquid into a sturdy mug. "I made hot cocoa." Heaping spoons full of whipped cream followed. "I thought you could use the pick-me-up."

It was just the thing. "Thank you." Lauren accepted the mug, drank a small sip. The heat and the chocolate sent warmth and comfort rolling through her. "Mmm. Perfect."

"You told him, didn't you?"

"Mmm," Lauren hummed. She had too much pride to bad-mouth the woman's grandson in her own home. "He's processing."

"He didn't take it well." It wasn't a question.

"Let's say he was shocked." The truth, and yet far short of everything.

Mamó nodded. "Which translates to being a jerk."

"I'll stick with shocked." Lauren sighed. "Now I've calmed down I recognize I was a tad hormonal and perhaps overly sensitive."

"All the more reason for him to take care of you." Sadness tugged at the corners of Mamó's eyes and her lips trembled as she sipped from her cup. "He's never cared much for surprises. I blame losing his parents at such a young age."

Lauren remembered the shock and horror of losing her high school friend to suicide in their senior year. It had consumed her whole world for months. How much worse would it be to lose family? To lose both parents at the same time?

"I don't even want to imagine the pain he must have experienced. And then Camilla pulled her heartless stunt. It's understandable he dislikes surprises."

Unfortunately she knew of no other way to deliver news of a baby. Especially an unplanned pregnancy.

"He told you about Camilla?" Surprise chased despair from Mamó's face. "He's never told anyone, as far as I know. Not even Ellie. I had to piece parts of it together myself."

"It's not a pretty story."

"Far from it. I was so proud of him. I knew how much he wanted to go to UCLA, how hard he'd worked for the Stahling Award. But he set aside his future in Hollywood for a future with his family. It was the smart thing, the responsible thing to do. It shattered him when he realized Camilla had murdered his child to mortgage her own career."

"Murdered…?" Lauren murmured. He hadn't used the word last night, but it sounded like Ray. It was very telling.

"His word." Mamó unknowingly confirmed it. "Most men would have been happy to get out of a forced marriage. Ray was committed from the beginning. I know my boy. I read all those tabloids where they call him a confirmed bachelor, and say how he prizes his privacy. They've got him all wrong. The truth is he has a big heart. He's just learned to guard it carefully."

"He's afraid of being hurt again." Lauren related to that sentiment. Better to be alone than to give up a part of your soul.

"You're different."

That caught Lauren's attention. "What do you mean?"

"The way he is with you. It's different from when he's with other women. He doesn't just look at you—he watches you as if he can't look away."

"Really?" She cringed a little at the hope in her voice.

"This isn't an easy time for either of you. I implore you to give him a chance. Your little ones deserve to have both parents in their lives."

"Lives?" Lauren croaked.

"Yes, dear. You're having twins."

Mamó says twins.

Ray read Lauren's text over and over. Twins. *Hell*. This was news he could have waited to hear. He couldn't stop thinking, wondering, worrying. Any minute now his head would implode.

When he couldn't take another second he went on the move. He rented a car, took the 87 in the Bronx and headed north. Blowing by Albany, he chased the Catskills, his mood black.

He took a curve, low and tight, and came out on a straightway. Punching the accelerator, he raced through the night, going faster than he should in an act Lauren would no doubt consider foolhardy.

His foot lowered, squeezing out a little more speed.

He was an adult. The last thing he needed was a woman telling him how to act.

The rental handled well, but his plan to go for a drive

in order to get away from his thoughts wasn't working out. Okay, it was a flawed plan. Where his head went, his thoughts followed. And, no matter how hard he tried to focus on something else, his mind kept wrapping back to Lauren and the babies she carried.

He tried thinking about his upcoming film and the sites he'd seen today, but honestly he didn't remember much after the bomb she'd dropped.

Mamó's condition couldn't even hold his attention. And the industry awards scheduled a few days away barely blipped on his radar—which peeved him, because he really wanted to sweep the season and this was the biggie. Not since his first film had he hit the trifecta of awards. To do so again would prove he had staying power.

Was it just yesterday he'd asked Lauren to go with him? This week stretched out forever in his head.

He ground his teeth, mad at the world, mad at himself, mad at Lauren, mad at life.

Mad at the world because, seriously, why him? The first time had completely undone him. He might not survive a second time.

Mad at himself because of the way he'd managed to muck things up. He wasn't handling it well, but he couldn't get a grip.

Mad at Lauren because she was the one doing this to him. No matter how cockeyed that thinking was. Which only added guilt to the mix as well. *Hello*.

Mad at life for the whole mix.

And now twins.

It only made the situation worse to hear the news here in New York, after spending half a week mired in memories he'd spent fifteen years burying skull-deep.

He slowed for another curve, flinched as headlights hit him in the eyes. It was the first traffic he'd encountered in a while—not surprising, considering the late hour on a work night. Soon he'd have to think about turning around and heading back to the hotel.

It might be a cop-out, but no way could he face cuddling up in his old bedroom with Lauren. At the same time he'd miss having her in his bed. It didn't make sense, yet it was one of the loops his head kept tracking.

That and memories of that horrific summer. He'd been shocked and devastated when Camilla had broken the news. He'd tried to hold it together, but in the end he'd bolted.

It had crushed his spirit to give up on UCLA, but he'd seen no other choice. The kid had to come first. How idealistic he'd been. But even in retrospect he couldn't see playing his hand any differently.

Except to wear a damn condom.

Resentment festered. Why did this keep happening to him?

He felt victimized, and yet there was no fault here. They'd had protected sex. Hell, *he'd* been the one to provide the condom that broke.

Fighting off weariness, he rolled his neck, stretching muscles, working out kinks. He owed Lauren a better apology. More, he owed her his support. She was just as much a victim as him. Yet deep down he couldn't help feeling as if she'd done this to him.

Because she'd kept the news from him.

He'd deserved to know as soon as she knew. The babies might be in her body, but they were as much a part of him as they were of her. He had *rights*, damn it. Being the last one to know, having no say in decisions, didn't sit well with him. How could he protect his children when he didn't know what was going on?

Anger lashed at his nerves.

Back to being mad at himself, because he couldn't stop being upset with Lauren. She might have been blameless in the conception, but she had withheld the news, taken the power of knowledge from him. Tried to push him away. Still was, come to that. Who knew how long she would have taken to tell him if Mamó's depression hadn't pushed them together?

Well, Lauren needed to adjust her thinking. He might be a perpetual bachelor, but he was damned if he'd be a sperm donor. If he'd fathered a baby—babies!—he'd be a part of his children's lives.

And, no, he didn't doubt the babies were his.

He knew Lauren—knew her integrity and the value of family to her. Never in a million years would she play false with the paternity of her child.

And she'd never hurt her child. *Children*. He believed that completely.

Yet he took little comfort in the thought.

Never would he have contemplated it of Camilla either. He couldn't conceive of it himself, so he had a hard time putting the unconscionable act in anyone's head. Then again, for Camilla the baby had been a means to an end—a tool to get what she wanted, never meant to see life.

And he had to put that aside.

The past had no bearing on the current situation. He needed to get past it and move on.

Desperate for a break, he took the next exit and pulled into the parking lot of an all-night diner. The waitress gave him a choice of the many empty booths. He slid into one next to the window, a distance away from the other two occupied tables.

"Coffee, please."

"Anything else?" the waitress asked. Young, slightly plump, with a high ponytail and pretty features, she waited patiently for his response. Her name tag read "April."

Had he eaten? He scrubbed his hands over his face, barely able to string two thoughts together. Whatever. He had no appetite.

"That's all, thanks."

She nodded and wandered away.

Ray turned his gaze to the window and got smacked with his own reflection. He looked haggard, but otherwise the same as he had this morning. That was just *wrong*. His life had changed; surely his appearance should show it?

April returned. She set down a big mug of steaming coffee and slid a plate with a large slice of chocolate cream pie in front of him.

He looked up at her. "I didn't order this."

"I know, but we're known for our chocolate cream pie. And you look a mite troubled. Pie always helps me when I'm troubled."

Looking at the whipped cream piled high, he felt his appetite come rushing back. He tipped his chin up. "Thanks."

"You want to talk about it?"

He tasted the coffee, hummed his approval as he shook his head. "Anything but."

"Okay, then." She leaned against the facing booth. "You're that director guy, aren't you?"

"I've made a few movies," he acknowledged. Usually he'd politely shut her down, but she'd brought him pie and he welcomed the distraction. "Are you interested in movies?"

"I like a good flick, but my passion is fashion design."

He recalled his trip to Eve's and seeing Lauren's transformation. *Passion* summed it up. "Well, April, that's a fine profession."

A huge smile lit up her face. "Let me know if that family gets too loud." She winked. "I'll bring you another piece of pie."

She wandered off and he glanced at the family: a mother, father, and three kids somewhere between the ages of five and eight. They chattered and laughed as they ate. The oldest, a boy, was telling the story of some ride where he'd been scared but his dad had been there so he'd felt brave and lifted his arms and felt like he was flying.

"And then *I* got scared," the dad said. "Because I thought you were going to fly away."

At that point the mom sent the kids off to the bathroom. Once they'd trooped off, she murmured something to the dad and they shared a laugh and a kiss.

Their unity got to Ray. Their love and camaraderie at the end of a long day. It shouted family with a capital F. And he realized he wanted that—the love, the togetherness.

April brought him a full to-go cup along with his bill. He left her a hefty tip. Time to head back. Running only worked so long before you had to step up and face what you were running from.

"Mamó." Lauren's voice shook. "I'm bleeding."

"Oh, my dear." Mamó came from the kitchen to take Lauren's hands and lead her to the couch. Sitting next to Lauren, she held her hands over her belly. "May I?"

Lauren nodded.

Mamó laid her hands on Lauren's belly and concentrated. Heart tripping wildly, Lauren waited breathlessly.

"I sense no distress," Mamó announced, and Lauren allowed herself to breathe. "Is it heavy bleeding?" Mamó asked. "Are you in pain?"

"Spotting, mostly. No pain. But it's not good, is it?" Lauren squeezed the words through a sand-crusted throat. She wished she'd been to the doctor, had some indication of what this might mean. "I've always heard bleeding is bad when you're pregnant."

"Some things are natural. But much has been learned since I had my babies. You will feel better if you see a doctor."

Lauren squeezed Mamó's hands. "I will, yes."

"Then we will go. You have been through much these last few days. I'm so sorry for my part in causing you distress."

"Mamó—"

"No." The older woman shook her head, swiped at a tear. "Ray was right. It is not okay. I've worked myself into a state, wanting great-grandbabies, but it's not fair of me to pin my happiness on Ray's life. Seeing the problems I've caused, I realize it's not healthy for either of us." She patted Lauren's fingers. "You stay here. I'll get Ellie and your purse and we'll be on our way." She bustled off.

Lauren wrapped her arms around her babies and sat perfectly still. If she didn't move, nothing could happen to them. Where was Ray? She longed for his strength and support—could really do with some of his take-charge attitude right about now.

Mamó returned with Ellie and her purse and jacket. Ellie was dragging Lauren's luggage.

"Hey, I'm thinking positive. In case you're good to travel you'll have to leave from the hospital."

Oh, right. Lauren had made a flight reservation after her assistant had called with an emergency. Lauren had handled it, but she'd decided she needed to go home. Ray didn't want her here and she was needed in California. It was after she'd finished packing that she'd noticed the spotting.

She'd hoped to see Ray before she left, but she really couldn't think about all that right now. She was too worried about the twins to focus on anything else.

Mamó and Ellie bundled her up. And they were off. Lauren tagged Ray with a text. Yes, it was cowardly, but she didn't feel like fielding a lot of questions she didn't have answers for.

And he should *be* here, damn it.

Suddenly chilled, she shivered. All night she'd lain awake, wondering what his "processing" might result in. Would their children—oh, goodness, she still reeled at the reality of twins—would their twins bring them closer or drive them apart?

Perhaps that was her answer. Never had she felt so alone

as she had sleeping by herself in his bed last night. Not that she'd slept much.

She should be more understanding. Recalling her own shock and her struggle to adjust to the life-altering news, she should have a clue what he was going through. And she did. But it didn't stop her from resenting his continued silence.

It might be unfair of her to think so, but there was a difference in being uncommunicative when the other party existed in blissful ignorance than when they waited in breathless anxiety. He'd been the one to pull back. The way she saw it, he needed to be the one to come to her.

Now would be good. She really needed him.

I'm bleeding. Mamó is taking me to the hospital.

Fear punched into Ray's gut as he read Lauren's text. He immediately tried her phone, but she didn't answer. *Damn it.*

He dialed his grandmother. She answered on the first ring.

"Mamó, how is she?"

"I don't get any sense of distress from the babies. And I believe I would if they were in true danger. But to be safe we're taking Lauren to Emergency."

"Let me talk to her." Muffled voices rumbled on the other end of the line.

"She doesn't want to talk to you."

Damn it. Add anger to the fear and dread forming a ball in his chest. His fault. He shouldn't have put her off with texts last night and this morning.

"Put her on."

"She's not shutting you out," Mamó assured him. "She doesn't want to talk because she doesn't have any answers. She's holding it together, but she's scared. It doesn't help that she's out of her element here in New York."

"Ask her what I can do."

This time he heard Lauren answer clearly. "Just tell him to get here."

"She said—"

"I heard," he cut in. "Text me the address. I'm on my way."

Ray explained the situation to the major's aide, thanked him for his assistance, and hopped in the car waiting for him. He gave the driver the address and instructions to hurry. As the car raced toward Queens he kept his mind off worrying about Lauren and the babies by looking ahead.

He'd need to get Fred and Ethel to baby-proof the house and grounds. Maybe they'd have a recommendation for a nanny. Or perhaps Lauren knew someone.

No doubt she'd want to be a hands-on mom, but he wanted someone available to help so she didn't get worn out. It was a given she'd continue to work.

Calculating dates, he figured Lauren would be due in seven months, give or take a week or so, which put him a month into filming here in New York. Maybe he should chuck the location shots?

His shoulders tensed at the notion. There was an authenticity that came with location filming that couldn't be captured on a back lot or in a substitute spot. He'd figure something out.

Because he wasn't missing the birth of his children.

And this—whatever it ended up being—was just a blip. Mamó would have sensed it if something were wrong. Battling another surge of fear, he clung to the fact she hadn't felt any fetal distress. Everything would be all right.

The car hit the bridge, and he made a proclamation and a prayer. He had to believe.

The alternative just wasn't acceptable.

The driver changed lanes, cutting off a delivery truck with inches to spare. Ray gritted his teeth and held on. They couldn't move fast enough for him. He hated not knowing. Hated not being there for Lauren. How he longed to have her safe in his arms right now.

Again, his fault. He'd been punishing her for…what? Thinking of herself first? Adjusting to the fact she was going to be a mother? Letting him deal with his grandmother and his past before learning he was going to be a father?

What a hero he was.

Finally he spotted his destination. The driver pulled right up in front of the emergency room at Queens Hospital and Ray hopped out. He spoke briefly with Mamó and Ellie, then waved down a nurse. He recognized the woman from the neighborhood, and for once he was happy for the connection as she personally escorted him to the cubicle where Lauren was being treated.

"How is she?" he asked, his heart running a marathon in his chest.

"The doctor has seen Lauren and she's fine. The bleeding was due to some natural adjustments of the uterus. Nothing to worry about. But to be on the safe side he ordered an ultrasound. The technician is in with Lauren now."

"Thanks." Relief left him breathless.

"No problem." Arriving at a cubicle, she pushed the curtain aside. "Mr. Donovan," she announced. She patted him on the arm, said, "Congratulations, Daddy," and left.

"Ray." Lauren gave a glad cry of relief and reached for his hand.

He stepped forward, wrapped her fingers in his. "The nurse said you were fine."

She lay on a gurney while the technician ran a scope over her belly and monitored the machine next to her.

"That's what they tell me. More important, the babies are fine. Look."

First he leaned down and kissed her on the top of her head, disguising his huge relief. Seeing her animation, touching her, reassured him more than any medical niceties could.

He glanced at the picture she indicated on the screen but failed to make out anything until the technician directed his attention to two little heads and two sets of feet, showed him the two beating hearts.

He slowly sank down on the side of the gurney next to Lauren, overcome by this visual evidence of his children. The twins were no more than a couple of inches big, but they packed a big wallop.

The picture blipped as Lauren scooted over, making more room for him. "Pretty awesome, huh?"

"Yes." The word *terrifying* came to mind. "I want to be involved."

It was a bald statement.

Her gaze flew to the technician. "We don't need to talk about that now."

For once he didn't care who heard his business. He'd never been more certain of anything in his life. "I've been an ass. I'm sorry."

"Stop." Lauren tightened her grip on his hand.

"I'll just check with the doctor." The technician handed her a couple of tissues for the gel on her tummy and made a discreet exit.

Ray took the tissues and wiped her clean, his touch warm after the chill of the gel. "Lauren—"

"No." She laid a finger on his lips. "Before you go on I need to say something."

Needing to feel more in control, she tugged her sweater down and sat up.

"Yes, I thought you were being a jerk, but I was wrong. And so were you. This is huge." She waved at the blank screen that had so recently held images of their children. "We're going to be parents. It's important, and it's not something to rush. I already made that mistake. And I'm sorry."

"I shouldn't have yelled at you."

"You were in shock. So was I. We need time, both of us, to come to grips with this change in our lives. And I mean more than a few hours—possibly more than a few days. And that's okay, because we have another seven months to figure everything out."

He lifted a sandy brow. "Ms. Clipboard? You're not going to be able to wait seven months for anything."

The corner of her mouth kicked up at that. "Probably not. But I know I want to do this right. And rushing isn't the way to do that."

"No rushing around for you, young lady," the doctor said, entering the cubicle. "You're carrying precious cargo."

He introduced himself to Ray.

"How are the twins, Doctor?" Ray asked. "Anything we should be concerned about?"

"Everything looks normal." The doctor included Lauren in his answer. "You'll want to see your doctor when you get home. In the meantime try to keep stress to a minimum—which means no rushing. But you're healthy…the babies are healthy. I see no reason why you can't fly."

"Thank you, Doctor." His assurances finally allowed her to relax.

"Congratulations to the both of you." He shook Ray's hand and departed.

"Well, that was good to hear." Ray helped her up. "Now, let's get you home."

"Listen, I'm not going back to Mamó's." She stood and looped the strap of her purse over her shoulder. "Something came up at work so I booked a flight earlier. I can still make it, so I'm going to go. It's for the best. It'll give both of us the extra space we need." She kissed his cheek.

"Wait, you can't go." He followed her out into the hall, pulled her to a stop. "We're just starting to actually communicate."

"We'll communicate better in Hollywood, when we're both back in the real world."

"You can't leave. You just got out of Emergency.

"And the doctor said I'm okay to fly."

"Come on, Lauren," he implored her. "It's not like you to pout."

"I don't pout."

Moving around him, she moved toward the lobby, where Mamó and Ellie waited. His arguments made her more determined to leave. She pulled her phone out and texted the cab company she'd called while waiting for the technician.

"What would you call running away? I thought you were done playing games?"

Serene mood shattered, she swung on him. "This isn't playtime for me, Ray. I'm not a paper doll. I've been there, done that, didn't like it. I won't apologize for making my own decisions." Not wanting to go there, she dropped her head on his chest, leaned on his strength. "You need to finish your visit with your grandmother, and I just want to go home."

His arms came around her, his hand fisting in her hair. "I don't need more time, Lauren. This scare has confirmed my feelings. I want to be a part of my children's lives. I'll let you go now. But factor me into your thinking—because I'm not going away."

CHAPTER TWELVE

RAY STOOD IN THE middle of his room, surrounded by emptiness. All evidence of Lauren's presence was gone. Only her scent lingered. Honeysuckle and soap. He stared at the too-small bed where even she had defied the rules she'd set down, curling so sweetly into his arms.

He didn't spend the night with women. And he didn't bring them home. Those two steps prevented any misguided sense of intimacy from developing between him and his companions. Those two decrees were the bedrock of his rigidly practiced relationship controls, followed by:

Never let sex control a decision.
Never get personal.
Never have unprotected sex.

Those few restrictions had helped him live an uncomplicated life for the last fifteen years. Yet from the very beginning Lauren had slipped past his shields. She'd blown through the first two in one night.

You couldn't get any more personal than having family over for Thanksgiving. He should never have invited them…her…not even to drag Garrett out of his funk. But, hey, he'd figured he had his attraction for her under control. Heck, she'd irritated him as much as she'd turned him on—if not more. And her family on the premises should have guaranteed nothing was going to happen.

Best sex he'd ever had.

It hadn't mattered that they'd been in the laundry room, or that her parents had been down the hall. One smart remark too many had sparked the flame of passion, incinerating the barrier of restraint, creating an urgency not to be denied.

He'd only meant to quiet her with his mouth.

The taste of her had ignited his blood.

It was the last coherent thought he'd had until, heart racing, he'd collapsed against her and let the washing machine absorb his weight.

At the end of the night he'd shaken it off. Okay, it had happened. Lesson learned. He'd keep his distance in the future.

Right.

It should have helped that she was having the same discussion with herself.

It hadn't.

Twice more they'd hooked up. The urgency just as strong. The sex just as good. The broken condom should have been deterrent enough to prevent a third session—but, no. He'd just been glad he'd had condoms on him when the mood had struck, because the passion was so overwhelming he couldn't claim he would have stopped.

Add sleeping with her to his list of violations. He'd taken just as much satisfaction in holding her as she slept as he'd taken in pleasuring her lovely body. The last rule broken. The contentment he'd felt waking with her in his arms had overridden any thought of self-preservation.

He'd always been a rule-breaker, but not about this. The way he'd blown through his own rules should have warned him against asking her to accompany him to New York. Arrogance again. He'd missed her, so he'd thought he could give Mamó what she asked for while seducing Lauren into a vacation fling. A win-win for him.

And now they were to be parents.

He yanked his bag out of the closet and started emptying the drawers into it. With Lauren gone he felt a need to follow her to Hollywood. He stopped packing to text his friend's pilot and got an immediate response that the plane would be prepped and ready within two hours. His flight set, he tossed in his remaining items and zipped the bag.

To the pit of his soul he detested the need to alter his life for another unexpected pregnancy. Yet the one clear thing he'd taken away from the last two days was the desire to be a part of his children's lives.

The juxtaposition twisted him up inside. Deep down he knew he had to get past the resentment or he'd poison any relationship he established with Lauren and his kids.

Still he lingered, his thoughts in turmoil.

He dropped down on the bed, dragged Lauren's pillow from under the covers and buried his nose in the softness. The heady honeysuckle scent went to his head. Through all the uncertainty the one thing he did know was she'd touched him in ways no one else ever had.

"Ray." Mamó appeared in the bedroom doorway a little winded from her trip up the stairs. She carried something red clutched under her arm.

"Mamó." He hopped up and led her to the bed to sit. She patted the bed beside her and he sat too.

"I'm sorry Lauren felt the need to leave early. Such a nice girl. I'm so glad you brought her with you."

"Yeah, it turned out to be more of a trip than I expected."

"I apologized to her and now I'll apologize to you. I'm sorry for my meddling, for letting my emotions get the better of me, for causing you so many problems."

"You may have caused a few complications. I managed the problems all on my own." There was a fine truth. In the scheme of things Mamó's preemptive engagement announcement had turned out to be a minor development. Hard to trump twins.

"I guess I don't have to tell you my news."

"Dear boy, I won't deny I'm pleased." She patted his knee. "I do regret my gift has been such a trial for you. To this day I mourn the part I played in ending your wedding."

"Don't." He draped an arm around her shoulders, took comfort in the strength of her thin frame. She was tougher than she looked. "None of what happened was your fault. I'm glad I learned the truth. If not for you, I would have married a woman I didn't love under false circumstances. The marriage would have ended anyway, because the child was the only reason I was with her."

"And will you propose to Lauren?"

A denial sprang to mind, yet he hesitated. "Truthfully, Mamó, I don't know how I feel. It's hard to unwrap the events of today from the events of the past."

"It shouldn't be. You were a boy then, just starting out. You're a man now, well established and successful in your field. Your feelings for Camilla were mild at best, your decisions based on honor and expedience. And she was using you. Your feelings for Lauren are deeper, stronger. She's successful in her own right. She's with you because she chooses to be, not because she needs you. You'll be partners in whatever manner you elect to go forward."

She made it sound so simple. But she didn't know the whole truth.

"Lauren came to New York as a favor to me." He explained the circumstances. "So, you see, we aren't actually romantically connected."

"Hmm. I think you're wrong. And you just proved my point. There was no need for her to help you. You may feel like you're caught in the same situation, but these women couldn't be more different. My advice is to stay focused on the present. Don't let the past cause you any more misery than it already has. Here."

She held out the red item she'd been carrying and as it unfolded he saw it was the coat he'd given Lauren. The one she'd refused. The one she'd looked so beautiful in when the weather had trumped her stubbornness.

His jaw clenched as he took it. Obstinate woman. He started to hand it back, to demand Mamó donate it to charity as he'd threatened Lauren he would. But he couldn't. He hated the thought of another woman wearing the coat.

A honk from the street announced the arrival of his taxi.

"There's your ride. Give me a hug." She wrapped him in her arms and for a moment he felt like he was ten years old again and she was his whole world.

He kissed her cheek. "You take care of yourself."

"I'll be good." She patted his cheek. "No more feeling sorry for myself. Besides, I have great-grandchildren to look forward to."

Well, *there* was an upside to the situation.

He helped her down the stairs, and then he was out the door and on the road.

A short while later he boarded the plane. He tossed his backpack and the red jacket into a seat and dropped down in the leather chair beside it. Soon they were in the air. The six-hour flight stretched ahead of him.

Leaning forward he stabbed his hands into his hair. Heck, he couldn't stand to spend any more time with himself. If he didn't find something besides his life to think about, he'd go insane.

"Good afternoon, sir." The flight attendant appeared. "Would you care for refreshments?"

Ray shook his head. "No thank you, Julie."

"May I secure these items?" She gestured to the backpack and jacket in the seat next to him.

"Leave them. That will be all for now."

The woman disappeared and Ray reached for his bag, drew out his camera and laptop. He'd organize his photos and video shots. That should occupy him for a while.

To start he sorted the work into three categories: family

and Mamó's birthday, the siting trip, and others. He soon noticed a commonality in all three. Lauren.

Grr... The point of this was to get away from thoughts of her. He began dropping all the photos of her into a separate file. It didn't take long to discover the problem with that plan. He lost nearly all his photos. Easily two-thirds of his pictures went into the "Lauren" file.

She'd obviously been a primary target for his lens.

Curious about what had drawn him, he went back and started looking from the beginning.

There were shots of her sleeping on the plane, pale and exhausted. He should have had a clue something was off right then. He called her Dynamite for a reason—because he never saw her going less than full out. She'd given him some excuse and he'd bought it, chalking her frailness up to pulling off her sister's big wedding, right during awards season, which would knock out any normal person.

Then came shots of her at the welcome party, surrounded by strangers, yet smiling and poised, all while under the duress of supporting a fake engagement. She really had been a good sport.

He grinned at the less than patient expression on her face in his bedroom as she tried to lay down her new rules. As if they could sleep in any sized bed without touching. He'd taken great delight in letting her break *that* rule.

Lauren at Mamó's party, looking elegant and feminine. He wanted to delete the picture of her with the hired dancer. But he left it as penance for the one of her with her head bent, hurt and sadness evident on her face and in her posture. His fault for insulting her matchmaking talents.

Not his best moment.

To make up for it he'd tried to tell Mamó he knew about her admirer before he left. She'd twittered and waved him off, saying she knew all about George's hot crush. And that someday she might do something about it.

Appalled all over again, he'd turned, looking for Lauren, and immediately realized his mistake.

Damn, he missed her.

Seeing her coat next to him, he curled his hand into a fist on the leather. Then he forced his fingers to loosen the fabric. He'd already sniffed her pillow today, like some lovesick pup. Besides, he could smell the honeysuckle from where he sat.

He wished she were here.

More shots of Lauren—in the hardware store, coming out of the spa, on the streets of New York, at the mayor's reception, stunning in that blue dress, flying over the city, on the boat to Liberty Island, in the crown… He'd even caught one of her when she'd wrapped herself around that newel post.

The fear on her face was stark. Real. Telling.

He looked into her eyes and adrenaline shot through his body as if he was prepared to defend, to protect, to battle—whatever it took to remove the anguish staring out at him.

Problem was he'd be fighting himself.

Lauren cared about him. It showed in every smile, in every indulgent look, in every censuring grimace—and she'd nailed him a few times—in every sultry glance.

His gaze landed on the one boudoir shot. He grinned, remembering he'd snapped it before she'd realized he held the camera.

She'd beat him back to bed after a steamy shower and sprawled half under the sheet, half on top, so the camera had caught the naked length of her back. Her blond hair was a messy knot on the top of her head, damp tendrils clung to her face and neck, and she looked directly into the camera, anticipating his return.

His blood heated and—

His breath caught.

He leaned forward. Blew up the shot. And stared right

into sleepy eyes, molten gold and shimmering with soft emotion.

Love.

He'd missed it at the time—damn camera—but there was no mistaking the intensity of emotion.

Satisfaction and something more filled him up.

Lauren loved him.

The question was what to do about it?

CHAPTER THIRTEEN

Lauren sat at her desk, carefully scrutinizing the event schedule, shifting people around, hiring more where necessary. It was the biggest Hollywood awards ceremony of the season, and By Arrangement would be hosting Obsidian Studio's huge after-party. She expected it to go on way into the next morning.

Usually they wouldn't attempt two events on such a big day, but a valued customer had called two days ago, requesting they handle a brunch for twenty on the day of the awards. Lauren hadn't been able to refuse. So she'd shuffled and shifted, authorized overtime, and wrung miracles out of vendors.

When her phone rang she lifted it to her ear, eyes still on the schedule. "This is Lauren."

"I leave for a week and you run off to New York and get engaged. To *Ray*. I knew there was more to that fling than you were admitting."

"Tori!" Lauren hopped up and closed her door. "I didn't expect to hear from you until you got home."

"I am back—well, in New York anyway. We'll be flying home later today." The second half of her honeymoon she would be attending the awards, and then settling into her new home with Garrett. "And I see I just missed you here. It would have been fun to spend the day together in New York."

"Honeymoon so boring you need company?"

"Uh, that would be *no*." Tori's merry laughter rang over the line. "France was fabulous. We had dinner at the top of the Eifel Tower the night before we left. It was breathtaking."

"So is New York from the crown of the Statue of Liberty. You should check it out if you have time."

"Hmm... So, are you going to tell me about Ray?"

"Oh, Tori. I miss you so much." Lauren forced a calming breath. "But I'm not going to intrude on your honeymoon."

"The only way you're going to do that is if you leave me hanging."

"I'm serious."

"So am I. Garrett went to the gym for a few minutes. Spill, already."

Lauren spilled everything. Taking the pregnancy test at Tori's wedding, Ray's request to go to New York with him, Mamó's announcement of their non-existent engagement, falling in love, Ray freaking at the news of the baby—which, hey, turned out was twins.

Tori let her talk, except for shrieking over news of the twins. In the end she went right to the heart of the matter.

"You've been through a lot in such a short amount of time. I heard you blow by that mention of love. I know you're hurt by his distancing himself, but do you love Ray?"

"Yes. No. I do, but—"

"No buts. Yes or no?"

"It's not that easy," Lauren protested. "I can't, Tori. I thought yes once before, and it was an illusion."

"Love isn't meant to be easy. I almost lost Garrett because I was afraid to trust him. Afraid to trust myself. I let a piece of my past stop me from seeing beyond the surface. I needed to open my eyes and my heart and take that final step into the present."

Lauren remembered. Watching her sister suffer and not

being able to help had been excruciating. But Lauren's situation was different.

"You don't understand. What I feel for Ray is so much more than what I felt for Brad. His reticence *does* hurt. It makes me worry I've given too much of myself away. I can't be in another relationship where I care more than my partner. If it goes wrong with Ray I'm not sure I could find my way back."

"Sis, you're stronger than you think. Brad was able to influence you because you believed you loved him and naturally wanted to please him. You never conceived of someone taking advantage of you in such a way. You're aware now. You need to trust yourself and trust Ray."

Lauren paced in front of her desk. "I don't know if it can work. He's manipulative and he likes his own way."

A snort sounded in her ear, and then Tori demanded, "What man doesn't? Let me ask you this: has he ever coerced you into doing something you didn't want to do?"

The whole New York trip came to mind. But, to be truthful, he'd accepted her refusal. She'd been the one to change her mind. He always seemed to be making plans she had issues with, but when presented with challenges he adapted well.

"Uh-uh." Tori finally cut off Lauren's search for an example. "You told me after we were engaged that you'd seen Garrett and I belonged together."

"I remember. You obviously cared for him, but I didn't want to unduly influence you. If you'd continued to be stubborn I probably would have said something eventually."

"I'm glad to hear you say so. I get the same feeling about you and Ray."

Lauren froze. "You're just saying that to get me to act."

"Maybe, but it's also true. Don't dismiss the significance of the bond just because it's not what you want to hear."

"He's back in town," Lauren volunteered. "Before things blew up between us he asked me to go to the awards show with him."

He'd called and texted every fifteen minutes for the past hour and a half. *Now* he wanted to talk. Finally she'd texted back that she was busy with work and she'd contact him on Monday. His response was that he'd leave a ticket for her at Reception.

"Wow. You've got to go. It would be perfect if we're both there, and then we can go to the party after. It's everything we've been working toward."

"Except for the pre-event work and the estrangement between me and Ray."

"Yeah, well, you need to get over that. You belong together, Lauren."

A deep male rumble sounded in the background. Then Tori's muffled voice.

"Give…minute…talking to Lauren."

A giggle.

"Always…that thought…shower…"

Then she was back.

"Lauren, think about what I said. Trust yourself, girl. The risk is worth the reward."

The happiness in her twin's voice reinforced her claim. She'd given Lauren a lot to think about.

"Hey, don't worry about me. Go take care of your man."

"I do believe I will. See you soon. Oh, and Lauren? If you don't allow yourself to love again, then Brad is still controlling you. And that's just sad."

Unsettled by the call, Lauren returned to her desk and the spreadsheet. Mouse in hand, she stared at the screen.

"If you don't allow yourself to love again, then Brad is still controlling you."

Tori's proclamation echoed through Lauren's mind again and again. The concept of him still having any influence on her raked across her senses like fingernails over a blackboard.

Neither did it sit well with her that he might triumph over Ray in any way. It wasn't true. Yet that was what Tori's words implied. Lauren's blood chilled at the very notion of anyone getting that impression, including her. *Especially* her.

She blinked and the schedule spreadsheet came back into view. By sheer strength of will she finished it and handed it off to her assistant, deliberately leaving Tori and herself off the assignment delegation. They'd both be there, but this way Tori got to enjoy herself. And Lauren could be wherever she was needed.

After the success of Obsidian Studio's event at the Hollywood Hills Film Festival, Obsidian's after-party was being hyped as the event not to miss. It was the pinnacle of By Arrangement's achievements. Not even her current heartache could steal her pride in their accomplishments. This party signified everything she'd been working for.

Logistics-wise, there really was no reason she couldn't attend the awards with Ray. With the adjustments she'd made, her assistant and Tori's should be able to handle both events without the company's owners. Plus, the two of them would be attending the Obsidian Studio party and could step in if needed.

But it was to be *her* night, *her* success, and she needed to be in the midst of it…

Still, she remembered the thrill when he'd asked her to attend the awards with him—the longing to go. Not because it put her closer to her career goals, but because she wanted to support him. His brilliance deserved to be honored and something instinctual in her demanded she be by his side.

Except the day had to belong to *her*. If she gave it up, did that prove she was right back to putting a man's desires before her own?

Not forgetting the fact that the world believed her to be his fiancée. How could she walk the red carpet at his side, pretending all the time they were together, when in truth they'd never been further apart?

By Sunday morning Lauren still hadn't made up her mind. Her emotions rode a teeter-totter ride—up one moment, down the next. She went from wanting to support Ray to needing the validation of self-worth that would come with working the party. Giving it up would diminish her power. Which was exactly what she feared happening.

Of course Ray completely ignored her attempt to put him off until Monday. At ten a courier arrived in her office with an envelope. Inside was her ticket to the award ceremony and a note:

> *It'll be a crush at the theater. I wanted to save you the trouble of going after the ticket. I'm hoping you'll be my lucky charm.*
> *Ray*

His lucky charm. No pressure there. And he didn't fool her—he wanted to make it easy so she had no excuse for not doing what he wanted.

Yeah, *that* was going to work. But along with annoyance came a little thrill of flattery. He really had no need for her to join him. He usually walked the red carpet alone. With her along the attention would flip from the potential of his movie winning to their faux engagement. She would literally be stealing his limelight.

An hour later another courier arrived, carrying three large stacked boxes tied with five-inch-wide red ribbon and a huge red bow.

"No. N. O. I'm not accepting this," she told the wiry teenager in a gray tee and jeans. "Take it back."

"Sorry, ma'am."

Ma'am? Seriously? Okay, yeah, she'd be a mother soon, but she was way too young to be called "ma'am."

"There's a no return flag. I'm not allowed to take it back." He gave her a big grin. "Got a *nice* tip, though. You enjoy, now."

He practically ran out the door. No doubt in a hurry to spend his "*nice* tip".

Hands on hips, body and soul at odds, she sighed, eying the stacked boxes. Her fingers itched to tear into the ribbon to see what the white boxes hid. A dress, for certain, and possibly shoes. A weakness of hers. But if she saw, she'd want. And he was manipulating her. Seducing her with niceties and beautiful things into going with him instead of working.

And he was getting to her. But she lacked the skill-set to spend hours in his company pretending there weren't unresolved issues between them. If nothing else the New York trip had proved that beyond all doubt.

She tore into the boxes. *Temptation, thy name is Ray.* And, yes, the biggest held a dress. An Eve Gardner. Oh, he was good.

She'd tried this black gown on in New York and it had fit like a dream, with a fitted bodice with narrow straps and a square neckline low enough to display the rising swell of her breasts. The dress had clung to her curves, the material flowing over her body with a soft sheen. Too daring for the mayor's reception…tame by Hollywood standards.

The smallest box held shoes—strappy silver heels, with rhinestones and a lifted sole that made her drool.

No fair. He knew her too well. And he'd hit her weaknesses dead target.

The last box surprised her. It held the red leather jacket he'd bought her in New York. The one it had broken her heart to leave behind. She clutched it to her like she'd found an old friend.

A note slipped to the table.

*Something to wear. And shoes, because a special
dress deserves new shoes. Or so Kyla assured me.
No lingerie, because frankly I don't care if you wear
any. And the jacket because I plan to buy you many
things through the years. Best to get used to it now.
Ray*

She folded the jacket and put it back in the box. Tucked
the dress and shoes out of sight too. His reference to
"through the years" yanked at her heart strings. A master
at setting scenes, his message today hinted at a future together. But she didn't dare assume.

She fingered the phone in her skirt pocket, longing to
call him.

But, no. Their conversation, when they had it, needed
to be in person. If she called he'd try to charm her into
going to the awards and all her progress would be lost.
Best to tough it out.

A task made more difficult when the staff spied the
boxes and demanded to see their contents. Oohs and aahs
echoed through the room, but what really cut through her
resolve was when her assistant, Maria, pulled her aside
and assured Lauren she could handle the party.

"I've learned so much from you. I can do this. You
should go to the awards—have fun."

"This is a big event. It's not fair to ask you—"

"You're not asking. You've trained us to be a well-
oiled machine. You should take advantage of what you've
wrought and live the life the rest of us only dream about."

"Thanks, Maria. I'll think about it." An easy promise
to make as her thoughts revolved around little else.

Just before noon Lauren stood at her desk, gathering her
things to move over to the Lowes Hotel—the venue for
tonight's party. It was adjacent to the theater which was
the home of the awards ceremony.

She glanced up at the sound of the bell to see two men in their display showroom. One wore an expensive suit and the other a security guard's uniform.

Smoothing her hands over her blue skirt, she went to greet them. When they saw her they advanced to meet her. On closer view, she noted that the guard was armed and the man in the suit carried a metal case handcuffed to his wrist.

Good gracious, Ray, what have you done?

"Gentlemen, I'm Lauren Randall—how can I help you?"

"Yes, Ms. Randall. I have a delivery for you. Might we go somewhere more private?" asked the suited man.

"This will have to do." Her office wouldn't hold the three of them.

"Very well." He set the briefcase on the nearest display table. "May I see some identification, please?"

"And if I say no…?"

"I've been instructed to stay with you until I've made the delivery."

"Of course you have." She went to her desk, grabbed her purse, returned to show him her ID.

Suit Man opened the case and lifted out a long, flat velvet jewelry box. With practiced ceremony he opened the hinged case and displayed the dazzling contents.

"The Sabina of the Claudia Collection, House of Brandia."

Diamond layers about an inch wide formed a pattern that reminded her of leaves. The avant-garde neck-piece was designed to flow around the neck and almost meet at the front. One point, formed of three oval rubies, would hit the center of her chest above her breasts, then the collar would wrap around her neck and the second ruby-tipped end would stop two inches above the first point, leaving an inch of skin between the two points. Matching earrings completed the set.

Speechless, Lauren simply stared. The set had a name—the Sabina. She loved the avant-garde design of the pieces.

But she couldn't wear them. Not in a million years. Not if its delivery required an armed guard escort. This went so far beyond the red jacket it was ridiculous.

What was Ray *thinking*?

"And there's this." Suit held out a small box.

Lauren's heart jumped into her throat. A tremble revealed her state as she reached for the ring box. It shook in the palm of her hand.

Suit reached into his front breast pocket. "Mr. Donovan also sent a missive." He offered the envelope with a flourish.

Missive? The dude clearly liked his drama.

As did Ray.

"You need to take this back," she informed Suit, and included Security Guard just to cover all bases. "I can't be responsible for this."

"May I suggest you read the letter, Ms. Randall?"

The hefty guard nodded.

Of course they'd stick together.

Turning away from the two men, she tore into the envelope.

Dynamite

Don't freak out. The jewels are on loan. Just a few baubles to add to your enjoyment of the night. I hope you like them. When I saw the necklace I thought of you. A special piece for a special woman.

The ring is my grandmother's wedding ring. She gave it to me fifteen years ago to give to the woman I would marry. Camilla didn't deserve it. I couldn't give it to her.

Will you wear it tonight? With you by my side I'll be a winner regardless of the results revealed on stage. Afterward we'll go to your party and I can watch you work. So sexy.

I love you, Lauren. I want to live my life with you

*and our twins and our future children. I admit it
took me a while to get to this point. But it feels right.*

   *We have much to talk about. Much to look for-
ward to.*

   Tonight our journey begins.
With all my love,
Ray.

Lauren opened the ring box, drew in a sharp breath.
Stunning—just stunning. An oval of small diamonds
framed three raised round diamonds, the middle one bigger than the top and bottom gems. Two rows of diamonds
flowed off each side into a platinum band.

   It fit perfectly on her finger.

   She was so lost.

From the vantage point of the Panorama Suite of the Lowes
Hotel Lauren watched the frantic activity down below as
the Hollywood elite started to arrive for the big night. The
limo line would be non-stop for the next four hours as the
five-hundred-foot red carpet and then the theater filled.
The people filling the seven hundred bleacher seats had
been in place for hours.

   Behind her the thirty-five-hundred square foot suite,
complete with baby grand piano, was ready except for the
food and servers—but this was just the escape route, or
more accurately the end-game.

   Downstairs her team was putting the final touches on
the transformation of the main ballroom into an upscale
club with a sexy edge. Music, dancing, and live perfor-
mances would take the party into the wee hours.

   Along with the Panorama Suite, Obsidian had taken a
full floor of rooms. Some were for performers, others for
executives, and half were set aside as changing rooms.
Many stars liked to change after the awards. Lauren had
convinced Obsidian to offer them a place to do so.

Her own finery was spread out on the bed in her room.

The problem? She still ping-ponged about whether to go with Ray or stay and work.

She'd texted him not to send a car for her; said she was working at the Lowes. Vague, much?

He'd proposed, sent her a beautiful ring she had yet to remove, had been the first to admit his feelings. Pretty brave, considering she hadn't spoken to him since leaving New York. She owed him a real response.

More importantly, she owed herself an honest response.

"Hey." Tori's heels clicked on the hardwood floor. "We're heading out. Garrett wants to get a quick bite to eat before we meet up with Ray in an hour."

"Have fun," Lauren urged without turning around.

"I'm still hoping you'll join us." Warm arms enfolded her in a hug. "I wish it were as clear to you as it is to me. You love him, he loves you, you're having twins. You belong together."

Lauren curled her arms over Tori's, savoring the familiar touch, the unconditional love.

"I wish it were that simple, too."

Suddenly bigger arms, stronger arms, enveloped the both of them as Garrett added his support. His deep voice sounded close to her ear.

"He's the best man I know."

"Of course you think so." Tears welled up. A half-sob escaped as her breath hitched. "He's your best friend."

"Yeah, but you're my sister now," Garrett said. "I wouldn't tell you something I don't believe to be true."

"Thank you."

His support touched her. A loving family was a new concept for him, so she knew what reaching out cost him. She turned around and hugged them both.

"I love you." She pulled free. "Now, go. I'll see you later."

After a last hug from Tori, they left.

At the door, Tori looked back. "Get out of your head. As long as you're replaying the same loop you're going to get the same answer." She waved and was gone.

Get out of her head? If only she could. Unbidden, Tori's words from yesterday came back to Lauren.

"If you don't allow yourself to love again, then Brad is still controlling you."

She clenched her hands until her nails bit into her palms. No way was she letting that happen. So enough, already. No more internal fighting. She needed to let go of what she *should* do and focus on what she *wanted* to do. In other words: get out of her head.

Eyes closed, taking deep breaths, she let it all go. Counting…ten in, ten out. Three times. It was the most peace she'd had in hours. Days.

Her hand found her stomach and she focused on the twins growing within her. She imagined holding them in her arms, guiding them through their first steps, trying to decipher twin-talk, taking them to preschool, ballet classes, T-ball, puppy dogs, high school drama and graduation.

She stopped there because she had her answer.

Through all her visions of laughter and chatter, pirouettes and proms, doggies and dugouts Ray stood by her side, guiding, dancing, scooping, and beaming: a family.

By her side. Not leading or directing, but sharing—a partner in life.

Tension drained out of her as she accepted the truth.

She'd been doing to him what she'd feared he'd do to her: punishing him for another's sins. She'd worried she'd lose herself to Ray's dominant personality as she had to Brad's. *Not going to happen.* As Tori had said, Lauren was aware. She knew what to watch for. The problem was she hadn't been paying attention.

Ray was a self-confident, take-charge kind of man, used to getting his way and directing events to his liking. Yes, he manipulated—but he did it in your face. No snarky, sneaky moves for him. And he'd never guilted or maneuvered her into doing something she didn't want to do.

That had been Brad's style. Always using faux understanding or disappointment as a tool to make her do as he wanted. He'd made it seem as if she were deciding to do something when he'd actually used her emotions against her to get his way. Her desire to compromise had eventually become habit, until she'd always deferred to his will.

In truth, the two men couldn't be more different.

She loved Ray. There was nothing wrong with wanting to be with him on this exciting day in his career. In fact it was normal.

With her decision made, she felt the anxiety surrounding her work disappear. Yes, this event represented everything she and Tori had been working toward. But just because she wasn't overseeing every little detail it didn't take any of the responsibility or success away from her. She'd built the business into what it was. And she'd be there. Available to assist if needed. The best of both worlds.

Ray knew how important her career was to her. He'd never try to get in the way of it. In fact he'd written something in that last note. What was it? She'd read right over it, too stunned by everything else in the message.

She found her purse and the note tucked inside. Now she was free of conflict the romance of it struck her anew. He'd honored her request not to contact her until Monday while completely disregarding it at the same time.

Here it was:

Afterward, we'll go to your party and I can watch you work. So sexy.

Her heart swelled even fuller. He was the best man *she* knew, too.

A glance at the clock revealed an hour had passed since

Tori and Garrett had left. They'd be starting on the red carpet soon.

She reached for the zipper on her dress, yanked it down as she kicked out of her heels. *Hurry!* Thank the angels her hair and make-up were already done.

The beep of her phone announced a text. From Ray.

Lauren. I'm at the theater and you're not with me. I understand. We have a lot to talk about. This changes nothing for me. I hold you in my heart, so you are with me even when you're not. It just means we'll have one more thing to celebrate tomorrow when we do get together. I'll see you at the party. You couldn't keep me away. Fair warning, Dynamite: Monday starts at midnight. I love you. Ray

Incorrigible.

Grinning, she wiggled and her dress hit the floor. Seconds later her underthings joined the dress. Naked, she slipped into the sexy gown. So naughty—but, oh, yeah, Ray deserved a thrill for the silent treatment she'd subjected him to all day long.

Ten minutes later she rode the elevator down and walked over to the theater. The crush of people grew thicker as she neared the red carpet. The public pressed against the barricades while the press jockeyed for position and Security tried to maintain control.

She finally reached the entrance and found more chaos. Someone took her ticket and sent her to the aisle that led directly into the theater. She was tempted to meet him inside, but he wanted her by his side. And she wanted to be there, too.

Just then she spied a friendly security officer she knew from events they'd both worked. Waving, she caught the plump African American woman's attention.

"Ms. Randall—wow, you are *rockin'* that dress. You need to be on this side of the carpet."

"Thanks. That's why I called you over. My date has already started down the carpet. Can you take me to him?"

"So it's true? You're engaged to Ray Donovan?"

"Yes!" Lauren held out her hand, flashing her ring. "I really need to get to him."

"You sure do, girlfriend." The woman ran a hand over her red dreads. "How can I help?"

"Can you take me to him?"

"Hmm. I really can't leave my post."

"Oh." Disappoint bit deep. "Okay. I guess I'll wait for him inside."

"Can't have that. You need to get to your man. Hang on."

The officer stepped away and spoke into her radio.

Seconds and then minutes ticked by. Lauren chafed under the wait. Finally a man the size of a linebacker came along, clearly someone with authority, and talked to her friend. He glanced at Lauren, then approached her.

He looked at the necklace she wore, consulted his clipboard. "Is that the Sabina?"

"Yes." Her hand flew to the jewels at her neck. "From the Claudia Collection, House of Brandia."

He nodded. "Ms. Randall, we're going to get you through." He unhooked the rope barrier and let her pass. "Bonnie will lead you to Mr. Donovan. He's about a quarter ways up the carpet."

"Thank you." Lauren followed Bonnie as she started up the carpet.

The red carpet worked efficiently by having the press and cameras on one side and the stars on the other as they strolled from photo point to photo point. To keep from photo-bombing half of Hollywood, Bonnie led Lauren down the press side, which involved evading cables, cameras, and lampstands as well as many members of the press.

Threading their way through, they caused a bit of disruption. A buzz started behind her and moved forward with them as she was recognized.

"We're causing a spectacle," Lauren told Bonnie. "Maybe I should just meet him inside."

"This is Hollywood, girlfriend. Everyone loves a good spectacle."

"Then let's hurry."

Picking up her skirts, she took off as fast as her heels allowed.

Ray stepped up to the next microphone in a long line of microphones. He greeted the host by name and complimented her on her dress. Gave silent thanks she didn't ask who he was wearing.

No, she went right for the kill.

"Ray Donovan, you have a chance to sweep the season with *War Zone* tonight. And we got news of your engagement this week. Where *is* the lucky woman? With the stakes so high for you, we were hoping to see her on your arm."

"Of course she wants to be here. But, as owner of the hottest event company in Hollywood, today is a busy day for her."

"I imagine." The woman turned to the camera. "We're talking about Lauren Randall of By Arrangements, which has been applauded for great premier productions. Her sister just married Obsidian Studios owner Garrett Black. These lucky twins are snapping up Hollywood royalty."

"I don't know about royalty," Ray demurred. Mention of the newlyweds had him looking around, hoping for a save. They were stuck one mic back. "Garrett is a good friend." He kept it simple. "Now we'll be family."

Or so he planned.

He hoped he hadn't put Lauren off with his persistence today. No lie: he had freaked when she'd refused to talk to him. Not that he didn't deserve it. Now he knew what *she'd* gone through while he'd kept her waiting in New York.

He'd hoped the ring would sway her, because he really wanted her by his side—now and forever.

"Well, good luck tonight." The woman waved, then put a hand to her ear. "What's that?"

Ray got the sign to move on, which suited him fine. He turned away, rolled his eyes when he caught Garrett's stare.

"Wait. Ray!" The woman caught Ray's arm. Then quickly dropped it as she flushed red. "There's a disturbance on the red carpet. It seems Lauren is trying to catch up with you. Why don't you wait…?"

Joy swelled up, lending Ray height as he leapt off the dais and backtracked to reach Lauren.

Progress moved at a snail's pace. He traveled against the flow of humanity, causing a commotion, and making it worse were all the friends and colleagues who wanted to greet and congratulate him.

All he wanted was to get to Lauren.

He picked up his pace.

And then he saw her. He came to a dead stop, awed by her beauty, by her grace, by her radiance. The dress hugged her curves, displaying her delectable cleavage, while the jewels drew attention to her uniqueness.

His soul shouted, *Mine!*

She looked up, saw him, and her face lit up.

Lauren looked up and there was Ray. Finally. Her heart sang. Feet moving with grace and balance, she danced her way to him and launched herself into his arms.

Applause broke out around them. She barely heard it, too busy kissing her man.

"You made it," he said against her lips.

"I wouldn't miss it for the world."

Neither spoke of the awards show. "I love you," he breathed into her ear, arms locked around her in an embrace meant to last forever. "I was punishing you for so many reasons. All wrong."

"Me too." She couldn't let him go—never wanted to let go ever again. "I was afraid to give you too much power because I gave too much to Brad. But you've never taken from me. You've always empowered me to be more, better, sexier. I love you, Ray Donovan, with all my heart and with all my head."

Lights and clicks flashed and binged from every direction.

He pulled back to frame her face in hands strong and sure, his love on full display. "Will you marry me? I'll get you your own ring—"

"Shh." She pressed a finger to his mouth, held up her hand so Mamó's ring flashed in the afternoon light. "This ring is perfect. It comes with a history of love."

His jaw clenched and then he was kissing her again, long and soft, with tenderness and devotion. She sighed inside, seeing the caress as a testament to his hope for the future.

He lifted his head, stared into her eyes, his eyes promising everything his kiss had just declared. "I wish we were alone."

"Not me. The world is watching, and I want everyone to know you're mine. Time to say goodbye to your bachelorhood, Mr. Donovan."

His eyes lit up at the challenge. "My pleasure, Mrs. Donovan-to-be."

He took her hand, kissed Mamó's ring, and turned them both toward the waiting crowd of spectators and press.

"Congratulate me, everyone. Lauren Randall has agreed to be my bride."

EPILOGUE

LAUREN REACHED THE DOOR, checked in both directions down the hallway and slipped inside. She flipped on the light and grinned at the spread she found already set up on the counter next to the washing machine.

Holding her extended belly, she waddled over to inspect the goodies. Cheese and fruit, some roast beef from last night's dinner. And—oh, yeah—pickles. She stole one and popped it in her mouth. Such a cliché craving for a pregnant woman—but, hey, clichés got to be known for a reason.

She started when the door opened behind her. Just Ray, sneaking in. He carried a bottle of sparkling apple juice and two glasses.

He came to her, bent over the twins, and kissed her softly. "Hello."

"Hello. Did anyone see you?"

"Nope. Tori and Garrett just got here. That'll give Mamó and your mother someone else to focus on for at least half an hour."

The newlyweds had announced that they were expecting at the last family get-together in July. Lauren's mom was in heaven, with both her girls married and starting families. She and Mamó had become best friends. Everyone was gathered at her and Ray's place now because she was scheduled to have the twins in two days.

"This was a great idea." She settled into the chair he

pulled out and opened for her, shifted trying to get comfortable. Her back had been bothering her all day. "I love the support and having everyone about. But I have to say I miss having you all to myself."

With so many people in the house, alone time had become impossible. So when Ray had suggested a laundry room tryst she'd jumped at it. The small room had become their little hideout whenever the house was full. Nobody looked for them there.

He sat next to her and she leaned against his strength. She rubbed her belly. "Two girls. Are you ready?"

"No." A touch of panic sounded in the one word. "Maybe we can put it off for another week. Maybe a month."

She laughed, then winced as a twinge rolled up her back. She groaned. "You wouldn't do that to me, would you?"

"I guess not." He watched her carefully. "Are you okay?"

"Just tired. You may not be ready, but I am. And so are the girls."

"They were restless last night."

"Tell me about it. I wasn't able to get comfortable all night. Two more days. I can hardly wait." She sympathized with his nervousness, but she'd moved on to the *I want them out of me* stage.

"Are you hungry?" He served her food and juice, watched over her every move. His care showed his devotion to her and their girls.

"You take such good care of me."

"Not too controlling for you?"

"Marrying you was the best decision I ever made," she answered, without looking up from the tray he held for her perusal.

It scared her sometimes, how close she'd come to walking away from him. Thank goodness for his persistence.

She picked up a thin piece of provolone, but almost lost her hold when the tray was yanked away. "Hey!"

"Hey, back." He took the cheese, tossed it toward the tray, kissed her long and deep. "I love you. Marrying you was the best thing I ever did."

She was so lucky, so loved. "Oh."

"Oh, you love me too?"

"No. I mean yes. I love you. But *oh* because my water just broke."

She watched him carefully, waiting for the hint of panic from earlier to take hold. It never came.

Ray went into director mode, herding her downstairs, putting the family to work gathering her suitcase, getting the car, the baby gear. Never once did he let her go. She relaxed and let him do his thing, confident he had everything under control.

Four hours later she cradled her first daughter in her arms. Looking down into her tiny features, she felt such love flowing through her she didn't think it could get any bigger, be any stronger. Then she looked up and saw Ray next to her, cooing at a second little girl bundled in pink, and her emotions doubled in an instant.

The doors opened and family flowed into the room to admire the new additions.

Amid the chaos Ray lifted blue eyes to hers and mouthed, *I love you.*

And her love grew even bigger.

* * * * *

"Do I scare you?" Drake asked.

"A little," Marly murmured. "But it's nothing you did. It's just… There's a lot of stuff I'm working through," she told him. "Sometimes it hits me harder than others."

Drake knew all too well about painful memories creeping up at random times, cutting you off at the knees when you least expected it. But he'd learned to conquer those demons when they threatened him. He was stronger than he'd been a year ago, and he wanted to help Marly build on her strength.

"I'm a pretty good listener," he said.

Drake stepped closer, fully aware that he was teetering on a thin line with her emotions. But that damn pull between them crackled in the air, making him want to hold her, to offer some sort of comfort.

"Sometimes it only looks like there's no hope," he told her. "Trust me."

Damp eyes came up to meet his and the punch to the gut was swift and unexpected.

The St. Johns of Stonerock:
Three rebellious brothers come home to stay.

THE FIREMAN'S
READY-MADE
FAMILY

BY
JULES BENNETT

All rights reserved including the right of reproduction in whole or in part in any form. This edition is published by arrangement with Harlequin Books S.A.

This is a work of fiction. Names, characters, places, locations and incidents are purely fictional and bear no relationship to any real life individuals, living or dead, or to any actual places, business establishments, locations, events or incidents. Any resemblance is entirely coincidental.

This book is sold subject to the condition that it shall not, by way of trade or otherwise, be lent, resold, hired out or otherwise circulated without the prior consent of the publisher in any form of binding or cover other than that in which it is published and without a similar condition including this condition being imposed on the subsequent purchaser.

® and ™ are trademarks owned and used by the trademark owner and/or its licensee. Trademarks marked with ® are registered with the United Kingdom Patent Office and/or the Office for Harmonisation in the Internal Market and in other countries.

Published in Great Britain 2015
by Mills & Boon, an imprint of Harlequin (UK) Limited,
Eton House, 18-24 Paradise Road, Richmond, Surrey, TW9 1SR

© 2015 Jules Bennett

ISBN: 978-0-263-25111-1

23-0215

Harlequin (UK) Limited's policy is to use papers that are natural, renewable and recyclable products and made from wood grown in sustainable forests. The logging and manufacturing processes conform to the legal environmental regulations of the country of origin.

Printed and bound in Spain
by CPI, Barcelona

Award-winning author **Jules Bennett** is no stranger to romance—she met her husband when she was only fourteen. After dating through high school, the two married. He encouraged her to chase her dream of becoming an author. Jules has now published nearly thirty novels. She and her husband are living their own happily-ever-after while raising two girls. Jules loves to hear from readers through her website, julesbennett.com, her Facebook fan page or on Twitter.

I dedicate this book to all the real-life heroes who
shine a light into someone's darkened world.
May you ever be blessed.

Chapter One

The firefighter was back.

Once again dressed in his blue cargo pants and matching blue polo with the Stonerock, Tennessee, fire department's seal embroidered on the left side of his chest...a chest that really maxed out the material of his shirt.

But muscles meant something entirely different now. A few years ago the well-sculpted body of a man would have had her appreciating the view. Unfortunately, her world had been vastly changed six months earlier, and now muscles, power and strength only reminded her of the scars she'd be wearing forever.

Pediatric nurse Marly Haskins moved farther into the private room of her six-year-old patient. The young boy had been badly burned in a house fire only a few days ago. The doctors were waiting to see how the wounds healed and pumping him full of antibiotics to ward off infection before discussing the use of skin grafts on his arm and torso.

Marly's heart ached for the boy, who had started kindergarten with her daughter, Willow, just a few weeks ago. This little guy should be at school running around on the playground, not recovering from a fire that had claimed his home.

As Marly approached the side of the bed, the firefighter raised his gaze to her. Those piercing blue eyes shouldn't make her belly do flips, but she couldn't control her body's reaction. Her mind, though… Her mind knew better than to be impressed by beauty, brawn and silent allure.

"Let me know if I'm in your way," he told her as his eyes drifted back down to the sleeping boy. "I just wanted to see him before my shift."

Other than family, no one had been by to see Jeremy. Marly had been told by Jeremy's parents that the fire chief was a close friend of the family and he would be visiting often. Marly didn't know his name, just that he was the chief—another man in a powerful position. A man whose physical appeal had her wishing she wasn't so cynical and jaded. Would she always look at muscles and power as a bad thing?

"I'm just giving him another round of antibiotics," she told him, hoping he didn't want small talk and thankful that he stood on the other side of the bed.

Marly wiped the boy's port with an alcohol pad and

injected the medicine before slipping the needle into the biohazard bin on the wall.

Jeremy slept peacefully, due in part to the pain medication he was on. This was the hard part of her job. The part where she imagined how easily this could be her daughter lying here and how fortunate Marly was that Willow was in school right now, safe and having fun with her friends…just as any five-year-old child should.

"I'm Drake, by the way."

Marly turned her attention back to the imposing man. With wide shoulders stretching his polo, his tall, lean build and those captivating baby blues, the mesmerizing stranger silently demanded attention. Her pulse kicked up whenever they made eye contact, and she hated the thread of fear that niggled at her.

He reminded her too much of her past life—a life she was still trying to escape. A life she was privately rebuilding one day at a time.

Guilt slid through her. Judging a stranger wasn't quite fair. After all, a stranger hadn't hurt her. The man who'd vowed to love, honor and cherish her, though, had nearly destroyed her.

"I'm Marly."

"I know." With a soft smile, he nodded toward her badge clipped on the pocket of her puppy-printed smock top. "I should've introduced myself before now."

"You were preoccupied." The man may be menacing in size, but the worry lines between thick, dark brows spoke of vulnerability. "I understand you and Jeremy's parents are friends."

Nodding, Drake gripped the edge of the bed rail and

stared down at the boy. "Yeah. I graduated with his dad, Shawn. I was on the scene of the fire."

Marly swallowed. Remorse seemed to envelop this man, and there was no doubt he was mentally replaying said scene in his mind.

She'd witnessed that level of sorrow many times over the years as a burn-unit nurse at a children's hospital in Nashville before moving to the suburb of Stonerock. And that was the only reason Jeremy was allowed to stay at this small-town hospital.

"I just wish I could do more," she whispered. "His parents…"

She trailed off, not wanting to get too emotional with this stranger.

Private. That was the theme for this stage in her life. She needed to remain private and locked in her own world, where she could protect herself and her daughter.

"They're having a tough time," he added as he pushed off the rail and came around the edge of the bed. "But you're doing all you can. Keeping their son as comfortable as possible is a blessing to them right now."

Marly nodded, Drake's large, looming presence causing her to step back. He'd done nothing to her, yet she couldn't help that proverbial knee-jerk reaction.

"Are you okay?" he asked, dark brows drawn together.

Easing her side bangs over a tad to keep her scar covered, Marly nodded. "Yeah, just worried. It's hard not to get swept into the lives of my patients."

"That's what makes a good nurse." His soft smile didn't quite reach his eyes, as if the gesture was only for her. "Getting emotionally involved is an occupational hazard."

On one level she knew he understood. After all, they were both public servants and protectors. But on another level, she really didn't want to bond with this man who had her emotions all jumbled up because of his gentleness and potent sex appeal. A lethal combo.

If she wasn't careful, she would find herself slipping into his personal space, and she'd promised herself no more letting herself trust—not yet and probably not for a long, long time. There was too much at stake in her life for her to let her guard down…with anyone.

"When will he be transferred to another hospital with a burn unit?" he asked, crossing his arms over his wide, taut chest.

"We'll have to wait and see if the doctor and his parents decide on the skin grafts."

She tried to ignore the way Drake's size dominated the room. Tried to ignore the way her heart kicked up at the way he seemed to study her.

"I think he needs to be transferred to a hospital that specializes in this type of care," Drake told her, crossing his arms over his wide chest.

Marly wasn't really in the mood to defend her medical position or to discuss her patient's needs with a non-family member. And she definitely wasn't up for being bullied by this man, who no doubt was used to getting his way. She didn't think he was posing for an argument, but he was making it clear his opinion mattered.

"For now he's fine to stay here." She forced herself to meet his gaze. She was no longer that meek woman who was afraid to stand up for herself. "I'm able to care for him because I was a nurse on a burn unit at a larger hospital before I moved here. But if his parents choose for him to have skin grafts, he'll go to a specialist."

"Why the wait?" Drake demanded. "Wouldn't he heal faster if he were with a specialist now?"

Fisting her hands at her sides, Marly shook her head. "The doctors here have Jeremy's best interest in mind, and he's getting the best possible care. And we can't transport him yet anyway."

Drake swore under his breath. "Shawn and Amy are self-employed, and this is really going to hurt them financially on top of all the emotional turmoil they're already experiencing. Never mind the fact they lost their house and they're staying with Shawn's parents."

Okay, so the overpowering man had a soft spot. Seriously, though, how dare he question not only her, but the doctors and Jeremy's parents? Perhaps he was just speaking out of worry, but still, Marly wasn't interested in this chief's medical opinions.

But he was right about one thing. Medical bills were going to flood their lives before they ever got their son home. Marly couldn't imagine the financial strain this would put on the poor family.

Since she'd run from her ex and left behind all the money and flashy things, she was having a hard time adjusting to her single salary, but it was hard to feel sorry for herself when a tragic case like this smacked her in the face with a dose of reality. There was always someone worse off. She had to remind herself of that when pity started to settle in.

"Can I talk to you outside?" Drake asked, intruding on her thoughts.

Surprised at his request, Marly nodded. This was the first real interaction they'd had since Jeremy had been admitted to her unit two days ago. Even though he'd been here both days, she'd made sure to just stick to the pleasantries, getting in and out of Jeremy's room quickly when Drake visited.

They stepped outside the room, and Marly eased the large wooden door closed behind her. Trying to come off as a professional was hard when your hands were shaking, so she crossed her arms over her chest and tipped her head to level his stare.

"Something wrong?" she asked.

"I'm going to be at the station for the next thirty-six hours," he told her, stepping closer so there was only a small gap separating them. "I know Shawn and Amy won't let me know if they need anything, but could you keep an eye on them when they're here? If they need food or a break, could you let me know? I can give you my cell. If I'm not busy I can run over or I can have one of my brothers stop by. I don't want Shawn and Amy to feel like they're in this alone."

Wow. He was serious. The fire chief was ready to drop everything to help a friend in need.

The cynical side of Marly wanted to know if he was using this opportunity for publicity in his position, to look good in the eyes of his superiors. Or did this man actually have that kind of a heart?

She shook off the pull to want to know more. The old Marly would've reached out, but that woman was dead, cut off from all the emotional tugs toward the wounded hearts of others. She had her own heart to heal.

Pulling herself back to his request and his intense stare as he waited on an answer, she smiled. "Of course I can let you know."

His mesmerizing blue eyes continued to study her, and she resisted the urge to reach up and make sure her side bangs were covering her scar. She didn't want to know what he was thinking, didn't want to know what he saw when he looked at her.

Her ex had used her as a trophy, only wanting her to look good at his side and remain silent. But, gone was that quiet, reserved, perfectly-coiffed woman. Now Marly kept her long blond hair in a ponytail, downplayed her voluptuous chest and wore little to no makeup. This was the real Marly Haskins.

"Did you need anything else?" she asked, ready to get out from under his questioning gaze.

Drake shrugged one shoulder. "Just wondering why you look so sad."

Taken aback by his abrupt, imposing question, Marly shook her head. "I'm not sad. I mean, I'm sad for Jeremy and his family, but that's all."

Reaching out, Drake slid a thumb beneath her eye. "No, you've got shadows and there's sadness there."

Swatting his hand away, Marly stepped back. "You don't know me, so I'd appreciate if you didn't analyze me."

Drake raked a hand over his closely cropped dark hair. "My apologies. It's second nature to worry. I just wondered if you were okay."

Was she okay? Far from it. Was she going to spill her heart to this charming stranger? Absolutely not.

But, oh, how she wished she had someone she could open up to. It was so hard being a single mother in the best of times, let alone when trying to keep her abusive ex from discovering where she was living and trying to remain strong and put up a cheerful front for strangers who had no clue the hell she'd endured.

She couldn't focus on Drake or his charms. She needed to concentrate on getting her life back in order and setting a stable foundation for her and her daughter. No room for a handsome stranger with vibrant blue eyes and a killer body. Those two qualities meant nothing in the long run.

Drake reached back and pulled out his wallet, producing a business card. "My cell is on there."

As she slipped the card from his grasp, her fingertips slid across his—the briefest of touches, but enough to have her pulling back. She hadn't touched a man in any way since leaving her husband. Her patients were all children and she'd made a point to stay clear of men at least until her mental state returned to normal.

Scars weren't always just on the outside.

"You sure you're okay?" he asked, brows drawn in as he leaned closer.

Great, now he was seriously concerned about her.

Forcing what she hoped was a convincing smile, Marly nodded. "Fine. Just thinking about Jeremy."

That answer seemed to pacify the chief as he pulled his keys from his other pocket. "Call me anytime. If I can't talk, I won't answer, but leave a message."

Marly nodded, still eager for him to be on his way. "I'll be back tomorrow," he said.

Yeah, that was what she was afraid of. Each time she saw him her heart would speed up and she'd find herself drawn deeper and deeper into his appeal. That type of mentality was exactly what had gotten her in trouble to begin with.

As Drake walked out of the cheerily painted pediatric unit, Marly couldn't help but watch him go. Those broad shoulders, that uniform, those dark forearms… Drake St. John was all man and all powerful.

But whatever fluttery feeling she got from being around him would just have to be ignored, because no way would she ever get involved with another man—especially one so sexy and powerful. That combination nearly killed her once before.

Chapter Two

Confident that the pretty nurse would notify him if Shawn or Amy needed anything, Drake felt a sliver of satisfaction. Marly, with her wide, chocolate doe eyes, may be leery of him, but he had to assume she'd keep her promise.

He mentally cursed himself for reaching out to her. Good Lord, she'd think he was some type of creep. But he'd seen fear spread through those beautiful eyes of hers when he neared, felt her stiffen beneath his touch.

Drake figured he intimidated her, which was a shame, but he couldn't figure out why. Someone or something had hurt her. The protector in him wanted to keep her safe, as strange as that may sound, considering he barely knew her.

He also couldn't figure out why he kept finding himself thinking about her when he'd leave the hospital. He'd seen her a total of three times—she was fairly new in town, according to all the chatter—but other than that, she was a total stranger he knew nothing about.

Well, he'd known when he'd stepped closer to her earlier that she'd smelled like strawberries; he knew she had a gentle, patient bedside manner; and he knew she was one of the most beautiful women he'd ever seen. With her long blond hair, dark eyes and creamy skin, Marly was a stunner, and he'd never even seen an ounce of makeup on her.

He'd not felt a pull toward another woman in over a year. Not since the day his fiancée had died. He never thought he'd feel for anybody again. In his defense, he'd even been on a couple dates since then, but nothing had ever come of them.

There was something pulling him toward Marly. Whether it was her underlying vulnerability or just the woman in general, he truly had no idea. But he knew he couldn't ignore it, either.

Drake pulled from the hospital parking lot, but before he went to the station, he swung by the courthouse to check on the status of the budget. Granted, the official meeting was tomorrow, but Drake knew the good ol' mayor already had some sort of clue as to what was going on.

Drake mounted the steps, waving to a few city workers as they exited the old historic building. Quickly making his way to the third floor, Drake went in and greeted the elderly secretary, who had been the smiling face of this office for the past forty years. No matter the mayor, Betty May Allen was the right-hand woman. That woman probably held more secrets than the Pentagon.

"Chief St. John." She beamed, sliding down her reading glasses to dangle off the pearl chain. "What can I do for you?"

"Is he in?" Drake asked, nodding toward the closed door.

With the frosted glass and large block lettering, Drake couldn't see.

"He is. You don't have an appointment, do you?" she asked.

"No. I'll just be a minute if he's free."

Betty May slid from behind her L-shaped desk and walked to the door, easing it open a crack. Her silver hair bounced as she nodded and spoke, but he couldn't make out what she was saying.

Turning with her signature smile, Betty May gestured as she opened the door wider. "Go on in, Chief."

"Thank you, ma'am."

Drake closed the door behind him as he took in the overweight, half bald, half comb-over man behind the large mahogany desk. The man looked every bit the part of a small-town mayor. Too bad he didn't play the part like one.

"What can I do for one of my city's finest workers?" Mayor Tipton asked, easing back in his chair hard enough to cause very questionable creaks.

Was it too much to hope the jerk would tip the chair too far and fall backward?

Gripping the back of the leather chair across from

the desk, Drake leveled the man's gaze, refusing to return the smarmy smile. "How's the budget looking? Are we going to be able to bring my men back on board?"

Tipton blinked. "The budget meeting is tomorrow."

Drake never did like a man who couldn't just answer a question straight-out. And he'd certainly never liked this lazy, selfish mayor. He hadn't voted for the man, and he sure as hell hated working under him.

"I'm sure you have some idea," Drake said, clenching the chair and trying to rein in his patience, as he had for several months now. "My department is suffering, and because of that we were shorthanded on the fire at the Adkins' residence on Sunday."

"Yes, I heard all about that." Mayor Tipton leaned forward, propping his flabby forearms on his cluttered desk. "I was told the young boy was severely injured."

Drake swallowed the bitter truth as images of that boy lying beside his bed as flames licked all around his room consumed him. Drake had dragged the unconscious boy out, praying the entire time that he hadn't been too late.

"The city simply doesn't have the extra money," the mayor was saying. "We had to cut somewhere, and unfortunately your department was one of the areas."

Fury bubbled within him, and Drake knew if he didn't leave he'd say something that may get him suspended. But he also wasn't going to back down, not when he had dependable men who needed the income, not to mention men that worked harder in one shift than this mayor did in an entire year.

"Did you happen to look at cutting your own income?

Or maybe the new landscaping in the park? How about those new streetlights that just went up around Main Street? None of that was ever considered? That little boy's injuries lie directly on your head, not mine. I did my job... Can you say the same?"

Drake didn't stop when the mayor pushed his pudgy frame away from the desk and stood. In fact, the idea of the mayor gearing up for the argument was rather amusing and fueled Drake even more. He was definitely teetering on a thin line here.

"Oh, I see where you're coming from," Drake said in his most condescending tone. Sarcasm had always been a strong suit for him and his brothers. "Why pay honest, hardworking men when we can make things pretty? I see that logic. Best to put lives in danger so we can have purple pansies and lantern-style streetlights."

"You better watch yourself, Chief." The mayor's face was slowly turning red, his gobbler neck wiggling back and forth when he spoke. "You always were a smart-mouthed hellion."

Ah, yes. The infamous St. John reputation he and his brothers had had to overcome in order to rise to their rankings in this small town.

Drake didn't care if his character came into play here. He knew he was right and the mayor was flat-out wrong. Drake also didn't care if Tipton got angry. Angry didn't even cover what Drake felt when he thought of the moment he'd had to tell three of his men that they were no longer needed.

"A young boy is lying in the hospital with second- and third-degree burns to his arm and torso," Drake went on, the image alone adding fuel to his anger. "We would've been able to get to him faster had all regular responders been available. We're shorthanded, Mayor, and it's time you realized just how dangerous those cuts have become. The guys left on staff are working overtime, and it's not safe for them or the public to have them so exhausted."

"I sympathize for the boy. The accident was tragic, but I am not to blame here. I have a job, just like you. I suggest you focus on that."

A whole new level of rage slid through him. "Are you suggesting I didn't do my job?"

With a slight shrug, the mayor merely stared across the desk.

Yeah, if he didn't leave, Drake would get fired...at the very least, because the urge to punch the guy in the face was too strong. Fortunately Drake had self-control and actually cared about protecting the people in this town. That right there proved he'd overcome his rebellious days. Once upon a time Drake and his brothers would punch first and discuss later.

"One way or another, my men will come back to work," Drake assured him. "Your term is almost up. Then we'll see who really cares about the safety of the citizens."

"Are you threatening me?"

With a slow grin, Drake raised his hands, palms out. "Just stating a fact. The voters will take care of you."

And with that he walked out, nodding to Betty May, who was wide-eyed, no doubt hearing the heated encounter—not Drake's first with the mayor, but perhaps the most hate filled.

Drake marched all the way back to his truck and slammed the door. Damn it. He had to figure out a way to get the city to allow him to hire his men back on. The men who were currently working were maxed out. They were tired and all feeling the extra stress… not good when lives were on the line every single day.

Drake clenched the steering wheel and stared out the windshield toward the old fountain in the distance at the park.

Andrea had loved that fountain. Had always said if she got married she'd do it there in the summer with all the beauty of the tall old oaks surrounding her.

Drake had every intention of giving her that dream. He'd had every intention of giving her everything she'd ever wanted.

But that dream had died in a fiery crash.

Starting the engine, Drake forced out the crippling images of that day. His counselor was right. Focusing on the past wouldn't help him rebuild for a better future. And he knew that Andrea would want him to move on; she'd want him to live his life. Besides, he had a department he needed to fight for and a boy in the hospital he cared about.

Which brought him right back to the pretty nurse who seemed a bit skittish when he was around. Her beauty was rather shocking, and Drake hadn't felt a physical pull toward anyone since Andrea. Which only made his mixed-up emotions even more confusing.

How could he find another woman so appealing in

such a short time? Should he ask her out? He had to keep trying his hand at dating if he wanted to truly move on.

But Marly was afraid of something. Perhaps he should approach this on a friendship level, because Drake knew one thing. He had to find out what had put the shadows beneath her pretty eyes.

Marly was thankful her supervisor gave her a few hours off to chaperone Willow on the kindergarten field trip. Marly knew it was going to be tough to hold a full-time job and be the parent Willow needed, especially after removing Willow from the only home she'd known.

So far Willow was adjusting perfectly, and today's field trip to the fire department was all her sweet little five-year-old could talk about this morning.

Marly left work early and pulled into the department lot just after the bus did. It didn't take long for Marly to zero in on the chief, and she cursed herself for instantly seeking him out.

Drake stepped up to the open doors of the bus and greeted the kids with a wide grin as they bounced off the last step and raced across the lot to the closest shiny red truck. Another group of men in blue polos and matching pants herded the children to the grassy area, where they had them take a seat.

As Marly got out of her SUV, her eyes locked on the chief. She hadn't seen him since that awkward moment in the hallway two days ago. He hadn't popped in yesterday like he'd said he would, and she hated that she'd had a sliver of disappointment when her shift had ended and she hadn't seen him.

Marly crossed the parking lot and headed toward the front of the bus to wait for Willow. Before she could spot her daughter, Drake raised his head. Even with his dark aviator sunglasses on, she knew he was looking right at her.

Sweltering heat from the late-summer sun did nothing to prevent the chills from racing through her. The instant reaction her body took to this man was unexplainable and unwanted. Yes, at one time she would've loved to have felt chills over the thought of a man like Drake looking at her, but that was years ago, before she'd married a monster.

Trusting her judgment now wasn't the smartest move. She needed to regroup, build a solid life on her own before trying to appreciate a man like Drake. Her personal life would have to come later—much later.

Such a shame, though. She didn't remember the last time a man had looked at her and made her feel anything but fear.

"Mama!"

Marly smiled as Willow came running up to her. "Come on." Willow started tugging on Marly's hand. "They're going to let us squirt the hoses in a minute, and the teacher said we may get to climb inside a truck."

Laughing, Marly allowed herself to be pulled toward the other smiling, wiggly kids. She passed by Drake, earning a devastating smile and a nod of his head.

"Marly."

Unable to help herself, Marly returned his smile. "Chief St. John."

Mercy. Just passing by the man and his spicy scent had Marly wondering where on earth her head had gone. Hadn't she scolded herself already? Physical attraction wasn't something she could indulge in. But just because she didn't plan on doing anything about this sudden on-slaught of emotions didn't mean she couldn't appreciate the view of such a spectacular man.

"I want to sit in the front," Willow said, taking a seat beside a little boy wearing his school spirit T-shirt. "This is my friend Alan. Just stand over there with the other moms, but watch me when I squirt the hose. Okay?"

"All right, sweetie," Marly agreed.

She stepped aside, but not too close to the other moms. She was only here to see her daughter, help if needed and snap some pictures of her baby's first field trip. What she wasn't here to do was make friends with other moms or spend her time fantasizing about Chief Drake St. John.

But as she watched him interact with the children, she found herself softening toward this local hero even more. The children all stared up at him with wide eyes as he projected his strong voice over the young crowd. They were his captive audience as he discussed how firefighters rescued people when they were scared and needed help.

Within moments he had donned full firefighting gear to show them how they may look scary, but all the equipment was to keep them safe so they could help others in danger.

That instant, Marly found herself drawn deeper into his world. Whether she wanted to or not, she was mesmerized and hung on his every word…just like the children.

Great. Now what? The emotions were there. No matter how she'd tried to dodge and deny them, they were in the forefront of her mind. So what on earth did she do with that revelation?

Drake absolutely loved this part of his job. He loved the interaction with the kids, enjoyed seeing their smiling faces as he explained the different tools on the different fire trucks; he even loved letting them play with the fire hose.

But today, all of that faded in the background. Marly had a child—a little girl who looked exactly like her. Once his initial shock wore off, he realized he was staring like a fool.

Drake wasn't sure if he was more shocked at the fact she had a child or the fact she was smiling so widely, so beautifully. He'd not seen her so happy before. Of course, he'd only seen her in her element at work, caring for Jeremy.

The second he'd spotted her, his heart had tightened, but when her face had lit up at the sight of her little girl, Drake had literally felt that punch to the gut he'd heard his brother Eli talk about.

Now that the children had gone through their tour and were starting to line back up for the bus, Drake realized Marly had pretty much stayed in the shadows. He'd caught her snapping photos of her daughter, and now she was holding the little girl, kissing her on the cheek. Drake lurched forward. He couldn't let an opportunity pass him by.

"Would you like a picture together?" he offered.

Marly's head whipped around. "Drake."

"You know the chief?" Willow asked, wide-eyed and obviously impressed. "Why didn't you say so? That's the coolest!"

Drake laughed. "Maybe your mom could bring you back sometime. I'm sure I can find time to take you for a ride in the fire engine."

The little girl's mouth dropped. "If you're kidding, Chief, I'm gonna be sad."

Drake couldn't help but reach out and give a tug on one of her long blond ponytails. "I would never kid someone so eager to learn about firefighting. But you have to promise one thing."

"Anything," she squealed and wiggled in Marly's arms. "What is it?"

"You won't try to take my job once you learn all this stuff."

He forced his eyes to stay locked onto the little girl, which wasn't a hardship because she was so adorable. But he could feel Marly's gaze on him, and he wanted to turn and see those dark eyes of hers.

"I promise, Chief," the little girl assured.

"Call me Drake." He held out a hand for her to shake. "And your first name is?"

Her tiny hand slid into his and she squeezed. "Willow."

"Nice to meet you, Willow. Your bus is loading, so how about I take a picture of you and your mom in front of the station so you guys can always remember this day?"

"Oh, Drake, you don't have to," Marly protested.

He cut his gaze to hers; thankfully he'd removed his sunglasses so he could see her with no barrier. "I know I don't have to. I want to."

Marly smiled as she handed over her phone. "In that case, we'd love a picture."

Drake made sure he took a couple. He knew from experience that most women wanted options. Sweet Willow, with her golden pigtails, gave her mommy a big hug and scrambled down to race to the bus.

Marly waved goodbye and turned to Drake. "Thank you. You're really good with children."

Shrugging, Drake rested his hands on his hips. "Kids are great. You just have to know how to treat them."

A shadow passed over Marly's eyes. "Do you have kids?" she asked, raising her arm to shield the sun from her eyes.

He thought of Andrea, of the dreams they'd had. The family they'd planned.

"No," he told her. "I'm an uncle to a beautiful baby girl, but none of my own yet."

Sliding her phone back into her smock pocket, Marly started to pass him. "Well, I need to get back to work. Thanks again for being so great with all the kids, and especially Willow."

"I meant what I said." He turned to meet her stare as she started to walk away. "Anytime you see my black truck here, swing in, and if we're not busy I'd love to give her a ride on the engine. I know she'd enjoy it."

Marly studied him for a moment before a corner of her mouth kicked up. "You really do love kids, don't you?"

Taken back by her odd question, Drake nodded. "What's not to love?"

There it was again, that ghost of an emotion taking over, and Marly's smile turned sad in an instant. "I agree. See you around, Chief."

Drake watched until Marly was in her car and headed down the street. A hand slapped him hard on the shoulder, and Drake turned to see one of his men grinning.

"She's a looker, Chief."

Drake nodded. No sense in denying the truth.

"Gonna ask her out?"

Shaking his head, Drake laughed. "I have no clue what I'm going to do. No clue."

And that was the honest truth. Because on one hand he wanted to see Marly on a personal level, but on the other hand she was scared of something—or maybe someone.

The pull Drake felt toward her, though, was only getting stronger. As much as he wanted to see more of the beautiful pediatric nurse, he also knew he needed to take things slow.

After all, he was still on shaky ground himself in regards to relationships.

Chapter Three

Those piercing blue eyes had penetrated her once again. If Marly thought Drake a big man before, now that she'd seen him in full gear, he was even more impressive. She knew broad shoulders lay beneath that bulky coat, and his towering height was only emphasized by his helmet.

What drew her to powerful men? Although she had to admit, Kevin's power was used to blackmail and lie to get what he wanted. From the little she'd seen of Drake, the man genuinely cared for his job, the people he encountered. Drake certainly didn't seem the type to use others for a publicity stunt.

Marly steered her car back into the hospital lot and found an open spot. Now that Willow had been given the invitation to go to the fire station, no doubt the rambunctious little girl would ask every two minutes when they were going.

Which meant Marly would have to go back and witness Drake in all his gorgeous glory. A part of her so wanted to address the tension that settled between them each time they were within breathing space of each other, but at the same time, she wanted to deny any attraction existed. She wanted to ignore the desire that seemed to creep up on her when she didn't have the mental strength to stop it.

Killing her engine, Marly sighed and rested her head against the steering wheel. No matter her sudden attraction to Drake, she had a war she was still fighting, and that had to come before anything else.

When her phone chimed to signal a text, Marly pulled the cell from her purse and cringed at the screen.

Call me. You can't avoid me forever.

That didn't mean she wouldn't try like hell.

Tossing her phone back in her purse, Marly stepped out of her car, welcoming the warmth of the midday sun. When she'd left Nashville, she'd found enough courage to force Kevin into letting her go, taking Willow and not disclosing her whereabouts in exchange for the pictures she had promised would not go to the newspaper or other media outlets.

Kevin didn't know she'd gone to the police… Of course, she figured he knew now. No doubt some corrupt cop who was friends of the family had called Kevin moments after Marly had left. Marly knew the power

Kevin's family held, so she also knew that was probably why the Nashville Police Department hadn't returned her calls and she'd heard no more on her case... if there even was a case.

Marly figured the only reason Kevin hadn't hired a PI and traced her phone was because of his powerful status and the fact that he tended to avoid public conflict. For once, his social standing was working in her favor.

Even with the sun beating down on her, she trembled. There was no way in hell she'd ever return to Kevin. If she had to stay on the run the rest of her life to protect her child, then so be it. She would never be another man's punching bag or pawn again.

The day after the field trip, Marly was stepping out of Jeremy's room when Drake came striding through the bright yellow walls of the pediatric unit. The cheery surroundings made him seem less intimidating, but the man's impressive size still dominated the space.

When his gaze met hers, his lips spread wide in a smile that hit her hard. Then she spotted the small stuffed Dalmatian in his hand and she couldn't help but return the grin. Why was she softening toward this man so fast? She'd learned her lesson, right? Just because a man was charming and good-looking didn't mean he treated women right when no one was looking.

But there was still that nugget of doubt that kept telling her Drake was nothing like the man she'd married. Nothing.

"You carry toys everywhere you go?" she asked, once he closed the gap between them.

Glancing down at the toy in question, Drake shrugged. When his eyes met hers once again, they held as his voice lowered. "My toys are a bit larger than this."

She shivered at the veiled flirting and innuendo. The part deep inside her that had thought no man would ever find her attractive again sparked to life. For so long she'd not even been given a second thought, other than being used as a pawn or publicity stunt.

But Drake had a way of making her feel... Just feel, and that was something she'd have to get used to if she was going to keep seeing him in this small town.

"I assume that's for our patient?"

With a nod, Drake asked, "How's he doing today?"

"Good. Amy just stepped out to get a bite to eat and Shawn ran home to shower. I nearly had to bribe them to take care of themselves."

Drake swallowed hard, glancing away.

"You okay?" she asked.

"Yeah, I just... This whole situation kills me. I don't know what to say to Shawn. Words won't fix what happened." He shook his head. "Talking to people after accidents is part of my job, yet this is on a whole new level of difficulty. Shawn and I are friends."

"You saved their son's life," Marly pointed out. "They're grateful."

"I know they are," he told her, waiting until another nurse went by before he continued, "I'm thankful I got to him in time, but the entire situation just sucks."

"You didn't tell me you were the one who pulled Jeremy from the fire. Amy was telling me earlier how she doesn't know what they would've done without you."

Drake's eyes held hers, but he didn't utter a word. A true hero was someone who didn't boast or brag of his achievements. A true hero did his job, though fear may overpower him. A true hero cared for others, put their needs first, even at the risk of being injured himself.

And before her stood a true hero.

"You can go in and see him, but I'll need to put the toy at the nurse's station with his other things. We've been keeping all of the balloons and flowers out here since his room is set up for his special needs due to the burns."

He passed the stuffed dog over, and Marly was careful not to let her hands brush his again. The less contact with this potent man the better. He was already wreaking havoc on her nerves and consuming way too much of her mind and she barely knew him.

"Go on in," Marly said, afraid of just how fast she was becoming infatuated with the town fire chief. "I'll be back in a bit."

She quickly rushed off and went straight to the employees' restroom. Flicking the lock, Marly sank against the back of the door. Drake St. John was becoming a bigger issue than she'd first thought.

When he'd first come into the pediatric unit she realized he was probably there to check on the boy because that fell in line with being the chief. But then when he'd been there nearly every day, he was great with Willow and now he'd brought a stuffed animal for Jeremy... He was becoming more and more real.

Marly sighed. Real? That sounded ridiculous. Of course he was real, but now he was even more genuine and melting away that layer she'd formed around her heart. She needed to be on guard, not to start feeling all schoolgirl over a handsome, charming fire chief.

No doubt, his physical appeal couldn't be denied, but how could she allow herself to be so taken with him so fast? She'd learned her lesson—the hard way—on big, powerful men. Right now she had to focus on rebuilding her new life and trying to keep custody of Willow. Kevin wouldn't stop at sending texts and voice mails. He'd take action by hiring a PI, if he hadn't already.

But it was getting harder and harder to focus when Drake came around. Between his easy rapport with Willow and his dedication to Jeremy's welfare, there was so much more to Drake than power.

Perhaps that was what scared her most.

Marly looked at herself in the mirror. In twenty-six years, she'd been through too much. All she wanted was happiness, a settled life in which she felt safe, protected and secure. Not only for herself, but also for her daughter.

She eased her blond hair back, facing the ugly, jagged scar that ran down her temple. Vanity had never been her thing, so the physical image wasn't what bothered her. Kevin's fists had taken so much more than physical beauty. They had taken away her freedom, her sense of self-worth and her courage. But she was getting those back. No way would she give Kevin the satisfaction of stealing everything from her.

Including her daughter.

Her eyes roamed down to the small scar on her chin. That one was impossible to hide, but at least it was on the underside, so it wasn't as noticeable and easier to chalk up to a fall from childhood.

Adjusting her hair back in place, she took a deep, calming breath and headed back to work. At some point she'd have to face the fact that she was finding herself more and more intrigued by—and dare she say attracted to—Drake.

She couldn't act on her unstable emotions. After all, how could she trust anything she felt after her poor judgment regarding her ex? On the other hand, she couldn't keep lying to herself about this invisible tug whenever Drake was around. She was a woman who had desires and eyes, for pity's sake. How could any woman not do a double take at Drake? And after that double take, the real problems started. Because the looks didn't make the man...the big heart and devastating smile did.

Drake eyed the young boy lying in the sterile bed wearing a sheet up to his waist, dressings wrapped around his torso and his left arm. Drake's heart literally ached for Jeremy, Shawn and Amy. Such a beautiful family living in a small town like so many others around the country, and now fate had turned their world upside down.

Someone needed to step up and help them. There was no way Shawn and Amy could take on this financial burden alone. Wasn't that what people in small towns did? Rallied behind each other when one of them was hurting? Besides, they needed mental support, as well. No one should ever go through a trauma like this alone.

Drake figured he'd get the ball rolling in the direction of a fund-raiser to assist Shawn and Amy. He couldn't just sit back and do nothing.

Drake wanted to drag the mayor from behind his desk and his cushy leather chair and show him the ram-ifications of cutting good, hardworking firefighters. Drake had zero tolerance for that man, and this was just another reason Drake couldn't wait until the next election when hopefully a new mayor was sworn in…a mayor who actually cared about the people of the town.

When Drake stepped from the room and eased the door shut behind him, Marly was nowhere to be seen. He walked up to the nurses' station and was greeted by a middle-aged lady wearing character scrubs with her hair in a tight, high bun.

Balloons, teddy bears and flowers were piled high on the back counter. Drake figured all of those gifts were for Jeremy, since Drake saw the stuffed toy he brought nestled in the mix.

"Excuse me," he said, leaning an arm on the top of the high counter. "Is Marly busy?"

"I haven't seen her for a couple of minutes. Maybe she's in the break room." The lady turned, gesturing behind the desk to a narrow hall. "It's the first door on the right. Go on in."

Drake smiled. "Thank you, ma'am."

Drake figured wearing his department logo on his shirt had gotten him the pass to the employee area. He went around the desk and into the break room but didn't see Marly. As he turned to leave, Marly rounded the corner to enter the room and plowed right into him.

Instincts had him reaching out, gripping her arms tight in an attempt to steady her. The second he grabbed her, she screamed and jumped back.

The color had gone from her face, and Drake held his hands out to his side. "Are you okay?"

A shaky hand came up to her heart as she nodded, her eyes not quite meeting his.

"Marly." He eased closer. The disturbing look in her eyes wasn't just shock at finding him in here, this was pure fear. "Come in and sit down."

After a moment of silence, she sought his eyes and shook her head. "No, no. I'm okay."

"You've gone pale and you're shaking." He started to reach for her, but she moved back. Dread settled deep in his stomach. "Are you afraid of me?"

Marly closed her eyes and sighed. "No," she whispered.

Drake had no clue what demons she was battling before his eyes, so he remained silent. God knew he'd never wanted anyone to witness his rough moments after Andrea's accident.

It wasn't long before she raked a hand down her face and opened her eyes. With her shoulders back and head high, Drake knew she'd pushed through whatever hell she'd entered into moments ago.

"Sorry," she told him, trying hard for a smile, but failing. "You just caught me off guard."

And she didn't like to be touched, apparently. There was a story there...a story he feared would make him want to protect her at all costs and dig even deeper into her world.

"It's okay," he assured her. "I was just heading out, but I wanted to run something by you."

Nodding, she gestured toward the table and chairs. "Let's have a seat."

He moved out of her way, letting her go where she wanted before he pulled out a chair across from her. The last thing he needed was her to worry about being alone with him. He wanted to gain her trust, and after what he'd just witnessed, he feared getting into Marly's inner circle would take more time and patience than he'd first thought…but something told him she would be worth the effort.

"Is something wrong?" she asked, lacing her fingers on the tabletop.

"No, I just wanted to discuss Jeremy with you."

He hadn't realized he was going to bring up the fund-raiser with Marly, but he found that he wanted to include her in the planning.

"You and I are both worried about his parents financially, especially since the doctor decided he'll have to have grafts. When he's transported to the specialist, Shawn and Amy will have added travel expenses." He eased forward in his seat, resting his forearms on the table. "What if we did a fund-raiser for them?"

Marly's eyes widened. "We? Like you and me?"

Smiling, Drake nodded. "Well, yeah. I'd appreciate your opinion. But if you don't have the time, I understand."

Marly rested her chin on her palm and seemed to process the idea. Drake didn't know what had come over him, why he wanted to work with her on this project, but he found himself holding his breath until she nodded with a smile.

"I'll do it. Willow can help, too. We could all work on this." A slow smile lit up her face. "What did you have in mind?"

Yeah, he hadn't got that far yet, but now that she was all in, he had to come up with something.

"I'm not sure yet," he told her honestly. "Why don't I come over and we can discuss it more? I'm off until tomorrow."

When she remained silent, he knew she was battling that same demon as moments ago. Someone had hurt her, someone had scared her, and he damn well wanted to know who. Another invisible tug pulled him toward her whether he liked it or not…whether he was ready or not.

He didn't want to push her, didn't want to scare her, but at the same time, he needed to let her know he wasn't going anywhere and he wasn't treating her with kid gloves. She was the type of woman who needed to find her courage again, and he'd damn well be the man to help her.

"I can bring pizza so you don't have to worry about dinner," he told her. "Willow seems like a kid who would love pizza."

"As if she didn't think you were cool enough already after the invitation back to the station," she told him with a slight grin. "I get off work at four and I need to pick her up from the sitter, so why don't you come over about four-thirty?"

Feeling as if he'd truly accomplished something, Drake came to his feet. "Sounds good. Any special requests for toppings?"

Marly rose as well and shook her head. "I'll eat anything, and if Willow doesn't like it, she'll just pick it off. But, if you want to gain extra points, she really loves banana peppers."

"I'm all about scoring extra points."

When Drake stepped closer, Marly's eyes widened as her head tilted up so she could look him in the face. That underlying vulnerability kept eating at him. He had no clue what she'd been through, it was none of his business, but he had a feeling whatever war she was battling, she wasn't finished yet.

Everything in him wanted to get to know her more. He knew he needed to move on, knew Andrea would want him to find happiness. And Marly was the first woman since Andrea who had sparked this much emotion inside him, so he couldn't ignore it.

What if he wasn't ready? What if he tried to get closer to a woman and he couldn't follow through?

Damn it, he couldn't live in fear. He wouldn't live in fear. Going slow with Marly, working on gaining her trust, was the best step to take.

He focused on those dark eyes as they looked back up at him. "Can I ask you something?"

Her gaze held his as she nodded.

"Do I scare you?"

"A little," she murmured. "It's nothing you did. It's just…"

Unable to help himself, he rested his hand on her shoulder, keeping his touch light when she started to tense. "I don't want you uncomfortable around me, Marly."

"There's a lot of stuff I'm working through," she told him. "Sometimes it hits me harder than others."

Drake knew all too well about painful memories creeping up at random times, cutting you off at the knees when you least expected it. He'd be lying if he said he was over Andrea's death, but he'd at least learned to conquer those demons when they threatened him. He was stronger than a year ago, and he wanted to help Marly build on her strength.

"I'm a pretty good listener," he said, giving her shoulder a slight squeeze, pleased when she didn't pull away.

"I'm sure you are, but I…" She shook her head and sighed.

Drake stepped closer, fully aware that he was teetering on a thin line where her emotions were concerned. But that damn pull between them crackled in the air, making him want to hold her, to offer some comfort.

His other hand came up to cup her other shoulder as he eased forward. "Sometimes it only looks as though there's no hope," he told her. "Trust me."

Damp eyes came up to meet his, and the punch to the gut was swift and unexpected.

"My trust was shattered," she whispered, keeping her wet eyes locked on his. "I can't face this… I can't get close to anyone, if that's what you were thinking."

Shocked that she'd called him out, Drake slid his hands from her shoulders and let them drop.

"I wasn't looking for anything more than friendship, Marly. I want to help Jeremy and I'd like to be your friend." He met her gaze, ripped apart at the sight of those big brown eyes brimming with unshed tears. "Before you can learn to trust others again, you need to trust your heart. What's it saying about me?"

With that loaded question, he walked from the lounge. His own heart beat fast in his chest as he made his way out to the parking lot and to his truck. Once he settled in behind the wheel, he took a deep breath, closed his eyes and leaned his head back.

When he'd told her to trust her heart, he'd been talking to himself more than anything…but now he realized it was solid advice.

Drake knew Marly was a strong woman, but someone had pushed that strength aside and had taken advantage of her. He intended to honor his promise of friendship and not press for more. Marly was special, she was worth being patient for, and Drake couldn't wait to see what happened next.

Chapter Four

What had she been thinking, agreeing to this plan? Hadn't she already mentally scolded herself for getting too close to Chief St. John? She should be steering clear of the man, yet when he'd looked at her with those mesmerizing eyes and offered compassion and support, she couldn't deny him anything.

Which was why she was now straightening her home like a maniac, picking up random toys and stray shoes while Willow ran the vacuum. Thankfully the rental home was small, so the cleanup wasn't too hard—it was more the pressure of having Drake in her home that had her nerves on edge.

The vacuum shut off and Willow wheeled it back through the hall and under the steps where the cleaning supplies were kept.

"I better get extra pizza for all that sweeping," Willow mumbled as she came back through the house.

Putting away the last of the clean dishes, Marly smiled. "I'll make sure you get extra. And maybe even dessert for all your help."

Willow's smile widened. "Like brownie delights?"

Marly shrugged. "I'm not sure if we'll make brownie delights or not, but I'm sure we can come up with something."

Climbing onto a wooden bar stool at the small center island in the kitchen, Willow rested her head in her hands. "What's the chief coming over for?"

"We're going to try to figure out a way to help Jeremy's family," Marly explained, hanging her plaid kitchen towel over the oven handle. "Medical bills can be expensive, and Jeremy will need a lot of extra special care to make sure he's all better."

"We've been making him get-well cards in class. Jeremy likes trucks, so I drew him a big red truck on my card."

Marly reached across the island and smoothed stray strands from Willow's forehead. This morning her blond mass had been tamed into two braids, but now, well, apparently recess had gotten the better of the hairdo.

A tap on the front door jerked Marly upright. Heart pounding heavily, she knew the second Drake entered her home, she'd start getting all fluttery, and the last thing she needed was her daughter picking up on any vibes. Not that a five-year-old was very in tune with adults' feelings, but Marly couldn't take the chance.

Kevin didn't need more leverage in his attempt to get full custody.

This was just an evening of acquaintances getting together to collaborate on how to make a family's life a little easier. Any feelings toward Drake that wanted to take root would have to be removed before they could grow. Any type of relationship at this point, especially with a man, was not a smart move.

When her doorbell rang again, Marly pulled herself from her thoughts. To assume Drake had feelings on his end was very presumptuous of her. Yes, he'd seemed interested, but did that mean he was going to act on anything? She was borrowing trouble when she had too much on her plate to keep her mind occupied already.

"I'll get it, Mama." Willow ran by her and headed to the front room. "Can I let in the chief?"

"Yes, and thank you for asking before letting someone in the house."

Marly smoothed a hand over her ponytail, then made sure her side bangs were covering the scar. Even though her hair was still in the same shape it had been in at work, she'd at least changed from her scrubs and put on her ever-dressy yoga capris and V-neck T-shirt. Hey, she wasn't inviting him over for anything romantic, and this was the real her. Nothing fancy, no jewelry, no makeup, plain-Jane hair.

The days of always worrying about her appearance had long since passed. And to be honest, she loved the Marly she was rediscovering.

"Wow, pizza?" Willow jumped up and down. "You're the coolest, Mr. Chief."

Marly stepped into the front room and smiled. The sight of Drake in a gray T-shirt pulled taut across his shoulders and faded jeans did nothing to help her motivational speech she'd just given herself about not having time to think of him as anything other than a friend.

How could she ignore such a visually tempting man? And the fact that he was concerned about a helpless little boy only made her heart clench more. Oh, and the way he'd handled a parking lot full of kindergarteners… Yeah, the man was fast becoming more and more appealing.

"How about you call me Drake?" he suggested to Willow.

Drake's lopsided grin and the way he ruffled her daughter's hair had Marly crossing her arms over her chest. "Thanks for bringing the pizza."

He nodded his greeting and held the pizza box in one hand while closing the door behind him with the other. "I hope you guys like fish eggs on it."

"Fish…eggs?" Willow asked, throwing a worried look to her mother, then shrugged. "I guess I'll try it."

"I'm teasing," Drake said with a laugh that showcased his wide smile and white teeth.

Darn him. Was there nothing about the man that wasn't perfect? Joking with her child and not acting as though Willow was in the way like…

No, she wasn't pulling Kevin into this evening. He occupied enough of her waking hours between the texts, voice mails and her mind working overtime on when he would start looking for them.

Right now, she just wanted a few hours of peace,

away from her monster ex and away from her own worried thoughts.

Marly shot a smile to Drake and pointed to Willow. "This kid would try anything. She's a tough one to scare."

Drake's bold eyes went back to Willow, his brows rose. "Really? A brave girl? I like that. You sound more like a firefighter than a kindergartener."

Willow beamed. "When can I take a ride on your fire truck?"

"Willow," Marly scolded. "I'm sorry. She was really impressed the other day at the field trip. She's hardly talked about anything else."

Drake moved through the living room and handed the pizza box to Marly. "I don't mind at all, actually. What kind of chief would I be if I didn't keep my promise to let such a brave girl take a ride on the truck? You may become a firefighter one day and you'll need the experience."

"Me?" Willow squeaked, jumping up and down. "A firefighter? That would be awesome!"

The man had been in the house for all of two minutes and had already captivated both women in the room, for totally different reasons.

"Come on in and eat," Marly suggested as she turned and headed toward the back of the house. "You two can discuss firefighter training over fish eggs."

Before long, paper plates were filled with chips and pizza. Marly pulled out two cans of soda and a bottle of water. They gathered around the small kitchen table and Marly resisted the urge to make everything perfect.

The man sitting across from her was nothing like the man she'd left. Nothing.

Marly highly doubted Drake cared if he ate off paper plates or fine china. He didn't seem the type to need a linen napkin over a paper towel. She refused to bow down to a man's every wish again. She would make Willow happy first, herself second, and if a man came along and could put up with being third on her list of priorities, then there was a slight chance that she would consider him in her life.

To be honest, she doubted the yearning to want another man would come for a long, long time. Yes, she found Drake attractive and had those tingles in her belly when he was around, but she wasn't ready for anything beyond that. How could she be? She was still recovering emotionally and physically from her last relationship.

"Everything okay?" Drake asked, pausing as he reached for another piece of pizza. "You wandered off for a bit."

Marly took a sip of her soda and nodded, forcing herself to be in the moment. "Just thinking. So what have you thought of for a fund-raiser?"

He slid the piece onto his plate and met her gaze. Those blue eyes could mesmerize a nun. She shoved a chip into her mouth to try to keep her mind on the task and not the man. Easier said than done when the man in question was as potent as Drake St. John.

"We need something where the town comes together," he told her, oblivious to the turmoil inside her. "The more people who pitch in, the more support Shawn and Amy will have. This isn't just about monetary needs, they need moral support and people to lean on."

Rocked by his selfless declaration, Marly nodded in agreement. "You're absolutely right. They will need assistance from all angles."

"How about a bake sale?" Willow chimed in around a mouthful of pizza. "The school had one the other day to raise money for books for the library."

"Honey—"

"Willow." Drake cut off Marly, giving her a wink. "I think a bake sale is a wonderful idea. Your mother and I were thinking of something really big for the entire town, but those people would love some treats, I'm sure."

Drake took a bite of pizza, took a full gulp of his soda before continuing, "What about something that incorporates several aspects of raising money? Maybe a dunking booth or three-legged races?"

Marly's mind started working overtime. Now, this was an aspect from her old life she was actually glad to have instilled in her. Planning, organizing a way to raise funds.

"Like a festival?" Marly asked. "That's great, Drake."

"A festival?" Willow smacked her hands on the table and jumped from her chair. "Can we have a Ferris wheel like the one we rode on a few weeks ago, Mama?"

Marly laughed. "Oh, honey. It would be quite expensive to bring in a Ferris wheel. The whole point of this would be to make money, so probably nothing like that."

As the pizza was devoured, Drake and Marly volleyed back and forth various ideas. Some were good, some not so good.

"I'll get you a pen and paper, Mama."

When Willow ran out of the room, Marly shook her head and started gathering the paper plates. "That child has more energy than I can keep up with at times."

Drake came to his feet and folded the chip bags. "Where do these go?"

"Oh, just leave them. I'll get everything." Marly tried to busy herself so she didn't have to look in his eyes, didn't have to talk about anything personal. "What do I owe you for the pizza?"

Drake rested his hands on his narrow hips and shook his head. "Absolutely nothing."

"I need to pay at least half," Marly told him, reaching for her purse on the counter.

He laid his hand over hers. She hadn't even seen him move toward her, but when she looked up and her eyes met his, she tensed. His hands were so big, totally blanketing her own. An image flashed in her mind of other large hands on her, hurting her. She forced herself not to completely seize up beneath his delicate touch.

Between that intense stare and the heat from his hand, Marly swallowed hard, trying to reinforce that pep talk she'd had with herself earlier.

Feeling anything toward Drake was a bad, bad idea.

"You owe nothing," he told her, keeping his eyes locked onto hers. "Maybe you can buy next time."

Holding her breath and praying her voice came out strong, Marly asked, "Will there be a next time?"

Before he could respond, Willow burst back into the

room. "I got paper and a pen," she yelled. "Now, spell everything slow for me and I'll make notes."

Drake's hand slid away from Marly's as she continued to stare at him. Willow was oblivious to the tension that had settled between them, but it left Marly… confused, intrigued…fascinated.

What was Drake thinking? Flirting was one thing, but the way he looked at her, as if he was attracted and ready to act on it… How could she cope with a man who wanted anything from her? She truly had nothing left in her to give. But, she vowed, she would never be this low again. She would never allow another man to break her.

Marly turned toward her daughter and concentrated on helping Willow write down some simple notes for the festival. If they were going full speed ahead with this plan, Marly feared there would most definitely be a next time she and Drake got together.

And Willow couldn't always pose as the chaperone.

What the hell had he been thinking?

Drake picked up another nail, positioned it against the two-by-four and hammered it home with more force than necessary.

"Whoa. Who are you pissed at?"

Drake glanced over his shoulder to see Eli standing in the doorway to the addition Drake was adding onto the back of his house.

"Nobody," he mumbled.

That wasn't true. He was beyond mad with himself for allowing his hormones to control his actions. He knew Marly was skittish, yet he'd still flirted, hoping to see a reaction. Her deer-in-the-headlights look when he'd placed his hand over hers was all he'd needed to know that she remained very cautious and scared.

"You're mad," Eli retorted, stepping into the room. He ran his hand along the already placed beams and glanced over the work. "Is it the mayor again?"

Drake grunted, driving in another nail. "It's never *not* the mayor."

"Something more than usual?" Eli asked.

Carefully dropping his hammer to the subfloor, Drake shook his head. "Nothing I can't handle. What are you doing here? Don't you have a clinic to run, wife to love on or baby to feed?"

Eli's smile widened. As the oldest brother, Dr. Eli St. John had been busy lately with taking over their father's clinic, marrying his high school sweetheart and becoming a father.

Nora and Eli had drifted apart when Eli had gone into the military. Nora had married Eli's best friend, but when Nora's husband was killed in action, she had discovered she was pregnant. Now that she and Eli had found their way back to each other, Drake had never seen his brother so happy.

"Actually Nora took the baby and went to visit Mom and Dad. I saw your truck when we passed by and since I hadn't seen you in a week, I told her I'd check up on you and be right back." Eli crossed his arms over his chest and leaned against a stud. "Care to tell me what's wrong?"

"Everything, actually." Walking over to the sawhorses with plywood on top for a makeshift worktable, Drake twisted off the cap of his water and downed half the bottle. "Jeremy is still recovering from that damn fire, the mayor is the bane of my existence and now Marly is consuming my thoughts."

"Marly?" Eli's brows raised. "Who's Marly?"

The St. John boys were known for being jokesters and hellions, but Drake was thankful for once that his brother didn't razz him about saying another woman's name.

"She's the nurse caring for Jeremy."

Eli continued to stare, as if weighing his words before they came out. "This is the first time you've mentioned any woman since Andrea."

Raking a hand over his head, Drake sighed and downed the last half of his water before tossing the bottle into the trash in the corner.

"I've been on a few dates," Drake commented. "Nothing has progressed beyond date one with anybody, so I never mentioned them."

"Is this nurse a serious thing?" Eli asked.

With a laugh, Drake shook his head. "She's skittish, she's a single mom to an adorable little girl and she's running from something. But as far as she and I go, we're nothing. She consumes my thoughts and I don't know if that's the protector in me wanting to know more and help her or if I'm actually attracted on a level I didn't think existed anymore."

"Wow, man." Eli sighed and walked around the spacious room that was now ready for the drywall. "I don't even know what to say. I mean, this is great that you may be finally moving on. You haven't even gone on a date with the woman and you're already torn up. It may not be serious to her, but it's turning into something for you."

"It's crazy. I barely know her, but everything in me wants to." Drake crossed his arms over his chest, twisting his neck from side to side to work out some kinks.

Holding his arms out, Eli shrugged. "Hey, I'm not judging the time frame. Just because it took me and Nora years to get it right doesn't mean you can't feel something for Marly this soon. You know Andrea would want you happy, would want you to move on."

Drake knew this in his head, but saying he could move on and actually doing it were two different things. He was much stronger than he was even a year ago thanks to his family and his therapist.

Yeah, he wasn't afraid to admit he'd had to see a shrink after Andrea passed. What man wouldn't have to deal with those demons? He'd loved Andrea with all of his heart and he'd blamed himself for so long for being unable to save her. But in the end, he knew there was nothing he or the first responders on the scene could've done.

The survivor's guilt would always be a nugget embedded deep in his heart, his mind, but Eli was right. Moving on was the only way he would conquer that nightmare. And Marly may just be the woman to help him do that…if he could get her to open up and relax around him.

"What makes you think this woman is running from

something?" Eli asked, turning back to face Drake. "Do you think it's something illegal?"

"No, nothing like that." Drake swiped his arm across his forehead to wipe away the sweat. "She's scared."

"Of you?"

His mind flashed to the second in the nurses' lounge when she'd gone pale after he'd gripped her shoulders, then again when he'd slid his hand over hers at her house.

"No, but I'm laying money some jerk has damaged her."

"So she's not from here," Eli deduced. "Is she divorced?"

Shrugging, Drake realized he didn't know too much about her personal life. He also figured Marly wasn't the type of woman who would give such information up easily, either.

"I assume so, but I'm not sure. She has a little girl."

Eli smiled. "Really, at this point, all you know is she's afraid of something, you're attracted to her and she has a kid? Yeah, sounds like your protective instincts are all over this."

Drake sank down on the bucket of plaster and rested his elbows on his knees. "I'm screwed, Eli. I've put myself in a position where I'll be seeing her fairly often, and each time I'm around her, I want to find more reasons to stick around. Maybe if she gets more used to me she'll feel safe, feel as if she can let her guard down a little."

"Do I need to call Cameron?" Eli asked, referring to

their other brother. "I mean, if we're having a Dr. Phil moment, I think it's only fair we include him."

Drake laughed. "I should've known your compassion would only last a minute before turning into sarcasm."

Eli slapped Drake on the back and settled down on the wood subfloor. "You wouldn't have me any other way."

Drake eyed his brother on the floor and laughed harder. "I'm not helping you up, old man."

Eli flipped Drake the finger. "So why the hell are you and Marly spending so much time together?"

Drake went into the details about the town festival, his harebrained idea to pull Marly in on the project and the fact that he'd found himself lingering at her house the other night.

What Drake didn't go into details about was how he'd felt the entire time he had to endure looking at her in those snug pants and T-shirt and how her bouncy ponytail had made her seem younger than he figured she was. Nor did he go into the whole saga of how fast she'd turned him inside out and twisted his insides all over the place with nerves and wants and needs.

How could he have slid down this slippery slope so fast?

At least his emotions weren't one-sided. He'd seen that pulse at the base of her neck quicken, the widening of her big brown eyes and the way she held her breath when he'd laid his hand over hers. She may have had a layer of fear masking her desire, but the passion was there nonetheless.

Chapter Five

Marly rested her hands on the edge of the counter at the nurses' station and sighed. Jeremy was going to be transported to Nashville Children's Hospital at the end of the week.

Now more than ever Shawn and Amy would need support. The fund-raiser couldn't come soon enough.

"Hey."

Marly lifted her head and blinked back tears that threatened to fall. "Drake," she greeted, trying to paste on a convincing smile.

His eyes studied her, seemed to see beyond the exterior as if he could zero in on her hurts. "Is it Jeremy? Did he take a turn for the worse?"

Marly shook her head. "No, no. He's still on the road to recovery. I just…" She trailed off and sighed as she turned to grab her purse from the desk chair. She'd laid it there moments ago and had wanted to look over one last set of patient's vitals before leaving. "I'm headed out, actually. Sorry if I worried you for no reason."

"If you're upset, I'm still worried, and there's definitely a reason."

Warmth spread through her. Beyond his physical appeal, Drake St. John truly had a hero's heart. And from the few encounters she'd had with him, she already knew he was a natural-born protector.

What did he see when he looked at her, though? Did he see the vulnerability she'd tried so hard to hide? Did he just see a single mom afraid to face each new day and the monsters that could creep up at any time and steal her happiness?

"Can you wait just a minute?" he asked. "I want to pop in to see Jeremy and then I'll walk you out. We can talk."

As much as she wanted to leave on her own, she figured if they were going to talk about the festival, this would be as good a time as any. If he wanted to talk about anything else, well, this would be the best place.

"I can wait," she told him.

She didn't wait long, but when Drake stepped from Jeremy's room, the man had that sad, lost look about him again. Something haunted him, as well.

Weren't they just a pair?

Those bright blue eyes met hers as he strode across the hall. "Ready?" he asked.

Marly nodded and waited until they exited the pediatric unit before she spoke up. "You know, if it bothers you to see Jeremy, maybe you should stop coming by every day."

Drake glanced down at her but kept walking toward the main entrance. "It doesn't upset me to see him. It makes me angry and frustrated. I've done all but tap-dance on the mayor's desk to get his attention that we need to hire the rest of my men back on the department, but he's a jerk and that's a story for another time."

The passion in his tone confirmed the man was a hero doing a hero's job and not just acting the part of a caring citizen. Drake St. John wasn't so complex. She had a feeling what you saw was what you got with him. Unlike her ex, who delighted in putting on a show for the public and turning into a monster behind closed doors.

As they exited the hospital, the late-afternoon sun greeted them, and Marly pulled her sunglasses from her purse. Before she could put them on, her cell rang. Juggling her purse on her forearm, her glasses in one hand, Marly pulled out her phone.

"One second," she told Drake as she answered without looking at the number.

"Hello."

"You've not returned my calls."

Chills crept over Marly despite the heat from the sun. "I've been busy working."

Her eyes darted to Drake, who was studying her. This was the very last thing she needed. Being humili-ated in private was bad enough; she refused to bring her dirty world out in the open.

"Too busy to talk to your husband?" he scolded.

Marly turned her back on Drake. "This is not a good time."

"You'll make time for me," he ordered. "We need to talk in person. I've allowed this charade to go on long enough. I am hitting the campaign trail hard shortly and my family needs to be with me."

"We're divorced," she whispered. "We're not a family."

"We are a family, and we will present ourselves as such. I've kept this divorce from the media, but you will stand by my side during these next few months."

Like hell she would. "I'm hanging up, Kevin."

Months ago she wouldn't have cut him off and disconnected the call, but she wasn't afraid of his wrath now. No, right now she feared that he'd use his power to take Willow away. Not that he was interested in a tomboy with pigtails. He wanted a refined family, a family that would make his image spotless and win over the voters. But he would try to use Willow as a pawn, and that was something Marly refused to allow. It was only a matter of time before he'd had enough, when he realized she wasn't coming back. Then he would exhaust all resources to find her and their daughter. Marly had to be ready and on guard.

After dropping her phone into her purse and sliding on her glasses, Marly took a deep breath and turned back to Drake, who had his dark brows drawn.

"Everything okay?" he asked, taking his aviator shades from his pocket and sliding them on to cover his vibrant eyes.

"Fine," she lied.

The wind started moving her hair about and she quickly reached for her side bangs, but they'd already flopped the other way. Marly jerked them back over and turned her head, hoping he wouldn't say anything, hoping he hadn't seen the puckered, jagged scar.

"Jeremy is actually getting moved at the end of the week," she told him, steering the conversation away from anything remotely regarding the phone call or the scar she figured he'd seen. "Were you able to talk with the mayor about having the festival in the park?"

Drake groaned and started heading toward the parking lot. "The mayor and I aren't exactly on great terms right now, so I sent someone else."

"Who did you send?" Marly asked, falling into step beside him.

"My brother, Cameron. He's the police chief, so I figured the chances of us getting the park for the day we want would be greater coming from the man who would provide some security."

Keys clutched in her hand, Marly gestured toward her SUV. "This is me. So you're the fire chief, your brother is the police chief. Anybody else in your family ruling this town?"

With a chuckle, Drake opened her driver's door after she clicked the button to unlock it. "No, but we do have another brother, Eli. He's a doctor and actually took over my father's practice just a few months ago."

Marly's head was spinning. Three powerful men, all pretty much holding vital roles in the town. Were his brothers handsome and potent like Drake? Marly couldn't even imagine. Surely all the single ladies in town were beating down the doors of the St. John brothers.

"So what did your messenger brother say?" Marly asked, tossing her purse onto the passenger seat and crossing her arms to face Drake.

"The mayor was completely on board. Of course, his reelection campaign is coming up, so anything to look good for the community."

Marly quirked a brow. "I'm assuming he feels just as warm and fuzzy toward you."

Drake's smile spread across his handsome face. "We're pretty much on the same page of warm and fuzzy feelings."

"So the date and the place are all set?"

Marly really tried to focus on the project, but Drake's broad shoulders and towering height blocked the sun and gave her ample opportunity to appreciate what great shape he was in. The man did physical labor, earning his muscles the old-fashioned way as opposed to in an air-conditioned gym like her vain, pampered ex. The list of differences between the two men was adding up quickly. Odd how at first she'd considered the two so similar simply because of their size and powerful positions. Drake and Kevin were at opposite ends of the male spectrum.

"The guys at the department are all on board, too," he went on. "One guy is already drafting up some flyers and another guy was calling some area businesses to see if they'd donate some prizes for an auction."

Marly smiled. "You're really taking control of this."

Shrugging, he added, "I have to."

She wasn't sure if he was blaming himself for Jeremy's accident, but she knew guilt and sorrow when she saw it.

"None of this is your fault." She reached out, placed a hand on his biceps. The thick muscle twitched beneath her palm. "Jeremy will be okay."

"I know this isn't my fault. This accident falls on the mayor's shoulders, since he cut funding and took three good men from my department." Drake glanced down at his feet, shaking his head. "I just hate that Jeremy will lose a good chunk of his school year and he'll be emotionally scarred from the nightmares of living through a fire, and then with all these upcoming surgeries…"

Marly squeezed his arm, waiting until he looked back up at her. "He's a strong boy," she told him. "He's young and healthy. He'll recover faster than you or I would in this situation. Trust me when I say you're a hero to him."

"I was doing my job, that's all." Drake reached up, took her hand from his arm and held it between his own strong, warm hands. "You're still new to town, so you should know, hero material is the last thing that comes to mind when people here think of me. My teen years set a precedent that I can't seem to shake. I'm human. I make mistakes."

He dropped her hand abruptly, leaving a shiver that coursed through her. What else was he referring to? He realized Jeremy's accident was out of his control, but there was something else that bothered him. He'd alluded to the fact that the residents of Stonerock knew, but what? What demons chased him?

"Sorry," he muttered. "I just...hate that label. I mean, I love my job and I'm good at it. I don't need to be elevated to a status beyond that."

Only a true hero would be so humble and sincere. Those defensive walls around Marly's heart continued to crumble.

"I'll talk to the art teacher at the school and see about maybe having a painting station set up or even face painting. Even if we just charged a buck, that would really start to add up."

Drake nodded. "Perfect. Cameron even mentioned having some guys from the department doing fingerprinting of the kids to keep on file for safety."

"That's a great idea. Not that any parent wants to think of their child missing, but better to be safe, and the kids would love it."

Marly hugged her arms tighter around her waist. Her daughter may not be taken by a stranger, but there was a very good possibility she'd be taken by a justice system that could be bought for the right price. Just the idea sickened her.

"You okay?" Drake asked, taking a step closer.

Her back was still against the open door of her SUV, and she hated how her body responded to his nearness. The overpowering man should frighten her, but other than his physical appearance, there was nothing intimidating about Drake St. John. The fire chief was all heart from what she could see. He truly cared and wasn't afraid to show it. And that made him infinitely sexier.

Which made her wish she were at a different point

in her life right now where she wasn't afraid to open up and let someone in. But she simply wasn't ready.

"It's just been a long day," she told him.

"Listen, I realize we don't know each other that well, but I told you before I'm a good listener and I can be a good friend."

Oh, how she wished she could trust him. She honestly had no clue how she'd fight this battle on her own, but dare she confide in Drake, who threatened her from so many angles?

The biggest threat was the feeling that slithered through her whenever she was around him. More than anything she wanted to take him up on that friendship proposal, and perhaps she could, but there were still things she couldn't discuss with him.

Would he think her a terrible mother for taking Willow away from her father? Would he think she should've stayed married for the sake of the child?

"I'm just having an issue with my ex," she told him honestly. "Nothing I can't handle."

"That who called you earlier?" he asked, straightening his shoulders. "Is he causing problems?"

Instantly he came to her defense, and she so wanted to share her fears, her worries. He had no idea what she'd done, what her ex had done...yet he was immediately on her side.

Still, Marly had to be cautious and keep her secrets close to her heart, because she couldn't drag Drake into her world, leaving him vulnerable to Kevin's wrath, because Kevin could have Drake off the fire department in the proverbial blink of an eye. Kevin wouldn't think twice about throwing his power around to prove that he could hurt anyone in Marly's life just because he wanted to.

"No more problems than usual." She took a deep breath, pleased that she'd shared a very minor part of herself with her new friend. "I need to get home to Willow. She's expecting dinner, and she's suddenly asking about fish eggs."

A corner of Drake's mouth tipped up. "Shall I bring a specialty pizza?"

Marly laughed and realized that she'd done more of that with Drake in just the short time she'd known him than in the past several months.

"No," she replied. "I'm actually going to cook a real meal, sans fish eggs."

Part of her wanted to invite him over, but the logical side of her brain told her she'd better steer clear of temptation.

And as much as she hated to admit it, Drake St. John was becoming more and more tempting by the minute. "Can I call you later?" he asked.

Surprised, Marly jerked back. "Um…"

"To discuss the festival," he added.

"Oh, yes. I put Willow to bed at eight on school nights, so if you want to call after that I'll be free to talk."

Her bangs started to drift in the breeze again, and before she could reach up to control them, Drake's hand came up, smoothed them down and leaned in within a breath of her as he removed his sunglasses with the other hand.

"You don't have to hide your scars from me," he whispered. "I carry my own, they're just on the inside."

His eyes landed on hers and Marly could swear he could see hers through her sunglasses. Could he hear her heart pounding? Could he feel the electrifying tension that crackled between them?

"I have a feeling we'll be better friends than either of us first thought." Drake slid his glasses back on and turned to walk away. "I'll call you later," he called over his shoulder.

Marly stood staring after him until he disappeared amongst the sea of cars in the parking lot.

When she sank onto the driver's seat, she quickly started the vehicle to get some much-needed AC flowing. Drake had not asked her about her scar; he hadn't stared at it like it was the ugliest thing he'd ever seen.

No, he'd been perceptive enough to know she wanted her hair to hide the ugliness. What he didn't know was that she wanted to hide the ugliness of the situation behind the scar, but there was no hiding or blanketing the truth of her past.

She'd been the abused wife of a powerful politician, and she was about to face down the enemy. There was no way in hell she'd ever return, let alone with their impressionable daughter. She'd fight the devil himself if she had to.

Marly feared she just may have to lean on someone for support. And, so far, the only contender in the "someone" category was the mesmerizing, somewhat vulnerable, incredibly sexy fire chief.

Chapter Six

"So tell me about this woman."

Drake groaned at his sister-in-law's abrupt statement and immediately eyed his brother across the dining room table. If the table weren't so wide, Drake would've given Eli a swift kick to the shins for opening his big mouth.

"What woman?" his mother asked, her fork clanging against her plate.

Drake narrowed his gaze at his brother, who merely raised his brows and shrugged. Eli was so going to get it after family dinner.

Drake turned his attention to Nora, who merely stared at him as if she had nothing else to do but wait for his response. If he didn't love her so much, he'd give her the same death glare he'd just awarded Eli.

"Don't get too excited," he started, wiping his mouth with his napkin and easing back in the dining room chair. "I met a nurse at the hospital who is taking care of Jeremy, the little boy from the fire two weeks ago. We're working together on a fund-raiser and festival to raise money to help Shawn and Amy with the expenses."

Mac St. John rested his arms on either side of his now-empty plate. "That poor boy. How's he doing?"

Mac was the retired town doctor, but only because his own doctor recommended he slow down since having quadruple bypass just a few months ago.

"He's getting better every day," Drake replied, thankful the topic had veered off course. "He's being transported to Children's in Nashville tomorrow."

"So sad," his mother said, shaking her head. "A mother's worst nightmare is to have her child hurt or injured."

Nora nodded in agreement. "I don't know what I'll do when Amber gets hurt for the first time."

Drake smiled. His little niece was taking a nap in the other room, but Drake knew Nora and Eli were awesome parents and would be able to handle future challenges. "What about this nurse?" Nora asked, resting her elbow on the table, her chin on her palm. "Is she married?"

Drake shrugged. "We're only planning a fund-raiser, not planning a wedding shower."

He hated how irritated this topic made him. He hated that he'd told his brother something in private and now his entire family was staring at him, minus Cameron, who was away working on some hush-hush big case.

Drake was talking with a woman. So what? Just because he hadn't really associated with a woman since Andrea had passed away didn't mean anything. Drake took a drink of his sweet tea and avoided the eyes around the table staring at him. Just because his attraction for Marly had grown each time he'd been with her didn't mean he would or even could act on them. As slowly as he was moving with her, the ball was in her court.

She was scarred, visibly so, and it made him want to tear apart the man who'd laid a hand on her. No wonder she was so skittish, so cautious. If Drake were a betting man, he'd say it was her ex who had abused her.

And that alone made Drake want to be closer to her, to protect her.

Suddenly he felt sick. Had Willow been a victim, as well? Any man that laid a hand on a woman or child wasn't a man at all, but a monster. Even if Willow hadn't been a victim, she could have witnessed her mother's abuse. There was no excuse for a woman or child to go through such evil.

If Drake found out who had harmed Marly, there wouldn't be a corner of this world the man could hide.

"You're looking pretty angry there, bro."

Eli's comment jerked Drake back to reality. "Maybe that's because I told you something that was private."

"Don't blame Eli," Nora said, coming to her feet and picking up her plate. "He tells me everything. I was the one who was curious."

"I'll have to remember to confide in Cameron next

time," Drake replied with a grin. "He'd only tell his best friend, Megan, but he's even too busy to see her lately."

"I'm still worried about him," their mother said. "I know he's busy being the police chief, but he's more out of touch than usual, and he's so closed off when I do see him."

Drake had noticed and he knew Eli had, as well. In fact, they'd discussed their mother's worries with Cameron several weeks ago, but the man was deep into some operation he couldn't discuss. Drake just prayed that by the time Cameron wrapped up this case he wasn't burned out on the job.

The only person Cameron seemed to keep in close contact with lately was Megan. Cam never kept anything from her. Hopefully whatever he was battling, he was at least confiding in Megan.

"He'll be fine," Drake assured his mom as he stood, too, and started gathering plates. "Dinner was great, as always. I'm going to carry these in, and then I need to get going. I'm covering for a guy tonight for a couple hours."

"Any luck with the mayor?" his father asked.

Drake's grip on the plates tightened at just the mention of the pudgy man who sat on his butt behind a desk all day. "About as much luck as getting money to fall from the sky. He's a useless politician and is only in the position for the name and recognition. Pathetic. I only hope voters see that come election time."

"I'm sure they will," Eli chimed in. "This town is too small and he's so lazy. His lack of effort hasn't gone unnoticed."

After Drake had stacked most of the dishes in the dishwasher, he gave his mother and sister-in-law a kiss on the cheek, said farewell to his dad, who was looking much better since his surgery, and eyed Eli across the room. With a nod, he silently bid his goodbye. He was still a bit ticked that Eli would tell Nora about Marly, but he supposed if Andrea were still alive, they'd be married and Drake would tell her everything.

But she wasn't alive.

Drake slid behind the wheel of his oversize truck and headed toward the department. Soon he'd have to touch base with Cameron about the festival anyway. Drake would just use that opportunity to discuss, once again, the worry their mother had. And Drake was starting to become concerned himself.

For now, he had his own issues to deal with, and figuring out what to do with his growing feelings for Marly was starting to take top priority.

Would she even let him in? Would she trust him enough to talk? Because Drake seriously wanted to know about those scars. There was no way around it. He wanted to know what had happened, wanted to know how he could make sure she was never victimized again.

But pressing Marly for details could cause further emotional damage. Drake knew an abused woman when he saw one, and his gut clenched at the thought of anyone's hands marring her perfect, delicate skin.

As he pulled into the station, he noticed two of his guys relaxing on the bench out front. This rarely happened, which meant the downtime was more than likely the calm before the storm, especially since it was a weekend night. Drunks were sure to be out, wrecks were bound to happen and the jaws of life were always at the ready.

Drake pulled into his assigned parking spot and killed the engine just as his phone vibrated in his pocket.

Sliding it out, he smiled at the display screen.

"Marly," he answered. "What's up?"

"Drake…um…hi. I thought I'd get your voice mail."

Intrigued at her hesitancy, Drake gripped the phone. "Is everything all right?"

Marly sighed, then hesitated. "I've been thinking about that friendship thing. I think I'd like to take you up on your offer."

Drake's heart started pumping faster, and a wide grin spread across his face. She was letting him in. He figured his olive branch would be dangling a bit longer, but he was glad she'd accepted it. He was also nervous about taking this next step with a woman who gave him the first set of attraction nerves since he'd met Andrea.

"I'm glad," he told her, finding that he was more excited than scared at letting someone into his own life. "But you sound a little, I don't know, sad. You sure you're okay?"

"Yeah, I just…"

"Marly." Worry settled in, and he wondered what she was truly battling. "Are you at home?"

"I am. I've just had a bad couple of days and I called you on impulse. I'm sorry."

No way was he letting her out of the conversation now that he'd gotten her this far. "Don't be sorry for calling me." He never wanted her to be sorry for anything where he was concerned. "Isn't that what friends are for?"

Marly's soft laughter filled the phone. "I suppose. Are you busy? I was wondering if you'd like to run over. Willow and I made some cookies."

Dropping his head against the back of the seat, Drake wished now more than ever the department had more manpower so he had the time off.

"I'm actually working."

"Oh, Drake. I'm sorry I bothered you. Why didn't you say so?"

"It's no bother, I just pulled into the lot. I'm covering for one of my guys for just a few hours, but why don't I run over after if it's not too late?"

"I'm sure you'll be tired, it's okay."

Her deflated tone was definitely not okay. She'd gone out on a limb—no way in hell would he turn her away. "I'll come over. I should only be here a few hours."

"Okay. I'll try not to eat all the cookies before you get here," she joked.

Drake didn't know what had her reaching out to him of her own accord, but he didn't care. If she had the courage to step out of her comfort zone, then so did he. And maybe this was what they both needed—a good friend to share things with, to possibly tackle those demons with.

The main problem, though, was that Drake was having thoughts about Marly that had nothing to do with friendship. He had no idea why this lady, why now, but he would follow her lead and figure out the rest later.

Chapter Seven

Marly was almost grateful that he hadn't shown. It was after nine and Willow had gone to bed an hour ago. After playing in her tree house all day, then baking cookies and watching a movie, Willow had fallen into Marly's bed with her cowgirl boots still on.

They'd had a really fun day, despite the fact Kevin had called again and threatened to show up at the door.

Marly learned quickly to return those threats, because anything that would tarnish his public appeal terrified him. All she had to do was threaten to have the local paper on standby and the man backed down…a little. But still, that was enough to give her the courage and the upper hand she'd lacked during their marriage.

She'd lived in fear too long, and she refused to do it

anymore. There was no way she'd raise her daughter to fear men or feel inferior.

A soft tap on the screen door jerked Marly from her thoughts. Instantly her heart pounded, and she prayed the visitor was Drake and not Kevin making good on his threat.

Padding barefoot to the front door, Marly glanced out the window to see Drake's big black truck in the driveway. A sliver of excitement and nervousness settled deep within her. She'd reached out to him after a moment of fear and panic, and now, well, she was glad she had. Being alone with a child was scary during the best of times. She needed a friend, and surprisingly, this powerful, strong man made her feel safe.

Marly flipped the lock and opened the door. "Hey," she said with a smile. "Come on in."

"I'm sorry. I just realized what time it is." Drake remained beneath the porch lights, making no move to enter. "I can come back tomorrow."

But her nerve might be gone tomorrow. "No, really, come on in."

She stepped back and allowed him to pass. And just as he did, she inhaled that masculine, woodsy scent that seemed to always envelop her when he was around.

"We got called out to an accident or I would've been here sooner," he explained.

Marly locked the door and turned to face him. "Don't apologize for doing your job. I hope it wasn't bad."

"Bad enough." Drake shook his head and sighed. "I believe I was promised some homemade cookies?"

Marly smiled, not pressing the wreck issue. She totally understood bad days at work. Unfortunately the bad days for a nurse and a firefighter usually meant someone died or was critically injured. No point in repeating the story and reliving the trauma.

"Why don't you have a seat," she told him, gesturing to the living area. "I'll bring you some."

A weary smile spread across his face. "You're going to spoil me."

Shrugging, Marly replied, "That's what friends are for, right?"

With a heart-stopping wink, Drake nodded. "Now you're getting it."

As he sank onto her secondhand sofa, Marly went into the kitchen and put several cookies on a plate and poured Drake a glass of milk. When she stepped back into the living room, she froze.

He had his head tipped back against her sofa, his large frame took up one entire cushion and those shoulders... Oh, my. The man was breathtaking, and she needed to remember that he'd offered friendship, which was the only thing she needed right now. But that didn't mean she couldn't take a visual sampling when the moment presented itself.

He lifted his head, caught her staring and lifted a brow. "You all right?"

Shaking off her thoughts—and her fears—Marly set the plate and glass on the coffee table. "I'm fine. Just not used to seeing a man on my couch, that's all."

She sat on the chair adjacent to him and tucked her legs up onto the seat beside her. Drake dug into the cookies and milk, and in no time they were gone.

"I take it they were good," she joked.

Smiling, Drake settled back onto the couch. "Home-made cookies are my weakness. My guys and I cook at the department, but it's just not the same. We can manage basic meals, but when we venture into the baking category, it's pretty bad."

"It's just following a recipe," she told him.

With a laugh, Drake shook his head. "Yeah, but the guys I work with would rather just throw stuff together without looking at directions. It never turns out edible."

He leaned forward and raked a hand over his head. "Like this one time, one of the guys wanted to make peanut-butter cookies. We were out of peanut butter so he used jelly."

Marly laughed. "Seriously?"

"You'd have to know Tyler. He can justify anything."

Marly listened to Drake's stories of his coworkers and found herself laughing more than she had in years. When she yawned, she slapped a hand over her mouth.

"Sorry." She forced back another yawn. "That's rude of me."

Drake glanced at his watch. "No, I'm sorry. I'm rambling on and on and you probably have to work tomorrow."

"Actually, I'm off."

Drake came to his feet and picked up his plate and glass. "I didn't mean to overstay."

"Don't be silly. I enjoyed talking with another adult who isn't a coworker." She reached for the dishes. "I can take those."

Maneuvering around her, Drake headed toward the

kitchen. "I can carry my own things to the sink. You've done enough for me."

Marly leaned against the door frame separating the kitchen and living area. She didn't mean to stare, but she'd never experienced a man picking up after himself. Then again, she'd never experienced a man like Drake St. John before.

When he turned back to her, the tension in the air crackled as his eyes landed on hers. Slowly, his long strides covered the ground between them. When he stood directly in front of her, Marly knew the fun atmosphere from the living room had vanished. They'd reached the point of the evening where it was time to say goodbye, which could turn awkward really fast... unless someone took charge. And she had a feeling that take-charge person was about to show his hand.

"I'm glad you called me," he stated, his tone low. "I had a good time."

"Me, too."

Heat radiated from his body. Marly noted navy flecks in his blue eyes and spotted a tiny scar she hadn't noticed before right on the edge of his eyebrow.

"I didn't give you a chance to say much." He rested a hand just beside her head on the wall. "Did you want to talk about anything particular?"

Marly shook her head. "Not really. I prefer laughing to dredging up my problems."

His fingertip came up, slid across her forehead, along the edge of her side bangs. "Problems that have something to do with this?"

Swallowing fear that was never too far away, Marly

nodded and resisted the urge to back away so he couldn't feel her imperfection. "Yes," she whispered.

His fingertip lingered on the side of her face. "And are these problems still a threat?"

Closing her eyes, Marly nodded. She wished they weren't, but she had to be realistic. She and Kevin shared a child and there was no way he would give up his family for good, not with the image he'd portrayed to the public.

"Marly." Drake tipped her chin up with his forefinger, taking his thumb and caressing the side of her jaw. "You know you don't have to live in fear, right? I can help."

Warming at the idea of just how simple Drake made the solution sound, Marly shook her head. "I wish you could. Honestly, I wish anybody could. But this is something I have to figure out on my own. I just need a friend, someone to get advice from. Nobody at work knows about my personal life and Willow is too young to know what all is going on. I don't want her afraid."

"No child should be afraid," he stated, his eyes leveling hers. "What can I do to help?"

Marly wanted to cry at his selfless gesture, his sincere worry. "You're helping more than you know. Just having someone I can talk to, someone who doesn't have a hidden agenda means so much to me."

Drake brought his free hand up to cup the side of her face. "I might have a slight agenda," he whispered as he closed the space between them. "If you want me to stop, you should say something."

Desire coursed through her as she remained silent and tipped her head up to meet his.

Drake's lips slid over hers, softly, gently. Marly fisted her hands at her sides, afraid if she reached for him, she may yearn for more than she was ready for.

Coaxing her mouth open, Drake angled his head the opposite way and slid one arm around her waist. One hand flattened against the small of her back and the other hand traveled around to the nape of her neck. He stepped closer to her, fitting her body perfectly against his.

That solid chest against hers felt so safe, so protective. Marly let herself feel, let herself get lost in the moment, in the man.

Drake nipped at her bottom lip a second before he eased back. Those dark eyes leveled hers.

"I've wanted to do that for two weeks," he murmured, resting his forehead against hers.

Between his declaration and those protective hands still molded to her, Marly trembled. "I have, too, but I've been afraid."

Drake shifted, easing back just enough to bring his hands up to frame her face. Those rough, calloused palms slid against her cheeks as he forced her gaze to remain on his.

"You won't be afraid as long as I'm here," he promised. "Tell me what you're up against. I can't help if I don't know."

Pulling away from his comforting touch, Marly shook her head. "I can't, Drake. I know you don't understand, but trust me when I tell you that it's best you don't get involved with my problems. Or me."

Crossing her arms over her chest, Marly waited for him to reply. Silence settled heavily between them, the soft ticking of the kitchen clock the only thing breaking the strained quiet.

Marly didn't miss the way his jaw was clenched, the way his hands fisted at his sides. That familiar thread of fear slid through her, and she moved back a couple steps.

"Don't." He shook his head, raked a hand through his hair and sighed before focusing back on her. "Don't look at me like that and don't step away from me."

"You're angry," she stated, lifting her chin. "I can't deal with that. I won't deal with it."

"I'm not angry at you, Marly." Drake threw his hands up, palms out. "These hands may have gotten into fights, and if you stick around long enough I'm sure you'll hear the tales of the St. John boys. But I've never, nor will I ever, use them in a harmful way toward a woman. Ever."

"We haven't known each other very long, but I believe you." Surprisingly, she did. "But I can't get beyond the fact I lived in fear for so long. I can't, Drake. I just can't let you in."

And that was something she hadn't anticipated. When she'd left Kevin, taking only her meager savings and Willow, Marly had never dreamed she'd find a man who made her want things, who made her passion come to the surface.

"I hate him," Drake said between clenched teeth.

"Whatever bastard put that look of fear in your eyes, I hate him."

Well, that made two of them, but she refused to give Drake any further details of who her ex was. Kevin could ruin Drake's career if he ever even thought Drake was coming around Marly.

Hugging her midsection, Marly glanced at her socked feet, then back up to Drake. "I'm sorry."

"What the hell for?"

"Leading you on. Kissing you."

With slow, easy strides, he closed the distance between them. "Baby, I'm not sorry at all. Kissing you was amazing, and you'll never know how much opening up to you helped me. You're not the only one with demons, but I've conquered mine. I just want to help with yours."

He had demons. She'd assumed as much. Of course a big, strong man like Drake had conquered his demons; he seemed in control of absolutely everything.

"Nothing can be done for mine," she whispered.

Drake slid her side bangs aside, his fingertips tickling her heated skin around her scar. "Something can be done, Marly. I'm not going anywhere, and when you want help, all you have to do is ask. I won't pry. I won't make you relive all the details. But I'm not afraid to battle your demons for you."

He laid a very tender, very brief kiss on her lips, stepped around her and let himself quietly out the front door.

Marly sank against the door frame that led to the hallway, her hand covering her trembling lips.

I'm not afraid to battle your demons for you.

Tears pricked her eyes. What man would say such things? What man would step in front of a woman and slay the past that threatened her future?

A man that wanted more from the woman than she was ready to give. What would he expect from her? If she could try at any type of relationship, she would try with Drake. But right now, friendship was even stretching it.

Swiping at her damp cheeks, Marly locked the dead bolt, turned off the lights and headed to her bed. Her sweet baby still lay at an odd angle across the bed, dressed in her horse nightgown and cowgirl boots.

Moonlight slanted through the window and cut across Willow's precious face. That right there was the reason Marly couldn't get involved with anyone. Not only would Kevin tear any man apart who tried to enter Marly's life, he would also use any means to steal Willow. Marly refused to allow her daughter to be a bargaining chip.

If Marly tried to move on and have another relationship, Kevin would surely use that as a weapon in his fight to get Willow. He'd twist the scenario to say Marly was unfit, or showcase her as a woman who brought men in and out of their daughter's life. He wouldn't care that Drake was a good friend. Kevin would spin their relationship into something ugly.

Marly had to put her own needs aside, no matter how much Drake made her realize there was more to men than evil and hatred. For the first time, Drake made her feel like a desired, passionate woman.

Unfortunately fate had other plans for her future, and Drake couldn't be part of them.

Chapter Eight

Jeremy had been transported yesterday, and Marly had already received an update from the children's hospital. Jeremy was all settled in, and the doctors would begin his first surgery as soon as next week.

Marly had just finished her break and stepped out of the nurses' lounge to see a huge smile on her co-worker's face.

"What?" Marly asked, figuring she had mayo on the side of her face or something equally as embarrassing.

"You have an admirer." Lori pointed to the colorful bouquet in a short glass vase that rested on the counter. "Apparently the fire chief wasn't here just to see our patient."

Marly eyed the card sticking out of the arrangement.

As she neared, she could make out the handwritten words.

Because we're friends
D

Even though her stomach was doing a nervous dance, Marly smiled as she turned to Lori. "He's a nice man. We're working on a fund-raiser to help raise money for Jeremy's family."

Lori sat down at the desk and typed in her password to log in. "Oh, Drake is a nice man, all right. But trust me, if he's showing attention toward you, and flowers are certainly attention, he's interested."

Yeah, Marly knew how interested he was. Her lips still tingled from the night before. The places on her body where his hands had been were now cold. He'd touched areas so deep within her she wondered if she'd ever recover. And all he'd done was kiss her.

Not only was she getting in deeper than she wanted to go, she was getting in deeper than she even thought possible.

"Good for him," Lori went on as she typed notes into the computer. "After Andrea was killed I wondered if he'd find happiness again."

That shocked Marly out of her own pity party.

"Who's Andrea?" *And how was she killed?*

Lori's hands froze on the keyboard, and she threw a glance over her shoulder. "He hasn't told you about Andrea? I forget you're not from here. Andrea was his fiancée. She was killed in a car accident over a year ago."

"What?" Marly gripped the edge of the other desk chair. "That's terrible."

A fiancée? No wonder he'd mentioned he had his own demons. He'd loved someone enough to want to spend his life with her and he'd lost her. A man like Drake would love with his whole heart, would die in someone else's place…especially those he loved.

Marly couldn't imagine what losing Andrea must have felt like. The only person who held such a high value in her life was Willow. Life without her would be unbearable.

Lori went back to typing. "Those St. John boys were always raising a ruckus as teens, but they've really grown into remarkable men."

Marly had yet to meet the other two brothers, but she was starting to get the impression the men were very close…and very potent.

"I keep hearing how they were hellions," Marly joked. "Were they that bad?"

"Oh, yeah. The irony of the positions they're in now is quite hysterical. Their father was the town doctor, and that poor man was always getting calls at his clinic." Lori laughed, typed a bit more and shook her head, causing the loose bun at the nape of her neck to wobble. "One time the boys stole a police cruiser and picked up a couple other friends from school. They claimed they were doing a public service by giving their friends better drop-off service than the school bus."

Marly smiled. She could only imagine the shenanigans three teen boys had gotten into. Their poor mother.

An alarm went off in one of the patients' rooms and Marly held up her hand. "I'll get it."

The rest of the day went by in a blur, and by the time she'd gathered her things—and her gorgeous bouquet—and headed toward home, she was flat-out exhausted.

Willow would be getting off the bus about five minutes after Marly got home, so there was no time for relaxing. Which was fine. She'd relaxed enough during her years of marriage when Kevin would insist on her going to the finest salons, getting facials and massages. All so he could brag about pampering his wife.

So being a single mom and being exhausted wasn't necessarily a bad thing.

Marly had just adjusted the beautiful flowers on the small kitchen table when she heard the bus pull up out front. Sometimes Willow would get dropped off at the sitter's, other times at home. The change in scheduling didn't seem to bother Willow, and she was adjusting remarkably well to living here.

Marly had never truly told her why they'd left, only that they were taking an adventure and Daddy couldn't come. Willow would ask about Kevin, but Marly would just say how he was busy with work and, because Kevin never put Willow ahead of work, that explanation seemed to pacify her. A shame, honestly, that being without a parent didn't seem to faze a little girl when she was at such an impressionable age.

Just then the front door burst open, and Willow tossed her backpack and lunch box aside. "This was the coolest day ever!"

Marly waited, always eager to hear how her daughter's day had gone. Luckily, Willow was always having "the best day." She loved school, loved her friends, freeing Marly of some of the guilt from upending her daughter's life.

"What happened?" Marly asked.

Willow shoved her wayward hair from her eyes. The once-adorable—okay, still adorable—pigtails were now slipping down from their place. "Chief Drake came to the school with another fireman, I don't remember his name." Willow put her hands on her hips and smiled. "And Chief Drake picked me out of all the kids in the entire kindergarten. He had me come up on stage in the gym and he said I had won the fire-poster contest."

"Oh, honey." Marly held her arms open and Willow launched into her hold. "That's wonderful. Is this the poster you told me you painted in art class?"

Willow eased back and nodded, sending more hair into her little face. "Yup. And Chief Drake said it was awesome and he was proud of me."

Marly listened as Willow went on and on about how cool the chief was and when could they go to the fire department for that ride she'd been promised and could he come over again and help prepare for the festival?

Such innocence, such excitement. Marly would love to have Drake over, would love to have Drake kiss her, touch her again.

She honestly couldn't remember a time when she'd been kissed so tenderly yet so passionately. Here she was, a twenty-six-year-old woman, divorced, with a child, and she couldn't recall being kissed from someone who actually cared about her.

That was just one of the many changes she was making in her new life. From now on, she would hold herself at a higher standard, expecting to be cared for by anyone who entered her life. She deserved nothing less.

Drake and Eli were just stepping out of the local pizza place when Marly and Willow came up the sidewalk. Drake clutched the boxes and stopped, experiencing that instant kick to the gut he always got when he was around her.

"What are you doing?" Eli complained, running into his back. "I nearly dropped the wings, dude."

Marly's eyes came up to meet his, and a slow smile spread across her face. "Drake," she said as she closed the space between them. "I see we're all on the same page with dinner."

"You're Marly?" Eli asked behind him.

Drake wanted to kick his brother in the jewels. Why ask like that? Why make it sound as if Drake had been chatting up Marly to him like some high school teen who had a crush?

"I am." Her smile widened as she took her daughter's hand. "And this is my daughter, Willow."

His brother moved around beside Drake, bent down and smiled. "I'm Eli," he told Willow. "It's nice to meet you."

"Are you a fireman, too?" she asked, her eyes wide and hopeful.

"No, I'm a doctor."

The little girl's brows drew in. "You give shots?"

Eli laughed, straightening to his full height. "Sometimes, but only so people can feel better."

"Um…thanks," Marly chimed in, her eyes only on Drake. "You know, for the flowers."

"Flowers?" Eli muttered.

Careful to keep hold of the pizza boxes, Drake rammed his elbow into his brother's side. Pleased when a burst of air expelled from Eli, Drake smiled at Marly.

"You're welcome."

Marly grinned, apparently not missing a thing. "Well, we won't keep you. I promised Willow we could eat inside tonight."

"Why don't you come back with us?" Drake asked before he could stop himself, though now that the invitation was out in the open, he wasn't sorry he'd asked. "We ordered plenty and we're just going to Eli's house to watch a game."

Marly shook her head. "I couldn't do that to you guys."

"My wife won't mind," Eli added. "She'd probably love to have female company."

"Please, Mama." Willow tugged on her mother's hand. "Let's go, and I can watch the game, too."

Marly laughed. "She loves football."

Drake smiled and looked down at Willow. "What do you say to some fish-egg pizza and a game?"

Willow's smile spread across her face. "Are you teasing me again, Chief?"

Loving that little girl's infectious smile, Drake shrugged. "You'll never know unless you come over."

Willow turned those bright blue eyes up to her mother. "Can we? Please?"

Marly looked between her daughter and Drake. With a sigh, she nodded. "It looks like I'm outnumbered. Are you sure your wife won't mind?"

"I'm positive," Eli told her. "Just follow us. I don't live far."

As Marly and Willow settled back into their car, Drake and Eli piled into Eli's truck. Drake knew what was coming. Knew there was no way in hell during these next few miles that Eli wouldn't give him hell.

"So...flowers."

Drake set the bag of wings on top of the pizza boxes and fastened his seat belt. "Shut up."

"Just making a statement."

"Keep your statements to yourself."

Bringing the engine to life, Eli backed out of the parking lot. "She's pretty. Little girl is adorable, too. You ready for a family?"

Drake held on to the food and glanced in the rear-view mirror to make sure Marly was back there. "I'm not getting a family, Eli."

"You haven't dated much since Andrea's death, you sent this beautiful nurse flowers, you've been to her house and you are obviously taken by that little girl. Sounds as though you're gearing up for a family to me."

Maybe so, but no way Drake would admit it aloud. After Andrea's death, he never thought he'd be ready to commit to another woman. He'd sworn she was it for him, and he could never even look at another woman with such emotions.

While he didn't have any thoughts of marrying Marly, he couldn't deny the strong pull, the intensity of his feelings and the anticipation of seeing where their relationship led them.

He may have not planned for another woman to impact his life, but he couldn't deny that Marly had sucker punched him in the gut with her beauty, her innocence and her vulnerability. No way in hell was he letting go of something that was building just because he was scared of taking another step into relationship territory.

Marly may just be the woman who had been placed into his life to help him get over that last hurdle he'd been afraid to face. Maybe this was the start of something he'd dreamed of, everything he'd wanted and never thought he'd have after Andrea.

Chapter Nine

At first Marly had wondered what on earth she'd been thinking agreeing to this, but after she and Willow had arrived at Eli's home, she realized it was a good idea.

After kissing Drake, wanting more and then pushing him away, the presence of other adults really lessened the awkwardness between them. Well, Drake may not feel awkward, but she sure did. Not a bad awkward, just…awkward. She didn't know what move to make or what he'd do next.

Being attracted to someone, knowing he felt the same way, was all new territory for her. Yes, when she and Kevin had first started dating and then gotten engaged, they had a level of attraction; she wouldn't have married him had there been no spark.

But the intensity with which Marly yearned for more

time, more kissing from Drake was beyond anything she'd ever experienced.

And now she had another layer of Drake St. John to consider. The man may be all strength and power, but he had a vulnerability that he held close to his heart. Losing a fiancée was unfathomable, and the fact Drake had been able to move on, pushing through what had to have broken him, only made her more aware of what a remarkable man he truly was.

"Sorry about that." Eli's wife, Nora, came back out onto the enclosed patio with a monitor in hand. "Had to get Amber down for her afternoon nap."

Marly smiled. "I understand. Too bad adults can't grab those afternoon naps."

Nora laughed, taking a seat on the floral-cushioned wicker chair. "So you're fairly new in town. What do you think of Stonerock?"

"I really like it," Marly answered honestly. "I wanted a small town and I wanted a nice school for Willow. We're both really happy."

That sounded convincing…didn't it?

"Where are you from?"

Marly slid her thumb over the condensation on her cup of lemonade, trying to figure out how much to reveal and still sound like a normal single mom just looking for a fresh start.

"Nashville."

"Oh, I love Nashville." Nora rested her elbow on the edge of her wicker chair and propped her head on her fist. "Were you a nurse there, as well?"

"For a few years. After I had Willow, I took time off to stay home and be with her."

Mainly because Kevin had threatened to have her fired if she didn't because he didn't want his wife working. That would look as if he couldn't take care of her financially, and image was everything after all.

"I'm so glad I'm taking a few months off to be with Amber," Nora stated. "Eli doesn't care if I return to work or not, but I love my clinic. Not that it matters. If I closed my office, my patients would just come here."

"You'd mentioned earlier being a vet. Do you love that?"

Nora nodded. "Every day is something different."

Marly took a drink of her lemonade, the tangy liquid reminding her of simple summers, and she was sorry that this one would be coming to an end soon.

"How long have you been divorced?"

Marly nearly choked on her drink at Nora's innocent question.

"I'm sorry," Nora said over Marly's coughing. "That was rude. I just assumed you'd been married and I shouldn't have done that. I was married before, but my husband was killed in the service. I hate when people assume."

Nora's backpedaling and apology gave Marly enough time to compose herself. "No, no. It's okay. I am divorced. I've been single about six months."

Longer than that, considering the loveless marriage. She'd raised Willow totally on her own, but there was no way Marly was getting into that.

"Well, you have one adorable little girl," Nora stated. "She really does love football, doesn't she?"

Marly nodded. "She does. Most people think she's this sweet, princess-type little girl with her blond hair and blue eyes. She really fools them when they realize she's a dirt-and-mud type of girl who loves sports and trucks."

"I love that you allow her to be her own person." Nora stroked the cat that had climbed up onto her lap. "So many parents try to mold their children into something they're just not meant to be."

Images of Kevin yelling about Willow's free spirit and blaming Marly played in her head. It was during one of those fights that he'd put that scar on her chin.

"Are you okay?"

Marly glanced across the patio to meet Nora's worried face. "Oh, yes. Just thinking. It is a shame when parents don't let their kids develop in their own way."

Shouting from the living room erupted, and seconds later the baby monitor lit up as the cries from Amber came through.

Nora groaned. "I've told him again and again he needs to tone it down during the games. He wakes Amber up every time there's an afternoon game."

Marly came to her feet. "Would you like me to go get her?"

"Oh, no. I'll go get her and take her to her daddy. He needs to be reminded what happens when you wake the baby," Nora smirked. "Be right back."

Marly sank back down on the wicker sofa and sighed.

This was what a family should be like. Give and take, good times with friends in a simple, loving atmosphere.

Before her parents had passed, she'd had that. Perhaps that was why she'd been so quick to marry Kevin. Marly had dreamed of raising her own family, mimicking the love and laughter she'd always known. Yet somehow she'd been blinded by a charming man with a dream for power who'd wanted her by his side. In theory it had all sounded so romantic… In reality it was a living hell.

One day at a time, she was crawling back to the life she'd envisioned for herself. And one day, perhaps she'd find her own happiness.

Drake stepped out onto the patio where Marly was obviously lost in thought. She stared straight ahead into the fenced backyard. Her legs were crossed and she absently toyed with her empty cup, spinning it slowly between her hands.

"Care if I hide here with you?" he asked, coming to sit beside her on the small sofa.

Her gaze jerked to his. "I didn't hear you come out. Um…sure."

"We woke the baby, so now Eli is being punished."

Marly straightened. "He's the baby's father, too. Is it just the mother's job to take care of the child?"

Drake held up his hands. "Whoa, I didn't mean that. I just meant because he woke Amber he would have to get her back to sleep."

Marly eased back against the floral cushion. "I'm sorry. I didn't mean to jump all over you."

"Never apologize to me," he told her. "You have nothing to be sorry for."

Her reaction told him everything he needed to know about the type of man Willow's father was. *Deadbeat dad* came to mind instantly.

"Aren't you watching the game?" she asked.

"It's halftime. Eli brought in Amber, and Willow was all excited about the baby, so she wanted to stay with them."

"Is she in the way?" Marly asked, her eyes wide. "We can go. I don't want to overstay our welcome."

Drake reached out, placing a hand on her knee. "You're not overstaying, and Willow is never in the way."

Marly's eyes held his for a second before she nodded. "Thanks."

He figured the kiss was still on her mind, which was right where he wanted it to stay, so he didn't bring it up. He wanted her to think about it, think about them. He sure as hell was.

So instead of bringing up the proverbial elephant in the room, he kept to a safer topic. As much as he wanted to dig deeper into her feelings, he also wanted to keep that line of friendship open.

"I have several items for the silent auction," he told her, pleased when she smiled. "I also rented a dunking booth, and the company was all too eager to let us rent it for half price."

"Oh, Drake, that's great." She shifted in her seat to face him fully. "I emailed the art teacher, and she was happy to have her high school class set up a face-painting station. A church in town actually contacted me about a bake sale."

"I'm picking up the flyers on Monday, and I'll bring some by your house when my shift ends. I think most people know by now, but it won't hurt to post some around town."

Marly tucked her hair behind her ear and reached to smooth her bangs. He had no doubt she did the gesture out of habit now. Every time he saw her trying to hide that scar, a new level of rage rolled through him. It absolutely sickened him to think of everything she'd endured…everything she still kept bottled inside.

"I'm excited," she told him. "I just know this will really help Shawn and Amy."

Unable to resist, Drake slid his arm across the back of the wicker love seat and toyed with the ends of her silky hair. "And what about you? What would help you?"

Marly tilted her head. "Drake, you've got to stop. You make this so hard for me."

"This what?" he asked, rubbing those golden strands between his fingertips.

A sigh shuddered through her as her eyes met his. "You make me feel things," she whispered. "I can't let this go beyond friendship."

"But you want to." He grazed the back of his knuckles down her delicate cheek. "I'm not trying to make this harder on you, Marly, but you have to know that it's been so long since I've felt anything for a woman. I can't ignore this."

Marly reached up and held on to his hand. "How long has Andrea been gone?"

Drake froze. Hearing his late fiancée's name on Marly's lips had his past and present colliding right in front of him.

"It's a small town," he told her, bringing their hands to drop into her lap. "I'm surprised you didn't hear about this before now."

Marly offered a smile. "We both have our own issues, Drake. I realize you're moving past yours, but my issues... They could destroy peoples' lives."

The reality of her words settled in and he shifted closer. "Are you trying to protect me?"

"You don't know what you'd be up against. Trust me."

The haunted look in her eyes, the sad tone of her voice had his blood boiling all over again. He'd climb these damn walls she'd erected and prove to her that real men didn't use their power to control women.

"Marly, I'm not afraid of anybody or anything." She started to look down, but he took both hands, cupped her face and forced her to look at him. "I don't know what kind of man you're used to, but I'm not a coward, and I stand up for people I care about."

Unshed tears sprang to her eyes. "He has the power to crush your career and take my daughter," she whispered. "Please, don't do this to me, to yourself."

Drake ignored her plea and closed the narrow space between them. Her mouth instantly opened to his, proving she wasn't speaking from her heart. Her heart was in this kiss, this moment. She'd become like a drug to him. The more he had, the more he craved. His hands slid into her hair, but she pulled away and came to her feet, turning her back on him.

"I won't do this to you," she whispered. "Don't ask me to."

And then she was gone. Drake sat on the sofa, wondering what the hell he could do to make her understand that he wasn't going anywhere, that he wanted to help her.

Beyond that, beyond the fact that he wanted to protect her, he had a feeling deep in his soul that Marly was a woman he could quite possibly fall in love with.

Was he ready to step into that type of commitment again? Could he open his heart fully and trust it not to be broken?

Chapter Ten

Two days later and Drake couldn't get Marly's haunting words from his mind. She was utterly convinced that if she started something with him, her ex would take action. He knew Marly was worried not only for herself, but also for Willow. Didn't she see that he wouldn't let anyone hurt them? Regardless of what happened between Drake and Marly, he refused to see any woman treated poorly, especially by someone who claimed to care for her. Drake refused to back down, and he refused to let Marly throw in the towel and give up on a life for herself.

If she'd said she wasn't interested, if she hadn't responded so passionately to his kisses, then he would back off. But Marly was just as interested as he was, and he would damn well find a way to get over this hurdle she'd placed between them.

Drake climbed the steps to the courthouse and welcomed the cool air-conditioning as he stepped into the marble, two-story entryway.

As if his mood wasn't crappy enough because of Marly's ex—a man he'd never even met—now Drake had to go meet with Mayor Butterball for a performance review. These were always a treat.

Bypassing the elevator, Drake took the steps and headed toward the mayor's office. Betty typed away at her computer, but looked up and offered a sweet smile when Drake entered.

How such a kind older woman could work for a man like Mayor Tipton was beyond him. The pay couldn't be good enough to put up with the lazy jerk.

"Chief," she greeted. "Go right on in. He's expecting you."

Goody.

"Thank you, Betty," he replied with a smile of his own.

Without knocking, Drake charged right in and closed the door behind him.

"Chief. Right on time."

Drake grunted as he took a seat in the worn leather chair. No extra words were necessary. Drake wasn't here to make friends, he was here to get this yearly review over with so he could head home and work more on his renovations. His ultimate stress reliever was pounding on two-by-fours and getting dirty and sweaty while blaring his music.

The mayor slid a folder across his desk and flipped it open. He pretended to be reading through the papers, but Drake knew full well the man had already looked over this stuff. He made it a point to be in Drake's business…and not just because he was the mayor and that was his job.

"Looks as though there was a problem at the Shack," he said without looking up.

Drake sighed. He knew this was coming. "This is the third time that restaurant has had an electrical issue. If they can't keep their box up to code, they can't stay open."

Tipton dropped the paper and glanced up. "That's the only place that the church crowd goes on Sundays. You can't keep closing them and fining them."

Drake eased forward in his chair. "Are you kidding me? Do you want a fire? Because I assure you, that will close them a hell of a lot longer."

"The Prestons are an older couple, Chief. They can't afford to lose the business."

"They can't afford to have their business burn to the ground, either." Drake's blood started pumping, as it always did around this moron. "I will continue to inspect them until I'm comfortable with their security."

Sighing, Mayor Tipton flipped the top paper over. "I also have a complaint from Helen Reed about one of your engines leaving a rut in her yard."

Drake laughed, shaking his head. "Seriously? She calls at least once a week because that damn cat of hers won't come out of the tree."

So embarrassing. He hated the stereotypical image

of a fireman getting the cat out of a tree, but the woman was nearing ninety and there was no way Drake could tell her no…even if she did complain.

"Be that as it may, you need to be more careful."

Drake clenched his fists, but said nothing. This "review" couldn't be over fast enough.

"I've also gone over the budget again for the next quarter, and I'm afraid we'll have to cut back one more man in your department."

Oh, hell no. Drake shot out of his chair.

"You've already pulled three," he retorted. "We're short staffed as it is. This is getting ridiculous."

"If the money isn't there, then there's nothing I can do."

Drake braced his hands on the desk and leaned in. "You could start cutting some of the hours of other city workers. You could start knocking off an hour from each employee in this building, and that would pay for one of my hardworking men to keep his job."

"I can't affect the lives of that many people," the Mayor defended. "It's easier to just remove one."

"Easier?" Drake laughed in disbelief. "You're all about easier. You sit behind this desk and dole out orders when you know absolutely nothing about what's going on in the town you supposedly care so much about."

"Watch it, Chief. You're treading a fine line."

Drake pushed off the desk, propped his hands on his hips and stared down at the man who had become the bane of his existence.

"I don't care about that line, *Mayor*, I care about the people who I took an oath to protect. I care about the men who work under me, who put their lives on the line every single day with little or no recognition." Drake's anger fueled his words and he couldn't stop. "What I don't care about is a lazy man who tries to play God and is more worried about image than people. And I sure as hell don't care about making your job easier. I will not sacrifice another of my men."

"Fine." The mayor pushed from his desk and came to his feet. "Consider yourself suspended without pay until further notice."

Stunned, Drake sank back on his heels. "You're not serious."

The smirk across Mayor Tipton's face had Drake resisting the urge to jump over that desk. The last thing he wanted was for his own brother to have to come arrest him.

"Oh, I'm very serious. Since you refuse to release one of your other men, you can be the one to go." The mayor picked up the file and tapped the edge of it against his desk. "I'll discuss your review with city council and we will take it from there."

"You do that," Drake said. "But I will be at that meeting. I will get my position back, and you won't be able to do a damn thing about it. Do you want to know why? Because you won't get reelected. I'll make sure of it."

Tipton's eyes narrowed. "Is that a threat?"

"It's whatever the hell you want it to be." Unable to resist, Drake swept his hand across the desk, sending papers flying. "Have a good day."

Pleased that he'd held his rage in check for the most

part, Drake stormed out of the office, the door slamming back against the wall.

He'd never been suspended before in his life. And suspended without pay? Whatever. He had a good chunk in savings, and at least his men would be able to hold on to their positions a bit longer.

But this sucked.

On the bright side? Now he had more time to devote to a certain blond nurse, and he intended to start right away.

Marly had just put brownies in the oven when her doorbell rang.

"Can I get it, Mama?" Willow called from her bedroom.

Fear settled in Marly's stomach. She'd had another threatening text from Kevin earlier, claiming he would find her if she didn't come back to him within a week. She knew he would make good on his threat.

"No, honey," Marly called back. "I've got it."

She'd been home less than an hour, but she'd promised Willow they would make brownies as soon as she'd gotten off the bus. Now the baked treats were in the oven and dinner wasn't even started. Priorities—they had them in order. Lately, due to all the stress, Marly was either cleaning or baking. One was by far better for her waistline, but not nearly as comforting.

Marly glanced out the picture window in the living room and couldn't help but smile when she saw Drake's truck at the curb. No matter what she said to him about backing off, deep inside she was glad he hadn't.

Since when did she turn into a woman who played games? She didn't want to be that woman. Damn it, she was all on board with the friendship thing, but then he'd gone and kissed her, making her forget everything but the fact she wanted him on a more intimate level.

But she wouldn't risk the inevitable action Kevin would take if Marly moved on with another man.

The thought had her shivering as she flipped the lock and pulled the door open.

"Hey." Drake smiled, but the gesture didn't quite meet his eyes. "Can I come in?"

Stepping aside, Marly motioned for him to enter. Before she could question what was wrong, Willow came riding through the house on a hobby horse, donned in her cowgirl boots and a Native American headdress made out of construction paper.

"Hey, Chief! Did you come for a brownie?"

Drake squatted down and held up a small red fireman's helmet that he'd had hidden behind his back. "I actually came to give this to you."

Marly's heart melted…as if there was much more to melt where this man was concerned.

The horse dropped to the wood floor with a clatter as Willow jerked off her homemade headdress and threw it to the floor, promptly putting on her new helmet. "This is awesome! Thanks, Chief."

Drake patted the top of her hat. "You look like a natural."

Willow peered up from beneath the brim. "Does this mean you're here to give me a ride on the engine, too?"

Coming to his feet, Drake sighed. "Sorry, sweetheart, not today. But, if you can give me and your mom five minutes to talk, I have another surprise for you."

Willow squealed and clapped. "I'll give you six minutes. Because six is bigger than five."

Willow bounced back down the hall toward her bedroom, counting in a singsong voice without a care in the world. But as Marly turned her attention to Drake, she knew this man with the worry lines between his brows had something weighing heavily on his mind.

Without a word, Drake walked over to her couch and eased down, resting his elbows on his knees and his head in his hands. He didn't look at her, didn't say a word.

"Now you're really worrying me," she told him. "You haven't even flirted or tried to steal a kiss."

The joke was meant to get a reaction, but...nothing. Then another level of fear rose to the surface.

"Did you hear something about Jeremy?" she asked, crossing to sit in the secondhand accent chair adjacent to him. "Talk to me."

"It's not Jeremy." Raking his hands through his cropped hair, Drake let out a sigh and finally turned those worried blue eyes on her. "I'm sorry I just showed up like this."

"It's okay," she told him. "What happened?"

"I was suspended without pay until further notice."

"What?" Marly sat up straighter in her seat.

"The mayor insisted we let go of one more firefighter and I disagreed and informed him I refused to lay off any more of my men... I may have said a few other choice words, as well. In the end he figured I was the best candidate."

Marly hadn't seen Drake's temper. Well, she had, but only when he'd learned the ugly truth behind her scars. She honestly couldn't believe this was a man who would get violent.

"How does he expect my guys to keep working endless hours, doubling up on shifts and putting themselves in the line of danger every day when they're running on empty?"

Marly jerked back and stared at him. He was worried about his men? He wasn't worried about the fact that he would have no income?

"I can't wait until the election in a few months," Drake added.

A chill crept over Marly. The election. The reason for Kevin's threats...or one of the reasons. He wasn't lying when he said he'd find her. And when he did come looking, she had no clue how she could fight him. Because he would come. And the longer he waited before he lost patience, thinking she'd return, the angrier he'd be when he finally found her.

Marly shifted toward Drake. "Did you get that helmet for Willow before you talked to the mayor?"

Shaking his head, Drake eased back on her sofa and stretched his legs out in front of him. "No. I went back to the department and broke the news to the guys. I grabbed some things from my locker and the helmet for Willow."

Tears pricked her eyes. "That may be the sweetest thing anybody has ever done for her."

Drake shrugged and glanced away. "It's no big deal."

Obviously he wasn't a fan of her praise, but what man would get suspended and immediately think of the men he was leaving behind and a five-year-old little girl?

A hero. The title fit him perfectly, whether he wanted to wear it or not.

"Are the adults done talking?" Willow yelled from her bedroom.

Marly laughed. "You can come on out, honey."

"Good." Willow ran down the hallway. "I smell the brownies. Can I have one when they come out of the oven?"

"I don't think so, sweetie. After dinner, though."

Drake came to his feet. "I'll go. I don't want to disrupt your dinner."

"You said you had another surprise for me." Willow came to stand beside Drake, her helmet still resting atop her head and blond curls hanging down her back.

"Willow," Marly scolded in a half whisper. "If Drake needs to go, you just be thankful he brought you the helmet."

"I don't need to go," he retorted with a smile. "I just don't want to be in the way."

"You're not in the way." Willow grabbed his hand. "You wanna stay for supper?"

Marly couldn't ignore that tug on her heart at the sight of Willow's hand in Drake's. She was so trusting, so innocent. In some ways that was a blessing, because Willow had no idea why they were away from Kevin.

"I'm throwing some chicken on the grill," Marly told

him. "You're more than welcome to stay. As you've heard, we have brownies for dessert."

Drake's smile spread across his face as he looked from Marly to Willow and back to Marly. "It's the best offer I've had all day. Let me run out to the truck and get the other surprise."

Chapter Eleven

"That's good, but hold the ball like this."

Drake squatted down and turned the football until the laces were out. Covering Willow's delicate hand with his own, he drew her arm back and helped her launch it across the yard. Well, maybe not all the way across, but far enough to get a whoop of delight out of her.

"You did it." Drake gave her a high five and watched as she ran after the ball. "Come on, we'll do it again."

After assisting her about three more times, he let her go on her own. Each time she launched it in the air, she was jumping up and down.

"Here," he told her. "Let me stand down here and we'll pass it back and forth now that you've become a pro on me."

Willow laughed. "You'd better back up. I throw it far now."

To boost her newly found self-esteem, Drake backed up, knowing he could move forward pretty quickly to catch it.

"Dinner is ready," Marly called from the small patio area.

"Mama," Willow whined. "We were just starting to pass."

"You can pass later."

Leaving no room for discussion, Marly took a plate of chicken into the house and left the back door open, an invitation for them to follow.

Teaching this sweet little girl to play football—while wearing her cowgirl boots, no less—and going in to sit down to a home-cooked meal with a family felt very... right.

Growing up, his mother had always stressed the importance of family dinners, and he'd always known he would want that same connection, that same ritual with his own family.

He couldn't help but feel that tug right now, but he knew to keep his heart on guard. No matter what he might be ready for or might be feeling, Marly was still running scared.

Honestly, he was scared, too, but he was ready... or at least he was ready to try for more. The time had come for him to move forward, and he knew in his heart that Marly was the woman to move on with. Now if he could only get her to trust him... He had to give this a shot; he couldn't let this second chance go when it was right within reach.

Willow was standing on a stool washing her hands at the kitchen sink, and Drake went over to help Marly get plates ready.

"I'll take care of everything." She waved a hand toward the table. "Go have a seat."

Ignoring her orders, he pulled cups from the cabinet and filled them with ice, then poured lemonade from the pitcher she had sitting on the counter.

All too soon they were all gathered around the table, eating and passing the food around, after Willow had said the blessing. Drake cut up Willow's chicken while she chatted about her school day and how everyone was excited for the upcoming festival.

"Oh, I've got those flyers in my truck." He cut another piece of chicken, so thankful he didn't have to head home and microwave a hot dog. "I picked them up earlier today, but with everything else, I forgot."

"When can I get that engine ride?" Willow asked, shoving more chicken into her mouth.

"Honey, I'm not sure—"

Drake held up a hand and cut Marly off. "I am taking some time off work, but if you wouldn't mind a buddy of mine giving you a ride, I can set that up one day after school."

Even though Drake was looking at Willow, he saw Marly's eyes go wide. "Drake," she scolded.

"Tomorrow?" Willow asked, wide-eyed.

"As long as he's not out on a call," Drake promised with a smile. He loved seeing that hope in Willow's eyes, loved seeing how excited she got when discussing his own passion. "I'll let your mom know tomorrow."

They finished dinner, and Drake insisted on helping with the dishes. After a bit more passing the football with Willow, he hadn't realized how late it had gotten until Marly yelled out the back door that it was Willow's bath time. Drake picked up the ball, and by the time he'd gotten back in the house, Willow was nowhere to be seen. He heard water running in the bathroom down the hall and he assumed Marly was back there doing her nightly ritual. Alone.

He admired her. Not once had she complained or even acted as exhausted as he knew she had to be. Being a single mother working a full-time job had to be trying...not to mention dealing with whatever weighed heavily on her heart that she kept bottled inside. Independent and strong, she chose to face her battles head-on. She was a warrior.

Drake pulled his keys from his pocket and set the football on the end table. He wanted Willow to keep it. Who knows? Maybe he'd be back to pass with her again.

Just as he opened the front door, Marly called his name. When he glanced over his shoulder, she was holding a towel and washcloth.

"Don't leave," she said. "Can you give me twenty minutes to get her into bed?"

He'd give her all the time she wanted because the fact she wanted him to stay was a huge step.

"Sure." Drake nodded, pretending as though this wasn't an important milestone.

He barely caught a glimpse of her sweet smile as she

disappeared back down the hall. Drake took a seat on the couch and realized that since he'd been at Marly's, he hadn't thought of the mayor or his absurd suspension.

Wait until Cameron and Eli heard about this. They'd explode. They'd head down to the city council offices and stage a two-man protest.

Of course, Cameron was still working the undercover thing, so who knew when Drake would hear from him to even tell him about the issue.

When his cell chimed in his pocket, he pulled it out, but nothing showed up. Then he saw Marly's phone on the side table, near his arm. The face was lit up and he honestly wasn't trying to be nosy, but the glaring message was hard to miss.

You have 3 days left. I'm coming for you.

Above the cryptic message was *Kevin*. Must be the ex. Even his name sounded like a jerk.

Drake resisted the urge to pick up her phone and send this Kevin guy a message, but he wouldn't do anything to hurt Marly.

He didn't have to wait too long before Marly came back down the hall. The bottom of her gray T-shirt was damp, her hair was falling from her ponytail, and even though she looked like she could drop to sleep at any moment, to Drake, she looked beautiful.

"I don't know what you did to her, but she was out before I could finish cleaning up the bathroom."

Marly dropped to the sofa beside him, tipped her head back against the cushion and sighed.

The column of her throat was exposed, nearly begging to be kissed. But that she'd invited him to stay didn't mean she had something more in mind than just talking. Marly had the lead here and he would just have to follow…no matter how difficult holding himself back would be.

"Thank you." Turning her head against the cushion so she could face him, Marly offered a sweet, tired smile. "For the helmet, the football…for coming here and talking to me. After the way I left things at Eli's house, I was worried that maybe you wouldn't want to see me again."

Drake shifted, pulling his knee up onto the sofa. "You left because you were concerned about me. I'd be a jerk if I decided you weren't worth the trouble of seeing again. Besides, I wanted to give Willow the helmet and the football. Seeing you again is just icing on the proverbial cake."

Marly started to adjust her bangs, but Drake intercepted her hand and pulled it into his lap. "You look fine. Whether your scar is exposed or not, Marly. It doesn't define you."

Those brown doe eyes studied his face. Drake wanted to know what she saw, what she thought when she looked at him. He prayed she saw a man who truly cared for her, a man who would go as slow as she needed if she would just give him a sign that she would eventually be ready to trust and open up.

"What will you do about the suspension?" she asked, obviously dodging the topic of herself.

Drake continued to hold on to her hand. "Fight it.

There's a council meeting next week, and I plan on being there. I also plan on writing up a letter stating what all the mayor has done since taking office—the layoffs, the budget cuts, the new lights and flowers all around town that could've been one of my men back on the job. They can't expect the town to remain safe and out of debt as long as he's at the helm."

Marly turned her hand over in his so they were palm to palm. "You're pretty amazing. It's a rare man who would be more concerned about an entire town than his own suspension. I can't get over how you still thought of Willow during all of that."

Drake laced their fingers together. "It's not hard to think of people I care about, no matter what's going on in my life."

He didn't want to bring the ex into the picture, but he did want to get her reaction and see if perhaps this could lead to that open door he'd been waiting for.

"Your cell went off while you were back there," he told her. "A text from Kevin."

Her eyes widened for a second, then closed as she nodded. "I'm sure you saw what it said."

"I did."

Lifting her lids, she met his gaze. "And?"

"You have three more days," Drake told her. "Has he been threatening you still?"

Marly nodded. "He never stopped. I blackmailed him into giving me a divorce, but he's still under the impression I'll come back home."

"How did you blackmail him?"

Marly's free hand toyed with the ratty hem of her

T-shirt. "I have pictures," she told him. "Of me. I took them to the police."

Drake squeezed her hand, wanting her to continue, but at the same time he feared what she was about to reveal.

"He has friends on the force," she went on, still looking down at her damp shirt. "They have put me off for months, saying they would look into my allegations, but each time I call, I get the runaround again."

"Do they have these pictures?"

Marly nodded. "I also have copies."

"So what else did you threaten him with?" Drake asked.

With a sigh, Marly met his gaze. "I don't want to get into that. The bottom line is I left after he hurt me."

Drake's heart literally clenched at her bold confession. "He hurt you more than once."

He didn't ask; he knew. But her nod just confirmed his fear.

"Mentally at first," she murmured. "He controlled me, wanted me to be the perfect show wife. I mean, I have the blond hair and the curvy build, why would I want to work and use my degree when I could be arm candy and entice voters? He was appalled that I wanted to continue my work in the burn unit at the hospital."

Drake stroked the back of her hand with his thumb. "You're an amazing nurse, Marly."

"I love what I do," she stated. "But when I got pregnant with Willow, he demanded I stop. That's when he started getting violent."

Drake wanted to rip this guy's head off. What lowlife hit a woman, let alone a pregnant one? There was no excuse for his behavior. Absolutely none.

"I don't want to get into the details," she added. "I've made a break, I'm trying to start fresh and give Willow a better life. She didn't witness any abuse—actually, her father ignored her most of her life. He didn't want to be bothered with annoyances such as teething, potty training, random sicknesses. He also wasn't thrilled that her personality tended to stray toward tomboy and not a meek, quiet little girl."

"The more I hear, the more I hate this man." Drake tried to keep his tone level, but he was seriously starting to feel his blood pressure soar. "I know I'm not Willow's father, but I just don't see how anybody could look at her and not fall in love. She's an amazing little girl, so full of life."

Marly's sad face softened with a genuine smile. "She's everything to me. I'm not sure I would've had the courage to leave if not for her. I just knew I never wanted her to see that, never wanted her to think abuse of any kind was okay. I want her to grow up and fall in love and not worry about saying or doing something wrong."

Drake couldn't stop himself from reaching with his free hand to stroke the side of her face. "And what about you? Do you want to fall in love and not worry?"

Marly closed her eyes, turning her face just slightly toward his hand. Drake cupped her cheek, stroking the dark circle beneath her eye. He hated how hard she worked, how much she pushed herself.

"I'd love to fall in love," she whispered. "I had a fantasy as a little girl that I would marry the man of my dreams. No little girl ever dreams of being neglected, taken for granted…abused. But I'm getting stronger every single day. I won't let myself get that low again. Ever."

She whispered the word *abused* as if it were a disease. In a sense, Drake figured it was. The word alone crippled her, made her feel inferior and less than who she was, which was a vibrant woman, beautiful and courageous.

"I won't let him get to you, Marly. You're safe here."

Her eyes searched his. "Nobody can stop him."

"I guarantee I'm more determined to keep you safe than he is to get you back." Drake would lay down his life for Marly and Willow. The raw emotions threatened to have him taking charge of her situation, but he knew she needed to remain in control. "Trust me."

Marly's hand came up to his face, the stubble on his jaw bristling beneath her palm. He loved those soft hands on him, loved how she was slowly reaching out to him, literally and figuratively. Little by little he was breaking her barriers of defense down, and he'd scale over anything that was left.

"I trust you," she told him with a smile. "You lost your job and immediately thought of everyone else around you. You're a good man."

Drake laughed. "I should've gotten suspended weeks ago. I had no idea that was what it would take to win your trust."

"I didn't expect to trust again, especially so fast." Marly dropped her hand and settled it over their entwined fingers still in his lap. "You do something to me, Drake. At first I was afraid of how fast my emotions were spiraling toward you. I mean, how could I trust anything I felt after what I'd lived through? But you're a different man than he was and I'm still getting used to the fact that you know how to treat a woman, and you know when to be patient."

"My patience skills are really being tested right now," he told her with a smile. "Because all I want to do is kiss you."

Drake was utterly shocked when Marly scooted in, held on to his hand and slid her mouth over his. As he opened to her he felt as if he'd won some sort of lottery. She was kissing him. She'd never initiated anything before, and here she was taking charge.

With his free hand, Drake cupped his hand around the nape of her neck and changed the angle of the kiss so he could get better access. With his knee between them, it was hard to get the closeness he craved, so he adjusted his body, putting his feet on the floor, and inched closer to Marly.

Her hands slid from his and traveled up over his T-shirt. She gripped his shoulders as she moved closer, as well. Her passion was evident, and Drake wanted more...as much as she was willing to give.

Drake broke free of her sensual lips and kissed his way down her neck. Marly arched her back, still holding on to his shoulders. He still needed more.

Snaking his hands up under her oversize shirt, Drake nearly whimpered when his fingertips came in contact with smooth skin. He traveled on up until his thumbs brushed the underside of her satin bra. He pulled her cups down with both hands and filled his palms with her softness. Marly let out a low moan that shot straight to his gut and had him lifting her shirt.

"You're stunning," he told her, ducking his head to taste her.

Marly cupped the side of his head as if holding him in position. With her back arched, Drake eased her down until she lay on the sofa. He brought himself over her, never breaking contact.

When her hands went back to his shoulders, it took him a moment to realize she wasn't clenching anymore but pushing. He lifted his head, glanced down at her face to see that she'd gone pale.

"I'm sorry," she whispered. "This is… I can't…"

He lifted himself off her, wondering what part had scared her.

"Don't apologize," he told her, reaching down to adjust her shirt. "I shouldn't have pushed."

With shaky hands, she smoothed her shirt herself and sat up…on the other end of the sofa. "No, no. You didn't do anything I didn't want. I just wasn't expecting to be so nervous. But when I felt your weight on me…"

Her voice cracked as she put her hand over her mouth and shook her head. The unspoken words slammed into Drake and he knew… Damn it, he knew full well what she'd endured at the hands of her ex.

Now more than ever he vowed she would not fall victim to that man again. He had to tamp down his fury, keep it hidden so as not to scare her further.

But he would be making a call to his police chief

brother to see what they could do, since he wouldn't allow Marly to live in fear any longer. Her superwoman act had to end because while he was perfectly aware she could stand on her own, he didn't want her to. He wanted to be the one she leaned on, the one she came to for support and when she was afraid.

"I'm not ready," she whispered, her voice thick with emotion. "I understand if that's not what you wanted to hear, if you want to move on."

When she turned to face him with tears in her eyes, Drake's heart broke for her.

"I mean, you're ready to move on, you've said that," she added. "Waiting on me would be like working backward."

Drake reached across the gap between them and held her face in his hands until she kept her watery doe eyes on him. "Waiting for you isn't working backward. Waiting on you is definitely a step in the right direction... for both of us. You need support, emotionally if nothing else, and I damn well will be the one to provide it. I won't do anything you aren't ready for, Marly, but I'm not walking away because you're vulnerable and you're afraid."

One lone tear slid down her cheek. "I wish I'd found you first."

Her bold, raw revelation pierced his heart. "You found me last. That's what matters."

Chapter Twelve

Drake slid another coat of mud on the drywall to hide the nails and the tape. Soon this room would be… something. He really didn't know what he'd do with the addition to the back of his house. He'd originally started this project as a way to vent after Andrea's death. She had died as a result of his driving, a detail from the accident that he liked to keep in the deepest, darkest recesses of his mind.

Using his hands, building something and actually having control over the outcome had been great therapy.

Now, however, the target of his rage was Kevin. The haunted, frightened look in Marly's eyes burned in his mind. Another man may have been the one to put that level of fear in her, but Drake would damn well be the man to take it out.

He hadn't been lying when he'd told her he was the last man to enter her life. He wanted to be that last man, and the revelation shocked the hell out of him…but in a good way.

Since Andrea's death, he'd been so cautious about whom he asked out, but everything about Marly seemed to click into place with his life and his desires. Definitely his desires.

On every level he wanted to make her happy, wanted to see a light in her eyes that he only saw when she spoke of her daughter.

And Willow? She'd totally stolen his heart from day one. How was she taking all of this? The move, being away from her father… Of course, if she was being ignored or brushed aside by her dad, perhaps she didn't even miss him.

The sweet girl had no idea the joy of that family bond. Drake had grown up with such a tight-knit family, between his affectionate parents and his hellion brothers. Of course they clashed at times—what family didn't?—but they were always there for each other, always supportive.

Drake swiped his wide spatula over the glop of mud and wiped the excess against the tray he held. He jerked his head around when he heard his front door open and shut. Heavy footsteps sounded down the hallway.

When his brother Cameron poked his head in, Drake went back to work.

"Grab that other tray and make yourself useful," Drake told him.

"Your warm greetings always make me want to stop and visit more often."

Cameron rattled around behind him and Drake smiled. He knew Cameron also chased demons away by doing physical labor. Of course, Cameron was private and nobody knew what was eating at him lately.

"It's looking good," Cameron commented. "Figure out what you're going to use this for?"

"Not a clue." Drake glanced over his shoulder and pointed with his spatula. "That bucket is the one I've been dipping out of."

"Heard you got suspended."

Drake cringed. "Yeah. Mayor Jerkwad decided that we needed another man in my department cut. When I refused to lay off another hard worker, he opted to remove me."

"This won't stick," Cameron assured him. "And he won't get reelected."

Drake nodded. "I know, but that man just lives to be a nuisance."

"Wanna talk about it?" Cameron asked.

"If I did, I'd go on some talk show and cry in front of the nation. I'm good."

They worked in silence for a few minutes. Obviously something was on Cameron's mind or he wouldn't have stopped by, but Drake knew his older brother well enough to know not to push.

"Hear you have a woman."

Drake laughed, dropping his spatula into the tray. "That's not what I thought you'd lead in with, but yeah, I guess I do."

"Heard she's a pretty nurse with a cute kid." Cameron turned, glancing over his shoulder. "You ready for all of that?"

Drake nodded. "I wasn't sure if I was at first, but I am now."

He moved on to the next wall and started covering up the nails. "While we're on the topic, I know you're swamped with whatever has had you away from us for months, but I need you to run a check on someone."

"Who?"

"Her ex."

"Come on, Drake. You can't be running a background check on an ex," Cameron complained with a snort.

Dropping his spatula into the mud, Drake turned and leaned against the dry part of the wall. "He's abusive, Cameron."

His brother turned as well and cursed beneath his breath. "All right. Give me the details you have."

"From what Marly says, he's powerful. I don't know what she means by that. His first name is Kevin."

Cameron's brows raised. "And? That's all?"

"Her last name is Haskins. I assume that's his, as well." Something clicked in his mind. "Kevin Haskins," he whispered. "Oh, hell."

Cameron's brows shot up. "You're dating the ex-wife of the state representative?"

Powerful, wanting a perfect family image... Drake should've guessed he was a politician. His gut churned, and everything she'd ever told him made him sick to his stomach.

"Damn it." Drake took a seat on the lid of a bucket of mud and sat his tray next to him on the subfloor. "No wonder she's afraid for me."

"Excuse me?"

Drake eyed his brother. "She told me I couldn't get involved because her ex would ruin me and my career. I had no idea he was that powerful."

"Are you going to back down?" Cameron asked.

"What do you think?"

Cameron laughed. "I think Kevin has one hell of a fight on his hands. The man's a politician. I've no doubt he's got some skeletons hidden in his dirty closet."

Drake nodded. "I don't care what you find, how minor it is, let me know. She's got pictures of the abuse."

"Why hasn't she taken them to the cops?" Cameron asked, finding the lid to the used bucket and putting it on so he could take a seat. "She could get a restraining order."

"She did take them," Drake corrected. "She was told they'd look into it and that was months ago. They keep giving her the runaround, and she figures Kevin has the Nashville PD in his pocket."

Cameron swore again, and the muscles in his tattooed forearm flexed as he tightened his grip on the tray in his hand. "I'll look into it myself. I'm busy, but not too busy to bury a dirty, wife-beating politician. The little girl... Did he ever—"

"No." Drake shook his head. "Marly said he basically ignored her."

"Well, that's something. I've got a good friend who's an investigator. He'll make this top priority."

"Let me know what I owe him."

Cameron nodded. "He works cheap for me, but I'll let you know."

"So what brought you here?" Drake asked. "Because I know it wasn't to spackle—as glamorous as this job is."

Cameron sighed. "I've just got a lot going on and needed a break. Figured you'd be here working."

"You want a beer?" Drake offered.

"Nah. I've got to be somewhere this evening and I need to be alert. Although having a couple of beers doesn't sound bad right now."

Drake came to his feet, stretching out the kink in his back from installing the new drywall on the ceiling last night after he'd left Marly's house.

"How soon will you be wrapping up this mysterious case?" Drake asked, picking up his tray to get back to work.

"I have no idea. Soon, I hope, but realistically, probably not for at least another month."

"Is something big going on in town, or are you working with another department?"

Behind him, he heard Cameron getting back to work, as well. "I can't say much, but it's my department and other law enforcement. If everything goes down as it should, this will be epic."

Drake knew Cameron's job was dangerous, hell, his own was dangerous, but he couldn't help but worry about his brother's state of mind. Going deep undercover wasn't something the chief did often, but Drake knew his brother wasn't about to sit on the sidelines and let other people go after the bad guys.

"Is there something in particular about this case that's bothering you, or is it just the overall red tape and jumping through hoops to make sure the suspect is brought down right?"

Cameron let out a faint laugh. "Oh, the jumping through hoops is always the bane of my existence, but there's more with this case."

Drake wasn't stupid, and knew his brother well enough to read between the lines. "A woman?" he asked.

"Possibly."

"She the perp?" Drake asked.

"No, but she may be getting caught in the middle."

No wonder Cameron needed to vent and blow off some steam. But there were other ways to do it besides putting up drywall. His brother was as much of a protector as Drake and Eli were.

"How about a game of one-on-one?" Drake suggested.

Cameron shrugged. "I suppose I could kick your butt before I head in."

"Please. You're an old man, exhausted from staying out too late. I'll win this match in no time and you'll still have time for a nap before you go to work."

Cameron flipped him the finger. Drake hated what his brother was going through, hated that he was torn between his emotions and loyalty to his work.

But Cameron was a strong man and an even stronger cop, and Drake had every confidence in the world that Cameron would find dirt on Kevin. Because even though Marly was afraid for him, he wasn't afraid one bit.

Angry, yes; ready to fight all of her battles, definitely, but not afraid.

Regardless, in the end, Drake would get what he wanted. And he wanted Marly and Willow in his life.

Chapter Thirteen

Willow had finally gotten her engine ride thanks to Drake's second-in-command, Tyler Warren. Tyler was a sucker for kids and Willow was one easy child to fall for…especially when she'd shown up in her worn cowgirl boots and the fireman's helmet Drake had given her.

Not only had Willow ridden in the engine, Drake and Marly had gone along for the ride, too. He wondered if the mayor saw him riding around in the engine. Honestly, he didn't care. He wasn't breaking any rules—he wasn't driving, he wasn't in any type of uniform and he hadn't even worn one of his SFD tees.

Regardless if the mayor saw them or not, Drake would still put Willow's wishes and his promise to her ahead of Tipton and his moronic rules.

"How about I take her on a tour of the station?" the

assistant chief asked. "I'm sure she'd love the behind-the-scenes tour we didn't give her class."

Drake looked at Marly. "I don't care," she told them. "I just don't want her to be in your way."

Tyler shook his head. "Impossible for her to be in my way."

Willow jumped up and down, holding on to her fireman's helmet with her hands. "This is the best day ever," she squealed.

Willow grabbed Tyler's hand and practically pulled him into the department's open bay. Drake laughed and turned to face Marly.

"He's a sucker for kids. He'll do anything she wants. Don't be surprised if she comes home with a T-shirt."

Marly smiled. "I'm just thrilled she's so happy. I worried about moving her out of Nashville, but she has really taken to the small-town life."

"Have you taken to the small-town life?" he asked, taking her hand and pulling her toward the back of the department, where there was a bench in the shade…and away from the street with nosy onlookers.

They took a seat, and Drake didn't even try to sit away from her. He wanted her to get used to the feel of him beside her. He wanted her to not worry about anything but the way they were so obviously meant to be on this path of healing together.

"I can't believe the festival is in just a few days," she told him, turning her face up to the soft breeze.

"I'll be glad when we can present a check to Shawn and Amy. They have to be running on fumes going back and forth, taking turns being with Jeremy and trying to keep their business up and running here."

Marly nodded. "I know. Good news, though. I called to check on Jeremy earlier today, and his first surgery went even better than the doctors had expected. He's doing really well."

Relief swept through Drake. "That's great, Marly."

Drake wrapped an arm around her and rested his hand on her shoulder. That was something else he wanted her to get used to—his random touch. Being near her and not seeking that contact was nearly impossible, but she needed to discover the positive aspect of touches from a man. She needed to know what a normal, caring relationship was about, and if he had to take baby steps to get her to that point, then so be it.

She stiffened just for a second, then relaxed against his side. "You're going to spoil me."

Drake grinned. "That's the plan."

She leveled him with her sweet smile, her eyes seeking his. "What else is in your plan?"

"To stop Kevin Haskins from getting near you or Willow."

Marly gasped, her eyes widened and she went pale. Damn it, he hadn't meant to blurt that out, but he wasn't thinking straight.

"Drake," she whispered. "Please, you can't."

Now that she knew that he was perfectly aware of who she was running scared from, Drake decided to lay it all on the line. She needed to know someone was fighting for her, needed to know that someone was him and that he wasn't giving up just because things may be getting a bit difficult.

"I can and I will," he insisted. "Kevin may be powerful, but I guarantee I've got more motivation and drive. Guys like him just pay people off, thinking that will get them ahead. You're living in Stonerock now, and he has no one on this police force in his pocket."

The determination in Drake's tone sent shivers through Marly despite the early-fall temperatures.

"You have no idea what you're up against." A tremble rippled through her at the endless, terrifying possibilities. "Have you involved your brother?"

Drake merely stared at her, not answering her question.

"You can't do this," she all but cried. "First of all, he will not only ruin your career, he will ruin Cameron's if he's gotten involved. Not to mention this will give him ammunition to take Willow. You can't just steamroll me and think you can decide what is best without talking to me."

"I talked to you, Marly. I've told you over and over that I wouldn't let anyone hurt you or Willow." Drake pushed forward off the back of the bench until he was leaning in toward her. "Just because I know who your ex is now changes nothing from my standpoint. I will still protect you, I will still keep you safe and I will still keep trying to get you to see that I'm not going anywhere."

Marly battled the urge to throw her arms around his neck and revel in the strength and protection he so freely offered.

Coming to her feet, Marly brushed her hair behind her shoulders. "I can't live through this. I can't be with someone who would go behind my back and try to control my future."

"And were you planning on being with me?" he asked, slowly rising to his feet. "Were you planning on fully taking that guard down and letting me in?"

Was she? She was certainly headed in that direction.

Marly smoothed her hand over her bangs and shook her head. "I don't know, Drake. I just know this is a mistake. Going beyond friendship is impossible."

Drake rested his hands on his hips, his eyes never leaving hers. "Fine."

Taken aback by his simple reaction, Marly crossed her arms over her chest. "Fine? That's all you have to say?"

Drake shrugged. "I can still care about you and respect your wishes. If friendship is all you can give, I'll take it. But I won't stop caring, so you can't ask me to."

The man was relentless. He knew what he wanted, had this notion that they could help each other. And he might be right, but...could she take that chance? Could she risk his life by pulling him into her nightmare?

"Let's take Willow for some ice cream."

Marly laughed. "What?"

"Things have been too intense with us lately," he told her with that grin that never failed to melt her. "We need to relax, just have fun. Friends go for ice cream, don't they?"

How could she argue with that logic?

"If Willow found out I turned down ice cream, she would never forgive me."

Drake held out his hand. "Then let's go get her. We'll pick up the ice cream and go sit in the park. There's a bridge there where you can throw bread crumbs and feed the ducks."

Marly looked from his outstretched hand to his eyes. "And you have bread crumbs on you?"

"No, smarty pants." He reached down and grabbed her hand when she didn't take his invitation. "We'll swing by the store and get a loaf. Have you taken Willow to the park yet?"

"We went there for a walk a few times, but we haven't fed the ducks. She'll love it."

Drake led her toward the front of the department, but stopped short of the open bay. When he tugged on her hand to turn her to face him, Marly put her other hand on his chest to prevent falling.

He tipped her head up and captured her lips in a brief, yet potent, powerful kiss. Barely lifting his head, he stroked her bottom lip, which was still tingling from the all-too-short encounter.

"You may be stuck in this friendship phase, but you should know, I've moved past that." He nipped at her lips once more. "When you're ready to catch up with me, let me know."

With that, he left her standing in the sunshine, wondering what in the world she was going to do with all of her emotions, her wants and desires.

How could they remain just friends when she'd had a taste of that sensual mouth, knew how arousing his touch could be, had experienced that selfless generosity he so freely gave?

Willow's sweet squeal sounded from inside the department. Marly smiled. Had her father ever gotten that reaction from her? Had her own father ever surprised her with anything so simple as ice cream and a trip to a park?

Something stirred deep within Marly. No matter what she told Drake, what barriers she tried to put between them, he'd managed to break through each wall. He'd managed to penetrate her heart.

God help her… She was falling in love with him.

The morning of the festival was already promising a beautiful sunny day. Marly stuck signs on each table, stating what each station was: face painting, pie tossing, bake sale, silent auction.

She'd had days to think about her growing feelings for Drake and she was still a mess. He'd not made another move, hadn't kissed her again and had been totally, 100 percent…friendly.

Darn that man.

Of course, she was giving mixed signals because her heart and her mind were battling for dominance. And her heart was winning.

Glancing around, she spotted Drake and his brother Eli speaking to an elderly woman. Marly smiled. The two strong men towered over the lady holding a rhinestone cane and wearing a hot pink skirt and…heels?

Marly laughed and turned just as a middle-aged woman came up to the table.

"You must be Marly."

Nodding, Marly smiled. "I am."

"I'm Drake's mother. You can call me Bev." Her eyes darted to the distance and back. "Bless her heart. Maddie Mays always bakes the most unusual breads and gives them as gifts. I suppose she's donating to the bake sale."

Intrigued, Marly tilted her head. "Unusual breads?"

Bev laughed. "Pomegranate pumpkin, kale and strawberries... Never just a traditional banana or zucchini."

Marly made a mental note to bypass those "specialty" breads.

"But she was my husband's best patient, and now she has a soft spot for Eli. Of course, she randomly injures herself pole dancing."

Marly froze, her eyes wide. "I'm sorry. Did you say..."

"Pole dancing," Bev confirmed. "She has a pole in her living room and that's how she says she gets her workout in."

Marly couldn't help the bubble of laughter that escaped. "Well, here I just walk or jog for exercise. Apparently I'm boring."

"According to everyone I've spoken to, you're far from boring," Drake's mom said with a soft smile. "I've heard you described as quiet, sweet, caring, a great nurse and wonderful mother. Sounds like quite a full plate of excitement to me."

Marly didn't say anything... What could she say? Drake's mother asking about her was exactly what

Marly would do as a mother. She couldn't blame the woman.

"Oh, I'm sorry," Bev said, patting Marly's arm. "I didn't mean to make you feel awkward. If it helps, I'm a little out of my element, too. I mean, it's been so long since Drake allowed any woman to occupy his time. I'm just so thankful he met you, and I had to see you for myself."

Marly smiled. "I understand. I have a little girl, so I get the curious-mom feeling."

Bev's smile was so warm, so caring. Marly knew this woman had her hands full with three boys, yet she still seemed…soft, sweet.

"Well, two amazing ladies standing by the silent auction table." Drake came up to stand next to his mother, giving her a kiss on the cheek. "People will pull out the checkbooks for you two, for sure."

Drake's mom smacked him in the stomach. "You hush. Nobody could afford us. Isn't that right, darling?"

Marly nodded. "Afraid so. Especially because I come with an adorable little tomboy."

"Oh, where is she?" Bev clapped her hands together. "I've heard just how wonderful she is and I can't wait to meet her."

Marly smiled, glancing over to where Willow sat beneath a large oak tree, petting a giant mixed-breed dog, which was just one of the many Eli's wife, Nora, had brought for kids to play with from the local no-kill animal shelter.

"That's her," Marly said, pointing. "I may never get her away from those dogs."

"She's an animal lover, huh?" Bev asked. "What kind of dog does she have?"

Marly swallowed. "Um…we don't have a dog. We just moved here and…"

"Mom, can you go help Eli?" Drake chimed in. "He was setting up the bake sale area and I have a feeling he'll be sampling the goods if you don't keep an eye on him."

Bev patted his cheek, as if Drake were still her little boy. "I know when you're trying to get rid of me, but you're right. With Nora busy, Eli will eat everything in sight if left alone." She turned and smiled at Marly. "It was a pleasure to meet you. Have Drake bring you by for dinner so we can talk more."

"I'd like that," Marly told her, realizing just how true the statement was.

Once she was gone, Drake turned to Marly. "Sorry about that. I should've warned you my mother would be here."

Shrugging, Marly shoved her hair behind her ears. "It's no problem at all. She's great."

"Yeah, she is, but I'm sorry about the dog comment. She has no clue about your history. She only knows who you are right here."

"Too bad I'm not that person for real," she muttered.

"You are that person, Marly," he told her, resting his hands on her shoulders. "You're the caring nurse, the festival coordinator, loving mother. You're out from under Kevin's thumb, so anything you're doing now is the real Marly and who you want to be."

He was right. This was her. The small-town life,

the laid-back atmosphere, the community where people came together to help when one of their own was hurting. This was what she'd yearned for while being a picture-perfect wife for so long.

Willow's laughter cut through the park, and Marly glanced over to see her getting her face licked by an adorable little puppy.

"I need to get her a dog," Marly murmured. "She's never asked. How could I not see this?"

Drake squeezed her shoulders until she faced him once again. "You were a little busy setting up a stable life and keeping you and your daughter protected."

"I know, but I still can't ignore the fact she's a child and it's my job to create memories for her."

Drake ducked his head just a tad until his bright blue eyes met hers. The smile he offered had her heart doing flips.

"You chose the rental house with a tree house, you're letting her help with this festival, we gave her a ride on a fire engine… I'd say she's already formed some pretty great memories since you've moved here."

Reaching up to hold on to his thick wrists, Marly tilted her head. "You're right. Parenting is hard. I just want to give her everything."

"You're doing an amazing job."

Marly glanced to the side and noticed a few older ladies staring in their direction. The women had purses on their wrists, pearls around their necks and smiles on their faces.

"We're being watched," Marly whispered.

Drake laughed. "Small-town life. Your business is everyone's business."

Groaning, Marly closed her eyes. "They think we're…we're…"

"Lovers?" he whispered next to her ear, his warm breath tickling the side of her neck.

Her eyes flew open; she dropped her hands from his wrists. "We are friends. That's it."

Drake's smirk had Marly backing up. "For now," he told her.

Squinting her eyes at him, Marly held up a finger. "Don't put words in my mouth. You know where I stand on this."

Laughing, Drake inched closer with each step back she took. "Oh, I know what you said, but I also know what you're not saying."

Holding up both hands, Marly gritted her teeth. "Stop. Right there. I've got things to do and you're distracting me."

"That's part of my evil ploy."

She turned, but stopped when he whispered, "If you stomp off, they'll think we had a lovers' spat."

Clenching her fists, Marly did the only thing she could think to do. She turned around and kissed him. Full on the mouth, hands gripping his shoulders.

Then she pulled away and gave him a shove.

"There," she told him. "Now they'll be all confused and ask you about the girl you're seeing. What will you tell them about us?"

His eyes widened; his nostrils flared. Desire settled into his eyes, and Marly turned and walked away before she did something really crazy…like drag him back to her house. Because lately, more and more, she wanted to do just that.

And now she had to figure out what she wanted. Did she want to live in fear or did she want to finally go after something that would make her happy, something that would make her future—and that of her precious daughter—brighter?

Chapter Fourteen

"Looks like a great turnout, Chief."

Drake cringed inwardly at the voice that was literally mocking him. He'd come over to the face-painting table to see Willow get transformed into a puppy, but now he'd have to turn and confront the one person he wished he could go the rest of his life without seeing.

On a sigh, Drake opted to be the bigger man here as he pushed away from the table and turned.

"That's what we were hoping for," Drake told him. "What are you into? Getting your face painted?"

Oh, the endless jokes Drake could come up with about options for the paint job. But for now he would play it like the upstanding, albeit suspended, citizen he was.

"Just came out to support the family in need," the mayor stated, his tone higher no doubt so people could hear.

Drake didn't miss the fact that the smarmy guy didn't even know Shawn and Amy's names. This little publicity stunt made Drake loathe the man even more.

Drake also highly doubted the jerk would take out his wallet to make a contribution of any kind. Oh, if the newspaper were around, he might.

"I trust you'll be at the council meeting on Monday?"

Drake gritted his teeth and forced himself to remain calm. "Wouldn't miss it."

Mayor Tipton leaned in and lowered his tone. "Just try to control yourself there, Chief. We wouldn't want you to get permanently removed from your position."

Drake reached behind him, absently reaching for a brush sitting in a cup of paint. His fingertips slid carefully along the table until he found one. Bingo. He swirled it around to get it good and coated.

"Oh, I can control myself," Drake stated with a smile. "Oh, here comes Carrie from the *Daily Times*. You'll want to make sure you get a good picture so she can write up all the lies you pay her to print."

His face reddened. "You better watch it. You're skating on thin ice."

Carrie approached. "Mayor, could I get a picture of you with the chief?"

Oh, the timing… Drake couldn't have planned it better himself. Just as she raised the camera, Drake pulled the brush from the cup and streaked it across Tipton's nose. And glory, glory—without even looking, Drake had been dipping the brush in hot pink.

"You…" The mayor stumbled over his words and Drake thought his head was going to explode. "How dare you."

Drake turned, placed the brush back into the cup and gave a wide-eyed Willow a wink. "It's paint. It'll wash off. Although I'm sure one of these lovely high school students from the art program would love to finish my masterpiece. I don't have time right now. I have to go check on the dunking booth. I assume you'll be heading there next to wash off the paint?"

The mayor's jaw clenched, his eyes narrowed. "I'll see you Monday."

Drake held out his hand for Willow to take, and he pulled her to his side. "Can't wait."

The pies were gone, the bake sale table empty, and the silent auction had raked in more money than they could have ever dreamed of. Marly couldn't wait to present the check to Shawn and Amy. Neither had been able to make it today, understandably, but it seemed as though all of Stonerock had come to show their support for sweet Jeremy.

Even Mayor Tipton had made an appearance…and the highlight of the day was when Drake had "accidentally" painted the man's face. Marly had mentally high-fived Drake for the genius move, knowing full well he couldn't help himself. Actually, the mayor should be glad Drake had only settled for the immature act.

Marly knew Mayor Tipton's type. He'd only come for the grand show of it all. He needed to be seen, have a few pictures taken and offer fake smiles and empty promises.

Yeah, she knew his kind all too well. And Marly knew one thing for sure: if she was still here when election time came around, he certainly wasn't getting her vote.

Drake and Eli were loading tables onto the back of Drake's truck. Willow was with Drake's mother, and from the looks of it, those two had become fast friends. The love these virtual strangers had shown Marly's daughter was overwhelming. They had taken Marly and Willow in without question…all because of Drake.

Marly loaded all the signs and the cash box into her car. After locking the doors, she set out to find Willow. Of course, she was still with Drake's mother and the two were headed her way…hand in hand.

"Thank you so much for staying with her while we packed up," Marly told Bev as they approached.

"Oh, she was an absolute delight. I raised three boys, so having a girl around is quite different, but fun."

Willow bounced from one foot to another. "Mrs. St. John said I could come over and spend the night. She said we could watch movies and make cookies and then for breakfast she would make her famous French toast."

Marly jerked her gaze back to Bev. "Oh, um…"

"I was serious," Drake's mother said with a smile. "I'd love to have her over, but I completely understand if you don't want her to. I mean, you barely know me."

Marly swallowed, more than surprised that this woman would welcome Willow into her home so freely.

"Please, Mommy," Willow begged, still holding on

to Bev's hand. "I promise I'll be a big girl and I'll be good for Mrs. St. John."

Torn, Marly looked between the older woman and Willow. Both held the same hopeful look on their faces. Marly couldn't help but laugh.

"Are you sure?" Marly asked. "I don't want you to feel put on the spot."

"Oh, honey. I invited her, she didn't ask me." Bev looked down at Willow and winked. "Besides, I just discovered my new friend here loves *Mulan*, and that happens to be one of my favorite movies."

"Because she's so strong," Willow beamed. "She doesn't care about a crown or a dress. She's the coolest."

Marly shrugged. "How can I argue, then?"

"Why don't I go ahead and take her home?" Bev suggested. "Take your time cleaning up here and just run her pajamas by anytime."

Bev gave Marly the address, and Marly barely got a kiss before Willow skipped away with Drake's mother.

No, Marly would never let Willow go to the house of someone that Marly had just met, but she was confident that Bev wasn't some ogre or would put her child in danger. The woman had managed to raise three strong, upstanding men.

Once the park looked back in shape, the random garbage was picked up, all tables were loaded and Cameron and crew had headed back to the police station, Marly found herself alone with Drake.

"Where's Willow?" he asked, shoving his hands into his pockets.

"Believe it or not, she went for a sleepover with your mother."

Drake laughed. "Oh, I believe it. She's been chomping at the bit to get grandchildren. My brothers and I have tried to rein her back in, but she's so excited. Now that Eli has one, she's backed off me and Cameron."

Marly yawned. "Sorry," she muttered around her hand. "I'm exhausted, but this was a good day."

"Any idea how much we brought in yet?"

Marly shook her head. "I know we have at least a couple thousand, but I plan on counting it all later once I'm not so sleepy."

"Need me to follow you home?" he asked, his brows drawn together.

His genuine concern continued to win her over.

"No, I'm fine. I'll call you later tonight or tomorrow with the amount and we can go present Shawn and Amy with a check when we can catch one of them at their store."

"Sounds good to me."

He stared at her for another moment. The sun had started setting, and the air had turned a bit cooler now. But the shiver that raced through her had nothing to do with the dropping evening temperatures and everything to do with the man who stood before her and had made it no secret that he wanted more than friendship.

"If you need anything or if you run into a problem, don't try to be a hero. Call me." Drake slid her hair away from her face, pushing her bangs away where she knew he could see her scar. "I expect nothing in return. You know that, right?"

Marly nodded. "I'll call if I need you."

And those words held so much more meaning than she'd intended.

"See you later," she told him, needing to get home and get Willow's things gathered.

Drake nodded his goodbye, and a part of Marly was relieved he was letting her go without the flirting. But then she realized he was giving her the space she'd requested, he was being noble and, darn him, he was letting her decide what she really wanted.

Marly drove home and grabbed some pajamas, clothes for tomorrow, a toothbrush and Willow's favorite pillow. After shoving it all in Willow's small horse tote bag, she headed back out. She'd stashed the money box in her bedroom and intended to count the proceeds as soon as possible. Hanging on to that much cash made her nervous. Money was Kevin's thing… It had never been hers.

Turned out Drake's parents didn't live far from Marly at all. That was an added comfort. The neighborhood with its tree-lined streets and simple cottages with window boxes full of colorful flowers and neatly manicured lawns just screamed small-town USA. Marly wanted to be a part of this community more than she'd first thought possible.

In the beginning, coming to Stonerock had just been a means of escape. But now that she was here, Marly realized she wanted to stay, wanted to put down roots here for herself and her daughter.

After Marly dropped off the bag and got in one more kiss good-night from Willow, she was more than ready to go home, soak in a tub and do absolutely nothing. When was the last time she'd done nothing? Or pampered herself? She didn't have to work tomorrow and she planned on taking advantage of that fact.

She started her engine and pulled out of the subdivision, but instead of heading home, she turned toward Drake's house. She'd never been to his house, but he'd told her where he lived and she figured she'd just drive by to see it…just in case she ever wanted to visit.

Oh, who was she kidding?

Pulling into his drive behind his black truck, Marly called herself all kinds of fool for being there.

But for once in her life, she wasn't going to second-guess herself. So before she could sit in her used SUV and talk herself out of it, she jerked open the door and marched right up to his entrance. She knocked on the door and waited. Nerves were starting to consume her, but before she could turn and walk away, the door swung wide-open and Drake stood there wearing only a towel and water droplets all across his bare, chiseled chest.

Marly's eyes widened as she took her visual sampling of the man who had consumed her thoughts, her fantasies, for weeks.

"You flatter me with that look," he said with a grin. "But I'm assuming you didn't come here to stare at my chest."

Digging up courage from deep within, Marly squared her shoulders and placed a hand on his chest. The hair between his pecs tickled her palm.

"That's where you would be wrong," she told him,

backing him into his living room. "I did come here to stare at your chest, and to take you up on your offer of going beyond friends."

His heavy hand came up to cover hers. "Not that I'm complaining, but why the change of heart?"

Marly focused on his mouth, his eyes. "Because I'm finally taking what I want. And I want you."

Chapter Fifteen

Drake had waited for this moment. Had fantasized about it to the point where it had become real in his mind.

But nothing had prepared him for the confident, passionate woman standing before him with determination in her eyes and a defiant tilt to her chin.

"Are you sure?" he asked, praying she was. "I don't want regrets later."

That delicate hand of hers rested against his bare chest—just that simple gesture had his blood soaring. He ached for those soft hands of hers to be all over him.

"I have no regrets where you're concerned," she told him, her voice husky with arousal.

This was the moment he'd been waiting for…a moment he didn't think he'd ever be ready for after Andrea died. But he'd gotten stronger each day, had finally come to realize that he was still alive, that he needed to move on.

Drake reached around her and gave the door a firm shove to send it closing with a click. Then he fisted his hands in her hair and set his mouth over hers, needing to feel her.

Stepping fully against her, Drake slid his hands down her back to cup her rear and tug her hips toward his. Her purse and keys fell to the floor as her arms wrapped around his neck.

"It's late. I probably should've called," she muttered against his lips. "I just didn't think…"

"Good." He tugged her long-sleeved T-shirt over her head and tossed it to the side. "When you think you start to pull back. You followed your instinct, your heart. And you're in the right place."

Drake stepped back, ready to take his fill of the woman who had caused him many sleepless nights and cold showers. A shiver swept through his body.

"Are you sure?" she asked, holding on to his shoulders and studying his face. "I mean, I assume I'm the first since…"

"You're the first since Andrea passed," he confirmed. "I haven't wanted anyone else."

Marly closed her eyes. "I hope you're not disappointed. I'm not that experienced, and I just want you to—"

He cut her off with another kiss, then eased back. "Doubts have no room here. Deal?"

Nodding, she looked up at him and smiled. "Deal. But you'll tell me if you don't like something, right?"

"There's nothing you could do that I wouldn't like."

Marly's fingertips trailed over his chest, down his abs, and he nearly fell to his knees right there. He was so in for it. Any control he'd thought he had was gone and Marly held all the power. This beautiful, vibrant, vulnerable woman had more power than she could ever imagine. She might not realize how far she'd come since she'd first jumped beneath his touch, but she'd scaled mountains. Here she was, standing before him with all the confidence of a woman taking charge of her life.

Her courage was beyond sexy.

"I've only been with one man," she told him, eyeing the knot in his towel. "I'm just scared, I guess."

Tipping her chin up with his thumb and finger, Drake bent his head to look her in the eyes. "Don't do this because you feel like you have to."

"I want to be with you," she told him. "I want to move on. I want to prove to myself that I can do this and not be afraid, that there's a man who will treat me like I should be treated. But most of all I'm done denying what I want. I need you, Drake. I just need you to go slow. Is that okay?"

"You humble me." Drake framed her face. "I'm nervous I won't make this perfect for you."

Marly slid her hands inside his towel until it loosened and slid to the floor. "Just let me be in charge for now and I should be okay. If you start getting too dominating, that may scare me. I'm sorry."

Drake glanced down to where her hands had rested on his bare hips. "If you want to take charge, baby, I'm certainly not going to stop you."

Laughing, Marly went to unfasten her jeans. "I should've known you'd be fine with being manhandled."

"Handle me all you want." Drake spread his arms wide. "Where do you want me?"

Marly shoved her jeans down her legs, toed off her flats and kicked them aside, leaving her standing before him in a pale pink bra and panty set.

She glanced down at her body and shrugged. "Cotton, sorry. I wasn't planning on this when I got ready for the festival. But that's me, so…"

"They're coming off, so I don't care what they look like," he told her truthfully, though he would say anything to put her at ease.

"I'm not sure what kind of woman you're used to, but I hope the added weight and stretch marks are your thing," she joked, but her voice was laced with insecurity.

"Everything about you is my type of woman." He slid his hands over her hips and up to her waist. "No matter what you look like, no matter what battle scars you sport from a pregnancy or from defending yourself, you're the exact woman I want."

Marly trembled between his hands, but he slowly ventured on up and reached around her back to unhook her bra. With her eyes locked on his, she held out her arms as he slid the garment down and discarded it somewhere in the vicinity of the couch.

"I need you against me," he murmured as he splayed his hands across her back and pulled her body flush against his. "You feel so good, Marly."

Damn it, his hands were shaking. He didn't want

to mess this up, didn't want her to worry about doing something wrong or not living up to his standards.

What the hell had her ex filled her head with? The man had obviously been mentally abusive, as well. But there was no room for him in the relationship Drake and Marly were building, so Drake shoved all thoughts of the ex aside and focused on the nearly naked woman in his arms.

Hooking his thumbs into the waistband of her panties, he shoved them down as far as he could and let her take it the rest of the way as he nibbled on her throat.

Marly arched her back, her breasts brushing against the hair on his chest and sending jolts of need through his body so intense he was afraid he would snap. But he had to rein his desires back in and take all leads from her.

"Where's your bedroom?" she whispered.

"Too far away."

Molding her breasts in his hands, wanting to feel all of her at once, Drake walked backward until the couch hit the back of his legs.

Marly smiled up at him. "You ready?"

"Baby, I was ready weeks ago, the second you started lecturing me about the healing of burns."

Flattening her hands on his chest, Marly gave him a shove, sending him back onto the oversize couch. Looking up at her, with her swollen lips, her disheveled hair and totally naked body, Drake wanted to take a mental picture because he never, ever wanted to forget this moment.

Drake grabbed hold of her rounded hips and tugged

her to stand perfectly between his legs. Her fingertips dug into his shoulders as he dotted kisses along her abdomen.

After a moment, he rested his head on her stomach and closed his eyes. He was falling apart. Inside, where Marly had penetrated so deep, he was crumbling, because he wanted to be it for her. Not just her protector or even her lover, he wanted to be it. As in, happily-ever-after.

What an awkward time to come to that realization.

Drake breathed in and exhaled. No way could he confess this to Marly. He wanted her to stick around, not run away.

"You okay?" she asked, sliding her fingertips along his shoulders.

"Yeah," he said, his head still resting against her stomach. "I'm just trying to take it slow. I don't want to scare you, and I'm holding on by a thread here."

Her soft chuckle vibrated him. "I'm not scared of you," she murmured. "But we need a condom before this goes any further."

Condom. Yes. Why hadn't he thought of that? Oh, yeah, because he'd been finishing his shower when she'd knocked and he'd lost all rational common sense after that.

He came to his feet. "Don't move."

In a mad dash to his bathroom, he grabbed a condom, slid it on and returned to the living room, where Marly literally hadn't moved.

Instead of sitting back down, he took her into his

arms Rhett Butler–style, earning him a squeal and a slight laugh.

"What are you doing?" she asked, looping her arms around his neck.

"I changed my mind. I want you in my bed."

His bed, where no other woman had ever been. He'd replaced the bed he and Andrea shared, just another way he had moved on.

Marly's openmouthed kisses along his neck had him nearly growling as he gently placed her on his bed and came down to lie beside her. He was very careful not to put any weight on her.

He stroked her hip, the dip in her waist and traveled on up to one breast. Her bright eyes held his as she trembled beneath him. Knowing she trusted him with her body, her heart, was beyond humbling. This woman wouldn't be here if her heart wasn't invested… and that silent fact made him even more excited about where this was going.

When Marly reached down to stroke him, Drake's eyes nearly rolled back in his head. He eased away, falling onto his back, and laced his hands behind his head. She wanted control, fine by him. Who was he to stop her?

Damn, that felt good.

When she slid one leg over his and eased up to straddle him, Drake opened his eyes, not wanting to miss a second.

Marly smiled down at him and settled her hands on his chest. "You should know, I'm falling for you."

Drake swallowed. "Yeah? You should know I fell for you a while ago."

When she sank onto him and began to move, Drake knew she was the woman he'd been waiting for. He knew she was the woman he was meant to move on with. Now he just had to make sure she kept on this path, the path that led the two of them into a future together and away from her fears and insecurities.

Drake reached up, pulling her head down so he could capture her lips. Their bodies moved perfectly, her soft little moans filled the silence.

All too soon her body tightened, her fingertips bit into his shoulders and Drake let himself go, too. Finally. He'd finally found where he belonged.

Marly rested her head in the crook of Drake's arm. She'd tried to move more than once, but he'd silently kept his arm around her and tugged her back in place.

Tears pricked her eyes. The man was absolutely perfect. Well, no man was perfect, but he was perfect for her. She never knew a man could be so selfless, so genuine, with no hidden agenda. She'd been living in a shallow, loveless world for so long…and that was on the good days.

"Don't bring anything of your past into my bedroom," he whispered into the dark. "It's just us. There's nothing to fear. There's no one to hurt you."

Marly slid her hand up over his taut stomach and up onto his chest. "Sorry. Just thinking."

"I'd rather you be sleeping. It's after midnight and we had a really long day."

Sleep? At a time like this when she'd discovered she could fall in love, for real this time, and she had to figure out a way to keep Willow for good, as well as keep Drake off Kevin's radar? Sure, no problem falling to sleep with all of that swirling around in her mind.

"What was it like growing up with brothers and a loving family?"

Drake slid his hand up her bare arm and settled it on her shoulder. "You really want to just talk?"

"Yeah."

She'd never made love with someone and then just settled in afterward to appreciate the special bond. This was a moment she wanted to capture, because she'd never realized just what she'd been missing.

"My brothers and I may have caused a ruckus in town a time or two when we were teens," he started. His low voice caused his chest to vibrate. "My poor mother, she took it one day at a time. My father, on the other hand, wasn't so lenient. I know we embarrassed him on more than one occasion. He was the town doctor, so he was well respected. Then the St. John boys came through."

Marly fisted her hand on his chest and rested her chin there. "And here you all are with powerful jobs in the town. What transformed you?"

"As hellacious as we were, we respected our father." Drake slid her hair over her shoulder and smoothed it down her back. "Plus we all joined the service after we graduated. That pretty much knocked the chip off our shoulders."

He'd been a soldier, fighting for others. Just another

layer to his selfless ways. The man was remarkable in the fact he was always putting others first, proving beyond a doubt he was indeed a hero to anyone who came in contact with him.

Which made her wonder…

"Tell me about Andrea."

He stiffened beneath her, his heavy-lidded eyes closed for a brief second. "Are you sure you want that here?"

"I'm sure," she told him. "She's a part of you. I want to know about her."

With a sigh, Drake continued to stroke her hair. "We met when I came back home from the Marines. She was actually new to the area and was a professor at the college. She loved Nashville, but wanted a small town to settle in. We were set up on a blind date and we dated about two years before we became engaged."

Drake's eyes drifted across the room. "We were only engaged about a month before the accident. We were headed to a fund-raiser for the department. I was driving, she was in the passenger seat putting on her makeup and—"

"You don't have to go into that," Marly told him, placing a hand on his cheek to offer support. "I don't want you reliving it."

His eyes sought hers. "I relive it every day. But I'm to the point I can talk about it without all the survivor's guilt I once had."

"How did you get past that?"

"Counseling," he admitted. "I fought it at first, was convinced talking to a stranger wouldn't change the fact that Andrea was gone. I still have some guilt—I always will—but I realized that I couldn't have saved her. The accident was the fault of the semi driver who ran the light, not mine. She was pinned, and thankfully had passed out."

His chin quivered, sending a knife of remorse straight through Marly's heart. "Drake, please. I don't need to know any more."

Through the moonlight slanting across his bed, she saw the shimmer of tears in his eyes. "You're part of my life, Marly. I want you to know."

Flattening her hand over his heart, she waited for him to continue. This was important to him, perhaps even to his ongoing healing process. And he was right. She was part of his life now, no matter how frightening and thrilling that may be. If he wanted to share the most hurtful part of his past, then she would be brave enough to listen.

"The flames appeared before I could even try to get her out. The semi had tipped and was leaking gasoline."

Drake closed his eyes, a single tear slipping down his cheek. "The hardest part was getting out of that car, knowing she was trapped inside and there wasn't a damn thing I could do about it. That image… It haunts me. But I know had I stayed, I wouldn't be here."

Marly swiped Drake's damp cheek and turned his face until he met her gaze. "You're the most honorable man I've ever met."

Taking hold of her hand and kissing her fingertips, Drake smiled down at her. "I'll never let anyone hurt you. You know that, right?"

"When you say the words, I want to believe."

"Then believe it. I'm not afraid of what Kevin could do to me or my job. He tries anything in this town and he will have to answer for it."

Marly said nothing, letting the implications and this entire situation settle in. She truly believed Drake would do anything in his power to keep her and Willow protected. But she worried this was moving faster than she'd ever anticipated.

"I don't want you to think I want to be with you out of my need to protect," he said, interrupting her thoughts. "I'm not replacing Andrea with you and I am not attracted to you because I think you need saving."

Drake shifted on the bed, scooting up until his back was propped against his pillow. Marly sat up, too, facing him with the sheet pulled up over her chest.

"I'm perfectly aware that you can save yourself," he went on, taking her hands and settling them in his lap. "You've done a remarkable job for so long, but you don't have to be alone anymore. I want to be with you. I want to provide support both emotionally and physically."

Marly squeezed his hands. "I admit I'm tired. Tired of worrying, tired of wondering if he's going to find me today or if his lawyer and a corrupt cop are going to show up at my door and take Willow."

"What's the status of the courts and custody?" he asked.

Holding the sheet between her arms and her sides, Marly shook her head. "Right now I have full custody. He honestly doesn't care about Willow. She's too rambunctious, too tomboyish and too much work according to him. But he'll take her out of spite just because I love her and she's my world. Anything that hurts me would bring him joy."

Something glinted from Drake's eyes that hadn't been there a moment before. Something darker.

"He'll find me," she went on. "He needs me and Willow to stand by him for this upcoming election. He only waited because I threatened to go to the press about the abuse and he thought I'd come back on my own. Now that he sees I'm stronger and I'm not coming back, he's forcing his hand. He wants to play up the angle of how he's turned his life upside down to accommodate his family and how he's made every effort to reunite us."

The thought sickened her. She'd die before she ever returned to his clutches again.

"I refuse to go back, and when he finally comes after me, he'll be even angrier."

Drake tugged on her until she lay sprawled across his chest. Comforted by his strong arms wrapped around her, Marly slid her leg up over his firm thigh.

"I don't want to think about that tonight," she told him. "My worries will be there tomorrow, and reality is pretty harsh in the light of day. Can't we just have us right now?"

When she tipped her head to look up at him, Drake cupped her cheek, stroking her bottom lip.

"That's the second-best idea you've had."

Smiling, Marly eased up to straddle his hips. "And what was the first?"

"Showing up on my doorstep on a mission."

He gripped her arms and pulled her down for a toe-curling kiss. Marly shoved thoughts of anything else aside as she fell deeper in love with her hero.

Chapter Sixteen

"I'm pretty sure I have stale cereal or possibly a moldy loaf of bread," Drake mumbled as the sunlight flooded his bedroom. "So what would you like for breakfast?"

Marly rolled over and sat up, her back to Drake. "As tempting as that sounds, I need to go pick up Willow. Supposedly your mother is making her French toast."

The bed jerked behind her, and Marly glanced over her shoulder to see Drake jump up. "My mother is making French toast? Throw your clothes on and let's get going. You've never had a breakfast like that in your life, I guarantee it."

"I'm not barging in there and asking your mother to make my breakfast," Marly told him, still holding the sheet up around her chest. "I can grab something at home, but I don't want your mom to feel as though she has to keep Marly all day."

Shrugging as he pulled on his boxer briefs, Drake said, "Trust me, my mother doesn't care, and I'm sure by this point my dad is wrapped around Willow's little finger."

Marly tugged the sheet with her as she came to her feet. Her clothes were still strewn about the living room, which had seemed sexy and romantic last night, but in the light of day and after the fact, Marly was feeling more insecure than anything.

"Drop the sheet."

Marly turned to stare at the half-naked, beautifully sculpted man. "What?"

His eyes roamed over her body. "Drop it. I've seen everything you have and there's no way you're going to be insecure around me. Any imperfection in your mind is beauty in mine."

Marly clutched the sheet tighter between her breasts. Could she just drop it? For so long she'd been told how out of shape her body was, how the stretch marks could be removed if she'd get a tummy tuck. Added to that, Marly hadn't been naked in front of a man other than her husband before last night.

Drake crossed the room, slid his hands over hers and gently tugged until the sheet slid away and puddled at her feet.

"I don't care what happened before," he insisted, his dark eyes focused on hers. "I don't care what you've been told or how you've been treated. From now on, you'll be treasured, appreciated and loved. I don't want any doubts. I don't want any insecurities. Got it?"

Swallowing past the lump in her throat, Marly nodded. Drake's hands roamed up her stomach, over her breasts and up to her neck, where he used his thumbs to tip up her chin.

"We may be late for breakfast," he murmured against her lips. "I'm in the mood for something else right now."

Marly smiled. "You're going to make me look bad if I show up late to get my kid."

Wrapping his arms around her and tossing her back onto the bed, Drake crawled over her with a wicked grin and a quirk to his brow. "You're going to look really bad when we show up together. No way am I missing my mom's French toast."

Marly laughed as Drake started showing her his idea of breakfast.

Okay, so they were kind of late and more than likely breakfast was all gone, but the morning spent in bed had been so worth it.

Drake escorted Marly up the stone sidewalk toward his parents' house. They were running even later since Marly had insisted on grabbing different clothes from her house because she refused to do the walk of shame up to his mother's door…as if his mother wouldn't take one look at the two of them together and draw her own conclusions. The woman had raised three boys—she was pretty smart.

Drake eased around Marly and opened the front door. The instantly familiar smell of home greeted him.

Laughter and chatter came from the kitchen, and Drake grabbed Marly's hand, leading her that way.

"Wait," she said, tugging on his hand. "I am fine with your mom knowing about us, but let me talk with Willow. I don't want her to think I've just replaced her father or that this isn't something special."

Drake turned, framed her face with his hands and kissed her forehead before enveloping her in a hug. "I will do whatever you think is best for Willow. You just tell me what to do or what not to do."

Marly hugged him in return and stepped back. "I'll talk to her when we get home, so keep those lips and hands to yourself while we're here. Got it?"

Drake took a step away and saluted. "Got it."

"Mama!" Willow ran through the living room and launched herself at Marly. "Mrs. St. John makes the best French toast ever. I told her she could show you and you could make them again for me."

Drake couldn't help but laugh. When he turned to go find his mom, he ran into Cameron.

"Hey, didn't expect you here." Drake slapped his brother on the arm. "Cameron, this is Marly."

"Marly," Cameron greeted. "I've heard quite a bit about you."

"Glad I could finally meet the final St. John brother," she said, flashing a wide smile.

"Is Megan here, too?" Drake asked. "Haven't seen her much lately."

"She's been busy," Cameron replied. "I haven't gotten much time in with her, either. Our friendship for the past few weeks has resorted to texts all hours of the day and night."

"Megan is Cam's best friend," Drake explained to Marly. "She's a therapist and has a very full schedule."

"Maybe I'll be able to meet her soon," Marly said, her weight shifting closer to Drake.

He slid a hand behind her back, silently stating just how serious they were. "You heard about Mom's French toast, too?"

Cameron shook his head. "Actually, I just got in from an all-nighter. I ran by here to see Mom and was heading to your place next before I run home and grab a few hours of sleep."

Drake glanced over his shoulder, saw Marly's questioning eyes on his. "I'll be back in in a minute."

"Everything okay?" she asked.

Drake nodded. "Yeah, just tell Mom I'll be right in."

With her hand on Willow's shoulder, Marly glanced between Drake and Cameron. "Okay."

Drake waited until she was in the other room and motioned for Cameron to follow. They stepped onto the porch and Cameron shut the door behind him.

Crossing his arms over his chest, Drake eyed his brother, who had circles beneath his eyes, wrinkled clothes, day-old scruff and disheveled hair. "You look like hell."

Raking a hand through his shaggy mop, Cameron sighed. "Trust me, I look good compared to how I feel."

Drake shifted his weight. "Man, you're killing yourself. I hope this case you're working on is ending soon. I've never seen you like this."

"It'll be over when it's over," Cameron muttered. "Anyway, I have information you need to know regarding your least favorite politician."

"I hope it's enough to keep him away from her."

"Maybe. I found a female who worked in his office several years ago. Supposedly she tried to file assault charges on Kevin, but then they disappeared and she suddenly left the office."

Drake gritted his teeth and glanced across the street as a kid went by on his bike and turned up a driveway. Another car pulled up to the curb a few doors down. Such a simple, mundane life he'd taken for granted, and Marly had endured hell. No more. He wanted this life for her; he wanted her to know simple and mundane.

Focusing back on Cameron, Drake asked, "So where is this woman now?"

"We're trying to find her," Cameron confirmed. "I should hear something in the next day or two. My friend is relentless, so he won't stop until he finds her."

"Good. I don't want Marly to know I'm having Kevin investigated." Drake glanced at the door, hoping his mother and Marly were bonding…or whatever women did. "He's been sending threats, and if he shows up, you better get there before I do."

"Oh, Drake, come on. Don't make me arrest you."

Drake fisted his hands on his hips. "If Marly and Willow are safe, I don't care what you do to me."

"Don't say that. Just let me handle this, all right?"

Drake merely stared, not saying anything else. Cameron knew full well that if Kevin stepped foot onto Marly's property, there would be no holding back for

Drake. He would protect what was his, and Marly and Willow belonged in his life now.

The swift revelation overcame him, and he knew right then that he would fight for her no matter what. He'd been given this second chance, and he wasn't going to throw it away because he was worried about his sometimes unsettling feelings.

There would always be that piece of him that missed Andrea. There would always be that piece of him that would wonder what would've happened if he'd been able to save her or if there'd been no accident at all. But he had to move on. Not just in small steps, but in this life-changing decision. At some point he would have to take a leap over that hurdle he'd placed before himself. So why not jump in and reach for the goal that was standing right before him?

"Dude, you all right?"

Drake glanced at Cameron, who was staring. "Yeah, sorry. Just zoned out for a minute."

"Anything to do with the fact you and the pretty nurse came to breakfast together?" Cameron asked with a knowing smile.

"Something like that."

Cameron smacked Drake on the shoulder. "Good for you. I knew you'd be able to fully move on once the right woman came into the picture. For what it's worth, and even though I just met her, I really like her. I'm a good judge of character, and Willow is a little pistol. She's adorable."

Drake couldn't help but smile. "She's pretty amazing, like her mom. I better get back in there. Keep me posted no matter how minor the information is."

Cameron nodded. "Will do. I'm headed home for a few hours of sleep before I hit the shift later. Text me if you need anything. Can't guarantee I'll get right back at you, but I will when I can."

"Just take care of yourself."

Cameron gave a mock salute. "Okay, Mom."

Drake gave him the one-armed man hug and headed into the house, where he found Willow on a stool at the sink washing dishes. Her nightgown sleeves were pushed up to her elbows, her bed head had been pulled up into a ponytail and she was just scrubbing away at the forks.

"This is how you wrap up a fun sleepover?" Drake asked his mother, who was putting fresh French toast onto plates.

"She wanted to do it," his mom defended.

Marly poured a cup of coffee and sat it in front of Drake. "Really, she loves doing dishes. She loves being a big girl and helping."

"I wanted to make the breakfast," Willow muttered with her back still to the room.

"It won't be long," Marly promised. "I'll have you making me breakfast all the time in a few years."

"So how was the sleepover?" Drake asked, pouring an insane amount of syrup onto his stack.

"Loud," his father said, stepping into the kitchen. "Those two laughed and talked until after midnight. I gave up and went to bed."

Drake saw Marly cringe, and he reached across the

table to pat her hand. "You're just jealous you can't stay up like you did when you were young," Drake told his father. "Put to shame by your wife and a little girl."

"Yeah, well, I found out that little girl is the best Go Fish player in the world." Mac St. John went over to the sink and patted Willow's head. "She beat me four times before I finally called mercy and asked her to leave me with some dignity."

Willow glanced over her shoulder. "He's really bad. I offered to give him lessons."

Marly relaxed a bit in her seat and started to cut into her breakfast. "Well, thank you so much for having her and for this amazing breakfast."

"Anytime," his mother said with a soft smile as she placed a couple of plates on the counter behind her husband for Willow to wash. "We loved having a young one in the house. Movies, cards, popcorn… We'll have to do it again."

Willow clapped, sending suds flying. "I can't wait!"

As much as Drake loved his mother's cooking, he couldn't help but sit back in his seat and take in the atmosphere of his parents bonding so easily with Marly and Willow. This was what he'd always wanted. When he'd grown up in this house, he'd known one day he would bring his family back here to spend time with his parents. Family meant everything to him.

Which meant now that Marly and Willow were part of his, he would stop at nothing to protect them and keep them safe. And soon he'd have to reveal to Marly that he wanted more. He wanted a future.

Chapter Seventeen

Marly had been home only a few minutes when her doorbell rang. Willow had just gone into her room to play, but knowing her daughter, she was probably worn out from the big night and would fall asleep amidst a pile of toys.

Marly headed toward the door, fully expecting to see Drake on the other side. But when she pulled it open, her heart literally jumped into her throat.

"Kevin," she whispered.

In a pale blue dress shirt and black pants, Kevin Haskins always looked like the smarmy politician he was. It nauseated her just to look at his flawless hair, perfectly manicured hands and that cocky way about him, now that she knew what lay behind the facade.

"I know I'm a day early, but I wanted to surprise

you," he told her with that sickening grin on his face as he pushed past her and looked around her living room. "I assumed you understood when I gave you another week that you would be getting ready to come home, but I can see you're not moving in that direction at all."

Marly glanced out the door onto the narrow street. Of all the times she wanted Drake to make a surprise appearance, this wasn't one of them. She couldn't let Kevin's and Drake's paths cross. She had to keep Drake protected, even though he was convinced he could handle Kevin.

"I see small-town life has changed you into a slob." His eyes raked over her hoodie sweatshirt and jeans. "Really, Marly. This is taking your independence a bit too far. Why on earth would you want to look like a suburban housewife with no care for herself?"

Marly crossed her arms and tilted her chin. "You need to leave."

Kevin jerked back as if she'd slapped him. Oh, the irony. She'd never talked back to him before. Never stood up and made a bold statement like that before. Damn…that had felt good.

"I'm not leaving," he all but laughed. "I'm here to get you and the girl and we're going back home."

Fury bubbled within Marly. "*The girl* is your daughter, and her name is Willow."

Rolling his eyes, Kevin sighed. "I don't have time for your games, Marly. For crying out loud, I had to drive all the way out here to retrieve you."

Retrieve her? Like she was a lost shoe?

"I'm not leaving, Kevin. We're divorced. No matter what you say to me, I'm not going with you."

Marly silently applauded herself for standing up to him. Years of marriage, being under his thumb and always being afraid to make him mad had weakened her. But since moving here, meeting Drake and seeing what love was, seeing how a man and woman should be together, Marly had a new outlook on Kevin, and she was ready for him.

"Hi, Daddy."

Marly turned and nearly cried. Willow stood at the end of the hall, almost as if she was afraid to come any farther. This was her own father, a man Willow hadn't seen in months. Just this morning Willow had been laughing and joking with a family that obviously loved her, and here the little girl stood before her own father and she was afraid to make a move.

All of those facts lined up to confirm that Marly had made the right decision in leaving and she'd made the right decision in moving on with Drake.

"Willow," Kevin said with a nod as if he were just greeting an acquaintance. "Your mother and I need to talk. You need to go play or something."

Willow looked at Marly and Marly offered a smile. "Go play, sweetheart. We'll build a fort in just a bit, so why don't you get all the blankets and pillows we need. Okay?"

"Okay, Mama."

Marly waited until her daughter was out of earshot before she rounded back on Kevin. "Don't be a jerk to your own daughter. I realize she's not what you wanted, but she's my world and you will respect her or leave her the hell alone."

Kevin stepped forward. Even though Marly wanted to step back, wanted to go straight into protective mode, she stood her ground. This was her house, her sanctuary, and he was not going to ruin what she was trying to build here. He was not going to come in and start taking charge. No more.

"My, my," he taunted as he continued to close the gap. "You've grown quite the backbone since you left. That's cute, Marly. Really. But we both know you'll come back to me."

"There's nothing you could do to make me come back."

That gleam in his eye made her nervous. Great, she'd just gone and basically challenged him. When he reached up to stroke her cheek, she gritted her teeth and held her gaze firm on his. She couldn't show any weakness or he'd completely turn this around and take all control.

"I'm sure I can get you to come back," he taunted as he continued to stroke. "I've known where you've been for a while now, actually. I know all about your little boyfriend. I know all about the young boy who was injured in the fire. I was at the festival yesterday. Across the street, actually, but I saw you."

Terror slid through her. He knew about Drake. Oh, no. Had he followed her to his house last night?

"You will come back," he continued, gripping her jaw with his crushing fingers. "Because I will donate enough money to this town to reinstate the men your boyfriend needs back at his department, and I will send a very generous check to the family of that boy who was injured. That's a lot of people whose lives could be changed for the better, all with one decision from you."

Marly hated him. She'd hated this man for a while, but right at this very moment she positively loathed him. She batted his hand away and took a step back.

"Get out of my house."

"I can see you're surprised by my generous offer. I'll give you two days to think about it before I come back."

As soon as he left, Marly's shaky legs gave out and she sank onto the floor. What would she do?

All of Drake's men would be back on the job, medical expenses would be not as much of a burden for Shawn and Amy and all Marly had to do was return to living in hell, living a nightmare.

"Mama," Willow called from the back bedroom. "I'm ready."

"Be right there, honey."

That sweet little voice, that precious, innocent little girl depended on Marly to keep her safe. There was no way she could return to the life she'd finally escaped from.

How could she fully explain this to Drake?

The two powerful men would inevitably meet. Marly only prayed Drake controlled himself, because the last thing Marly wanted was for him to be arrested by his own brother.

Drake pulled up to the curb at Marly's house with strawberry cupcakes. Apparently, when Willow had stayed over at his mother's house, the little girl had mentioned that her favorite dessert was strawberry cupcakes. He was such a sucker for a cute little girl with lopsided pigtails and cowgirl boots. He was a sucker for her mother, too.

Why hadn't he heard any news from Cameron? Not that Drake wished a woman to be another victim, but perhaps if the woman was willing to step forward, they could build some sort of case against Kevin so he would stay away from Marly. A man like that needed to pay, needed to be held accountable for his cowardly actions.

But right now, he was going to focus on building his future with this amazing woman who'd swept into his life and instantly had him reevaluating his priorities. She'd put light into the darkest corners of his heart he never thought could be touched again.

And sweet Willow thrown into the mix was just the cherry on top.

Drake held the cupcake box in one hand, rang the doorbell with the other and was a bit surprised when Marly's soft tone came from the other side of the door.

"Who is it?" she asked.

"It's me."

The dead bolt slid back, a chain jingled against the door and finally the door opened. He knew she'd been frightened, but this was a first for all the locks and her extra security.

She turned when he entered. After closing the door behind him, Drake glanced around. "Where's Willow?"

"She's in my room watching a movie." She still kept

her back to his. "We were having movie night and I was about to make some popcorn."

When she went into the kitchen, Drake followed again. He sat the cupcake box on the kitchen table, wondering why this felt so…off. Something was wrong.

"I brought strawberry cupcakes," he told her, watching as she reached up into a cabinet to grab a box of popcorn. "My mom said Willow mentioned they were her favorite, so I thought she may like some."

"That's sweet. I'll go get her."

Her clipped words, her lifeless tone had Drake crossing the small space and grabbing her elbow until she turned to face him.

When he caught sight of her pale face, her swollen eyes, fear gripped him. "What happened?"

That quivering chin of hers nearly did him in. "It's nothing. I just have a lot on my mind."

"You've been crying. Talk to me."

Her face searched his and for a moment he thought she'd open up, but she shook her head. "I… It's nothing."

So they were back to that. Disappointment slid through him, making him wonder how they could've taken such giant steps forward and suddenly be taking more steps back. She'd erected that wall again.

Hadn't she just left his bed that morning? Was she having delayed regrets? Something other than the usual issues was troubling her enough to bring her to tears. And not just a few tears, but enough to have her eyes puffy and red.

"If you shut me out again, I can't help you," he whispered.

Marly's face crumbled, and he quickly wrapped her in his arms. Before he could do much more than run his hands up her back, Willow, with her lopsided pigtails, came skipping into the kitchen.

"Hi, Chief. Why is Mama crying?"

Marly started to straighten, but Drake held her tight. "These are happy tears," he explained with a smile, hoping she'd buy the lie. "She was so excited about the strawberry cupcakes I brought, she just started crying."

Willow's eyes scanned the kitchen until they landed on the box on the table.

"Can I have one?" she cried.

Marly sniffed into his chest as Drake continued to stroke her back. "Sure," he told her. "Go ahead and take it on back, but try not to make a mess, okay?"

Quickly, she tore into the box and chose the perfect cupcake and raced from the room.

"I hope you don't mind you're probably going to have strawberry-cake crumbs in your bed."

"I don't mind." Marly wrapped her arms around him. "I'm sorry. I don't mean to fall apart on you. I was back there in the dark and Willow didn't notice I was upset. I thought I could keep this to myself, but..."

Easing back just a bit, Drake tipped his head to the side to peer down at her. "But what?"

Wet eyes came up to meet his. "I need you. I thought I could do this, I thought I could save you, but I can't do it alone."

"Save me?" he asked.

Marly bit her trembling lip and glanced away for a

moment. But that was enough for Drake to see the round bruises along her jaw.

Stroking the spot lightly with his finger, Drake asked, "What's this?"

A deep breath sent a shudder through her body that shook him. "Kevin was here earlier."

Rage like Drake had never known rolled right through him. "He was here? He put his hands on you?"

"Please, stay calm," she pleaded, a fresh round of tears filling her eyes. "I can't do this if you're going to get all Neanderthal on me."

Barely able to rein his temper back in, Drake nodded. "Fine. Did you at least call the cops?"

Marly shook her head. "He wasn't here but just a few minutes."

"Enough time for him to put his hands on you." Drake glanced at the bruises again and nausea settled deep in his gut. "Damn it, Marly."

"I wanted to handle this all myself," she told him, easing back and wrapping her arms around her waist. "I didn't want to run to you to save me or you to ride to my rescue, but he gave me an ultimatum."

Drake didn't give a damn what this ultimatum was, he was going to track down Kevin and see just how well he liked having someone else's hands on him. Drake couldn't wait to meet the man and finally put this nightmare for Marly to an end.

"What did he say?"

Drake almost didn't want to know what this man was threatening Marly with now.

"Basically he wants me to come back and when I

cooperate he will donate enough money to your department to reinstate the three men you had to lay off, plus he'll make a very generous donation to Shawn and Amy for medical bills."

Drake cursed beneath his breath and gripped her shoulders. "You do understand you're not going back? No matter what he promises, you will not go back to him."

Marly nodded. "I know. I battled back and forth. I could save several jobs and help Shawn and Amy, but at what cost? I can't put myself in danger again and I refuse to bring my daughter back into that hell."

Drake let out a breath he hadn't realized he'd been holding. At least she was thinking straight and not trying to play hero by sacrificing herself.

"I'll notify Cameron." He held up a hand when she opened her mouth. "I'm just letting him know Kevin is in the area and that he threatened you. I'll need those pictures you have, and I want to take pictures of your jaw."

"It's just a bruise," she told him. "There's no need for a photo."

Meaning she'd lived through worse, and that thought infuriated him. "It needs to be documented that he was here for a short time and already put his hands on you."

Drake clenched his fists at his sides, trying to control his fury. She didn't need to see that; she needed him strong and thinking rationally. "I need those pictures," he told her. "I need to show Cameron."

Marly nodded and left the room. By the time she'd come back, Drake had almost calmed a tad, but then he took one look at the images and gritted his teeth so hard his jaw popped.

"I want you to let Cameron handle this," she told him, placing a hand on his arm. "I don't want Kevin to ruin your career, which is already teetering on a thin line with the mayor. And I want this to be handled the right way. I need Kevin to stay away from Willow."

Drake nodded. "I won't mess this up, Marly. He will be taken care of properly."

"He was so cold to Willow," she whispered. "No hug, barely a hello. I know he hates me and wants to control me, but she's his own flesh and blood. How can he be so heartless?"

"He won't be a problem again, Marly. I swear." Drake wrapped her in his arms again. "I'm staying here tonight."

This wasn't up for debate, and he wasn't asking. No way in hell could he go back home and leave these two on their own.

Marly gripped his shirt and held on tight. "I was hoping you'd say that."

Finally, he'd fully penetrated that wall of defense. Now if he could just handle Kevin, get his job back and convince Marly they belonged together long-term, he'd be all set.

One hurdle at a time. The first thing he would take care of was the ex. No way would that man lay another finger on Marly again.

Chapter Eighteen

Drake convinced Marly to call off work Monday morning, and he personally drove Willow to school, briefly discussed the issues with the principal and alerted him to potential problems with Kevin. Though Drake didn't think the lowlife would be brazen enough to show up at the school, Drake wasn't taking any chances at all with the family he'd come to think of as his own.

Back at Marly's house, she was a cleaning machine. Apparently she was relieving stress by sweeping, dusting, scrubbing showers and mumbling to herself as she went from room to room.

Drake ducked out onto the front porch to call Cameron. He figured his brother would be in the midst of either heading to the station or crawling into bed. Quickly dialing the police chief's cell, Drake took his gaze from one end of the quiet street to the other. Nothing out of the ordinary stood out, but then again he highly doubted a coward like Kevin would show his face with Drake here. Kevin was the type of man who opted to only prey on innocent women and children. No way would he actually want to go up against someone who would put up a fight.

"Yeah," Cameron answered.

"Kevin showed up at Marly's yesterday."

Cameron cursed under his breath. "Did he do anything to her?"

Images of those fresh bruises marring her skin had that pit in his stomach tightening all over again. Not to mention the pictures she'd brought out to him. He would never get those images out of his mind. Her nightmares were now his, and he planned on taking them away from her for good.

"He left some bruises," Drake informed his brother. "She's fine, but he did try to blackmail her into leaving. He's using me as the material."

"Real powerful man to use a woman as his shield to get through life. Let me call my investigator and I'll be over there in about an hour. I want to see those pictures and see Marly's new injuries."

"We aren't going anywhere."

"Have you thought about taking her to your house?" Cameron suggested.

"Apparently the bastard has been in town awhile. He knows where I live, I'm sure. Besides, Willow is used to this being her new home and I don't want her scared or confused."

"Understood," Cameron replied. "Be there as soon as I can."

Drake hung up, knowing his brother was running on empty, but also knowing there was no way Marly and Willow could get through this time alone. The sooner they got the threat of Kevin out of the way, the sooner they could move on with their lives.

Drake also had the council meeting tonight, but until this issue was resolved with Marly, he refused to leave. He would make calls, write letters or send someone in his place, but he wasn't leaving his family.

Yes, they were his. He'd grown to love them, cherish them and would always put their needs first. Starting with tonight and missing the meeting. If he lost his job over protecting his family, then so be it. He'd find other work. As much as he loved firefighting, he loved Marly more.

He wasn't going to let another person he loved slip through his fingers when he could save her, build a future with her and love her forever.

Ready to fight for another chance at love and happiness, Drake vowed to let nothing stand in his way.

Marly was utterly humiliated. She sat on the edge of the ottoman in her living room while Drake and Cameron pored over her pictures and asked her questions.

This was why she wanted to handle Kevin on her own. For one thing, she hated for anyone to see that side of her. The broken, vulnerable, helpless side.

For another thing, the look in Drake's and Cameron's eyes, the anger and fury that poured off them, scared her. She wasn't worried for herself, but feared what they would get into if they approached Kevin.

Kevin certainly wasn't a man to use violence against other men; he was too much of a coward for that. But he could use his power, his name and his old money to influence nearly anybody.

"Get that look off your face," Drake scolded.

"I was just going to tell you the same thing." Marly crossed her arms and leaned forward over the tops of her knees. "I don't care what you do by legal means, but do not start a fight, and please don't risk your careers. Either one of you."

Cameron shook his head. "You aren't the first battered wife I've seen or talked to. But I will say you are the first one that has really hit close to home with me. I won't risk my career, but I won't let Kevin continue to threaten you, either. He'll be dealt with properly."

Drake practically fumed, but Marly trusted them both to heed her request.

"Can I take these?" Cameron tapped the images on the table. "I promise they won't get away from me and no one who isn't pertinent to the case will see them."

Marly chewed her lip, knowing that this was too big for her to handle on her own. "Okay."

Cameron came to his feet. The poor guy looked so worn out and absolutely exhausted. Drake had mentioned that his brother was working some intense undercover case. Marly couldn't imagine laying your life on the line every day for your job.

"I need to speak with you outside," Cameron told Drake. "We'll just be a minute."

Once the guys left, Marly went to get the money bag from the festival. With all the unexpected chaos, she hadn't been able to get the cash deposited in order to write Shawn and Amy a check.

She'd counted all of the bills and was separating out the change when Drake came back in. Whatever he and Cameron had discussed had at least relaxed him a bit.

"Well, you've stopped clenching your jaw," she murmured. "That's a good sign."

He turned a kitchen chair around backward and straddled it. "I totally forgot about counting this. I'm sorry."

Shrugging as she stacked quarters into neat piles, she said, "No big deal. I'm almost done."

By the time he pitched in and they finished, they had more than either of them had thought in the first place.

"This will be a nice surprise for them," Drake told her. "We can bring the check over tomorrow if you'd like. I think Shawn said he would be at the store tomorrow and Amy would be there on Wednesday."

Marly nodded. "Sounds good. I want to get it to them as soon as possible. Why don't you go ahead and take out the money you put in for supplies?"

Drake pushed up from his seat. "Absolutely not."

Glancing up, Marly sighed. "You put in a good bit of materials for flyers, signs around town and quite a few other things."

"I won't take a dime from this, and I'll actually be adding to it."

Noble to a fault. The man was also stubborn, but how could she not admire and love every part about him?

"Need I remind you that you're suspended with no pay right now?"

Drake offered her a crooked smile as he reached for her hands and pulled her to her feet. "No need to remind me, but I also have a nest egg in savings. I'll be fine. They need the money way more than I do anyway."

Marly reached up, stroked his stubbled jawline and returned his contagious smile. "So what did you and your brother talk about?"

Drake's hands came around to her backside; he pulled her flush with his body and nipped at her lips. "Now, why would I want to talk about my brother when I've got a beautiful woman in my arms?"

Marly didn't miss the way he'd totally dodged the question, but the way he held her, the way he cherished her had her realizing this was so much more important than whatever they'd discussed.

"I'll let you skip the question," she murmured against his lips. "But only because this feels too good."

Running his arms up the back of her sweatshirt, Drake's fingertips expertly flicked her bra open. "Things are about to feel a whole lot better."

"But what if—"

Drake cut her off with a kiss. "Don't say his name. He's not coming as long as my truck is here, I'd guarantee it. Right now it's only me and you. Willow won't get picked up from school for a couple hours now and I want to be with you, just you, with nothing else getting in our way."

Marly wrapped her arms around his neck and arched into him. "Then why are we wasting our time talking?"

Drake took her words to heart when he stripped her down in record time and hoisted her up onto the kitchen table. To know she had such control over him that his own control snapped sent a quick bolt of arousal through her. Never before had she been so reckless as to have sex on her kitchen table in broad daylight, but Drake didn't seem to mind as he removed all of his clothes and piled them with hers across the kitchen floor.

As frenzied as Drake was at the start, when his hands slid up her body and to her face, he was so gentle, so… soft. Those fingertips glided over where she knew those bruises were.

"Nothing else but us," she reminded him.

He captured her lips and pulled her forward until she wrapped her legs around his waist. "Always us," he murmured as he joined them together. "Always."

Chapter Nineteen

Drake had dropped Marly and Willow off at Eli and Nora's house. He wasn't comfortable leaving them alone and he had business to attend to.

Granted, he was on his way to find Kevin, but Drake still didn't think leaving Marly alone was a good idea. For one thing, she didn't know he was going to see Kevin and Drake didn't want her worrying about him. For another, Drake had no clue what minions the creep may have brought with him, so he wanted to cover all his bases.

Oh, the bastard had no clue Drake was coming, or that his police chief brother was meeting him there. The element of surprise was on his side, and he fully intended to keep the upper hand at all times from here on out.

Cameron had informed him earlier that morning that Kevin was staying just outside of town in a nicer hotel that was closer to the city. Of course he wouldn't want to degrade himself and stay at the local hotel that was family owned.

Drake had also learned quite a bit about the woman who had originally filed assault charges against Kevin… the charges that had suddenly disappeared were surprisingly found once Cameron's investigator started digging deeper.

Drake entered the hotel, met Cameron in the lobby and followed him toward the elevators.

"My investigator said Kevin is staying in Room 801. It's a suite, of course."

Drake clenched his fists, still not sure exactly what he'd say to the man who'd made Marly's life a living hell for years. Not to mention the fact that he'd utterly ignored Willow…which was probably a good thing, except for the fact he was using the innocent child as a pawn to lure her mother back.

"You may want to simmer down a bit," Cameron muttered as they stepped into the elevator. "We're just presenting him with his options."

Drake snorted. "Options? He has one. Leave Marly the hell alone and get out of town."

"Why don't you let me talk?"

Drake shot his brother a narrowed look as he exited the elevator. No way in hell would he let Cameron fight his battles. Cameron was here as a witness, to make sure Kevin understood all the damning evidence they had uncovered. And to make sure Drake didn't kill him.

Cameron tapped on the door and Kevin opened it just enough to peer beyond the chain. "Yes?"

Cameron flashed his badge. "Stonerock Police. I need to speak with you, Mr. Haskins."

Drake loved the authority in his little brother's voice. Loved how Cameron could put the fear of God in so many people.

"What can I do for you?" Kevin asked, still not opening the door any wider than the chain would allow.

"I just have a few questions for you, sir. Would you mind if I came in for just a minute?"

Drake stayed off to the side; there was no way he wanted Kevin to see him. Although, if the man were smart, he'd already know that Cameron was Drake's brother, but Drake wasn't anticipating that Kevin had done a great deal of homework on Marly's new life. He had tunnel vision, and that tunnel led straight to the election. "I suppose," Kevin said.

The door closed while the locks were cleared away, and Cameron shot Drake a look. "Stay calm or I'll pull you out of here," he whispered.

Drake nodded. As much as he wanted to go charging into that room and tear Kevin apart, Drake wouldn't do anything to put Marly in any danger or jeopardize her case in the custody proceedings.

When the door swung open, Cameron stepped in first, and just as Kevin was about to close it, Drake slammed his hand on the door and pushed his way through.

Kevin's eyes widened. Oh, yeah. The jerk knew exactly who Drake was. Good.

"Mr. Haskins, come have a seat," Cameron said, breaking through the tension.

Kevin's wide eyes jerked to Cameron. "You said you were with the police."

"I said *I* was," Cameron corrected. "My brother is the fire chief…but you probably already knew that."

Drake closed the door behind him, keeping his eyes on Kevin the entire time. "You'll want to sit down. We may be a while."

Kevin went into the living area and took a seat on the navy sofa. Dressed in black dress pants and a dark gray shirt with the cuffs turned up, Kevin looked like a typical polished businessman. Unfortunately, Drake had seen photos that proved this man was anything but typical or polished.

Arms crossed over his chest, Drake leaned against the TV stand directly across from Kevin. Cameron took a seat in a wing-back chair and held up a folder.

"This contains some pretty damning information, Mr. Haskins," Cameron started. "First of all, I know you visited Marly yesterday."

Kevin laughed as he eased back on his cushy sofa. "You're wasting my time because I visited my wife?"

"Ex-wife," Drake quickly corrected, barely managing not to leap across the room and punch the smug smirk off Kevin's face. "She divorced you when you beat her and didn't take her for treatment and the wound on her head didn't heal properly."

Kevin narrowed his gaze at Drake. "Is that what she told you? She's always fabricating stories."

Cameron reached into the folder and held up a photo

of Marly with a bloody head. "Did she fabricate the pictures, too? That's a lot of work to go through for one story."

Kevin eased forward, his confident demeanor starting to crack. "What do you want?" he asked.

"It's not what I want," Drake chimed in before Cameron could go all cop on him. "It's what is going to happen. You will leave Marly alone. She isn't coming back to you. You also will drop this custody battle, because you don't give a damn about your own daughter."

With a laugh, Kevin shook his head and sighed. "Who is going to stop me from taking everything I want? You two? Aren't you suspended from your job? What power do you hold anyway? And your brother is a small-town cop who can't do a thing to me for visiting my own wife. Your threats are wasted here."

He started to rise and Drake took a step forward. "Sit down."

Obviously the tone did the trick because Kevin eased back into place. Drake rested his hands on his hips, continuing to stare the other man down.

"I have a statement from Janet Days that states you assaulted her when she worked in your office back when you were a lowly commissioner." Cameron pulled out a sheet of paper. "Here it states exactly what you did to her and her injuries, and she even reported that she feared her accusations would disappear and nothing would come of it."

Kevin tensed, and suddenly that cocky smirk was gone, replaced by fear. Drake still wanted to pummel the man.

"It's her word against mine," Kevin defended. "And apparently the police didn't take her seriously."

"Interesting," Cameron went on, holding up a hand to Drake, who had just pushed away from the TV cabinet. "My investigator also found another woman who was working in your office only two years ago who said the same thing. I have to say, Mr. Haskins, these ladies who don't know each other at all, both had quite similar stories."

Kevin came to his feet. "Get out. You can't arrest me and I won't say anything without my attorney anyway."

Drake shot across the room, his fist connecting with Kevin's jaw until the man fell back onto the sofa.

"Damn it, I told you to stay calm," Cameron shouted.

Shaking his hand, Drake shrugged. "I was calm for nearly ten minutes."

"I'll sue you," Kevin whined. "I'll press charges."

"I'll arrest him if you want me to—"

Drake smacked Cameron's shoulder. "The hell you will."

"But," Cameron continued, looking between Drake and Kevin, "I think you'll want to hear everything I have to say before you make any decisions about pressing charges."

Cameron stepped between where Kevin was rolled into the corner of the couch holding on to his jaw and Drake.

"These ladies I've found have agreed to come forward and testify against you if you choose not to leave Marly alone," Cameron stated. "Once they heard about your wife and why she truly left you, they were all too eager to discuss their forgotten cases."

Kevin narrowed his eyes. "She's my wife."

"She's your ex-wife and your former punching bag." Drake gritted his teeth. "And you'll drop the custody case, too, because we both know you don't want Willow. You've never been a hands-on dad, and she wouldn't be comfortable with you anyway. For once, think of the child."

Drake wasn't leaving this room until he was satisfied Kevin was out of Marly's life for good. He refused to let this jerk hold any power over Marly for one more second of her life.

"So what do you say?" Cameron asked, stepping forward and looming over Kevin. "You ready to get yourself back to Nashville and leave this town for good?"

Kevin glanced from Cameron to Drake. "You can have her. She's not worth the fight."

Drake stepped around his brother, came right to the edge of the sofa and leaned down within a few inches of Kevin's swollen face. "She's worth everything. You were just too cowardly and arrogant to realize that."

"Get out," Kevin spat. "I won't come into your ridiculous town again, but threaten me again and I'll have both of your jobs."

Drake laughed, pushing away from the couch. "You don't have a leg to stand on, Haskins. The charges we can bring against you would ruin any pitiful reputation you think you've built. So take your threats and get the hell out of Stonerock."

Pushing aside Cameron and maybe stepping on Kevin's feet, Drake headed to the door. "I'm done with this garbage."

He stormed out of the room before he really did something stupid like punch the man again. Because as good as it had felt to hit him once, Drake truly wanted to go full-on assault on the loser.

But, having respect for Marly and not wanting to stoop to Kevin's level, Drake was ready to close this chapter and move on. Drake knew the Nashville PD already had a warrant waiting for Kevin when he arrived back home, because Cameron had called a contact he knew for sure wasn't corrupt to handle the case. Kevin wouldn't be hurting any more women, and he certainly wouldn't be running for reelection.

Drake glanced at his watch and realized there was no way he'd make the council meeting.

Drake waited at the elevators for Cameron. If Drake had to go to the city offices tomorrow and explain why he was absent, he would. But right now, all he cared about was getting to Marly and building up a solid foundation for their future.

He was so quiet on their way home from Eli's house. Whatever had happened while he'd been gone had really upset him.

Marly let herself into her house and asked Willow to go on back and start getting ready for bed. Marly needed a few minutes alone with Drake.

After he closed the door behind him, he sighed and leaned against it.

"You weren't reinstated, were you?" she asked, almost afraid of his answer.

His brows drew in as he pushed off the door. "What?"

"The council meeting that was tonight. They sided with the mayor, didn't they?"

Drake closed the space between them and rested his hands on her shoulders. "I didn't go to the council meeting. I honestly have no clue what they've decided."

"What? Where were you?"

Those intense eyes held hers as he squeezed her shoulders. This couldn't be good. Fear pitted in the depths of her stomach.

"Drake?"

"I went to see Kevin."

Her entire world tilted. Marly swayed just as Drake's arms came around her. There was no way he'd gone behind her back and gone to see her ex-husband.

"Sit down." Drake ushered her to the couch where he sat down beside her. "Before you get upset, please hear me out."

"Upset?" she repeated, clasping her shaky hands in her lap. "I'm not upset, Drake. I'm hurt you didn't tell me that was where you were going. You let me assume you were going to fight for your job."

He gripped her shoulders and turned her to face him fully. "I went to fight for you, which was a hell of a lot more important than any career."

If she didn't love the man before now, the fact he'd laid literally everything on the line for her had her heart tumbling over in her chest.

"Do I want to know what happened?" she asked, almost afraid of his answer.

Drake tipped his head and offered her a grin. "The CliffsNotes version is Kevin is out of your life. You don't have to worry about anything else."

Questions, scenarios bounced around in her head. "What about the custody? I can't let Willow—"

Drake's finger covered her lips. "Taken care of. When I say I'm going to take care of what belongs to me, I mean it. I had Cameron do some digging, and he uncovered more women who stepped forward, willing to give their statements. The Nashville police are waiting for him and he won't be a problem for you anymore."

Tears instantly pricked her eyes. "I can't believe you'd do this for me."

His hands framed her face. "I did it for us," he said, sliding his lips over hers. "I did it because I love you."

A shudder rippled through her, vibrating against his body. "Oh, Drake," she cried, clutching him tight. "I love you. I love you more than I thought I could ever love a man."

He nipped at her lips again. "That's good, considering you'll never be without me."

Chapter Twenty

Standing outside this house that had once served as her prison, Marly smoothed her dress down and knocked on the door. She was ready once and for all to face her past and move on. With Kevin's power, he'd been given house arrest until the arraignment. She needed closure, needed him to see that she was strong, needed to prove that any power he'd ever had over her had disappeared. Most of all, she needed to put their marriage behind her so she could move on with her new life…her happy life.

The wide mahogany door swung open, and Kevin stood before her. One side of his face was swollen and bruised. Shock registered first, followed quickly by a sense that Drake had doled out his own brand of justice.

"What do you want?" Kevin growled. "I already told

your boyfriend and his brother I was out of your life for good."

Oh, the images that flooded her mind of Kevin facing down two St. John boys were almost comical.

"I heard that you opted to be smart for once." Marly smiled, knowing full well for once in her life, where this man was concerned, she held the upper hand. "I'm here to make sure you are fully dropping the custody dispute with Willow. I want to hear you say it."

His eyes narrowed. Well, one eye was nearly swollen shut, but the other one narrowed into a slit. "You can raise your kid any way you want," he told her. "You've ruined me and my career."

Crossing her arms over her simple wrap dress, Marly shrugged. "I think we both know who's to blame for your career spiraling out of control."

"Get the hell out of here, Marly."

Oh, yes, the fact that he was afraid shouldn't make her feel so happy. But for once in his life, he was scared of something, and that something was her and the power she now had over him.

And because she was feeling so powerful and wickedly happy, Marly took a step forward and stared him straight in the eyes. "If you come near me or my daughter again, I can't promise what Drake did to your face won't seem like a day at the beach."

As she turned on her heel and left this house for the final time, Marly realized she'd never felt so liberated, so free and happy in all her life.

Now she could truly start building the life, the family she'd always wanted.

* * *

Drake had never been so nervous in all of his life. He stood outside of Marly's house and rang the doorbell. The sun was just starting to set, and he hoped he wasn't interrupting dinner.

Willow answered the door and her sweet smile hit him square in the heart. "I have a loose tooth," she declared as she opened the door. "I've been wiggling it all day."

The innocence of a child. Drake stepped into the house and instantly smelled something baking.

"This is your first loose tooth," he told her, squatting down to look into her mouth. "What a big deal."

Willow nodded and snapped her mouth closed. "I can't wait for the Tooth Fairy. I might get a whole dollar like some of the kids in my class."

Laughing, Drake came to his feet just as Marly stepped into the living room, wiping her hands on a towel.

"Drake." Her smile spread across her face. That smile reached her eyes, and for the first time showed no sign of fear or worry. "I was going to call you in a bit to come over."

He hadn't been able to stay away. Not after he'd come to a life-altering decision.

"Hope I'm not interrupting."

"Not at all." She turned to Willow. "Go finish wiping off the table, please."

Willow ran past her mother and into the kitchen. "We're baking cookies," Marly said.

"You're always baking something."

"Well, these are chocolate chip, and I happen to know a certain firefighter who loves homemade cookies." She tossed the towel onto her shoulder. "What brings you by?"

"I wanted to know if you and Willow would like to go look at a litter of puppies with me."

Her face lit up. "Oh, you're getting a dog? That's great. Willow would love to go look at puppies."

Drake swallowed, knowing this moment was going to change his life…one way or another.

"I have a friend who found a litter on the side of the road and he's looking for homes for them." Drake ran a hand across the back of his neck, never dreaming he'd be this anxious or nervous about being there. "I also wanted to run by my house to show you the addition, now that it's nearly done. I need a woman's opinion on the paint color. I'd actually like Willow's opinion."

"Willow's opinion?" Marly laughed. "Be prepared for a shade of blue or green."

"That would be fine with me." He stepped forward, taking her hand in his. "I was also hoping that once I get the puppy I want and take him home, that maybe you and Willow would like to come home with me, too… you know, permanently."

Marly's eyes widened, then watered. "Drake," she whispered.

He dropped to his knee and pulled the box from his pocket. "I got this the other day, but I wanted to wait until you were ready. I don't expect you to answer me right now, but will you wear my ring? Will you consider moving in with me and the new addition can be Willow's room? Will you marry me one day?"

Marly dropped to her knees as well, and clasped her hands around Drake's and the box. Instead of answering his questions, she said, "I went to see Kevin earlier."

Fear threatened to creep up. "What?"

"I'm not scared anymore," she told him. "I'm not afraid to move on, to let you help me face my fears. Willow and I were planning on bringing you the cookies and telling you that I'm—we're—ready to move on. With you."

Relief swept through him. He took the ring from the box and slid it onto her finger. The thick band with a simple inset of diamonds fit her perfectly.

His hands shook as he held on to hers. "I saw this set and it looked just like something you'd wear. Simple, elegant."

Those watery eyes came up to meet his. "It's perfect. You're perfect."

"Why are you guys on the floor?" Willow asked, coming over and trying to wedge herself between them.

Drake laughed. "Because we're weird," he explained. "What do you say to helping me pick out a dog?"

"Seriously?" she asked.

Drake nodded. "I also need you to pick out your favorite paint color because I have a new room, and it can be yours, if you want."

"We're going to live with Drake," Marly explained. "Mama and Drake are getting married. What do you think of that?"

Willow let out an ear-piercing squeal that penetrated

his eardrums. "A loose tooth, a puppy, a new room and a cool new dad all in one day? This is the best day ever."

Drake kissed Marly over Willow's head. "I couldn't agree more."

* * * * *

MILLS & BOON®

Classic romances from your favourite authors!

40% OFF!

3 in 1 GREAT VALUE

The Jarrods: Temptation

MAUREEN CHILD   TESSA RADLEY   KATHIE DENOSKY

By Request

The Australian's Desire

MARION LENNOX   LILIAN DARCY

By Request

Royal and Ruthless

ROBYN DONALD   ANNIE WEST   CHRISTINA HOLLIS

By Request

Whether you love tycoon billionaires, rugged ranchers or dashing doctors, this collection has something to suit everyone this New Year. Plus, we're giving you a huge 40% off the RRP!

Hurry, order yours today at
www.millsandboon.co.uk/NYCollection

0215_INSHIP2

MILLS & BOON®

Two superb collections!

40% OFF!

Would you rather spend the night with a seductive sheikh or be whisked away to a tropical Hawaiian island? Well, now you don't have to choose! Get your hands on both collections today and get 40% off the RRP!

Hurry, order yours today at
www.millsandboon.co.uk/TheOneCollection

0215_INSHIP1

MILLS & BOON®

First Time in Forever

Following the success of the Snow Crystal trilogy,
Sarah Morgan returns with the sensational
Puffin Island trilogy. Follow the life, loss and
love of Emily Armstrong in the first instalment,
as she looks for love on Puffin Island.

Pick up your copy today!

Visit
www.millsandboon.co.uk/Firsttime

MILLS & BOON®

Why not subscribe?

Never miss a title and save money too!

Here's what's available to you if you join the exclusive **Mills & Boon Book Club** today:

◆ *Titles up to a month ahead of the shops*
◆ *Amazing discounts*
◆ *Free P&P*
◆ *Earn Bonus Book points that can be redeemed against other titles and gifts*
◆ *Choose from monthly or pre-paid plans*

Still want more?

Well, if you join today we'll even give you
50% OFF your first parcel!

So visit **www.millsandboon.co.uk/subs**
or call **Customer Relations** on **020 8288 2888**
to be a part of this exclusive Book Club!

SUBS_2014

MILLS & BOON®

Cherish™

EXPERIENCE THE ULTIMATE RUSH OF FALLING IN LOVE

A sneak peek at next month's titles...

In stores from 20th February 2015:

- **The Renegade Billionaire** – Rebecca Winters
  and **Her Perfect Proposal** – Lynne Marshall

- **Reunited with Her Italian Ex** – Lucy Gordon
  and **Mendoza's Secret Fortune** – Marie Ferrarella

In stores from 6th March 2015:

- **The Playboy of Rome** – Jennifer Faye
  and **The Baby Bonanza** – Jacqueline Diamond

- **Her Knight in the Outback** – Nikki Logan
  and **From City Girl to Rancher's Wife** – Ami Weaver

Available at WHSmith, Tesco, Asda, Eason, Amazon and Apple

Just can't wait?
Buy our books online a month before they hit the shops!
visit www.millsandboon.co.uk

These books are also available in eBook format!